W9-BUG-747

Monday's Warriors

By the same author

Monday's Warriors

A NOVEL BY

MAURICE
SHADBOLT

David R. Godine, Publisher

BOSTON

First U.S. edition published in 1992 by

DAVID R. GODINE, PUBLISHER, INC.

Horticultural Hall
300 Massachusetts Avenue
Boston, Massachusetts 02115

Originally published in the United Kingdom by
Bloomsbury Publishing Ltd.

LIBRARY OF CONGRESS CATALOGUING-IN-PUBLICATION DATA

Shadbolt, Maurice.
Monday's Warriors / Maurice Shadbolt. — 1st U.S. ed.
p.   cm.
ISBN 0-87923-915-8 (alk. paper)
1. New Zealand—History—Maori War, 1845–1847—Fiction.
2. Maoris—Fiction.   I. Title
PR9639.3.S5M66   1992
823—dc20   91-55521
CIP

FIRST U.S. EDITION
Printed in the United States of America

For Kevin, not before time;
and for Elspeth, none too soon.

Author's Note

Where this story most seems fiction, it is fact. Otherwise it is folklore, leaving a novelist with few liberties to take. I am indebted to historian James Belich for his generosity with research material, especially his provocative M.A. thesis *Titokowaru's War* (1979); also to Kendrick Smithyman, for his scholarly tracking of Kimball Bent through the undergrowth of the nineteenth century; and not least to military historian Lieutenant Colonel Christopher Pugsley for patiently walking me over warrior ground. I must also thank the English Department of Auckland University and the New Zealand Literary Fund for providing me with time and travel to mount my own search for Bent and Titokowaru.

*Failure or success seems to have been
allotted to men by their stars. But they retain
the power of wriggling, of fighting with their star
or against it, and in the whole universe the
only really interesting movement
is this wriggle.*

E.M. FORSTER

Monday's Warriors

One

It was the year that a distinguished British general, seldom menaced by more than a hundred warriors, took ten embittering weeks to march four regiments just sixty New Zealand miles, and at last found a war worth leaving unwon. It was the year before his substitute, no martial novice either, likewise learned that glory was the lesser part of an antipodean crusade; he rather magically managed to lose most of an army to belligerent ravines and insurgent vegetation without engaging his enemy.

Between one luckless general and the next there is a fleck of fable in history's eye called Kimball Bent. A son of Sodom Docks, Eastport, State of Maine, Private Bent had ostensibly aided and abetted Britain's legions in the reddening of the world's maps, sweating and swearing in Cork and Poona, Calcutta and Pondicherry, and now even more remote estuaries of empire. This was due to a day in 1859 when, lit with Liverpool ale, Kimball thought the Queen's shilling a tolerable price for a ragged and starving stowaway. He was then twenty-two years old and powerfully stirred by a recruiting sergeant's promise of a scarlet outfit and British beef in his belly. In 1865, stiffened with six years of scar tissue, he was sadder and not usefully wiser.

That was the year Kimball ended his loveless connection with Her Majesty's 57th Regiment of Foot. Garrison duty never became Private Bent, nor much else of military nature. Two years of subduing mutinous Indians and four of fighting inflamed Maori left him with the suspicion that life minus uniform might be more rousing than menial chores and mayhem. Even when he was at pains to excel the result was regimental uproar.

1

He had recently served forcefully enough as a sentry to shoot a drunken sergeant who failed to identify himself as friend and not foe. Right had been on Kimball's side, but not might, especially not the sober sergeant's perjury that he had thrice answered Sentry Bent's challenge. Maiming of a sergeant, by the eighth company's least animated marksman, could not be condoned. For attention to duty Kimball was awarded fifty lashes and six months' prison.

Earlier attempts to refund the Queen's shilling had been as injurious. Garrisoned in the town of Cork, defending Ireland against the Irish, Kimball sighted a vessel shipping to Salem. He secreted himself aboard, but found the world outside Cork Cove filling with ferocious Atlantic rather than freedom. Leaking impressively, the vessel listed back to port in time to rendezvous with a punitive party of soldiers patrolling Cork's quaysides for martial absconders. His prison term, though not his maiden lashing, was cut short by his regiment's posting to India. That humid land had much to dispirit an ambitious deserter; there was nowhere one with a white face might remain inconspicuous or, for that matter, alive. New Zealand, such of it as he had seen beyond punishment triangles, prisons and parade grounds, was a land with less grievous prospects. For one thing the place was filling with white faces. There were green woods, ferny valleys, unsettled shores, and winters cool enough to put him in mind of Maine summer. With a few acres of land, grass seed, sheep and a horse, he might perform marvels as a fugitive pioneer. In the port of Auckland, where the 57th disembarked, Kimball scuttled to freedom and hid for a month in a house of considerate whores. His diminutive stature, apprehensive face and appreciative smile won him more than mere sanctuary. This colonial idyll ended when an unclad colour sergeant of the 65th spied inhabited boots beneath a hired bed; he hauled Kimball out by the hair. At his first New Zealand court martial he was given to understand that Christian civilization could not suffer shirkers, not even of the North American kind. Knotted to the regimental punishment triangles, he survived his first lashes in New Zealand without lamenting more than most; the drummer who laid on the lashes was a man notoriously sensitive to the requirements of civilization. So was Colonel Hazzard of the 57th, who prescribed the punishment as an inducement for Private Bent to perform more convincingly in defence of Queen Victoria's realm. To see his point made Colonel Hazzard inspected Kimball while he shuddered and bled.

'It would seem', the colonel observed, 'that you hate our service with all the disloyalty and hatred for discipline that characterizes the republican rabble of your continent.'

'I can't speak for none but myself, sir,' Kimball whispered. 'But right now I can't say I'm in love with the army. No, sir.'

'You think a discharge might be timely?' The colonel was curt.

'Yes, sir,' Kimball said with hope.

'Over my dead body,' Colonel Hazzard announced.

There was a silence of a shaky sort.

'Then, sir,' Kimball ventured, 'there's one thing I will say for the likes of me. Americans, sir.'

'And what would that be, Bent?'

'That it's not a hundred years since us rabble whipped the likes of you good, sir.'

That failed to win a kindly smile.

'So long as I have command of this regiment,' the colonel said, 'let there be no further fancies of a discharge. You hear?'

'I heard, sir. Over your dead body.'

'That is no idle phrase,' the colonel warned. 'We of the 57th are not known as the Diehards for nothing. We live hard. We fight hard. And by God we die hard. We never ask less of officers or men.'

Colonel Hazzard seldom failed to note Kimball's existence thereafter, presiding with further satisfaction in the affair of the drunken sergeant. Private Bent was gainful to the health of the regiment, a man privileged to suffer for the villainy of his ancestors and the vice of his comrades. Whenever he seemed due a change for the better, fate had gone fishing.

3

Two

In April the warm weather thinned. The lone and ornamental cone of Mount Taranaki, most of two miles tall on the north horizon, glowed with the first snow of the year. The eighth company was under canvas on a coast of roaring sea and eroding cliff, three hundred feet above the mouth of a murky river. Forested terrain inland was as menacing as the rest of the North Island's heart. After five years of siege, skirmish and ambush, the Maori who rode the region had yet to be persuaded that the Queen's writ ran in their vicinity. While ungovernable tribesmen north and south now saw a surly cease fire as more propitious than strife, those under Mount Taranaki perversely made themselves more lethal. Once the most conscientious Christians in the colony, they were now the most pious killers. Pledged not to part with land for British pounds and pence, they fought tribal neighbours who thought to, and chanced the bullets and bayonets of Britons arriving to take it anyway. When imperial regiments razed their churches, Taranaki's rebels salvaged such of the scriptures as served sudden death and discharged Methodist clergy from further duty. Lay preachers were reborn as warrior leaders. Their new jury-rigged religion turned a penny dreadful war into a shilling shocker. Rebel allegiance was now to angry angels sailing the four winds. Taranaki's tribesmen called on other, exhausted warriors to unite under their enigmatic banners, to join in their occult chant of *Hau* and *Hau*. At first it was thought that the chant might ward off shot and shell, but graves in growing number soon said not. More formidably, these Hauhau Maori souvenired the heads of soldiers they slew, smoked them to traditional recipe, and marched such prizes into native regions seen in need of a new faith.

4

Meanwhile the soldiers of the 57th commanded as much of the region as came within range of their carbines. After levelling coastal villages and rebel crops, the regiment now served the muddy avenue of empire won between the fortified colonist communities of Wanganui and New Plymouth. Their chore was to keep armed convoys safe and the colony's communications in sufficient repair to please politicians. This meant ducking shot from rebels drifting through the hills to light defiant fires on the land they had lost; on the other hand it meant no disheartening assaults on Maori hilltop citadels. Aside from horsed pickets sniped from their saddles, and rebels tomahawking forage parties, excitements were few. Convoys came. Convoys went. Junior officers saluted senior officers; men saluted both. Messages were read and orders of the day given out. Men drilled twice daily, felled firewood, and fished. Mostly they stood sentry. There was always one posted to watch another. Desertions imperilled the regiment more than melancholic rebels.

'This is our lot,' Connolly confided.

'Of what?' Kimball asked.

'This war,' Connolly said. 'I got eyes to see. Ears to hear.'

They were sharing sentry through a morning of slow drizzle. On such duty, in fair weather or foul, Kimball was never one to argue with a comrade's eyes and ears, not even those of a gormy jeezer like Connolly. A flutter of foliage might herald a bird; it might also disclose a tomahawk.

'Colonists could do this job cheaper,' Connolly explained. 'Colonial militia. Playboys.'

'Playboys?'

'Not the likes of us. Real soldiers cost. They'll soon be shipping us out. There's talk.'

Kimball was quiet. So much for lucrative acres. He could also kiss the South Island's new goldfields goodbye. Arrivals from Australia and California were battling up nugget-strewn heights and storming through gleaming canyons; men made fortunes in minutes. Most deserters from the 57th had bolted in that direction. Their hunters had a Chinaman's chance of sniffing them out among steamy thousands of gold-seekers. Officers, not to speak of sergeants and corporals, were now alert to fidgets among men of footloose character.

'Where would we be shipped to?' Kimball asked.

Connolly shrugged. 'Maybe India again. Who knows?'

'India?' Kimball said with mixed feelings, mostly of dread.

'Or China,' Connolly suggested.

Kimball thought it unlikely that the populace of China pined for him any more than the inhabitants of India. Since he lofted his last shot at a Maine duck, and watched it spin from the sky, his luck had never been leaner. His parents were two headstones shaded by maples in Eastport's burying ground. The 57th was the most he could call kin. Even so only Colonel Hazzard saw him as having much point. In the day's one ray of sunlight he heard a free burst of birdsong from a nearby tree. The bird then launched itself toward forest and hill, soon lost in haze. There was rain, more rain, and wind. He and Connolly shivered out another hour, until relieved, and then looked for warmth and a crust in the cookhouse. They shed damp clothes, sat in their long underwear, and smoked. Kimball found a muddy newspaper to decipher. For illiterate Connolly's benefit Kimball laboured through the print in loud voice, enlightening his companion in respect of retired rebels vowing loyalty to the Queen, quiet frontiers, and new gold discoveries in the south.

'Read me that last again,' Connolly pleaded.

Kimball reported that mariners were wrecking their ships in icy rivers in their haste to dump men of all nations and most vocations on the South Island's western coast. It seemed vessels crowded with colonists were leaving North Island ports for the goldfields; entire towns were emptying. Kimball's voice dropped to a whisper.

'What is it?' Connolly asked.

'I'm just piecing it all out,' Kimball insisted.

Certain slabs of print promised sea passage to the goldfields. If Kimball put his arse behind him, and pointed himself toward the port of Wanganui or the port of New Plymouth, he might board a fast vessel. Wanganui, to the south, seemed a saner proposition. New Plymouth, to the north, lay along the con-tested coast road. Hiking lonely that way a man might lose his head to Maori rebels. In the other direction his hide was in hazard. Wanganui was a garrison town, with two companies of the 57th trawling the territory around. A truant might be hard pressed to bypass their patrols. He chanced putting the case of the devil, then that of the deep blue sea, to Connolly. Connolly was a devil's advocate.

'Wanganui by far,' he muttered furtively. 'Me, I'd work inland a little. Keep to the woods and clear of the road and convoys. Maybe make tracks past Wanganui for Wellington. Bigger. Fewer soldiers down there. And more ships south. You wouldn't be thinking of it?'

'I'm thinking of India,' Kimball confessed.

'And I'm thinking I don't need to know,' Connolly said even more shiftily.

That was as much conversation as martial need permitted. Joyless Corporal Flukes, no friend to a weary soldier, discovered them warm, dry and idle in the cookhouse.

'On your feet,' he ordered.

Connolly rose quickly.

'Me?' Kimball queried.

'You too, Bent. You.'

Kimball rose slowly beside Connolly.

'There is', Flukes disclosed, 'the matter of a firewood detail.'

'In this rain?' Kimball asked.

'All the more needed,' Flukes confirmed.

'We're soaked from sentry,' Kimball protested. 'There's some never been out of their tents today.'

'Did you speak, Bent? Did I hear you?'

Kimball looked to his rear and saw no one else likely. 'I reckon,' he said.

'And who, Bent,' Flukes asked, 'has not been out of their tents today?'

'You for one,' Kimball suggested.

'You're telling me something,' Flukes decided.

'Me and Connolly froze our arses for the Queen this morning. We left the Empire like we found it.'

'And?' Flukes asked.

'Go fuck yourself,' Kimball said. He had heard the words in his head a hundred times; mysteriously he seemed to be saying them. With his situation past repair he resumed a sitting position.

Flukes said, 'Connolly, is this your word too?'

'Never,' Connolly said with terror. Having hauled up his breeches, he tugged on a tunic. 'Rely on me, corporal. I'm right for a detail.'

Soon afterwards Connolly departed axe in hand for nearby forest and was never again seen by the 57th. Kimball, confined to the guard tent, took Connolly's absence more personally than most. In fancy he followed Connolly through hills, fern and scrub, evading the coast road and convoys, missing the port of Wanganui and its patrols; he toiled on to Wellington behind Connolly and wriggled breathless aboard a southbound vessel. There was a lesson in it of sorts. Literacy didn't butter the parsnips. Reading the ground made more sense.

Meanwhile there was Kimball's third New Zealand court martial. Colonel Hazzard left his soft bed in Wanganui and pushed his horse sixty miles up the coast for the privilege of again avenging Britain's loss of its American colonies. Unable to storm Massachusetts and levy a new tax on Boston's tea, he could mount a punishing campaign against Private Bent. With the colonel sat two lieutenants and the eighth company's new and dapper Captain Clark, a fair-haired and handsome Canadian, an officer Kimball found more bearable than most. Not that the most benevolent officer could save him now. A surgeon was at hand to announce him fit to flog.

Corporal Flukes testified that he had located the prisoner, Bent, idle in the company of the recent deserter Connolly; that he had given the aforesaid soldiers a firm and clear order. Connolly had complied. Bent had not.

'There was no room for misunderstanding?' Captain Clark inquired.

'There was not, sir,' Flukes replied. 'He made a lewd proposal.'

'Lewd?' Captain Clark leaned forward with interest.

'Of impractical nature, sir.'

'It might not be thought that Bent was unduly under the rebellious influence of the deserter Connolly?' Captain Clark mused.

'Not to my way of thinking, sir,' Flukes replied. 'Connolly took my order right smart.'

'And is now not on the strength of the 57th?'

'I was not to know his sly game, sir.'

'Naturally. But it can be counted possible?'

'If you insist, sir. The way things are, most things can.'

'The way things are, Corporal Flukes?'

'No one would have thought the regiment would still be

8

fighting New Zealand niggers after five years. No one would have counted that possible, sir.'

'Perhaps not, Corporal Flukes. You would argue, then, that the strain of antipodean service might be telling?'

'It's not for me to argue one thing or the other, sir. There's no denying men are getting difficult, especially in bad weather. But that's a horse of a different colour, sir.'

'Possibly,' Captain Clark smiled. 'Possibly not. Thank you, Corporal Flukes.'

Kimball understood that someone was trying to save him. Colonel Hazzard's face, on the other hand, still said the worst. So did his voice.

'Are you offering a defence to the charge, Private Bent?'

'Not that I know, sir.'

'You are aware of your rights in this respect?'

'I am, sir,' Kimball agreed.

'And of your duty here as soldier of the Queen?'

'I know I'm not in Washington County, sir.'

'So the facts of the matter are not in dispute,' said the colonel with satisfaction.

'Not about Corporal Flukes being a fair bastard, sir.'

'I fancy I did not hear you, Bent.'

'Corporal Flukes has always been an aggravation, sir.'

'Corporal Flukes is employed to be, Bent.'

'Yes, sir.'

'And you would not argue, as has been suggested here, that the deserter Connolly might have misled you?'

'No, sir. He just had the same fill of Flukes. My mistake, sir. I didn't know what was good for me.'

'Meaning?' Colonel Hazzard asked.

'It looks like I should of took off too, sir.'

'That was an unfortunate reply, Bent.'

'You asked the question, sir.'

'Bent by name and hell-bent by nature. Do I have it right?'

'You'd be the best judge of that, sir.'

'Just so,' Colonel Hazzard said. 'You may stand down.'

The colonel looked to his fellow officers. 'Need we confer, gentlemen?' he asked.

'I would appreciate the opportunity,' Captain Clark insisted gently. 'And in the absence of the prisoner, sir.'

'If you must,' Colonel Hazzard said with irritation.

9

Kimball was removed to the guard tent. 'Chokey for you, old son,' his escort promised. 'That's after your chat with the cat.'

The surgeon, a shaky little man with a whisky breath, appeared in the guard tent. 'Off with your tunic,' he ordered Kimball, and then considered the young back beneath. 'Yes,' he decided. 'No.' Then, 'Perhaps.' He left to rejoin the conferring officers. Finally Kimball was marched before Colonel Hazzard again.

'It will come as no surprise to you, Bent,' he said, 'that you have been found guilty of wilfully disobeying an order.'

'No, sir,' Kimball had to admit.

'The sentence of this court, Bent, is fifty lashes and six months' prison. Does that sound familiar?'

'Now you mention it, sir,' Kimball allowed. Mild Captain Clark must have gone for nothing.

'However,' the colonel continued, 'it is also the view of this court, given the unusual circumstances, and the desertion of your comrade Connolly, that part of the sentence be suspended. On Captain Clark's representation the prison sentence will be held over conditional on your making yourself receptive to orders. You will also give your solemn undertaking to Captain Clark to uphold the honour of the 57th in future. Are we understood?'

'Sir,' Kimball agreed.

'As to the remainder of the sentence,' Colonel Hazzard said, 'we seem to be in the hands of our surgeon. He appears rather humanely to feel that a long lashing would follow too soon on your last. Twenty-five will therefore be conditionally remitted. Should there be another disciplinary breach, however minor in character, the punishment will be administered in full without further court hearing or surgeon's inspection. I shall instruct the drummer to examine the instrument of discipline for signs of wear and tear, and to replace all leather frayed. I shall further instruct Corporal Flukes to maintain his commendable interest in you. Think yourself the most fortunate soldier in the British army.'

'I'll give it a try, sir,' Kimball promised.

'And remove yourself from our view lest we change our minds.'

'Thank you, sir,' Kimball said. 'Captain Clark too.'

'You may salute the court,' Colonel Hazzard said. 'It might suggest, Bent, that you are of a mind for a bold new beginning.'

Kimball was of a mind for much the next morning, and mainly for murder. The minute of his day worth recalling came with Captain Clark's visit to the guard tent. Kimball stood and saluted. 'Remember it's only twenty-five this time,' the captain said with a pleasant smile. 'Bear it in mind that some have survived hundreds and lived long and happily.'

'Yes, sir. I must have a good time coming.'

'Meanwhile you might make the most of this before the formalities.'

Kimball found a small flask in his hands. Also a silver coin.

'This shilling', the captain explained, 'is not to be considered the Queen's. It is easier to bite than the bullet, according to men of experience. The tongue is thus less in hazard from the teeth as the lashes fall. Do be careful not to swallow it. That is the disadvantage of the coin.'

Kimball felt obliged to ask, 'Why all this, sir?'

'I recall many a merry picnic in Maine, Bent. I have family in New Brunswick, just across the border.'

'I see, sir.'

'Meanwhile consider that I might well be serving my own interest too. I am fresh to this command; I should like a company with a less imposing desertion list. Colonel Hazzard and I are not obliged to agree in matters of charity. Sparing the rod need not spoil the soldier. Do we understand each other?'

What Kimball understood was that he was talking to an officer after all. But the rum and the shilling would not go amiss.

Captain Clark also took Private Bent's shoulder firmly. 'On some future and happier occasion', he proposed, 'we might share a small patrol, perhaps. And talk of woods and fields more familiar to us than here. Perhaps even of New England wildflowers.'

'By all means, sir,' Kimball said.

The grip on his shoulder was now exceptionally affectionate. Kimball had more to understand by the minute. Immoderate martial cordiality could earn more than a lashing; with an

11

officer it likely meant five loaded rifles or a length of hemp. He disengaged from Captain Clark tactfully. 'If it's all the same to you, sir,' he said, 'I'll drink down my rum quick now.'

'Good fellow,' Captain Clark said. 'Courage, mon brave. En garde. Show us the stuff you are made of.'

'I thought that was the notion, sir,' Kimball suggested, finishing the flask somewhere between the third gulp and the fourth.

Captain Clark lifted the flap of the tent and called, 'Corporal Flukes? Bent is your man now.'

It was not the time or place to argue. The bugler was sounding the fall-in for the eighth company; the punishment parade had begun. With men shuffled into ranks, and officers placed to advantage, Corporal Flukes and his detail marched Kimball toward the triangles. Tonks the company drummer, a Yorkshire hewer of coal who now split the backs of his fellows, stood ready with the cat of nine tails. Kimball's tunic was peeled off, his back exposed to the cool Taranaki wind, and he was tied to the triangles with respectable efficiency. His teeth were tight on Captain Clark's shilling. Flukes and the punishment detail stepped aside to allow Tonks room to flex.

'Is your instrument tuned, drummer?' Colonel Hazzard asked.

'And ready to sing, sir,' Tonks reported. Tonks was famous for never delivering sweetheart blows.

'Excellent,' Colonel Hazzard said. 'Give it air.'

Tonks drew slowly back and bounced swiftly in; there was a hiss of high-flying leather. Ripples of pain signalled a high tide of hurt. The first five lashes took old scars; the following five parted virgin flesh. After ten strokes the leather began lifting stickily from blood and fragments of skin. When the supervising sergeant's count reached fifteen, Kimball was ready to meet his maker, but interested himself ardently in first viewing Colonel Hazzard's dead body. Flecks of blood found his face as his rear was reliably shredded. It was not until the seventeenth that he felt the world shifting, and not until the twentieth, or thereabouts, that he left it. The last lashes were counted in his absence.

He woke on his stomach in the hospital tent, to Captain Clark's voice; his head was being lifted toward a replenished flask of rum. 'You have had a big day, little man,' Captain Clark was saying. 'You may recall the instruction of the court that you are to give me your solemn word in connection with the honour of the regiment. Now might be as good a time as any.'

If Captain Clark's little man gave anything, it was an authentically solemn obscenity which said the honour of Kimball Bent might be an issue. He failed to return Captain Clark's bitten shilling.

Three

It was most of two weeks before his back quit weeping and scabs formed a reliable crust. On attentive Captain Clark's order he was free to roam an area not exceeding twenty paces from the hospital tent. Kimball eased himself gingerly into such sunlight as he could locate in a New Zealand May. He watched Mount Taranaki glimmer above dark forest and cooled his mind with cloud and bird. Something better than bile in his belly might also be helpful when his hour came. To this end he stealthily filled three canteens with rum from the hogshead which warmed sergeants and corporals. His steadfast face was reserved for Captain Clark.

'I suspect desertion no longer tempts you,' the captain observed.

'Not now, sir,' Kimball promised. 'The fact of the matter is that I got no home but the regiment. My parents, they both caught a contagion. I never got on good with my brother and sister, and I don't know as I got any but buttonhole cousins alive. There's nothing back in Maine for me. I don't even remember Eastport right. There was ships, and a harbour, and Canada wicked close across the water when there wasn't no mist. The rest I don't remember.'

'Not the woods?' Captain Clark said gently.

'Nor the rivers,' Kimball insisted. 'Not even the lakes and islands.'

Kimball managed a crack in his voice and even a slow tear.

'We must put that to rights,' Captain Clark said.

'By talking more of Maine, sir?'

'By making more of the present, Bent. True that our situation leaves much to be desired. The woods and waters may be wilder, but there are ferns, and little streams. With serenity of soul you may yet reconcile yourself to your present lot.'

'The way I've heard it, sir, that might be time wasted. Men say we might not be in New Zealand much longer.'

'The fate of the fighting man, Bent. Always ready to travel where duty bids.'

'Then it is true, sir?'

'And perhaps sooner rather than later.'

'How soon, sir?'

'Not next week, Bent, nor even next month. But surely next year. This colony's politicians are pleading poverty. Some argue that they can police this place cheaper than we. Meanwhile we may be prevailed upon to scupper a few more rebels before bills fall due. Talking of which, tomorrow I am to scout to the south in anticipation of the next convoy passing through. I have instructed Corporal Flukes to give you release from hospital. You will be of my party.'

'As scout, sir?'

'Just so, Bent. The mission may give you more to think on than here.'

Kimball was not one to doubt it. 'Which way will we be scouting, sir?'

'To the south, for what it is worth. Toward Wanganui.'

Kimball was even more thoughtful.

'Furthermore,' Captain Clark said, 'the mission may help you establish a more becoming record with the regiment. There are some twenty-five lashes still in reserve.'

'I'm thinking on them, sir,' Kimball confessed.

'Capital,' the captain said. 'I shall see you a soldier yet.'

Colonel Hazzard was fond of saying that the British army was only as strong as its weak moments. Wistful Captain Clark might make a minute.

Four rode to the south. Two veteran scouts of the 57th named Fisk and Murphy jogged outside Kimball and Captain Clark. They kept a sulky distance, making their displeasure with the presence of the regimental Jonah plain. Their silence said they were cool about poetic officers too. Some of the coast route to Wanganui lay through untidy scrubland; some took in long beaches of black sand. Aside from villages lately looted and razed the landscape remained much as it was when God gave

15

up on sour apples. Ferny forest spilled down steep gullies to the sea. The terrain, even where level, was never easy. At noon, having scouted ground to the limit of the eighth company's responsibility, they rested their horses. Captain Clark used binoculars to consider the territory around. 'We can pronounce it safe,' he decided. 'You may smoke.'

Fisk and Murphy produced pipes. Bread, cheese and a rum ration also appeared. Kimball was chosen to remain on watch while others partook. It was a bright day, with sharp wind, the mountain tall to the north, the coast empty to the south. Kimball had never looked on land more lonesome. A shiver grew in his gut.

Fisk put it in words. 'Sometimes, sir,' he was telling Captain Clark, 'I get the feeling there's always eyes in the hills. That we're watched all the way down here, and all the way home, with them waiting their chance.'

'The worst misfortune is that which never befalls us,' Captain Clark argued.

'If you say so, sir,' Fisk said, unconvinced.

'You may now take sustenance, Bent,' Captain Clark ordered, 'and leave our diligent foe to Private Fisk.'

Kimball sat gratefully beside his commander. Rum did much to muffle his shiver.

'I trust this excursion makes you feel a shade more charitable toward the army,' Captain Clark observed.

'It gives me more to think about, sir,' Kimball said honestly. 'How many miles to Wanganui from here?'

'More than enough.'

'To Wellington, sir?'

'Now we are considering a hundred or two.'

'And all country like this, sir?'

'A shade more civilized to the south, beyond Wanganui. Colonists' dwellings become more conspicuous. And the natives more benign. What is your interest?'

'Knowing where we are, sir.'

'That is something you might well leave to me.'

'Yes, sir.'

'For my part I propose pushing no further than needed today. And certainly no nearer Wanganui and Wellington.'

'Yes, sir. And the South Island, that would be a fair piece further?'

'A march, Bent, of which Our Redeemer might be proud.'

'Our Redeemer, sir?'

'He walked, so far as was observed, a few yards of water. Not a score of miles.'

'Thank you, sir. It's all straight in my mind now.' The rum cached in his saddle bag should make the first hundred miles tolerable; nourishment for the next hundred would mean foraging and felony. The twenty nautical miles remaining should not slow a seasoned stowaway. The problem was whether his horse was spirited enough to outdistance the mounts of Fisk and Murphy. Pursuit by passionate Captain Clark had to be considered too. Also the worth of shots discharged to his rear.

'It might not hurt', Captain Clark observed, 'to make a more considered reconnaissance of this area. It would lend more credence to our report that the coast road remains peaceful. Fisk and Murphy, you shall wait on watch with the horses. Bent and I will venture inland and win a little height on the subject. We should not be longer than an hour. Should we suffer a problem, you will hear our shot.'

'Yes, sir,' Fisk said. His face was puzzled. 'It's not your usual form, sir. Is there some special reason?'

'Bent is,' Captain Clark disclosed. 'I think it time to break him in as scout. He may learn that there is less to fear than he supposes in New Zealand's wilds.'

'I see, sir,' Fisk said, and looked knowledgeably at Murphy.

Kimball looked even more knowledgeably at his feet.

'Come,' Captain Clark urged. 'And do not forget your weapon.'

They climbed a long ridge, Kimball cautiously to the captain's rear. The lifting landscape left them breathless. Wiry vegetation had to be forced aside. Foliage whispered in gullies right and left. Water rang over rock and shingle. Fisk and Murphy, with the horses, were fast out of sight. Even the coast was soon beyond greenery. Captain Clark elected to halt in a burn by the bank of a stream. A Maori fire had stormed out of control there. Lifeless and largely limbless trees rose from terraces of fern and tough native grass.

'You see,' he proposed, 'it is all quite accommodating.'

'Yes, sir,' Kimball said, feeling a protective grip on his arm.

'One can breathe the silence,' Captain Clark went on. 'Listen, Bent. Listen.'

Listening, Kimball was most aware of companionable breathing near his neck.

'This as far as we're going, sir?' he asked.

'I am making the point, Bent, that New Zealand woods may hold more than obstinate Maori rebels. That it may well hold moments rich in wonder.'

'Yes, sir.' Kimball sensed something beyond his means approaching. Captain Clark was now stroking his arm.

'You shiver so,' he said with sympathy.

'Yes, sir.'

'You might care to tell me about it.'

'Nothing I can put in words, sir.'

'You know you have a friend in me, Bent.'

'I'm getting that feeling, sir.'

'A good friend, Bent. With your interests at heart.'

'I thought we was going higher, sir.'

'And we may well, Bent.'

'And making this territory safe, sir.'

'As indeed we are. But that is no reason not to rest our weapons and unbuckle a little. Garrison life is seldom conducive to privacy.'

'Not with the likes of Corporal Flukes, sir. No.'

'Corporal Flukes is a long way from here.'

'Yes, sir,' Kimball said with surprising regret. Captain Clark's hands were alarmingly intimate.

'We can unburden ourselves, Bent. Be ourselves, in short.'

Arranging his sword and revolver neatly on the grass, and similarly disposing of Kimball's carbine, Captain Clark began to unbuckle quite literally. Unbuttoning was soon in progress too.

'Sir,' Kimball protested, more or less.

'Quick,' Captain Clark commanded.

'Sir,' Kimball said again, with no useful result. His own belt was winning attention.

'What is it, Bent?'

Kimball grabbed up his breeches before full unveiling. 'You might be yourself, sir. I don't know as I am.'

'Love begets love,' Captain Clark promised. 'It asks only faith, and faith asks firmness.'

He pressed warmly against Kimball, lacking nothing in firmness, and altogether trouserless. His breathing was even more heartfelt.

'Is that an order, sir?'

'By all means see it so,' the captain whispered with warmth.

Collapsing under his commander, Kimball sent up a prayer for Flukes and a firewood detail. His word against an intemperate sergeant's had gone for nothing; his word on unseemly sociabilities with a captain would likely count less.

Sinking still further under his superior, Kimball's left eye was taken by a dead and darkly weathered tree to the side of the clearing. For one thing, it was sprouting limbs, then something similar to a human head. For another, it was raising an article roughly like a firearm. It looked for all the world like a murderous Maori warrior. Then it wonderfully was.

Captain Clark mistook Kimball's cry as masculine ardour and answered with an endearment. The Maori tree, still in Kimball's sight, was given further time to place a telling shot. Even Kimball's second anguished shout did not divert Captain Clark. The firearm then gave up flash and smoke. This spurred the discharge of two or three other weapons in the vicinity. Captain Clark's mission in the woods ended inelegantly; it was he who now yelped as a bullet clipped his exposed rear. There was the wind of other shot into surrounding scrub and fern. An imperial arse made a rousing target.

'Dear God,' Captain Clark said, clutching up trousers and weaponry. There was a long moment before Kimball persuaded his legs to answer the helm. The Maori fire was from inland. He pointed his feet seaward.

'Wait,' Captain Clark pleaded.

Kimball looked back with reluctance. Captain Clark, in mounting panic, was holding his trousers high, wheeling wildly, presenting his revolver at all possible points of menace. A second shot undid him more damagingly; blood surged from a shoulder wound and coloured his tunic. The revolver fell from his limp hand. Captain Clark, after teetering, dropped too. He looked in appeal to disappearing Kimball.

'Where is your loyalty, Bent?' he gasped.

Kimball hesitated. Captain Clark became bolder.

'Answer their fire,' he ordered. 'Give fight like a Briton.'

Circumstances allowed Kimball poor opportunity to argue

that Maine no longer bred loyal Britons, nor to announce that the sour Yankees of Washington County had fought the King's bastards back into Canada with flintlocks, pikes and pitchforks, and taken scalps too. Any thought of a sentimental farewell was halted by a red streak racing along Captain Clark's blond scalp. As Kimball shortened the distance between himself and the nearest vegetation, he heard the captain begin to sob. Then he was aware of no sounds save his own. There were scarring encounters with low branches and crippling connections with logs; evil foliage lashed his face. Only one shot whipped near; he deployed himself even more resourcefully in a downhill direction. He imagined he heard a faint cry, perhaps Captain Clark's last as a tomahawk took him, but the fancy was not to be lingered on. Tumbling over a sheer bank, rolling muddily to its foot, he met Fisk and Murphy making a slow advance uphill with carbines cocked.

'They got the captain,' Kimball shuddered.

'Maoris?' Fisk asked.

'Over yonder,' Kimball said.

'Many?'

'Something wicked,' Kimball explained.

'A bad business,' Murphy muttered. 'Losing a captain.'

'Worse is a whole patrol,' Fisk concluded. He looked coolly at Kimball. 'Where's your gun?'

Kimball found no quick answer.

'You cut and ran,' Fisk decided. 'You left the captain to it.'

'There'll be questions,' Murphy darkly foresaw. 'An inquiry.'

There was just zeal between Kimball and his next arrest. 'He sent me to fetch you fast,' he announced. 'An order.'

'You just said they got him,' Fisk argued.

'Pinned down, that is,' Kimball said patiently. 'They got him fairly pinned down. Last I saw, he was holding them off. He told me to fetch you and look to the horses.'

Fisk gazed at Murphy. Murphy gazed at Fisk.

'Orders are orders,' Kimball said firmly. 'If there's questions I'd have to report what Captain Clark ordered.'

'You would?'

'Not without I'm in more trouble,' Kimball said. 'You know your duty.'

Murphy and Fisk had just one alternative. That was the quietening of Kimball. There was a long, thoughtful pause.

'Then look to the bloody horses,' Fisk said sourly. 'Bring them up fast.'

'I don't like this at all,' Murphy said. 'We been caught with our pants down.'

Kimball thought better of informing Murphy further on that score. 'I heard backs to the wall is when Britons fight best,' he said.

'It's gone queer quiet,' Fisk noted. 'No more shots.'

'Like I said,' Kimball insisted, 'he was holding them off. He might have them sized. Maybe they ran.'

He continued downhill with care. Murphy or Fisk might yet find it better to place a bullet in his back than join battle on behalf of Captain Clark. With horses in sight, Kimball sprinted. He looked back the once to see Fisk and Murphy warily entering the forest. The shooting began soon afterwards. What he failed to foresee was the wheeze of a tired bullet across his path as he arrived at the horses. It meant there was a divided party of Maori afoot in the area. Some had made a meal of Captain Clark, and were now mincing Fisk and Murphy; the others were heading feloniously for the horses and saw Kimball as a spoiler. He unhitched his horse, hauled himself into the saddle, and pointed the beast in a direction other than that from which bullets were beginning to nag. One warmed his right ear; he crashed his horse to the left. He was aware of grass and greenery rearing away on one side, cliffs and bright sea on the other. Whether he was travelling toward the port of Wanganui or that of New Plymouth was now of no importance; long anchorage in Hades looked more likely. Passing Maori shots, backed by unsociable cries, caused Kimball to swerve his horse in several directions. He guessed he had a hundred yards on his pursuers, at least until they mounted the captive horses. Altogether too late he observed a deep and unbridged gully ahead. There was no room for retreat; it was yards too wide to leap. His horse baulked, snorted, slithered in soft ground, and despite its best intentions hurtled into the gully with a crack of equine bone.

Kimball heaved himself from under the grieving beast and reviewed his situation so far as safety allowed. His carbine was abandoned beside Captain Clark. Even with a weapon a last stand would be unpromising. He unfastened and grabbed up his saddle bag, counted the canteens within intact, and then headed up the gully, between boulder and water, toward the best-looking trees.

Half his life later the Maori quit circling their fresh horses, whooping, and discharging shots into foliage. If their thought was to flush their quarry from cover, they were too hopeful by far. Numb Kimball was unable to expose himself sufficiently to pass urine without soaking his breeches. Among the firearms they were discharging were carbines just acquired from the 57th Regiment. The quality of Captain Clark's sword was being proven on saplings. Parting leaves, he watched the Maori agreeing to call him a lost cause. When their hoofbeats were distant, he lowered himself from a branch, sank in a smelly sea of leaves, and sighed. Duty said he should find the cadavers of Fisk, Murphy and Captain Clark and confirm their decease. He saw no joy in dwelling on events. There was worse than losing a patrol single-handed; colonels mislaid regiments in less time than it took them to lunch. Not before time, Kimball remembered the canteens in his saddle bag. Provided he met no further vexation, his soldiering days were done. He drank to that notion, and drank yet again, until rum lifted to a worthwhile level in his gut. So much for Private Bent's last fight. He drank to that too.

Four

Kimball woke streaky. Liberation was less giddying in dank
and cool dawn. Canteen still in hand, he was glued to a good
hundredweight of forest trash; never in Maine's mud season
had he been greasier. His head was hell, his vision hazy, and his
belly empty. Birds sang inconsiderately loud overhead. He felt
for his trimmed ear and confirmed it mostly in business. Rising
on unreliable legs, he considered his reduced circumstances.
One dim tree looked like another and rank undergrowth rose
chest high. It seemed sun might be a long time coming. The
57th, on the other hand, might not. Officers and men could
soon be roaming the coast in search of the missing patrol. It
was not Kimball's thought to provide an accounting. Meantime
sober bearings were needed. He pointed himself skyward,
ducking low limbs and pulling apart foliage, slithering into
creeks and crawling up banks. Against his better judgement
he breakfasted on two mouthfuls of rum. With hands scratched
and heart thudding, he finally rose on a rocky bluff feathered
lightly with vegetation. The forest fell away from his feet.
The sea was bold in the distance; tall to the west was Mount
Taranaki with a turban of cloud. It was as fine a day as any to
be alive and unfettered. By way of celebration he transferred
more rum from canteen to belly. He looked to his pipe. His
tobacco had survived saturation; he found a dry match to
strike.

If Connolly had it right, Kimball had to career wide of coast,
with its convoys and patrols; of any land likely to bristle with
rifles loyal or rebel. That meant hiking territory fit to make a
wild hog weep. On six sides he had a hell's kitchen of ridge,
ravine, river and tree. To find Wanganui, then Wellington, he
would have to study the sun's situation, push the mountain

to his rear, and keep his wits working. Oiling them a little more, and smoking his pipe, the prospect ahead became a shade less satanic. The pale winter sun said it was something past noon. Meditating a minute longer, Kimball saw movement on the coastal ground below. A horseman appeared, then several. Finally there were at least a score of men, capped and uniformed, fanning out among fern and bracken. The 57th was looking for its lost sons. Three headless torsos could soon be discovered. They might lose interest in finding a fourth. On the other hand it was Kimball's last chance to present himself as an undaunted survivor of ambush. He weighed the misty terrain ahead, then the proximity of Corporal Flukes and Colonel Hazzard. They did marvels. He took a large and sweet breath, swam two rivers, waded four creeks, scraped over more hogbacks than he cared to count, and put all of fifty New Zealand yards to his rear. When dark came, he rolled himself under a rock overhang beside a swampy creek and gathered twigs for a fire. He was not the first to shelter there. The walls of the overhang were worked with carvings of cruel lizard-like monsters, the work of lonely Maori hunters bewailing their lot in stone. If their situation differed from Kimball's, it was because they surely had fish and fowl and knew where they were; he had neither and didn't. He collected and roasted small tips of tree fern. It was difficult to argue them down his throat without further draughts of rum. In the firelight the carved lizards seemed to writhe, to rear, to stare. They were enough to make Maine's foulest witch fall from her broomstick. Finally he jumped at sight of his own shadow.

Next morning the vegetation at the mouth of the overhang was faint in mist. Kimball tried to recall his approach to the shelter, better to arrange the new day's direction. His suffering head was no help. He was surprised to find an entire canteen empty, and the contents of another already investigated. With no future in the forest, he hiccuped, shouldered his saddle bag, launched out, and was felled by four trees in fewer minutes.

By middle morning mist had lifted enough for Kimball to see ten yards ahead; by noon twenty. Toward dark he came upon human prints among crushed undergrowth and snapped saplings. It seemed Connolly was showing him the way to Wanganui. Kimball sped on, his breath coming fast, and arrived at another overhang in which carved lizards dwelled. Another?

There, as he left it, was an empty canteen beside the cold ash of his fire. Kimball set about emptying another in shorter order. He supped on fern-tips again; they failed to improve on further acquaintance.

Dawn called for thought. He struggled down to a stream and there sluiced his innards with most of a gallon of icy water. His lost day said he would win no ground without the sun to his left, the sea to his right, and the mountain to his rear. He headed up the creek in the hope of sighting all three. Some hours and lacerations later he found the sun overhead and then, from a roost higher, the distant sea and the mountain too. The difficulty was that the way to Wanganui still ran uphill and downhill under dark trees. He would have to map sun, sea and mountain in his mind through mazes of gully and creek.

That was the second and third day. The fourth and the fifth were no improvement. On the sixth, after a night in a hollow tree with an angry boar rooting nearby, Kimball thought there might be more to life than banging about like a toad in a tar bucket; it was time to take an interest in his progress. For buoyancy he broached the surviving canteen of rum. The uphill climb was steep, and there were no more than wisps of sunlight to be seen; he often slumped gasping and for longer and longer. From a weathered summit of sorts, where wind-bent scrub grew, he won sight of sun, sea and mountain.

They made no sense at all. The sun had reversed to his right, the sea to his left, and the mountain, rather than to his rear, rose dead ahead. More lunatic still, it had grown larger. He was slower to take account of patches of white fluttering in the far corner of his left eye. It took him much of a numb minute to identify a collection of tents. It was the eighth company of the Her Majesty's 57th Foot Regiment under canvas on the western coast of New Zealand's North Island. He had quit walking small circles to wander in large. Private Bent was all but back again, with an unedifying tale of privation and survival to tell; Colonel Hazzard was unlikely to find it endearing.

When Kimball had sworn himself out, he sat silent on his summit until dark. The last of the rum, as it sank, said that he might be better with the devil he knew. Even Tonks couldn't whip worse than New Zealand wilderness. He let himself slide slowly downhill, until trees made a roof, and slept where he stopped.

His eyes opened to black branches, dripping leaves, and day. In the distance he heard a bugle rousing men of the 57th to duty. Food and warmth were a short walk away. Even a prison diet looked promising. Yet his Yankee ancestors had a case to state too. They said that no man of Maine was ever bested by the British. Trying not to hear, he tested his feet to see where they took him. The soles of his boots flapped and the rags of his uniform rustled damply as he limped. Clutching creeper for support, he staggered breathless from tree to tree. Here the land rose; here it fell. Here Kimball rose; here he fell. At length he rose no more. The birds grew quiet. Then the trees dimmed.

There were hoofbeats and voices and, when his eyes opened, faces. The faces were those of mounted Maori with muskets and shotguns. Three or four of those firearms were trained. Tomahawks were also on show. A dismounted warrior knelt above him with an especially bright blade. This fleshy fellow had a belly-long black beard and was whispering sorrowfully, in splendid mission English, 'Soldier, soldier, what are you doing here?'

Kimball had to think too.

'Come,' the Maori urged. 'We don't have all day.'

Feeble Kimball found words; he failed to push them past his rattling teeth.

Long Beard looked up at his fellows and shook his head eloquently. 'Louder,' he told Kimball.

'I'm a bolter,' Kimball whispered at last.

'Bolter?' the Maori asked.

'From my regiment,' Kimball said. 'I been bolting six days. Maybe seven.'

'You did not bolt far,' the Maori observed.

'No,' Kimball grieved.

'Your gun?'

'Lost,' Kimball confessed.

'You are offering no fight at all?'

'Hell, no,' Kimball said with passion.

Long Beard looked up at his menacing fellows, and spoke to

26

them in Maori; the nature of the conversation was no mystery. Firearms were lowered. Tomahawks were not.

'I'm not fighting no more,' Kimball quickly disclosed. 'That was why I was bolting. I'm no soldier no more.'

'How do we know that?' Long Beard said.

'Look at me,' Kimball suggested.

That produced a helpful pause.

Kimball took breath. 'I hate the buggers,' he confided.

'The British?'

'Aside from an Irishman or two.'

'How can this be?' the Maori asked.

'When you're not British,' Kimball said with spirit. He saw surprise in his inquisitor; it looked useful.

'Then who are you?' Long Beard asked. 'From where?'

'No place you'd know,' Kimball said. 'A pretty little place, down east of Boston. Eastport, they call it. Washington County, State of Maine, U.S.A.'

'A Yankee? You?'

'Yes, sir,' Kimball agreed.

'In the British army?'

'The buggers borrowed me when I wasn't looking.'

'Interesting,' the Maori said. 'I once sailed to California with a cargo of potatoes and corn. San Francisco I consider an amicable place. If I had a second life I should be an American. Even now I wouldn't say no.'

'Then you'll see what I mean,' Kimball argued. 'We're not with the British. Not these last hundred years. We fought them good, and then some.'

'Better than we?'

Kimball thought on that, and was tactful. 'There's room for improvement,' he said.

'For example?'

'We did it quicker,' Kimball said.

'And we are taking too long?'

'No one's perfect,' Kimball said, warming to the notion. 'The fact of the matter is that this war has become boring. Not that it don't have moments. I seen enough.'

'You bolt because of this boredom?'

'Maybe,' Kimball said cautiously.

'Not because of us?'

The Maori looked disgruntled. It seemed better to please.

27

'You're not helping any,' Kimball said.

'Good,' the Maori said.

'The fact is', Kimball explained, 'I got my own bone to pick.' He rose on shaky legs. 'Take off my tunic,' he urged.

The Maori obliged. The sight of Kimball's sliced back silenced even the warriors interested in his head.

'And they call us barbarous,' Long Beard sighed. He replaced Kimball's tunic more gently than he had removed it.

'That', Kimball said, wondering where the notion came from, 'is why I been trying to join up with you.'

'Join with us? You?'

Kimball nodded.

The Maori sighed again. 'I feared that was what I heard.'

'What's wrong?'

'You make things difficult,' Long Beard said. 'We can ill afford not to abandon you mutilated somewhere near your regiment's camp. We are here to leave grief.'

'You got the wrong man,' Kimball argued.

'How so?' the Maori asked with surprise.

'There could be considerable celebration when the regiment sees my head gone. An extra rum ration too.'

Convincing Long Beard was difficult. 'The fact of the matter', he said patiently, 'is that every time we take a British deserter we hear the same sorry tale. That he was really coming over to join us. There are times when one wishes to believe the Irish. They plead that they are likewise oppressed by the British, and therefore deserve mercy. The fact is, however, that they wear British uniform and have white faces. We are not in a position to interest ourselves in their grievances; we have enough of our own. Besides, they are moody losers.'

'Not Maine men,' Kimball said.

'No?'

'We're winners. We beat the French, the British twice, and Boston too. We fight each other when there's no bugger better to beat.'

'You are trying to tell me something.'

'I could make myself useful,' Kimball said.

'To what end?'

'Bashing the bloody British. Especially one or two I could name.'

'You sound more belligerent than we,' Long Beard said.

'Try me,' Kimball suggested.

'You know we are the most terrible of Maori rebels? Of the Hauhau faith?'

'I know you're not pretty. No, sir. The more terrible you are, the more you suit me.'

'What faith is yours?'

'You could say I got no quarrel with Jesus.'

'Ours is no white man's faith.'

'It wouldn't worry me none,' Kimball promised. 'I mightn't be as white as I look.' He felt fresh inspiration arriving.

'Surprise me no more.'

'The fact of the matter', Kimball said, 'is my mother was a half-breed. I got Red Indian blood. My father never liked talk of it. I never told no one till now.'

'This is true?'

'I'd swear on my mother's grave.' It was true that he'd told no one till now. It was also true that he'd swear to most things as long as his legs lasted, and his head. Meanwhile the hunting he had done with Micmac tribesmen up the Quoddy might now serve larger ends than a side of moose.

'How do I know you're a Red Indian?'

'You ever seen one?'

'I think not.'

'An Indian needn't have no trouble with the Hauhau,' Kimball promised. 'They make a hellish din about things too. And they're buggers for mutilation.'

'They?'

'We,' Kimball said, his knees beginning to go.

'Perhaps,' the Maori mused, 'spiritual authority might take a hand here.'

'A hand?'

'Or a head,' the Maori explained.

Something unholy then did. Wilting Kimball felt words fail, his wit, finally his feet. He fell forward in an even more numbing faint than his first.

Halfway to heaven, he woke as a corpse slung across an unsaddled horse. The horse was led by a long-bearded Maori at the head of a cautiously moving convoy of warriors. After long hesitation Kimball felt for his head. It was there. Heaven wasn't. That was worth a third faint.

Five

Fed, and feebly propped upright before Long Beard, Kimball was given a loftier view of captivity.

'Riding beside us', Long Beard said, 'are men anxious to dispatch you. More so if you think to take a direction other than ours. You understand?'

'Ample,' Kimball said.

'Mercy is not to be seen as weakness,' Long Beard explained.

'It never crossed my mind,' Kimball said truthfully.

'We are just a little at sixes and sevens.'

'Like how?'

'Some chiefs think to continue warring; others think peace.'

'You?' Kimball asked.

'I act mad,' the Maori said. 'I am not crazy.'

When British coastal posts had been considered, and enough fires left warming the hills to please Long Beard, they turned inland. For Kimball the journey faired things out some. Halts were frequent for consumption of salt pork, wood grubs and water-cress, potted pigeon and potatoes. Wolfing down everything edible, then anything likely, he was soon less spectral. There was American tobacco and Australian rum, and dry caves and strongly fashioned forest shelters in which to bed; their clandestine trails were tolerably organized. Kimball's stiffest problem was pumping ship while armed warriors tallied his performance down to the last drop. Taking his time on a turd was a nightmare too. There were sighs and grumbles and inspections by his captors to determine that his pleas to excursion into the fern had substance. Long Beard could be apologetic.

'Hauhau policy', he explained, 'does not provide for trust. Or, for that matter, moderation.'

'You should see Flogger Tonks,' Kimball argued.

'On the other hand,' Long Beard said, 'your situation is not one I would wish my worst ally.'

'I guess not.'

'The longer you are with us, the more needy your demise may be. You know too much. You know our trails. Soon you will be familiar with our camp, and our numbers.'

'Who could I tell?' Kimball asked.

Long Beard was thoughtful.

'Your secrets are safe,' Kimball pointed out.

'The truth of the matter', Long Beard sighed, 'is that we have little to hide. We are as you see. Wanderers. Roamers and raiders. We can enliven the British. We cannot engage them. As for pushing them into the sea, that is all wild dream.'

'You're telling me you're finished?' Kimball asked.

'I am telling you I am a dreamer,' Long Beard said. He was not the happiest of men.

A Maori village rose at the end of a wooded valley. It sat across a long and bald plateau lifting three hundred perpendicular feet above winding green river. In places the flanks of the plateau were eroded down to rock, with just fern, plumed grass and a few cabbage palms finding soil to take root. There was clearing and cultivation below the plateau, and a steep bridle-path wound into the defence works on the summit. There were stockades made of large tree-trunks reinforced with cross-rails and lashed with native vines. There were also moats and ditches to slow attackers. The entrance to the stronghold was a low gate. Among rising uproar Kimball was dragged from Long Beard's horse and his hands bound behind him. With guards on each side, he was marched through the gate and between thatched dwellings and cooking fires. Shaggy and half-naked rebels and their mountainous womenfolk bustled around, laughing fit to kill, and likely wanting to. Children grappled with his limbs and pinched his pale skin.

'You bring music into their lives,' Long Beard explained. 'Show them a smile.'

Kimball at least bared his teeth.

At the centre of the village stood a beflagged pole, most of thirty feet tall. Cross-trees pointed to the four quarters of the compass, with strange four-fingered hands at the end of each. At its foot stood a shawled and white-haired old man. His face was almost pure purple with spiral tattoos. Holding a Maori club of shiny greenstone to his chest, he looked on Kimball with interest as the dismounted war party moved across clear ground.

'Your general?' Kimball whispered.

'Alas no,' Long Beard said. 'Our priest. The next minutes may not be among the most pleasing in your life. Nevertheless they could prove your most memorable. Warned of your coming, he sees the chance of a performance.'

'Performance?'

'Of a purifying nature,' Long Beard explained. 'His chances to be talkative have become few and brief. Your fate will be weighed with much care.'

'By him?'

'By the legion of angels he is about to call down. Should the rustling of their wings, as they pass, cause the flags to flutter in an incorrect manner, it will suggest that you are best cleansed with fire. Should the flags fail to float in other than the prevailing wind your prospects are other than fatal. It is in your favour that we have a reliable westerly today. There is also the risk that the Holy Ghost may put in an appearance. That is more clear-cut. The Holy Ghost is heralded by a roar of air. It is unmistakable and, for that matter, never heard. Were we playing poker, I would say the best cards were yours.'

Kimball didn't seem to be holding aces when villagers clad in flax mats and blankets reappeared. Their faces were enriched with red ochre; they had feathers in their hair and weapons in hand. Near the foot of their flagpole brushwood and logs were stacked and a fire quickly lit. Smoke gusted hot into Kimball's face. The old priest gave out an order to have the prisoner seated at the foot of the flagpole, nearer the fire. Long Beard, whose company might have been helpful, was soon beyond haze.

Meanwhile men, women and children of the village ranged about Kimball and began a brisk barefoot march. This mounted in speed as the priest leapt among them with a flourish of club. With his urging chanted prayers rose louder. Now and then Kimball imagined he heard familiar words floating free. Then he did. They were English words. Some were scriptural; others concerned trees and rivers, sun, moon and sky. It seemed the world was arguing the whys and wherefores of Private Bent. 'Hau,' the tribesmen shouted at the end of each prayer. 'Hau.' As chanting grew, they pointed the finger in his direction. More logs were dropped unpromisingly on the fire. Kimball waited for a shift in the wind, likely his luck, or worse for the roar of air heralding the Holy Ghost. Coughing his way through fumes, Long Beard reappeared.

'Common sense tells me', he said, 'that charity may prevail over commotion.' He stripped Kimball's tunic and marched him around the circle of villagers. His tattered back hushed all prayers and chants.

'I present you', Long Beard whispered, 'as an ally ill used by the enemy and therefore deserving of thought.' Finally they took stance by the flagpole alongside the priest. Long Beard orated at length. At intervals he coughed, cleared his throat, and paced back and forward. He pointed heavenward, earthward and windward; finally he called on the sun as his witness. The fire began to burn low, and Kimball to feel faint. Then Long Beard finished and sat.

'What have you told them?' Kimball whispered.

'That you are seen best as an omen,' Long Beard said calmly. 'You are here, I explained, to help us win our war both as a Yankee rebel and as a man descended from a Red Indian tribe noted for its cruelties. I have also argued that the angels may well hide their faces and weep should we destroy you. We of the Hauhau rejoice in headless corpses but dislike weeping angels.'

The priest was now pronouncing on the captive's future. His club rested briefly on Kimball's bare left shoulder, then on his right; at length it descended lightly on his skull and lingered. Oratory ebbed. An interesting hush grew.

'It would seem', Long Beard interpreted, 'that you are welcome as a Hauhau warrior.'

'Me?' Kimball felt breathless.

'As such it will be necessary to put you to the test.'

'I can't get along without being a warrior?'

'It would not be beneficial,' Long Beard said. 'The oath you must once have sworn to Queen Victoria can be forgotten.'

'I was fresh out of booze and hungry,' Kimball protested.

'You may have a minute to make yourself understood,' Long Beard warned. 'Less if there is a change in the weather.'

Kimball decided to make himself understood. 'What do you want said?'

'That you forgo the cause of white colonists to side with the angels to the world's end. That should serve for the moment.'

'You believe in all this?'

'That is your difficulty,' Long Beard pointed out.

The priest had grown restless. He raised his club from Kimball's head and let it fall lightly. Kimball fast allowed that he could be considered a Hauhau warrior.

'To the death?' Long Beard asked amiably.

'To the death,' Kimball promised.

'Smile,' Long Beard urged. 'You are to be protected from the savageries of Queen Victoria's servants. Your case touches us. We can be uncommonly sentimental.'

Kimball smiled warily. 'So what happens now?' he asked.

'What happens now', Long Beard explained, 'is a firewood detail. You report to Corporal Taipo for duty. Taipo, by the way, means demon. I warmly commend him.'

That evening Kimball's first Hauhau mission ended when he limped back to camp under a punishingly large log. Other warriors bore lesser limbs, some no more than bundles of brush. Airing injustice was out of the question. So were questions. Sleek and lean-legged Corporal Demon was a warrior of few words, all of them morose and most of them murderous. This had to do with past connections. He had risen to corporal while serving the British as a native auxiliary, and saw no reason to surrender the rank because service to the Hauhau was less disenchanting than loyalty to Queen Victoria. The bitter silence of fellow sufferers told Kimball that Demon was not Long Beard's most beloved lieutenant.

Meanwhile Demon hurled Kimball into an empty hut neighbouring the village centre and instructed him to persist there on pain of slow maiming. He smelled food cooking; he heard tribesmen making weary table talk at day's end. No one came near. As a white warrior it seemed he ranked lower than turkey turd.

At the point where he seemed forgotten, other than by a staunch Hauhau flea in his crotch, matters took a likelier turn. There was a rustle at the door of the hut and, in the faint light, a happily shaped young Maori woman made a showing. She bore a flax basket of meat and sweet potato. 'Eat,' she whispered. Kimball saw possibilities of more than a culinary kind. Life with the Hauhau might not be as desperate as first impressions said. He smiled at her. She smiled winningly back. Further accord was halted by Long Beard looming in the door of the hut.

'This', he announced, 'is my daughter. I am trusting her with your requirements.'

Kimball made no protest. 'Thank you,' he said.

'Be warned,' Long Beard said. 'She is here because I trust sadly few others. She will see you are fed and have a blanket for warmth. Tonight she will sleep across the door of your hut. Her first duty is to cry alarm should you think to desert us as you did the British. Her second is to give warning of young Hauhau thinking to claim their first soldier.'

'I got just a girl as a guard?'

'They know that should they interfere with my daughter, they will be unmanned. That will also be your fate should you be tempted. It would be best if you did not speak to her either. Do we understand each other?'

'Fast,' Kimball said.

'A wife, if natural need arises, may be arranged later. We have many widows.'

'I'm in no hurry,' Kimball argued.

'Sup well and sleep well,' Long Beard urged.

Kimball supped indifferently. The meat was old and cold and the sweet potato half-cooked. As for sleep, he might have managed a fretful minute before first light. The breathing of his guard was torment. When she moved her limbs beneath her blanket she was even more intolerable. Worst was when she sighed in her sleep. Kimball found natural need growing again and again. For a time he could see no end to the night unless an apprentice warrior came hunting his head. He met morning red-eyed. The village was alive with smoke and children. Long Beard's daughter sighed, stretched lazily, and sat up. She had humorous eyes and the boldest smile Kimball had seen on a girl.

'Your name?' he whispered.

'Rihi,' she informed him, in a voice quite as low.

'I'm Kimball,' he told her.

'What kind of name is that?'

'A good Maine name. It don't bother me none.'

35

'I might get to like it,' she decided.

'What about me?' he said.

'You could improve too,' she judged.

'That's all right, then,' he said. 'I reckon I'm in love.'

She was silent.

'What is the matter?' he asked.

'I have difficulty with English,' she said.

'It doesn't sound that way to me.'

'Maori is more to the point,' she explained. 'Why talk love when a wriggle is what you mean?'

'A wriggle?'

'Fornication,' she translated.

Kimball would have been lost in any language.

'We might', she pointed out, 'have wriggled the night away.'

'I'm sorry,' he said.

'I'm sorrier,' she taunted.

Through the doorway of the hut Kimball saw Long Beard arriving.

'Is he as bad as he seems?' Kimball asked.

'Worse,' she warned.

Then Long Beard filled the hut. 'You slept well?' he asked Rihi.

'Well, father,' Rihi told him.

'You?' he asked Kimball.

'The night through,' Kimball lied hoarsely.

'Since Rihi's virtue is famed, your word is acceptable. You have passed a sterner test than most Corporal Taipo will provide.'

Kimball was not inclined to argue. He was inclined to grieve.

Long Beard ordered, 'Perform your ablutions and report to Corporal Taipo and me for duty. There are matters of urgency afoot.'

'A battle?' Kimball asked.

'God forbid,' Long Beard said. 'You may make a seemly farewell to my daughter. We will be absent some days.'

'We have only just got here.'

'And we are only just going,' Long Beard sighed. 'War is not to anyone's convenience. Mine least of all.'

Three horses stood saddled at the outer gate of the fortress. Kimball recognized the piebald Long Beard mounted as the late Captain Clark's; the sword Long Beard carried was a similarly recent Hauhau trophy. Kimball thought silence wise as he, Long Beard, and Corporal Demon pushed their horses down from the fortress and forded the river below.

'You ask no questions,' Long Beard said.

'Not if I can help,' Kimball agreed.

'Let it be said that there are problems. Every time I absent myself, with the thought of harassing the British, I find peace breaking out behind my back. Another ten men have fled to the peacemaker's camp. It is time to have it out with all of them. Your report on British intentions may prove precious.'

'Mine?'

'It may win a little more fight from the enfeebled.'

Kimball was awed. 'I'm the last to know what the British are up to, and aren't.'

'You will see which tack to take,' Long Beard promised tersely. 'Mention of being a descendant of American rebels will not go amiss.'

'You want me to keep your war going?'

'You have the idea,' Long Beard said.

Corporal Demon rode spleeny alongside them.

Most of the morning their route was uphill. Then, travelling down a long ridge, they met the mountain. It took more and more of the sky as they moved; snowfields soared above bright beards of vegetation.

'It is taller today,' Long Beard said. 'What do you think, Taipo?'

Corporal Demon said the mountain was surely so.

'How do you mean?' Kimball asked.

'Just that,' Long Beard said.

'Mountains don't grow taller nor smaller,' Kimball argued.

'Then you do not know ours. When feats of arms have been accomplished, our mountain swells with pride. There is no mistaking its new height.'

'It sounds heathen to me,' Kimball said.

'Quite so,' Long Beard said. 'Tell him again, Taipo.'

'The mountain is taller today,' Corporal Demon repeated weightily.

There was a lengthening silence. It seemed they were waiting on Kimball to differ.

'I don't know if it's taller,' he allowed, 'but it's no God damn smaller.'

'Good,' Long Beard said. 'A warrior with no vision is of small use to me.'

Tangled woods and precipitous terrain diminished; their path meandered into muddy lowland. There was river, swamp, and greasy lakeside. It was near nightfall before they sighted the fires of a village.

'Remain near as we ride in,' Long Beard told Kimball. 'If you think we are wild men, wait until you see the peacemakers.'

Kimball fitted his horse prudently between Long Beard's and Demon's.

'And beware most of my cousin,' Long Beard added.

'Cousin?'

'Imagine your worst dream.'

'I thought I was in it,' Kimball said.

'One further warning,' Long Beard said. 'When you face him say only what I would wish you to say. Otherwise matters might become tiresome on Corporal Taipo's side. Is that correct, Taipo?'

Corporal Demon agreed that such was the case.

They rode into the village of peace.

This encampment sat in the bend of a slow-flowing river. There were no defence works; the lowland site left it looking even more inoffensive. But there were the same whooping children, scarred rebels, and considerable womenfolk; Kimball set off commotion here too. Long Beard, Demon and Kimball tethered their horses, and walked between dwellings. The village centre was commanded by another Hauhau pole, with a few faded pennants still flying. Watchers must have given warning of their arrival; a party of warriors waited on them. In the firelight it was difficult to discern chiefs from tribesmen; one tattooed face looked as unfortunate as the next. Speeches were made, all of them lively and none of them short. Finally it seemed a presentation was to be made. Corporal Demon unshouldered a canvas bag he had nursed on the journey from the interior and passed it to Long Beard. Long Beard, in turn, shook the bag over the trodden earth. One, two and then three martial heads thumped out. Kimball gazed down on the smoked countenances of Fisk, Murphy and Captain Clark.

Long Beard gave the bag a further shake and Connolly's head rolled shockingly free. Kimball wasn't permitted a moment to mourn. Long Beard grabbed his arm and thrust him forward. As a head on the hoof it seemed he was also to be tallied among the spoils of war. Parley of a poisonous nature began again. This proved, after hours, to be about postponing parley till morning. Corporal Demon, his gifts finding no takers, had to bend to the heads and bag them away again. Meanwhile Kimball was aware of a lean mystery of a man under a blanket at the centre of things, his face in shadow, who let lessers do the talking. Most of the passion was aimed at him. He may have nodded; he never muttered. When he shifted position, others shifted too; there was always a space around him. When he departed, his companions followed at a distance.

As the gathering ended for the night, Long Beard gripped Kimball's arm. 'Don't think I have forgotten you,' he said. 'You saw my cousin?'

'I didn't hear him,' Kimball said.

'You will,' Long Beard promised. 'As a Methodist preacher, his sermons were sometimes the equal of mine.'

Kimball woke between a flax mat and a woollen blanket in the guest hut he shared with Long Beard and Demon. His fellow travellers were already awake and arguing. They ignored Kimball when he disappeared from the hut to empty bladder and bowels at the village latrine. No guards followed him; none had been placed. Outside, the day was frosty and the mountain glittering; pigs grunted, dogs barked and fowls squawked. Villagers with their own problems were willing to let Kimball dispose of his. Even children now gave him no more than a sour stare. He might have put some distance between himself and the village before his absence was noted. On the other hand Long Beard was now his lone friend the length of New Zealand. He tramped back to the guest hut and found food steaming, flax baskets filled with dried shark and corn; Long Beard and Demon were munching with no pleasure and arguing between mouthfuls. Neither rejoiced in Kimball's return to custody.

'You again,' Long Beard sighed.

'What is happening?' Kimball asked.

'See for yourself,' Long Beard said.

'I see bugger all,' Kimball confessed.

'Quite so,' Long Beard said. He looked in powerful pain.

'What is wrong now?'

'Taipo tells me we are wasting our time here. That we will win no men back into the field again. They are all tired. Too many battles.'

'Your cousin?'

'No warrior has been worse wounded. There is now none more weary.'

'Does he say so?'

'He doesn't need to,' Long Beard said.

Debate began again in the village centre. Positions were resumed, villagers on one side of an invisible line, visitors on the other. Demon, again with his bag of heads, sat restless beside Long Beard. The man who mattered had yet to arrive. Little was said. A chilly breeze blew off the mountain, lifting the rags on the Hauhau flagpole; the sunlight was feeble. Shivering Kimball waited for something to happen.

What did, mainly, was an English gentleman. The Holy Ghost could not have made a more magical approach. A small and leathery Maori of middle years, he wore a bowler hat and dark suit and black shoes with high polish; a gold watch-chain was looped between the fob pockets of a burgundy waistcoat. The fault in the spectacle was facial. Kimball had never seen a man uglier, not even among mangled lumbermen up the Passamaquoddy, or for that matter down in Lubec. Long Beard's cousin had no warrior tattoo and didn't need one to make an impression; he had been left hideous by a firearm at short range, his right eye shot from its socket. His good eye, on the other hand, lacked nothing in ill will. It roamed over the assembly, rested chilly on Kimball, and for a time flickered into far distance. With a show of weariness he exchanged his silver-capped cane for a carved Maori staff reddened with parrot feathers. Finally, with a sigh, he removed his watch, considered its dial, and returned it to his pocket. He raised his staff and brought it heavily to earth. 'Korero,' he announced in the deepest voice Kimball had heard in his life. It seemed talk could fairly start.

Long Beard stood first to speak. After a long hour, with the morning no warmer, he appeared to be coming to the point; he lifted Kimball up by the ear.

'Tell them what you know,' he commanded.

'About what?'

'The British leaving soon.'

'It's what I heard,' Kimball agreed. 'Not just men are saying it. Officers too.'

'Louder,' said a deep voice. Sighting on Kimball again, One Eye spoke an English as civilized as Long Beard's. 'Let us all hear,' he told Kimball.

'Everyone is saying it. Most in the 57th reckon to be leaving soon.'

'And desertions have been many?' Long Beard asked.

'More than enough,' Kimball agreed.

'Would you think it a happy army?'

'Even officers are bored to buggery,' Kimball said with authority.

Long Beard turned in triumph to One Eye. 'There,' he continued in English. 'Warring will speed them. They no longer have nerve. And soon no longer men.'

One Eye continued in English too. 'It can be seen other,' he argued.

'Other?' Long Beard asked.

'If we leave well alone, so may they. But for your patrols, peace begins to breathe. On their side there is less excuse for a large army. On our side there is less excuse for many things, not least the taking of heads.'

'We are warriors or worms.'

'You are flies on the hide of a bull.'

'My flies still sting.'

'To what end? To madden the bull?'

'A maddened bull moves. This one begins to.'

'And which way?' One Eye asked slyly.

'Where flies linger less.'

'How talk of war with men numbered by the dozen?'

'Where is the warrior who said the smallest wedge could split the greatest log? My scouts say your people have been seen selling food to soldiers and colonists. This causes me melancholy. Are we poor pedlars now?'

'We are as the world makes us.'

'When was that a warrior excuse?' Long Beard asked sourly.

'Full British bellies are better than empty. Hungry men might look to our acres. Let the British be fed.'

'You survived a dozen battles for this?'

'And twice as many skirmishes,' One Eye agreed.

'I remind you that a British bullet took your eye.'

'Better to see with the other,' One Eye said. 'Each year we are fewer. Each year our lands less.'

'I hear words from my mouth,' Long Beard said.

'So see with my eye,' One Eye suggested. 'The British Empire is no passing breeze. Trees failing to bend also fail to rise when storm ends.'

'You wish to bend? You?'

'To sway a little,' One Eye said.

'Their Empire is made only of men,' Long Beard protested.

'Not men of a mere tribe.'

'Men nonetheless.'

'Of regiments. Behind one there is always another.'

'What are you telling me?'

'When the first arrive with shot and shell they shall find meat and potato in their path. Easier to kill them with kindness.'

'Kindness?' Long Beard asked in pain.

'So to speak,' One Eye said. 'And up to a point.'

'What point? When we are down to bare bone?'

'Dead warriors have no land.'

'Nor soon will live ones.'

'Our best ambush is a pleasing face. The British have seen the worst we can do. Let them have their highway. But let them long remain wary. They may think to live and let live.'

'You would risk all on this?'

'We have risked all on worse.'

'Meaning the Hauhau faith?'

'In short,' One Eye agreed.

'I hear no prayers in your camp,' Long Beard said. 'I see no priest.'

'His chants failed to melt British bullets.'

'You have banished him?'

'The man had no light and joy,' said One Eye, the last one to talk.

'And you have taken spiritual authority also?'

'Better to melt British hearts,' One Eye explained.

'Tell me I am mistaken, cousin. Tell me I do not hear Methodist talk again.'

'You hear my talk,' One Eye claimed.

42

Long Beard despaired. For his last throw he again hauled Kimball upright. 'Tell him,' Long Beard said. 'Tell them all as you told me.'

'We beat the buggers,' Kimball announced in his boldest voice. 'We gave the British hell until they quit. There was a thousand men of Maine at Valley Forge.'

'Must we let this Yankee shame us?' Long Beard asked.

'You, cousin, play games with this boy,' One Eye pronounced. 'Silence him quick.'

'Taipo,' Long Beard ordered.

Corporal Demon stood and kicked Kimball's legs away. He fell face down into mud and recalled Colonel Hazzard's court martials with more affection.

'If the British are departing,' One Eye went on, 'it is a fruit of quiet. Never of your campaign. Let this be seen.'

'Then let this word be mine,' Long Beard protested. 'We shame our mountain.'

'Believe that which you must,' One Eye said.

Long Beard lifted the bag from Demon. 'This', he announced, 'is what I most believe.' He was about to repeat his performance of the past evening, to scatter his harvest of heads defiantly before the peacemakers.

One Eye held up an open hand. 'We should return them to the British with apologies,' he said.

'Then I believe nothing,' Long Beard sighed.

'But', One Eye said, 'this one interests me. This head.' He was looking at Long Beard's captive. Kimball felt frost in his belly.

'I would', One Eye went on, 'find him an interesting gift.'

'You wish his head?' Long Beard said, amazed.

'The whole,' One Eye said.

'For what?'

'To show I mean what I say. The British may see that those who come in peace find men of peace. Besides, I have long wished a white of my own. It might permit me new fluency in the English tongue.'

'His vocabulary is poor,' Long Beard protested. 'I suspect he is lacking in literacy too.'

'You would not argue that he is safer with my people than yours?'

Long Beard did not quibble.

'More,' One Eye went on, 'if he survives your day of judgement, he will not survive long in the hands of his regiment. They would have a short way with a deserter in service to their foe.'

'That is his misfortune,' Long Beard said.

'You have won all you wish from him?'

'For what it was worth,' Long Beard agreed bitterly.

'What further use do you have for him?' One Eye challenged.

Long Beard considered Kimball and found nothing to say.

'The matter is settled,' One Eye announced. 'Your goodwill, cousin, is appreciated. The Yankee is mine.'

'He could flee your village,' Long Beard argued.

'Where to?' One Eye asked drily.

'Very well,' said Long Beard in poor temper. 'Keep him.'

Kimball stood. 'Can I have a say?' he asked.

'No,' One Eye said.

'No,' Long Beard said.

Corporal Demon kicked his legs away again.

Six

He who suffers long lives long. By spring Kimball had staked out a considerable old age. As a prophet of peace One Eye asked more of his tribesmen than a mere seer of slaughter. With other villagers Kimball was roused at dawn to labour to dark. Water had to be humped from the river, firewood lumped from the forest. Bush was cleared for cultivation, berries harvested and birds trapped in the trees; eel and fresh-water crayfish were snared in river and swamp. God never sent Sunday. Malingerers were mocked and, at worst, driven out. Kimball had the suspicion that he too might be sent packing.

'I am watching you,' One Eye warned. 'If you sadden me, I could put you to better use.'

'Like what?' Kimball asked with foreboding.

'Such as returning you to your regiment. I have a reputation as foul tempered. It helps sometimes to prove it.'

'You can't send me back,' Kimball protested.

'I might', One Eye mused, 'better be seen as a man of goodwill.'

'By the British?'

'Who else?'

'Is that why you wear smart English clothes?' Kimball asked.

'They speak peaceful intention,' One Eye agreed. 'Clothes, the English say, maketh the man.'

Meanwhile they were minting Kimball. When the last of his martial rags floated free he went bare to the waist in a tribesman's flax kilt. In rain and raw wind he wore a tunic stitched from old blankets and as a last resort a fibrous cloak. His beard grew to his chest and his hair to his shoulders. Sweating in kumara cultivations, he darkened with sun. Maori

45

visitors to the village soon mistook him for one of their own, and spoke in kind. As a tribesman he was a sight more trustworthy when Maori consonants made truce with Maine vowels.

Names also came easier. One Eye was more than a ruined face. His name was Titokowaru, Titoko for most tribal purposes, and it was not one to be forgotten. His cousin Long Beard, who rode regularly down from the hills, was more than whiskers hiding a big belly. His rightful name was Toa. Titoko and Toa were not kissing cousins. Toa was Titoko's lesser in warrior judgement. Therefore Toa's attempts to unite the tribe and win Titoko back to war were not occasions of joy. Nor did he find toiler Kimball a winning sight. 'With me you were a warrior,' he said. 'I see you a slave.'

'I'm not complaining,' Kimball said. Complaint in Titoko's vicinity might mean Corporal Flukes, Colonel Hazzard and Drummer Tonks, in that order.

'Never mind,' Toa said. 'When the folly of my cousin is seen, you may well have the worst of both worlds.'

'How would that be?' Kimball inquired.

'The difference between a dead warrior and a dead slave is difficult to see,' Toa explained. 'Demon, by the way, sends his good wishes. So, most unreasonably, does my daughter Rihi.'

'I'd like to see her again,' Kimball confessed.

'In that case,' Toa informed him, 'I must ensure you do not.'

He pointed his horse toward the hills again. So much for friendship.

Days lengthened and warmed. In the cultivations one large individual neighboured up to Kimball more often than not. This was one of Titoko's lieutenants, a Hauhau campaigner about as wide as he was high; and not sensationally short. His body was a map of the New Zealand wars, with skirmish and battle scored in his flesh by bullet and bayonet. In ugliness he was Titoko's one rival under Mount Taranaki. In bulk he was unbeatable. He didn't mount a horse; he overflowed it, with the beast peering between his thighs. A garden hoe in his hands was a twig in a tide of blubber and brawn. His eyes were heavily lidded; his face seldom enlivened by more than a leer. So far as he had a smile, it was no change for the better, and mostly a show of missing teeth. Conversation began by way of grunts leavened with fierce Maori expletives and fouler Maine curses.

46

The Maori found Kimball's obscenities more heartfelt than his own, and nor was Kimball averse to a trade. After two terse weeks the Maori invited Kimball to share his tobacco.

'My name', he announced, 'is Big Hitoki.'

'Hello, fucking Hiroki,' Kimball said.

'Big Hiroki to you,' the Maori said. 'Yours?'

'Kimball.'

'What piss-drinker's name is that?'

'Bugger off, shit-eater,' Kimball said.

With intimacy won, the Maori swung the first blow. Kimball, with disadvantage in height, ducked quick and butted the Maori hard in the belly. Then, with his knee, he scored radically enough in his opponent's family jewels to fancy success. The rest of Big Hiroki, however, remained a Maori wall.

'Very fucking good,' he judged.

His second assault, much like being leant on by a landslide, left Kimball ready to be carried home from the cultivations.

That evening Kimball woke from ragged rest to find Big Hiroki sitting cross-legged and patient, his size even more aweing in candlelight. Appearances said he was ready to take the offensive again.

'No,' Kimball pleaded. He found another tooth floating free in his mouth.

'Fucking yes,' Big Hiroki said.

He invited Kimball to consider a heap of articles arranged beside his sleeping mat. There were four gold watches, as many pipes, and an expensive pair of cuff-links; there were also two Colt revolvers and several rounds of ammunition.

'Choose,' Big Hiroki said.

'Me?'

'You,' Big Hiroki confirmed.

'Why?'

Big Hiroki shrugged.

Kimball reached cautiously for a watch, with Big Hiroki's approval.

'A pipe too,' he suggested. 'As for the cuff-links, they are no fucking use to a Hauhau fanatic.'

'I got no use for them neither,' Kimball protested.

'Take them,' Big Hiroki ordered with truculence.

Kimball lifted the cuff-links.

'Good,' Big Hiroki said. 'Now a gun.'

47

'The boss might have something to say.'

'Titoko?'

'He watches me close.'

'I', Big Hiroki warned, 'watch you for him.'

He took one of the Colts, inserted a round, rolled the chamber, cocked the hammer, and trained it between Kimball's eyes.

'If the British march again,' Big Hiroki explained, 'I might have to kill you. Or you, me.'

'It looks like I got myself a gun,' Kimball decided.

Big Hiroki, as he handed over the revolver, had an expression passing for pleasant. 'Nothing more you want?' he asked.

'No more than a new nose,' Kimball whispered.

'You and me, we are fucking all right?'

'I reckon,' Kimball said with a prayer.

'It could have been worse,' Big Hiroki suggested.

'Like being dead?' Kimball asked.

'Half dead. Dead is easy.'

Kimball thought it safer to dwell on gifts. 'Where'd you get all this stuff?'

'Robbing in peace.' Big Hiroki shrugged. 'Raiding in war.'

'You killed for it?'

'In war.'

'What's that make you?'

'A robber in peace,' Big Hiroki explained with patience. 'A raider in war.'

'When do you know the difference?'

'In war loot is of poor quality. Too many thieves.'

'In peace?'

'No cutting of throats.'

Kimball was quiet.

'If you wish dead men's boots,' Big Hiroki said, 'I have a pair of good character. It might be poor fortune to spurn them.'

'I'll try them when I look out my legs,' Kimball promised.

'And just call me Big.'

'Just Big?'

'Big.'

'I won't forget it,' Kimball said.

Titoko, after weeks of silence, found something worth saying to Kimball. 'I am told that you are first to forsake the cultivations at dusk,' he said. 'You have also been seen asleep in daylight hours.'

'I don't sleep so good at night.'

'What troubles you?'

'Luck. I must have killed a Chinaman. Or maybe broke a mirror.'

'That needs remedy.'

'You mean Maori medicine?' Kimball asked with apprehension.

'The best,' Titoko said.

'I can get along without,' Kimball decided.

'I have always failed to,' Titoko said. 'You will have no further excuses.'

He sauntered off, swinging his silver-capped cane, to menace more of his tribesmen.

That evening Kimball returned to his hut to find an unfamiliar sleeping mat arranged on the earth floor. There was also a bright woollen blanket and a perilous wooden pillow. A fire had been lit to warm the dwelling; food steamed in a flax basket. He was given no time to think on these favours. A larger gift, heralded by tobacco fumes, grew from shadow. If she didn't stand six feet it was because she soared an inch or two more. Candlelight showed a deeply chiselled chin tattoo. Her lips were full, her nose flat, and her hair greasy. If she was shy of fifty, she didn't show it. She was slow to remove the pipe from her mouth.

Kimball backed toward the door, faster when she smiled.

'I got the wrong hut,' he said.

'No,' she said, her smile no smaller.

'Then it's your mistake,' he argued.

'No,' she said.

'Something's to hell,' he said.

Her silence said not.

'Who', he ventured, 'are you?'

'Your wife,' she explained.

His retreat to the door slowed. 'How's that?'

'Wife,' she said, and relit her pipe.

'That's fairly fascinating,' he decided.

'For me too,' she said with mischief.

'Someone might have told me.'

'It was', she said, 'to be a surprise.'

'That would be about right,' he said. 'I don't even know you.'

'You are about to,' she promised. 'My name is Moana. The sea. The ocean.'

The tide, so far as he could see, was on the rise; her arms opened wide.

'The fact of the matter', Kimball said quickly, 'is I'm not a good bet.'

'Bet?'

'I still got a lot of settling down to do.'

'I shall see to that,' she told him. 'Move nearer that door and I kill you.'

'Look,' he said, 'this needs talking over. With my boss, for example. I'm Titoko's slave. He should have a say.'

'He has,' she told him. 'He chose me.'

'Titoko?'

'By now you should know that his wish, in all things, is final. If he says war, there is war. If peace, peace. If marriage, marriage.'

'I'm getting the idea,' Kimball allowed.

'It took ten bullets to lower my last husband. Titoko wishes my new marriage to honour his memory. Do you wish to pain Titoko?'

Kimball was quiet.

'Or to dishonour a brave warrior?'

Kimball looked for escape.

'Hello, husband,' she whispered.

With a suspicion that nuptials were near, Kimball made ground to the door as she moved. Her feet, however, had more purpose. She stepped to the left, by way of feint, and came in hard from the right. His arms were taken and his legs left earth. Hardly a moment airborne, he slammed into a corner pole of the hut. He lay there with more bruising than breath. As ceremony went it was tolerably quick.

'Eat your food fast and get on your back,' she ordered. 'A hungry husband is a feeble one.'

Titoko inspected limping Kimball next morning. 'You slept?' he asked.

'When I was lucky,' Kimball said.

'Men free to choose find bright parrots of the morning turning swamp hen by night. Beauty is not what it might be; the parrot hides the hen. I have your interests at heart.'

'Thank you,' Kimball said with difficulty.

'If you wish a second wife, that too can be arranged. We suffer a lack of men. It might also rest me.'

'I'll get along,' Kimball promised with speed.

'So you are not one who lusts for all Eve's daughters?'

'Not so you'd notice,' Kimball said.

'Such ambition is mad. There are too many women.'

'I guess you'd know,' Kimball said cautiously.

Squinting skyward, however, Titoko looked to have finished with the subject. The mountain was murky. 'Rain?' he asked.

'If it looks like rain and it don't, it won't,' Kimball said.

'My cousin Toa may well feel it in the hills. Speaking of my cousin, you met his family?'

'His daughter,' Kimball recalled wistfully. 'Rihi.'

'Not his wife?'

'I wasn't around long enough.'

'You thought Rihi splendid?'

'Fairly,' Kimball conceded with care.

'If you saw her mother,' said Titoko reflectively, 'you might think different.'

There was a silence, and regret in the air.

'What's wrong?' Kimball asked.

'Peace,' Titoko sighed.

'I thought you were for it.'

'War has one thing to be said in its favour.'

'I must have missed it,' Kimball said.

'It frees men from lust.'

'It frees them a little from living too,' Kimball pointed out.

Titoko ignored him. 'When you look at our mountain, Yankee, what do you see?'

Kimball looked. The peak was a ghost among cloud. 'A mountain,' he announced.

'I', Titoko said, 'see sin.'

'Sin?'

'Fornication. Adultery.'

'There must be more going on up there than I knew,' Kimball marvelled.

'You don't wonder why our mountain sits far from others of its kind?'

'It doesn't prey on my mind,' Kimball admitted.

'It rests much on mine.'

Kimball thought the mountain worth a second look, and again failed to see more than mist, snow and rock. 'You reckon?' he said.

'The truth of the matter', Titoko explained, 'is that a wriggle put it there.'

'A wriggle?' Kimball said with disbelief.

'A wriggle,' Titoko agreed.

'The day I see a mountain hump', Kimball said, 'is the day I seen everything.' He judged, 'You are telling me a story.'

'A sad one,' Titoko said.

'And I guess I'm going to hear it.'

'When you're ready.'

'I'm ready,' Kimball decided.

'When young and lusty our mountain lived with others as splendid, in the heart of the land. One day his longing for a passionate female peak could not be denied. Her husband was wandering. So Taranaki took her to bed. Her husband returned to find Taranaki about the work of love. Entrance had been accomplished, but not satisfaction. With the husband loud behind, Taranaki raced across the island and came to rest here. The fluid of love left great rivers flowing until he had no more to lose. And here he sits alone to this day.'

Kimball saw the mountain afresh.

'Think on it,' Titoko advised.

'On what?'

'Wriggling wisely and well, but most of all wisely. A man enthralled by his balls is not his own master.'

'Looks like I'm safe,' Kimball said wearily.

'My thought too,' Titoko said with sincerity. 'I envy your freedom.'

Conjugal duties, when not disabling, ensured that Kimball was by far the first to the kumara cultivations in the morning, and seldom seen speeding home at dusk. Big, no friend in adversity, seldom hid his leer, and never his laugh.

Seven

Spring had its say. Soon it was summer's. Snow peeled from the mountain until only patches crusted its cone. Moana failed to see why hot days and humid nights should make Kimball less distinguished a lover. In fear that he was ailing she brewed him fierce Maori tonics. He never lacked nourishment and ran no further risk of embittered bachelorhood. Marriage, on the other hand, was a mix of boon and battle.

'You are happy?' she menaced.

'You bet,' he told her.

'That is no lie?'

'No,' he insisted.

'So I am beautiful?' she asked.

'Yes,' he agreed.

'Louder,' she suggested.

'I am happy and you are beautiful,' he told her.

'Liar,' she said, and felled him again.

Notions of another existence were no longer a problem; getting the right side of this one was enough. Maine's misty coast was fainter still. Even the rest of New Zealand was remote. All he knew of the land now amounted to a few Maori miles. Peace persisted on the Taranaki plain, in the hill country behind, even on the coast. Toa continued to challenge it only by way of fires lit on prudently distant heights, so serving notice on the soldiers of the Queen that they still had a reliable rebel. For the most part the British remained encamped and wary; Toa remained entrenched and weary, Titoko looked to his harvests and, though not one to say so, found less to grieve him than suited his sorry face.

*

Battered Kimball sat smoking with Big in the shade of a large-leafed berry tree. Under the mountain's snowless slopes, heat sat thick on cropland and village. Summer's virtue was still to be seen. If Kimball's rumour was right, it might be the imperial army's last in the land. Tribesmen travelled carefully outside the village. Scouts watched the coast road and noted no more than careful convoys. Titoko sent parties to sell produce to British outposts; they reported no agitation. It seemed Titoko's peace might last, perhaps even his land.

Big scratched his belly and said, 'A hunting trip will suit you. Women are not welcome on my expeditions. Your safety is sure.'

'I have permission?'

'I asked Titoko to note your new scars and told him your loyalty was proven. With more to fear from Moana than the British you might have made your escape. He was thoughtful.'

'When?' Kimball asked.

'Would morning be too soon?'

'Yesterday wouldn't,' Kimball said.

There were a score in Big's party. Most were barefoot, and wore kilts and capes; a few were clad in torn British tunics and poor-fitting colonists' garments. All carried flax baskets and calabash gourds. They were armed with muskets, shotguns, fowling pieces, and carbines. As if in pursuit of more than pig and wild honey, they jogged silent and single file through the forest fringing the plain. Big's discipline was cruel. The more his men sweated, the more he rejoiced. They swerved this way, then that, and on his command loosed fire on a fat boar seen bolting for cover. Before it was dismembered, Big noted the shots which had found their mark and lamented those which had not. As warriors, he informed them, they had become a babbling band of old women. Over the campfire that night he listed personal shortcomings at unloving length. Kimball was not excluded. His pace, Big announced, had been woeful; his companions had too often been obliged to wait on him. Such delays could be killing.

'How?' Kimball protested.

'In time of trouble.'

Kimball sulked. 'No one told me this was a war party.'

54

'Maori wisdom is to think it might,' Big said. 'He who wears the thickest cape fears not the rain.'

'Tell me in English.'

'It means, you fucker, that the warrior who puts high fern behind his arse lives longest. If the British march again, you will need speed.'

Kimball was quiet.

'You wish me to explain?' Big asked.

Kimball thought not. Next day he kept pace with Big.

On the third day of the hunt they burst upon foul swampland. From one horizon to the next there was mud, greasy water, fluttering colonies of flax, and reedy islets. Here and there were dead trees silvering or slumped. Big gave the place a name. 'The great mire,' he said.

Kimball's nose wrinkled. The place wasn't any too fragrant.

'You know the story of our mountain?'

'I heard it had a hard time.'

'Some say it took its last piss here. Others say the last shit. Either way, it was a last gift. All things we hunt here have our mountain's flavour. In seasons of war our tribe found safety here too. Tales tell of enemies swallowed down.'

They followed an old and mostly hidden tribal trail, winding over crumbs and crusts of firm earth. It led them to a long island at the mire's heart. There were rough shelters waiting for seasonal occupation. About them lagoons and streams rippled with fat eels; the sky shadowed with distressed duck and heron as men made themselves known. Eel were hauled by hand from hiding, beheaded and split, and hung over fires for curing. Nor were noosed birds longer lived. They were grabbed up as they flapped, then strangled and heaped for plucking and dressing. For every living thing taken, there were teeming thousands more. Men were soon as awash with slime and blood as the creatures they slew. To Kimball's right and left his fellow men rose and fell, with curses and cries, like terrible-eyed beings born of the ooze. Toward night fires were lit on the island. Bird carcasses were sealed in clay and rolled into embers for roasting. The hunters were festive, with feats of carnage recalled in the firelight, and bellies soon bulging. The night was moonlit and thick with mosquitoes. Morning, with the sun's first light colouring lakes and streams, promised a day even more murderous. Hunters were wading into the swamp when a far cry was heard.

Moving along the level horizon, leaping from islet to islet, were two youths of Titoko's village. They paused to wave and shout with passion.

'They bring nothing sweet,' Big foresaw.

The pair arrived breathless. 'You got to come home,' one announced.

'Who says?'

'Titoko.'

'Ah,' Big said.

'It's the British,' the second youth explained. 'Titoko says come home.'

'For what?'

'For whatever may be. Titoko also wishes the stranger.'

'Him?' Big said, meaning Kimball.

'Him,' the youth confirmed.

'Of what use is he?'

The youth shrugged.

'So we move,' Big decided with reluctance. To Kimball he said, 'Why should he want you?'

Kimball didn't dare think.

Big struck camp in minutes, and urged his burdened party out of the swamp and through forest. Next day Titoko's village, much as they left it, was again in sight. Titoko sat outside his dwelling in a cane armchair, wearing tweed jacket, quill trousers and riding boots, and beside a woman in favour. No panic was apparent; he lit his pipe and invited Big and Kimball to sit. 'The hunt was good?' he asked.

'Until ended,' Big said with grievance.

'I regret that,' Titoko said. 'Your passion is better spent on bird and beast.'

'What is this of the British?'

'Who knows?' Titoko said.

'Yet you send for us.'

'True,' Titoko said, and let his smoke curl.

'You sent', Big persisted, 'two urgent messengers. Yet here we find calm.'

'I wish knowledge.' Titoko looked to Kimball and said, 'When you came among us it was with the tale that the British were departing. Is that not so?'

'It was,' Kimball agreed with unease.

'I wished to believe you. Yet travellers say that to the south there are more British than before to be seen moving on the coast road.'

'I can't account for that,' Kimball said.

'Nevertheless,' Titoko informed him, 'you must.'

'Me?'

'The bearer of unreliable tidings must return to the spring to refresh his story.'

'You're asking me to go back to the British,' Kimball protested.

'As wisdom allows,' Titoko agreed. 'I need to know what is afoot on the coast road, and why. I wish you to pass into British lines, using your eyes and ears to consider their intentions, then to return with speed.'

'Why me?'

'You look more British than Big.'

'How can I do it?'

'That is your difficulty. You have another. Big will be your companion until it becomes unwise for him to proceed further. He will be there to see you find your way to the British and find your way back. His instruction is to give the British no offence; not to slay a single soldier. He may take one life in the event of problems. That life is yours.'

Big was silent, Kimball too.

'Have I made myself plain?' Titoko asked.

'I kill no one else,' Big said. 'Just him.'

'On sign of treachery,' Titoko confirmed. 'Or should he prove too difficult to rescue.' To Kimball he added, 'Think on it this way. You might yet perish with a warrior's mana.'

Kimball, considering Titoko, then Big, was less visionary. 'When?' he asked faintly.

'You take a splendid interest,' Titoko said.

They mounted two able horses and rode in easy stages toward the coast. Open ground was ducked; they wove through tall scrub and shady fern and camped their first night on forest edge, with their fire early damped down. Big was less easily cooled; he streamed sweat until dark. If it was fair to suspect British thinking, he said, it was even more fucking fair to suppose British patrols were looking over the interior.

57

'For what?' Kimball asked.

'A line of march,' Big said.

'You think they are coming?'

'That is for you to learn.' There was a pause. 'You have your Colt?'

'What do you think?'

'It is time to return it.'

'You have yours?'

'With one round in the chamber,' Big said.

'Fair is fair,' Kimball argued.

'Give me yours,' Big said.

Kimball removed the revolver from his saddle bag and passed it to Big. After thinking on the weapon for some time, Big spun the chamber and emptied it of all but one round. Then he returned it to Kimball.

'Fair is fair,' he agreed.

Next day, through an antique telescope, they had their first sight of Kimball's old regimental outpost. Beyond it late afternoon sun burned low on the sea. There had been change, not of a promising kind. Large new earth ramparts had been thrown up. Fresh tents had risen, and a more considerable cookhouse; there were swarms of men on view. Big had even more reason to mop his face. 'Well?' he asked.

'There's things going on,' Kimball said.

'A fool can see that,' Big said.

'There's more than one company camped there now.'

'To strengthen the place, or more?'

Kimball shrugged. He watched a horseback party cantering in from the south. Steadying the telescope, sighting through flashes of sunlight from river and sea, he considered far figures and faces. At the heart of the party rode officers. There were too many majors, captains and lieutenants to be tallied. He adjusted the telescope further and felt his mouth dry. One of the officers, moustached and menacing in the saddle, was Colonel Hazzard. He disappeared in a blaze of sun. Then another figure moved into Kimball's view. A man broad-shouldered, chunky, plump, and sizeably bearded; not a man who lacked nourishment or, for that matter, rank. Pushing his horse with more purpose than those alongside him, he vanished even faster into the dazzling light. A couple of colonels then passed. Not officers Kimball knew, but two colonels too many. Kimball's eye sought the mysterious man in the middle again; this time he found only an energetic back rising and falling. Fife and drum from the outpost began telling him more than the telescope. A makeshift band, with trumpeters far from fluent, was airing a martial melody as the party rode in. Men were massed in tight company squares, ready for inspection, with colour sergeants faced out from the four corners. Captains and lieutenants on horse, swords to hand, were taking stance for salutes. There was bellowing of orders, clashing of arms and thumping of boots as rifles shifted from the slope to the present. A group bearing regimental colours moved across open ground and the colours were slowly lowered. The Union Jack, on the other hand, continued to drift high overhead. Kimball observed proceedings with an estranged and wondering eye. British ceremonial made Hauhau rites look playful.

'So?' Big asked.

'They got a fresh general,' Kimball said.

Big was thoughtful. 'What else?'

'The makings of more than one regiment.'

Big was silent for some time. 'We need to know more,' he decided.

'Something told me you were going to say that.'

'Tomorrow we get closer to them.'

'Something told me that too.'

'Good,' Big said. 'You need no further orders. When I say we, I bloody mean you.'

They retired into the forest, found their tethered horses, and made cautious camp. Morning promised to arrive in a mortal rush.

'I can't get among them with no uniform,' Kimball protested.

'That could be arranged.'

'Titoko said no killing.'

'That,' Big conceded, 'is a bugger. We shall have to find a lone soldier for an accident. Drowning, perhaps.'

'The 57th is still in camp. My face wouldn't get five yards.'

'Then a uniform', Big observed, 'won't save you one way or the other.'

59

'Come to think,' Kimball sighed.

'Good,' Big said. 'Another difficulty gone.'

Next day, after morning drill in hot sun, sweaty soldiers made their way down to the river to strip, wash and swim. Private Bent, when he rose disrobed from waterside shrubbery, was just one among hundreds of naked men. He stole a towel here, soap there, and shied away from known faces. He placed himself between strangers, a skinny Irishman and a hairy Yorkshireman. The Irishman turned a bleak gaze on Kimball. 'And who'd you be with?' he asked.

'The 57th,' Kimball said quietly. 'You?'

'The 14th,' the Irishman said.

'Ah,' Kimball said. 'The Old and Bold. So you buggers finally got here. Not before time.'

The Yorkshireman bridled. 'What's that supposed to bloody mean?'

'You been long enough about it. We been doing the work in this territory. And losing good men.'

'We been here helping out for weeks,' the Irishman said. 'Where's your bloody eyes?'

'Sorry,' Kimball said. 'I took a fever. I'm just back from hospital. No one tells me what's going on. What is?'

'Tell us and we'll all know,' the surly Yorkshireman muttered.

'With more and more men,' Kimball argued, 'something has to be happening.'

'Something will soon enough,' the Irishman promised.

'Like what?'

'Jollying up the niggers. What else?'

'Which niggers?'

'All the same to me. I heard it said they been getting away with murder hereabouts. You was only just saying so yourself.'

'So we're cracking the whip along the coast road again?'

'Not the way I heard it.'

'How did you hear it?' Kimball asked.

'This new general's hell for leather. He wants to tidy the territory before the army goes home. He can't win nothing more on the coast, can he? You ask me, he's heading up the guts.'

'Up to the mountain?'

'Everywhere the niggers are arsing about. We have to be here to give them a bloody big kick in the goolies. See for yourself.'

What Kimball saw, as he raised his eyes to judge the situation further, was Corporal Flukes. Flukes was no more than five paces off, ballocky bare, and flanked by Tonks the flogger. There was a pause in which Flukes seemed to be looking on a ghost, and sure as hell was. Tonks was sinisterly slack jawed too. It was a precious interval for Kimball. He lobbed his soap into Flukes' face, lofted his towel over Tonks' head, and in retreat bowled the skinny Irishman into riverside rock. Kimball made a respectable thirty yards up the north bank of the river before Flukes managed an audible shout. Startled men on sentry began to place shots in the vicinity of Kimball's pink arse as it twinkled away into the trees. Man born of woman arrives in the world in the buff, and leaves in little more. With one last and large leap, as bullets scattered twig and leaf, Private Bent was lore.

Big was waiting in greenery with horses. Still without a stitch, Kimball vaulted toward him and threw himself across a beast's back. 'Bloody hell,' was all he offered by way of intelligence. Bitter shots sounded behind. Big had a dangerous expression, his revolver, and Kimball's too.

'Tell me,' Big asked, 'are you a problem to rescue?'

He passed one of the revolvers to Kimball. They levelled them, one at the other.

'Let's get it over,' Kimball argued. 'There's two regiments on my back. Maybe a general too.'

'So shoot first,' Big suggested.

Kimball failed to.

'Then you've got another problem,' Big announced. He lowered his weapon, lifted reins, and pointed his horse home.

'Like what?' Kimball asked.

'A fast ride on a blistering bum,' Big said.

Eight

A cool wind blew from the mountain and gusted between the dwellings of Titoko's village; summer's dust flew from the ground and stung the eye. Titoko needed a morning to think on the news that the British were mustering for more than a flag-flying march. He called out Kimball and Big again. To Kimball he said, 'So they are to push inland?'

'The way I heard told.'

To Big, Titoko said, 'My cousin must be enlightened. Toa is the one who most dreams war. He may now wake to it.'

'What happens here?'

'To leave would be to starve.'

'To stay might be worse,' Big argued.

'We let them see peace. We ask them to observe harvests. They profess Christianity. Kindness to children, and loving of enemies. We give them a second chance.'

'After their first?' Big said with surprise.

'We give no cause for annoyance. We will not.'

Big shrugged. 'I have seen the British gathering.'

'So?'

'Your talk is too brave.'

'What talk is left?'

'And you wish me to tell Toa?'

'My word is that he must pull the forest over his head. To fight would be folly.'

'I ride now?'

'With your witness.'

'And return?'

'I need my best by me,' Titoko agreed. Looking at Kimball, however, he continued beadily, 'Much might be unpleasant if the British view you.'

'I guess,' Kimball had to agree.

'I see wisdom in your taking to the forest with Toa.'

'I'm obliged for the thought.'

'I'm not thinking of you,' Titoko said. 'I am thinking of us. Giving shelter to a rogue soldier, now a seen spy, could be called hostile.'

Kimball shifted from one foot to another. 'You mean I'm not wanted?'

'Not much,' Titoko agreed.

'Come,' Big said. 'You have a minute to farewell your wife.'

Moana made it an hour, and wept. Kimball found tears helpful too.

With fresh horses, Big and Kimball wound upland. It was a more rambling route than Kimball recalled riding before. They forded a score of streams, and all but shouldered their horses up steep faces. Big was in powerful sweat again as he considered untidy terrain through the telescope.

'What are you looking for?' Kimball asked.

'Death,' Big said, and dripped more.

'Today?'

'There are better days for it.'

'When?' Kimball challenged.

'I see a rocking chair, a quart of whisky, and grandchildren. And an old warrior's lies.'

'What lies?'

'About fearlessly battling the British.'

'Some of it will be true.'

'About the battling,' Big said.

Sweat continued to speed down his face.

'This is the warrior life?' Kimball asked.

'By the bucket,' Big said.

Next morning they looked down a valley at Toa's tall fortress, and slow smoke from cooking fires. The river curling about the fortress shone silver; the sunlight was warm.

'How does today look?' Kimball asked.

'Better without tomorrow.'

'What is the problem?'

'Poor dreams,' Big explained. 'Worse thoughts.'

'About tomorrow?'

'And the days after. Titoko may be wise to choose peace. He may not.'

'What do you think?'

Big thought. 'No warrior wishes a poor tomorrow.'

'You too?'

'Me too.'

'For what?'

Big steered his horse downhill. 'A last chance not to tell lies,' he said.

Toa needed no intelligence. His scouts had also been out. Bloodless shots had been bandied with British patrols pushing high into the hill country. True that Toa had no spy behind British lines, but his information was sobering. Gun carriages had been observed moving up the coast road. The British lacked little in firepower. There was news even less rousing.

'Two hundred Maori moved into their camp yesterday,' he announced.

'Whose?' Big asked.

'Wanganui's,' Toa said bitterly. 'Under Kepa.'

'Kepa?'

'The British now call him Captain Kepa and treat him as one of their own.'

'His tribesmen are with him?'

'For three British shillings a day, then more.'

'More?'

'Loot, women and land. They have long wished our territory. Now they can storm it behind British guns.'

Big was pained. 'So Maori fights Maori.'

'When was it other?' Toa asked.

'And when was there triumph?'

'There will be none on the plain,' Toa insisted.

'Titoko asks you to fall back into the forest.'

'To become lost beasts?'

'Live men.'

'I do not hear Titoko. He does not hear me.'

Big sighed. 'What must he be told?'

'That I acknowledge his mana. That his people need him most here. Our feud has been fair, but is better forgotten. The British wish triumph to take home, the colonists need corpses.

64

With Maori swearing love for the Queen and looking to win land, what have we left?'

Big shrugged.

'A fight,' Toa said.

'With more women than warriors?'

'Alas,' Toa agreed.

'Do you hear what you are saying?'

'Never better,' Toa boasted.

Before Big began his lone ride back to the plain he took Kimball aside. 'Getting yourself killed will be the easy half,' he warned.

'Tell me the hard.'

'Shitting yourself so your neighbour does not notice. Then trying not to smell him.'

'I'll clear my throat early,' Kimball promised.

'If you meet the Maori they call Captain Kepa, you will need more than one change of clothes,' Big said. 'Better still, wings.'

There was one smile among the overcast faces in Toa's fort.

'Your Maori has improved,' Rihi said.

'My English has come on considerable too,' he reported.

'Travellers say you are married.'

'I didn't sign no paper. Nor see no minister.'

'Married is married. This isn't Titoko's village. Here no man may wriggle with more than one woman. My father is fierce about anything which weakens his warriors. Adultery brings out his black side.'

'I wasn't suggesting it,' Kimball told her quickly.

'A pity,' she said.

Toa took Kimball from peril. 'Today', he warned, 'you make yourself worthwhile. Report to Corporal Demon for duties.'

Demon had not improved much in mood. He was heaping menace on those slow arriving uphill with fresh timber to reinforce palisades. Women were carrying calabashes of water for storage in the event of long siege. Trenches were dug deeper, with logs and layers of earth for overhead protection. Rifle-pits were growing in number, with fields of fire down to the water. Kimball looked downhill and foresaw ranks of men in British uniform pushing from the forest and pausing to fix bayonets. He fancied no further and looked for reassurance in Demon's dour face. Inside the stronghold warriors were sweaty over fires, casting bullets from melted metal scrap; others were laboriously packing cartridges. The sum of their toil was nothing special; there looked to be no more than a bullet apiece for the first wave of Britons.

'I', he volunteered, 'could help some with that.'

It was lighter work than lurching uphill with logs, and less menial than carrying calabashes.

'You?' Demon said.

'When my father wasn't smuggling,' Kimball said, 'he was the best gunsmith in Eastport. I had to help. Men rode miles to get their guns fixed and buy our ammunition.'

'You did such work for the British?'

'I only took orders,' Kimball said.

'Meaning what?'

'No bugger asked.'

Near nightfall, after tests on a dead tree, Demon pronounced Kimball's ammunition less unreliable than some, and more damaging than most. Toa found Kimball still diligently slaving, in the light of the casting fires, close to midnight.

'You have a gift for this work,' Toa said.

'I got a wicked good gift for staying in one piece,' Kimball explained.

Morning was as busy. Demon made inspection after inspection; his fear seemed to be that Kimball might faint away before he was finished. The frisky babble of prematurely heroic tribesmen preparing for strife creased his brow too.

'There are times', he lamented, 'when I long to be back with the British.'

Considering they had a fort to defend, it was like a loud fart in church. 'Why would that be?' Kimball asked.

'They know war a business. They know killing is work.'

'I guess,' Kimball allowed.

'When one soldier falls, there is a second paid to rise.'

'And warriors?'

'The next warrior remembers his fish-trap is full and his garden needs weeding.'

'You fought for the British because they warred better?'

'And paid.'

'So what kind of rebel are you?'

'A moody one,' Demon explained.

Rihi joined Kimball for a time. Talk was often halted by martial hue and cry. Silent Demon got on with the real work; it was Toa's task to bluster. He appeared, disappeared and reappeared, braving men for battle. Scouts had returned to report commotion in the British camp, with shouting on the part of sergeants, officers saddling horses, and men running this way and that.

'I have told my mother of you,' Rihi informed Kimball.

'I been hearing about her,' he said.

'She thinks you may be hungry. She says I must stand over you while you eat this.'

She presented a flax package of wild pork and thistle.

'I guess mothers are mothers,' Kimball said. 'Tell her I'm beholden.'

'She thinks you a poor motherless boy. I never mention your evil thoughts.'

'What evil thoughts?'

'Yours. When you see me.'

'My thoughts are my own,' he argued.

'So you think,' she said.

'We better quit this. Your father might hear.'

'You are thinking,' she persisted, 'of how you would like to get me alone in the forest.'

'Never,' Kimball claimed.

'You are thinking how you would slowly remove my cape and skirt.'

'Stop,' he whispered.

'You are thinking,' she continued, with even less mercy, 'how firm my young breasts would feel in your hands. You are thinking how you would push into me and wriggle like thunder.'

'Dear God,' Kimball said, enfeebled.

'And that is not all,' she insisted.

'No?' Kimball asked with some disbelief.

'You are thinking how we would then bathe in a stream, splash each other with cool water, and laugh. And how we would wriggle, more slowly, over again.'

She stood, considered him thoughtfully, and drifted away.

Kimball, trying to concentrate on cartridges, found his kilt unmentionably moist; his first change of garment was needed.

'The British, if they are serious, must strike here first,' Toa predicted.

'Perhaps so,' Demon said.

'If they lower us, they can have their way with our kinsmen on the plain.'

'What are you telling me?' Demon asked.

'That it is time to be good,' Toa said.

The two warriors stood within earshot of Kimball as he fervently encouraged fellow armourers. By his happiest estimate they were still a thousand rounds short.

'Today?' Demon said.

'Or tomorrow.'

'Women and children, and the old?'

'Have them begin leaving. Tell them to keep travelling.'

'All women?'

'Every woman,' Toa confirmed. 'All warriors must be one of heart when British guns sound.'

'Your wife must leave too?'

'And my daughter,' Toa said.

'Guarded?'

'Would that we had the warriors. Arm the old men, and my wife. Most surely my wife. As for this one, perhaps he should be sent away too.'

He meant Kimball.

'I need him,' Demon said.

To Kimball, Toa said, 'You wish to go with the women?'

Looking from Toa to Demon, then back to Toa, Kimball found himself in difficulty. The fact was that he did; the truth was that he couldn't.

'Well?' Toa demanded.

'I guess we got a few more cartridges to make,' Kimball announced.

'I need more than a few,' Demon grumbled.

'There's one I got to take time over,' Kimball explained.

'One?'

'Maine men', Kimball said, 'grind their own bait.'

He had his first sight of Rihi's mother, Toa's wife. There was no mistaking her as she sailed with shouldered rifle through the uproar of the refugee column. There was grieving among womenfolk as they farewelled their men, also among aged warriors claiming to need a last shot at the British. A cool clipper of a woman, Toa's wife made most females look lumpy square-riggers. She had Rihi's mouth and eyes; she was even as shapely. Where the daughter was mischief, though, the mother was magic. A long greenstone pendant fell between her half-covered breasts. There was a fine tattoo chiselled on her chin. Talking to Toa, her eyes were brazen and her mouth mocking; Kimball found it difficult to look elsewhere.

Someone shook his shoulder. 'Remember me?' Rihi asked.

'For a fact,' he lied with dry mouth.

'I told my father we should be taking you with us. He said you refused.'

'That would be about right,' he allowed.

'Why?'

'A man in the market owes me for a couple of hides.'

'You wish to prove yourself a warrior?'

'I never was much of a soldier,' he said.

Toward dark, after the women had left, Demon rose above Kimball again. 'Work must be ended and fire extinguished,' he said. 'The British must think us gone.'

'They are near?'

'Near enough.'

'A few minutes more,' Kimball pleaded.

He softened a small shiny object and hammered it into form; Demon was slow to identify it.

'A shilling?' he asked.

'Tested with my teeth,' Kimball said.

'And who is this for?'

'Maine mostly,' Kimball explained. 'Then me.'

Soon afterwards he had another visit. This time from Toa.

'We respect your interest,' he said, 'but it is no wisdom to hand a weapon to an unproven renegade.'

'See what I can do with it.'

'That is my worry. In the heat of battle you could fell me to return to British good graces.'

'The men of Washington County', Kimball argued, 'make a particular point of never shooting their hosts. Moose all the time. Hosts never.'

'And you are good shots?'

'The best,' Kimball bragged.

'What of you in the army?'

'I aimed where sergeants said.'

'You were no sniper?'

'I kept my arse clean.'

Toa stroked his whiskers.

'Perhaps one chance to show your worth,' he decided. 'One gun. One round.'

'That's how I had it thought,' Kimball said.

'There will be warriors to your left and right,' Toa said. 'It would be wise to discharge your weapon well.'

'I have to,' Kimball said.

At more or less the hour reckoned, in the first light of the day, men in British uniform made a stealthy showing on the riverside below the fortress. First singly, then in twos and threes, they were seldom more than fleetingly seen between clumps of foliage and fern. Toa and Demon raised their hands silently to remind warriors entrenched beyond palisades that fire was to be held. The voices of sour sergeants and sullen men floated uphill. They made no move from the vegetation, attempted no river crossing. Here and there drifts of tobacco smoke rose. Toa was making use of his telescope, and passing it often to Demon. Kimball saw why. On the far side of the river, on another flat-topped hill, horses and men were heaving gun carriages into view. One gun carriage, then two. Finally three. Men slashed at saplings so that the guns might be sited to advantage. Others were humping mortars uphill, and containers of shot. Toa's face was intrigued, and Demon's rueful; both seemed impressed.

'All men into tunnels,' Toa whispered. 'We alone remain.'

Warriors scrambled into trenches with overhead cover. Kimball saw no point in a tomb before time.

'You too,' Demon told him.

'I got an interest in this,' Kimball argued.

'Who does not?' Demon asked.

'I want to see the order of battle. Where regiments are placed, and colonels.'

'Colonels?'

'Especially colonels. Especially one.'

'What is he to you?'

'A discharge.'

'Let him stay,' Toa sighed. 'It helps to know who we are killing.'

The first British ranging fire, from a field gun, arrived within the hour. Debris and dirt billowed up just outside the defences; whoops of approval rose from across the river. The next fell within the fortress. There was a cracking of timbers, a small storm of dust. Then mortarmen tried their luck, and proved shatteringly competent. Rivalry between gunners was soon deafening. The soldiers lofting the shots were in range of a reasonable marksman. Demon fidgeted with the loaded carbines before him, more so when a mortar shell roared near.

'No,' Toa told Demon. 'They must see us dead.'

'As we will be,' Demon warned, when a shell fell closer. A slow trickle of urine warmed Kimball's left leg. There was a sudden, shivering silence. Dust wisped away. It was possible to hear cicadas, birds and soldiers' voices. It seemed British commanders thought the fort decently ravaged. A shaky regimental bugler soon said so too.

'There,' Toa said to Demon with satisfaction. Then, to Kimball, 'Who?'

'A bugger that always plays flat,' Kimball whispered. 'We got the Diehards.'

Demon called men back into open trenches.

'Make yourselves comfortable,' Toa told them, 'and enjoy the first volley. No man will have the excuse to miss. The second will need thinking if you are to hear the third.'

Demon surely meant to. He had his first choice of firearm trained downhill. Judging him the most reliable companion in the coming commotion, Kimball edged nearer. To share Demon's field of fire, he forced an opening between timber and vine and screening brushwood and found a vista of hillside and river. The sun shimmered off bracken and grass; there was a flutter of silver on the water.

'Do they still attack from the front?' Demon asked.

'In style,' Kimball promised.

There was a pause of minutes. Field glasses glinted on the plateau across the river; British observers were satisfying themselves that there was no life in the fortress.

'A man who breathes is a dead man,' Toa promised.

Another pause, and a subaltern pushed his horse off the plateau to report to his superiors.

'Good,' Toa sighed. A half hundred warriors breathed.

Foliage rippled along a hundred yards of riverside; line after line of British infantry shook into view. The first waded waist-deep across the river, teetering among rocks with weapons held high. Beginning the steep rise to the fortress, they became better targets. Men of the 57th were taking first bite at the cherry, with a company or two of the 14th rearing behind. Flukes and Tonks were both in full view. To the left a roaring officer rose among men. Colonel Hazzard was puffing uphill with pistol and sword, urging his men on. Kimball was unmoved by Demon's mutter that there were now most of three hundred madmen storming uphill. He sighted only one.

Again Toa signalled fire to be held. The British remained in blasphemous argument with the terrain, exhausting themselves as they slithered, slid, and again pointed themselves skyward. Valour was on the wane in places. Gaps grew in the first rank as it climbed close. Colonel Hazzard found an elevation from which to cow shirkers and curse shameless cowards. Waiting until the first rank was reinforced by the second, then thickened by the third, he raised his revolver and placed a round in the sky. 'At the double,' he ordered.

With ground levelling off, the British had a few easy yards to trot toward earthworks, palisades and Maori marksmen. Kimball had a last and lively view of his regiment. Some were shouting, some baring their teeth. Older faces were resigned to more misery. Two new young Irish recruits were streaming tears as they stumbled nearer. Kimball lifted the muzzle of his firearm as Colonel Hazzard loomed at short range. In the corner of his eye he saw Toa shaking his head, and finally trumpeting, 'Now. Yes. Now.'

Flame leapt from fifty firearms, then fumes. Repaying his shilling, Kimball saw a rose-shaped patch of red grow on Colonel Hazzard's chest and bloom to the size of a sunflower. The colonel's eyes were large with surprise as he sank to his knees and pitched slowly forward. Matters were further dimmed by flash and fog. Britons still afoot were in loud disarray and then in louder retreat. There were a dozen limp on the ground, and others crawling and whimpering. Toa and Demon were urging warriors to mount more fire as British backs departed.

'Here,' Demon told Kimball, offering another carbine. 'Yours.'

Warriors were leaping from trenches and scrambling under the palisades, no longer in need of cover, using their weapons to wilder effect. No one was crying enough. Kimball was thinking to make his second shot kinder when one Briton, more vengeful than his fellows, turned to duck fire, raise his rifle and show fight; the face behind the rifle, flinching as shot flew overhead, belonged to Flukes. He was steadying himself to let light into Kimball.

'Bent,' he gasped. 'Bastard.'

Kimball swerved sideways, making himself thin, and fired in much the same moment as Flukes. Both swayed in shock, and survived.

'See you in hell,' Flukes hissed.

'When it freezes,' Kimball promised.

Flukes skidded downhill in pursuit of his platoon.

The British assault sank with no further ceremony. Kimball, returning to cover, knelt to prone Colonel Hazzard and judged him more lifeless than not. The 57th might still muster a corporal too many, but the regiment was direly in need of a commander. It was a long haul from Lexington, but it looked like the last shot of the American Revolution had fairly been fired. The colonel's pistol and sword had already been lifted by a fast-fingered warrior. There was nothing for ex-Private Bent to take but a large, shaky breath.

'You got your discharge,' Demon noted.

'Over his dead body,' Kimball allowed.

Inside the fort, Toa was issuing loud and confusing orders. Thirsty and dusty warriors were emptying calabashes of water and reloading weapons.

'What now?' Kimball asked Demon.

'We leave while we're lucky,' Demon disclosed.

'And give up this fort?'

'Forts are built to wave luck goodbye.'

Across the river there was a boom, then long echoes, as the British turned to artillery again. There was a second boom too, but this time no echoes. Kimball was sprung from the ground, and bundled beneath tribesmen and timber. There was a reek of cordite; the men with whom he shared blast and burial were mostly slack flesh, though some moaning grew. Then Demon was hauling him out by the heels. The dead were laid out roughly, the wounded arranged on litters. British shells were dropping even more ruinously.

Toa and Demon broke their surviving warriors into three parties. The first was made of weak and wounded; the second of younger warriors who had the right to die another day. Toa would push these parties toward safety. The third, Demon's rearguard, was of warriors longer in the tooth; their mission was to persuade the British of peril while the first parties cleared the fortress and found trees. Kimball, limping back and forward in the turmoil, loitered long enough to find himself in the rearguard too. The first parties stumbled away down a long trench line dug for escape. As they left Demon called men back to rifle pits and palisades and ordered shot placed among riverside trees, to further dishearten Britons resident there.

Three of the enemy, however, were not daunted. They rode down to the riverside together and looked up the steep hillside on which dead and wounded were scattered. Rebel shot failed to shift them. Kimball recognized one of the trio. Short, energetic, and violently gesturing, he was making it plain to his companions that the assault on the fortress was short of pleasing.

'Their general,' he told Demon.

Demon was loading weapons. 'Look to the others,' he warned.

The horseman to the general's right was a beamy Maori with a lank beard and a British forage cap tipped to the back of his head. He wore no more than a light cloak and kilt, with his bare brown legs clamped to an unsaddled horse. Otherwise he was an armoury, with cartridge belts crossing his chest, revolvers, sword and tomahawk strung at his waist, and a carbine upright before him. He had the hungry look of a hunter who liked gunning in close. His horse twitched nervously; his face never.

'Captain Kepa?' Kimball asked.

'One Maori never short of a shilling,' Demon said bitterly. 'He still owes me two weeks' pay.'

'He was your boss?'

'When we rode together,' Demon said.

'I'd give up on the pay,' Kimball judged.

The general's other companion was mystifying. With elegantly pointed beard and long ringleted hair, he was dressed in blue colonial bush-fighter's garb, bowie knife and ivory-handled revolver in his belt, a flashy orange kerchief around his neck. He had a pad of sorts before him, and a pencil, and his hands were at work as he looked over the hill. Kimball didn't care for the cut of his jib either.

'As for Many Birds,' Demon said, 'we might have expected him.'

'Many Birds?' Kimball asked.

'Major Many Birds. He flits here, he flits there. He fights as an angry flock of birds. His true name is von Tempsky. Those hired to kill for the colonists call him the Prussian.'

'I thought colonial troops were playboys,' Kimball said.

'Not Many Birds,' Demon said. 'He uses wild dogs to hunt rebels.'

'What's he up to now?'

'No good,' Demon said with authority.

'He's keeping himself busy.'

'He's keeping himself cool.'

'With what?'

'The plan for his next painting. He has a pretty trade in warriors dead and dying. If he can't string us from a tree, he can hang us on colonist walls. Who knows? A dead renegade could fetch a lively price too.'

The general was pointing to right and left of the fortress. Demon judged him to be ordering flanking parties.

'Enough,' he decided. 'Show me a Maine marksman at work.'

'Show me a Maori,' Kimball challenged.

Demon fired first. His bullet clipped a branch above Captain Kepa's head. Kepa didn't think even to lower it as leaves floated down.

'Do better,' Demon urged.

'Who?' Kimball asked.

'Try a general,' Demon said. 'Colonels are easy.'

'I got a corporal in mind.'

'The general,' Demon ordered.

Kimball pushed his shot at the man in the middle. The British commander leapt with a yelp and his breeches, freed of a belt buckle, dropped to his boots.

'Almost good,' Demon said grudgingly.

Recovering his decency with earnest profanities, the general urged officers along the riverside to form men for another frontal attack.

Demon, for his part, ordered warriors to place farewell shots and evacuate the fortress.

'That's it?' Kimball asked.

'Unless you pray,' Demon said.

The escape trench gave out on to a clearing; fifty yards of open ground had to be crossed before greenery was gained. As Demon's rearguard thumped across it, a volley sounded and shot fizzed among them. Warrior after warrior staggered and fell. Shooting couldn't have been cleaner, nor killing much quicker. The rowdy ambushers were Maori, Captain Kepa's tribesmen. Those who survived Kepa's fire to their left reeled back into shot placed by Many Birds' irregulars from the right. Demon saw no cause to detain the poor score of warriors left in his command. 'Fight with your feet,' he urged.

Men knew an order. They ran until they crashed into Toa's parties groping toward the interior. They then had to turn. 'Stand,' Demon ordered. 'Fight.' They stood and fought, stood and fought again, until there were no hours left in the day. Dark slowed the killing, but not fever. There was the flash of firearms among leaf and vine until ammunition was spent and chopping and grunting began. Time and again Demon took the fight to the pursuers, to terrify them and rally his own; time and again the pursuers became the pursued. Anything with an edge in Demon's clutch was soon worth its weight in gore. Slicing a fillet here, a rasher there, finding sinew and vein and finally lopping away limbs, he seemed fascinated by the number of ways men might be divided. Slimy with blood and forest filth, finally with blades blunt and chipped, they fought for four days more. Then the forest held only faint birds, festooning creeper, a flutter of sunlight and a cluster of corpses. Flies fell noisily on drying blood. Demon tottered a little, looking about with disbelief, and then toppled to earth. Though he wasn't seen counting, he could now tally only five warriors in his rearguard, one of them white. Kimball sagged to ground too.

'How did you do it?' he whispered.

'I was a Catholic,' Demon said. 'Methodists aren't serious.'

Nine

Demon's survivors finally joined with Toa's people. Together they climbed into the tall interior. Wounded and wobbling warriors were gathered in as they went. Daylight was fitful through mists of foliage. By night they had the flare of torches. First they waded up stony rivers and creeks to leave no footprints. Then vines were slashed for paths along which litters could be carried. When death slowed them, shallow graves were dug; tears were few and rites short. It was a week before Toa and Demon agreed a favourable distance from the coast won. A riverbank campsite was decided, and fires lit; festering wounds were treated with the juice of boiled flax root. Meanwhile huts of sapling and thatch grew. A forage party was sent out. Another party was told to scout back to the fortress, to bury dead and determine pursuit ended. This left the camp with few men fit and free. Toa and Demon still had to win all their scattered people back from the wilderness, especially the women. A choice of men was made for the search.

Toa considered Kimball. 'You too,' he decided.

'Me?'

'I wish my woman,' Toa explained. 'Also my daughter. Above all I wish them as they were. Especially my daughter.'

'I'll do my best,' Kimball promised.

'Your least will be splendid,' Toa warned.

Those trusted to win back the women wormed their way through neighbouring valleys at first light. Kimball started out in a party of four and soon mislaid his morose companions among unfriendly growth. He followed up a creek, looking for signs of human travel, and fetched up under a slender waterfall in late afternoon. It fell all of fifty feet into a deep green pool. Cliff flecked with moist fern rose tall on each side. Enough was enough; he could push no further. He sat and lit his pipe. Lifting his eyes, he sighted a ladder of chopped saplings and vine dangling down cliff face on the far side of the waterfall. He could have sworn that it had not been there a moment before. But it was surely there now. Someone agile must have clambered up the cliff to set the ladder in place. The climb remained a test even so. He swayed from foothold to foothold, snatching at fern for support, rising giddily higher with the waterfall soaking his left flank and the slippery ladder likely to unravel. There was little day left when he crawled bruised and sodden on to clifftop, and no sound save that of water pitching away to his rear. Too late, he wondered if he might have toiled into a snare. His last yard was unpromising. The vine ladder ended at a tree. Beside the tree were Maori feet.

Braced for grief, he lifted his gaze higher. Rihi, her mother's gun on her shoulder, was smiling.

'We've been looking for you,' he said hoarsely.

'That is happy,' she said. 'We have been looking for you.'

'You've been watching me get up here?' he said with grievance.

'Shaking the ladder,' she confessed.

'Thank you,' he said bitterly.

'You are alone?'

'I lost the sods with me.'

'That is happier still.' She began unburdening herself of the gun.

'Happy how?'

'I no longer need this ugly thing. I was left here to take up the ladder in case we were followed.'

'You're alone too?'

'Even more happily.'

'Where's your party?'

'Safe. Some way from here.'

'Mine's a fair piece back too.'

'More to the good,' she said.

'For what?' he asked warily.

'Our wriggle,' she suggested.

'I thought there was a war on,' he said.

'Not here,' she promised.

Upstream, the last of the sun still lit a ferny site. Rihi flung herself down. Kimball stood his ground, limp.

'I think you fall on top of me,' she said.

'You think?'

'If you know a better way to begin, I am willing to listen.'

'Folk mess around a bit first,' Kimball explained.

'Mess around, then,' she sighed.

'I never done much girling,' he admitted. 'As for whoring, I never met one who messed.'

'The woman Titoko gave you?'

'Not so you'd notice.'

There was a bleak silence.

'I thought you would be reliable,' she said.

'For what?'

'My first,' she confessed.

'You mean you're just talk?'

'Chief's daughters,' she reported, 'don't wriggle about.' She looked away; a tear trickled.

Kimball thought comfort timely. 'Things could be worse,' he judged.

'How?' she asked bitterly.

'Think of the hole I'd be in if it was my first too.'

'I am thinking of the hole you are not in.'

So was Kimball.

'Maybe we should start over and move along slow,' he said. 'Tell me hello like we only just met.'

She took a quiet breath. 'Hello,' she told him boldly.

'Hello,' he said, and fell on her fast.

His day couldn't have taken a fancier turn. Rihi was capable of considerable commotion. Trying to hold her in place was like keeping a mad ship on course in a Maine blow. With his lower deck awash, not a star to steer by, he rode it out on a storm-jib. His body became a long sigh, with Rihi pitching in too, and for that matter most everything.

When they rolled apart it was near enough dark. Pale sky above black hills promised a moon.

'What are you thinking?' she asked.

'Wriggling takes your mind off a fight.'

'And you think you are going to sleep now?'

'You reckon about right,' he said.

'You are not,' she promised. 'Now wriggling's over, you talk love.'

'There's a time and place for everything,' he argued.

'Go on,' she said. 'Whisper sweet things.'

'What things?'

'To keep war away.'

'It sounds like you got something against it,' Kimball said.

'Haven't you?' she asked.

On second thought Kimball found sweet things coming easy. They nested together the night through.

In the morning they worked upstream to the camp where the weak, the aged, and the women were camped. Old warriors on guard lowered their guns. Otherwise the first face seen was that of Rihi's mother. She had no smile. Nor was there a glimmer when Rihi announced that Toa had survived the fall of the fortress and was now in nearby forest, and safe.

'Where', she asked her daughter, 'have you been?'

'Helping him find us,' Rihi said.

'All night?'

'Most of it,' Rihi claimed.

The mother considered her elated daughter, then guilty Kimball, and came to an intelligent conclusion.

'You father will kill you,' she told Rihi. 'Then me.'

To Kimball she said coolly, 'My name is Hine. We have not met.'

'My bad luck,' Kimball said.

'It is not improving,' she warned. 'What have you been about with my daughter?'

Kimball was quiet.

'Well?' she asked.

'You wouldn't believe a little praying for peace?'

'No.'

'That's how I had it figured,' Kimball said.

'For your health,' Hine sighed, 'let there be no talk of this. And no further lost nights.'

Rihi turned away with a pout.

'So who', Hine asked, 'still lives of the warriors?'

'Those fast on their feet,' Kimball said.

'Which means not many?'

'There could have been more,' he agreed.

'And my man managed with no wound?'

'Not so you'd see.'

'He wanted war,' she said. 'Perhaps now he is happy.'

'He's not making a show of it,' Kimball said.

It took all the hours of light in the day to move Hine's party down past the waterfall toward Toa's camp. The old had to be helped, and young children nursed. The last of the journey was torchlit. Then the brighter fires of Toa's riverside camp began burning beyond trees. There was much pressing of nose on nose, and sharing of breath. Reunions were loud. So was grief for those lost.

'My woman and daughter are in order,' Toa told Kimball. 'It is possible you deserve praise.'

'I don't mind one way or the other,' Kimball insisted.

'Conscience tells me that my unkind thoughts about you have been uncalled for. I am talking of Rihi.'

'If I said your daughter was nothing to look at I'd be a liar.'

Toa's face grew less genial. 'You are not hiding lust for her?'

'I was just being honest,' Kimball argued.

'Honest?'

'Man to man.'

'Christian gospel told us that honesty is its own reward. For myself, I have never found it sufficient. In your case it deserves much respect.'

'Like what?' Kimball asked.

'I will instruct Corporal Demon to free you from menial duties.'

'Thank you,' Kimball said. Rihi looked his for the asking.

'Instead,' Toa said, 'you will join him in finding a route through the forest and down to the plain.'

'I have only just got here,' Kimball complained.

Toa failed to hear. 'On the plain,' he said, 'you will observe how Titoko's people are surviving the British. Demon will return to report to me. You will remain.'

'With Titoko?'

'With your woman,' Toa said.

81

'You didn't say Rihi would be travelling with me.'

'That is correct,' Toa said, even cooler. 'I did not.'

'I don't understand,' Kimball said.

'My feeling is that your talents are suited to Titoko's village. Your place is with your woman there.'

'You are kicking me out,' Kimball mourned.

'As a poor omen,' Toa acknowledged. 'Since you joined us little has gone well.'

'I'm to blame for everything?'

'A warrior does well to remove those things which may not be auspicious. A white skin seems likely.'

'So I go.'

'With regret. I can ill afford to lose another pair of warrior hands. Your genitals, however, are the root of the problem.'

'That's your last word?'

'Just so,' Toa said. 'As for Rihi, I wish no noisy farewells.'

'Give me a second chance,' Kimball pleaded.

'That might be more painful,' Toa said. 'Emasculation is final.'

Horses had been lost with the fall of the fortress. Other things had been too, among them knowledge of their present location. It was generations since the tribe had hidden so far inland. To find lowland and mountain, then Titoko's village, Demon and Kimball needed the rising sun to their rear. They set out afoot at first light, with a rifle apiece and next to no provisions. They would have to fend for themselves in the forest, or fall to swift rivers and barren heights in finding familiar country. For Rihi, however, the worst had already arrived. When she learned of Kimball's banishment her grief sent birds speeding to safety. The morning and most of the camp came to a halt. Tribesmen and tribeswomen gathered to wonder.

'You', she told her father, 'are a slimy old eel.'

'Bail out your mouth,' Toa said.

'You are the arse-faced son of a boar and a sow. You fart through your teeth.'

That seemed tolerably final.

'Get her away,' Toa ordered.

Hine and other senior women hurried to help; Rihi was dumped in a hut, and muffled. Hine emerged to turn a loveless gaze on her husband. She didn't look any less handsome in rage.

'You', she said, or near enough, 'are all piss and wind.'

'So this is what it has come to,' Toa sighed.

'It is what you have come to,' she observed. 'A girl is a girl, even your daughter.'

'What are you asking?'

'It is what you ask of her.'

'Only respect.'

'Win it,' she suggested. 'All this because your daughter, as daughters do, wants a man to call her own. A man who is not you.'

'Him?' he asked, meaning Kimball.

'Even him,' Hine said.

'Where is his warrior line? What canoe did his ancestors sail?'

'I heard no such questions when he returned us to your camp.'

'Unnecessary. All know him an outcast of low reputation.'

'Recent days say he has uses.'

'I shall be the judge of that.'

'I think your daughter a better.'

'She will want the man I want.'

'When you are down to your last warrior,' she mocked. 'When you wish to favour the wretch with Rihi so that he might return to the fight.'

'I will have respect from you too.'

'That day has gone,' she said. 'Or have you not noticed?'

Demon whispered impatiently to Kimball. 'Move. This war makes others look clean.'

Demon's strategy in rough country did not favour skirmishing. He pushed forward the way he was pointed, seldom looking for saddles or easy slopes; he refused to let landscape interfere with a mission. If a summit sat in their path, the summit was stormed. Cliffs were never outflanked. He spent little time looking for safe fords even if a river was roaring. He and Kimball would march across it with a pole gripped between them and, in the last resort, swim. That might mean being swept downstream, battered by boulders. It often meant Kimball spitting out much of the river as he rose bobbing from rapids to

83

find tall Demon tugging him out by the hair. In the evening they sheltered under rock overhangs and ate fern root, forest grubs, berries and possibly a pigeon if long-striding Demon allowed a pause to snipe one from a bough. Demon, with seldom more than a grunt, then tumbled asleep for a few hours. He was mean with conversation, and made no exception for matters on Kimball's mind.

'I don't think I've been treated fair,' he confided.

'You are alive,' Demon said tersely.

'If you say so,' Kimball mourned.

'Such was never the case, in the past, when a war chief was crossed. You risk Toa's standing. Yet his orders did not appear to include the instruction to dispose of you mortally.'

'You would?'

'With no joy.'

Joy never got a great showing in Demon's face anyway. Even with his fellow traveller snoring, Kimball was slow finding sleep; he could never quite calculate his chances of another dawn. On the other hand Demon might not muster enough treachery to take him unawares.

'So what is it with Toa?' he asked at the end of another day's travel.

Demon shrugged.

'I mean about Rihi,' Kimball prompted.

'A spirited daughter can be worth more than a warrior son. She might be worth a good hundred.'

'Meaning?'

'If Toa wishes to war further, he needs an alliance.'

'With who?'

'Titoko, for best.'

'He would offer her to Titoko?'

'To make the tribe one. Titoko's weakness for women is not hidden.'

There was a lengthening pause.

'Shit,' Kimball said.

Ten

On a mild summer morning, as they battled through growth, the summit of the mountain, surely no taller, showed through breaks in overhead foliage. Trees thinned, and they sighted lowland. Demon considered western sky. Short of the mountain, thick smoke lifted.

'Guests,' he grunted.

'British?'

'Still on the march.'

The two had shaken off forest further north than Demon expected. If he read the smoke right, the British were raking around for rebels old and new to the north. Titoko's village was to the south. Demon and Kimball were safe unless they fell in with British flying patrols.

'That', Demon said, 'could be sad from your point of view.'

'Yours?'

'I can give the Queen a second chance,' Demon said, surging downhill.

They travelled past the great mire that afternoon. After surprising a pair of slow-rising duck for supper they pushed toward Titoko's village. When dark slowed them they ate, slept, and next day travelled on in a dawn loud with birds. The sun was well up the sky before they rose on a ridge and looked on the bend of stream where Titoko's village had been sited. The site was there; the village was not.

'No,' Kimball whispered.

'Yes,' Demon sighed.

A little charred timber rose askew in sooty rubble. Otherwise the village was levelled to the last latrine. As they closed with the place a breeze played with cinders. The prospect, daunting enough from a distance, began to give up stench. Humming flies heralded rotting horses and cattle; there was worse. The smell of cooked meat rose from the corpses of people suffocated within their dwellings when the village was torched. Those overcome were heaped where stumps said doorways had been. Elsewhere in the debris were the bodies of women split by shrapnel and men more pitilessly divided. Even dogs feeding on the dead had grown disgusted; they had already moved on.

'So much for Titoko,' Demon said. 'So much for peace.'

Kimball's mouth was too full to speak. When he opened it, his breakfast leapt free. Sooner than look out the remains of his hut he walked from the village to the cultivations in which he had sweated. No crop was visible, nor would be this summer. Gardens had been left waste by scores of trampling horses. He slumped in the berry grove where he and Big once hid from labour.

Perhaps an hour later Demon found him there.

'It could have been worse,' he announced.

Kimball was not impressed. Demon sat, lit his pipe, and smoked.

'Perhaps fifty dead,' he said.

'How worse is worse, then?'

'A hundred.'

'What makes fifty so fair?'

'They failed to finish ours. They bettered their count here.'

'And that's supposed to be all right?'

'In the warrior way,' Demon said.

Kimball was silent for a time. 'Bugger warriors,' he decided. 'I saw a British colonel fall. Regret is late in the day.'

'You're telling me something.'

'Your hand is on this too.'

'Enough,' Kimball pleaded. 'I'm in so many minds I'll never be mad.'

'I must have missed it.'

'There is a bright side.'

'My reckoning', Demon went on, 'says many have flown.'

'Titoko? Big?'

Demon shrugged. 'They may be safe.'

'Are we?'

'It is not helpful to think on it,' Demon suggested.

'What would you call helpful?'
'Burying the dead,' Demon said.

Kimball fearfully searched for his own hearth. One patch of debris looked much like another. His was signalled by a silver gleam in the ash. It was one of the cuff-links Big had given him. He searched further and found the second shining too. There was no more to salvage, and no scrap of flesh.
'There,' Demon urged. 'No laments.'

Their toil was no easier the next day, in summer sun, and even more foul on the third. With another five graves dug, there were always five more. They took themselves upstream to a swimming hole where air was sweet and water ran clear. Demon, though, was never far from a firearm.
On the fourth day they covered the last of the dead.
'One difficulty remains,' Demon said.
'What would that be?' Kimball asked.
'You,' Demon said. 'You cannot be turned loose.'
'What makes that a problem?'
'If I return with you,' Demon observed, 'Toa may kill me. If I don't, his womenfolk will.'
'I'm glad it's your problem,' Kimball said.

They slept in forest edge on the far bank of the stream. Kimball woke to find the sun bright, the mountain clear, and Demon cleaning a carbine.
'If you were to flee,' Demon proposed, 'it might help matters.'
'Flee?'
'I cannot leave you to be taken alive by the British.'
'You're talking a bullet in my back.'
'If you were to oblige,' Demon confirmed.
'No,' Kimball said.
'I thought not,' Demon said.
After they breakfasted, Demon found cause to climb to his feet and look north through a rusty pair of field glasses.
'Two horses,' he said. 'Two riders.'
'British?'
Demon shrugged. 'Perhaps Kepa's.'
'We move?'

'Not until our first shots have taken their horses out from under them as they ford the stream,' Demon insisted. 'We fell them with our second.'

Kimball loaded weapons while Demon kept watch. There was a punishing pause. Then he heard Demon's intake of breath.

'Titoko,' he marvelled. 'Big too.'

Noses were pressed, and sharing of breath long. The four sat, smoked for a time, then ate, drank, and talked. Titoko wished news of Toa's people, of the fall of the fortress and the flight, before an accounting of his own grief. When the British column made a showing, he ordered most villagers to persist in residence. Then he dressed in a quality English suit, knotted his tie, and chose Big and others as dependable to advance on the Queen's army. Titoko's men were unarmed; all carried calabashes and baskets brimming with fruit and vegetables, preserved birds and berries. They halted two or three hundred paces out from the village to form a party of welcome. When British skirmishers closed, they were harangued by a stylishly clad Maori and surprised by a salvo of potatoes, onions, and the sweet kumara for which Titoko's village was now famed. For the most part the puzzling missiles fell harmless at British feet. Some appeared to suspect a hellish Hauhau ruse; superstitious Irishmen burst into sweat and began breaking. The skirmishers were withdrawn so that British officers could reconsider the human barrier. Finally orders were given, field guns set up, and shells slammed into breeches. Titoko, waiting on a British messenger, ordered his warriors to stand their ground. There was no messenger; there was, all the same, a message. Shell after shell sped over the heads of Titoko's party to drop in the village. There were people shouting; there were people running. It was also seen that Captain Kepa's Maoris were pushing toward the village from the flanks; Titoko's men were about to be mired between flaming guns and falling tomahawks. Titoko ordered his party to retire. Those fast enough to find horses rescued their families; those slower and horseless perished with the village. The survivors looked back to see Kepa's auxiliaries making free, finally reducing dwellings with fire, while screams grew fewer and the British stood off until death and destruction were sufficient. The smoke rose most of a mile tall.

'So,' sighed Titoko. 'It is done.'

'Are you?' Demon asked.

Titoko made no answer.

'Where is character in peace?' Demon prompted.

'And where in war?' Titoko said.

He looked for shade, spread a blanket, and slept the day through.

While Demon kept watch, Big walked Kimball to the village site; they stood together in ash. 'I found these,' Kimball said, and showed his companion the scorched cuff-links. 'They brought me no luck.'

'I can take one back,' Big offered.

'One?'

'Poor fortune is better shared. My right arm is yours.'

'Thank you,' Kimball said.

'First see what use I have for your left.'

They were quiet. 'You wonder about Moana,' Big said.

'I reckon,' Kimball admitted.

'Kepa's men would have taken women thought useful.'

'Moana too?'

'She can fill a man's belly.'

'What else is possible?'

'Many women without men have flown to look for new in the north. Better than see the sky fall, they kept travelling with the British behind.'

'Travelling where?'

Big shrugged. 'As far as their feet take them. Sight of the mountain means grief. Sight of Titoko too.'

'Titoko?'

'Many now see a man of no mana. A man who can no longer war with the world, or fight fortune.'

'Who can?'

'A man of mana.'

'And Titoko is not?'

'Now most fucking not.'

'You think Moana thinks worse of Titoko too?'

'Who knows? You look to be free.'

'It is not something I asked for.'

'It is what you have got,' Big said. He kicked a crumbling timber. 'Travellers tell the same elsewhere. Not a village unburned.

Even those Christian and wanting no war. All under Taranaki are now tame.'

'Titoko too,' Kimball suggested.

Big shrugged. 'He says nothing.'

'I can see that.'

'He sleeps much. Always alone now, no longer with women.'

'Is that a good sign or bad?'

'It depends on his dreams. I would not wish them.'

'Why is he back?'

'Because he looks for something lost.'

'Like what?'

'Himself,' Big said.

That night Titoko stirred enough to join them at their fire. He took food without speaking, and afterwards turned his good eye on Demon. Finally he said, 'The split tree asks the axe. Likewise split tribes.'

'I hear you,' Demon said.

'My people must now join Toa's, and his mine.'

'You talk war?' Demon asked.

'I talk tree and tribe,' Titoko said. To Big he added, 'You will travel with Demon and see it done.'

'You?'

'I have business.'

'Here?'

'Elsewhere.'

'You have not spoken of this.'

'I speak of it now,' Titoko said.

'Bonding the tribe is not a matter for a lieutenant,' Demon argued. 'Toa will have much of a mocking kind to say.'

'I will have more,' Titoko promised.

'There is one problem,' Demon said.

Titoko lifted his gaze from the fire. 'Of what nature?' he asked.

'Of human nature,' Demon said, with a hand on Kimball. 'Toa wishes to be rid of him. He sees a poor omen.'

'He loses his fort, half his warriors, and frets over one small Yankee?'

'You may value this man more than Toa. It is better that Toa is not displeased.'

'Has this one not served your people well?'

'He thinks to serve Toa's women better.'

'Hine?' Titoko asked with a one-eyed gleam.

'Surely the daughter.'

'Ah,' Titoko said.

'Toa has plans for Rihi.'

'He keeps a poor secret,' Titoko said.

'His prospects are few. Without a daughter, they are fewer.'

Titoko was thinking more on Kimball than Toa. 'Must I have him on my hands?' he asked.

'It would be no kindness to leave him walking the territory.'

There was a pause in which Kimball's lot was considered.

'Well?' Demon asked.

'He may prattle less than a Maori,' Titoko decided. 'He travels with me.'

Next morning Demon and Big rode north to begin joining the tribe. Titoko and Kimball watched them ride out of sight.

'What now?' Kimball asked.

'Speak only when I wish it,' Titoko announced. 'Even so, give it thought.'

'That's no problem,' Kimball said.

'It will be,' Titoko warned.

They walked west. At times they followed dusty dray roads; at other times trails fainter wound through tree and scrub. Their direction was soon plain. Hourly the mountain lifted higher ahead. They passed charred villages, shredded crops, and saw no living human other than a lone Maori rider, a man not of Titoko's people, looking for villagers missing.

'The British?' Titoko asked.

'Lost also,' the horseman said. 'They thought to follow my people up into mountain forest. They now pick a fight with the mountain. It defies them as no human can. Presently they seek guns fallen down ravines and sup poorly on their own horses.'

'So we are safe,' Titoko concluded.

'Unless you fall over them as they crawl home,' the horseman said.

At noon next day they arrived at the mountain's foot. Eroding rock faces reared from foliage, and fast water roared. The rain forest was silvered with the limbs of long-dead trees; moss cushioned their footfall and flimsy fern and beards of lichen fogged their route. After the heat of the lowland the air was clammy and cool, with a sour odour of rot. Their path, turning this way and that, was plain only to Titoko. They had gone some distance before crushed leaves and bent branches told Kimball that men must long have made a habit of travelling this way. They began crossing bridges of slashed creeper swung across stream and gully. Birds scattered noisily from tree-tops, and flightless feathered things skittered away in undergrowth. The summit was only to be seen from sites where storm and torrent had left the forest roof tattered. Titoko's silence was even more sobering as they pushed higher. It was late afternoon before he called a hard-breathing halt.

'You wonder what we are doing here,' he observed.

'I guess,' Kimball admitted.

'So do I,' Titoko said.

Dusk found them still besieged by forest. They ate leanly, unrolled their blankets, and looked for comfort beside a fire lit in the lee of a large rock. Soon small bats began rustling between trees. As their fire burned low Titoko took Kimball's shoulder. 'Wait,' he whispered. 'Watch.'

A marvel began. A spectral light fluttered from the earth; decaying trees and mouldering debris teemed with tiny points of phosphorescence. As the bright tide lapped to their feet, Kimball's scalp promised to part company with his skull.

'What is it?' he whispered.

'Life beyond fate,' Titoko said. 'It still burns.'

Mounting higher next morning, they moved through mammoth trees in moist gowns of lichen. Then growth shrank to scrub. Finally scrub too became sparse, making room for wiry mountain grass, moss of many colours, and shy herbs. The bright summit, among tossing cloud, lit the sky like a torch; wind blew cool in their faces. Far below, woody lowland unfurled to bright coast. Titoko's feet led them past crevice and shingle slide, finally to caves closed with rock. Titoko paused at one, then at another, and took breath outside a third.

'Ancestors,' he thought to inform Kimball.

'Hauled all the way up here?'

'Warriors thought worthy,' Titoko said.

'They must have been wild buggers,' Kimball suggested.

Titoko's silence seemed to say so.

Kimball finally asked, 'What is it you want with them?'

'What they want with me.'

They climbed on. Titoko finally halted in a waste of rock where next to nothing grew.

'What now?' Kimball gasped.

'You remain here.'

'You?'

'I travel higher.'

'All the way?'

'Until quiet ends.'

'What quiet?'

'That in my head.'

Kimball shifted mountain debris into a shelter and watched his companion climb further. The wind began whining more dourly. Titoko was soon a flea on a far mountain ridge as he rose closer to streaky snowline. Then a gust of cloud hid him altogether. An hour passed, soon several more. Sunset was colouring the sky before rattling stones signalled his return. He limped to ground beside Kimball, and sat silent for a time. 'I need your shoulder,' he announced.

They found a path downhill until dark made movement too dangerous, and camped among scrub hard by the bed of a stream. While Kimball lit a fire, Titoko slumped with his head between his knees. He did not look up long to take food.

Finally he whispered, 'Even Hauhau frown on old superstition.'

'You're telling me something.'

'Aged men of the tribe say that when the old gods were spurned, they looked out a tall dwelling.'

'War gods?'

'Waiting their call.'

'Up here?'

'Some say as mist and rainbow.'

'You believe that?'

Titoko shrugged.

Most of a minute passed.

'You will not speak of this,' Titoko said.

A minute more passed.

Kimball confided, 'I got a temptation on me to ask a question.'

'One,' Titoko said.

'This quiet in your head,' Kimball began.

'What of it?'

'Did it end?'

Firelight fluttered over Titoko's spoiled face. Even on a good day he would scare Satan back to church.

'Not so I heard,' he sighed.

The wind muttered through alpine grass. Rocks shook loose and rang down valley. Kimball found sleep with chattering teeth.

When he woke, it was in morning mist. Their fire was cold. Sleepless Titoko sat in the same position, a cloak tight around his neck. Kimball had never seen him more haggard.

It seemed he had missed something. 'What is it?' he asked.

'Nothing,' Titoko said.

'Nothing?'

'Nothing. It becomes less easy to look into.'

'All night?'

'All night.'

'I guess it must,' Kimball said.

As they travelled down to the plain, Kimball risked another question.

'Is it peace or war?' he asked. 'What are you talking?'

'The eating of shit,' Titoko said. 'We cannot spit it all out. A little swallowed now might later seem sweet.'

'So you wish peace.'

'I wish a woman,' Titoko said.

Eleven

A long walk later they came to the forest clearing where Titoko's people and Toa's were camped. On Titoko's arrival there were further laments for those fallen to the British. On Toa's part there was grief for one who had not.

'Must I have the Yankee?' he asked Titoko.

'If you would have me,' Titoko said.

'He is nothing much,' Toa argued.

'Nor are we,' Titoko said.

Kimball saw Hine before he glimpsed Rihi. Hine had words. 'Think no more of my daughter,' she warned. 'You will suffer less hurt.'

'I been hurt by experts,' Kimball argued.

Hine shrugged. 'Whatever happens,' she said, 'a reliable male never goes amiss. The world has no shortage of women.'

She had a smile cool enough to tease the buttons off a man's trousers.

'What women were you thinking of?' he asked.

'Those who think to show a sad male that all is never lost.'

'To make it up to him, you mean?'

'That is one way of putting it. Showing him where to put it.'

Kimball wasn't shocked more than middling. Maori, even pious Hauhau, were not famous for calling a spade a hayrake.

'You wouldn't be telling me', he asked cautiously, 'that there are one or two like that around here?'

'You have only to ask,' she said.

Once his sweat dried his problem was winning Rihi's eye without grief. Whenever she was in sight, so also was Toa. A show of virtue seemed called for; he remained bungs up and bilge free the day long.

That night, at the campfire, senior tribesmen gathered to hear Toa and Titoko.

'The British gun unites us,' Toa told those assembled. 'Must ours now fall quiet?'

Titoko's deep sigh was heard.

'My cousin', Toa continued with irritation, 'spoke of trees bending. We have seen his dead bend. We have still to see his dead rise.'

Titoko was quiet.

Toa taunted, 'Did the British spare those who spoke with the green branch and gifts?'

Tribesmen, mostly Toa's, muttered as one that the British had not.

'Then', Toa said, 'let it be seen that we bite.'

Lingering fervour was apparent, at least among Toa's people.

Titoko rose wearily. 'My cousin has spoken,' he said.

Tribesmen, again in unison, agreed that his cousin had.

'The bird flies,' he said, 'but where is the branch?'

No tribesman answered.

'With no branch we fall to earth,' he argued.

Tribesmen were quiet.

'We have been a tribe of two tongues,' Titoko proposed. 'We mutter peace and whisper war. British ears are deaf to the difference.'

'So I am to blame,' Toa said bitterly.

'I spoke nothing of blame,' Titoko insisted.

'Then speak shame,' Toa scoffed. 'Your peace was the work of weakness. The British fought because we were feeble.'

'That was yesterday,' Titoko said. 'This is today.'

'Enlighten us further, cousin,' Toa suggested.

'Tomorrow we have a lean winter.'

'And why?'

'Because starvation is what the victor now wishes. If we sow seed again, and not fear, we defy them. If we fail to perish, we foil them. If we live, we win the larger war.'

'What talk is this?' Toa protested.

'The talk of the eel who knows the river dry. Tell me other, cousin.'

Toa, for the moment, could not.

'Alive we are a difficulty,' Titoko argued. 'Dead we oblige them.'

'To live as the creeping octopus?' Toa asked.

'To live,' Titoko said.

'Taranaki's warriors die as the shark.'

'Tell your fatherless daughters.'

'Does Titoko speak with the voice of women now?'

'Titoko speaks with his own voice, and will.'

There was stalemate, with both Toa and Titoko sullen. Titoko was first to find voice again.

'There have', he said, 'been six years of war. What does six say?'

Opinion, so far as it made itself heard, favoured the idea that six was one up on five.

'What comes after six?' he challenged.

There was a wary silence.

'Seven?' he asked.

Even Toa found it impossible to say different.

'What does seven, then, say?' Titoko went on. 'Christian and Jew have a seventh day, a day of rest. Their God saw seven as a holy figure. The warrior sons of our tribe have had six years of war, never one of peace. Let this be the warriors' sabbath. Six years for the lion, the seventh for the lamb. Six years for the sons, the seventh for the daughters.'

Kimball saw Titoko's mountain meandering might not have been waste. The notion interested even warriors weathered and bitter. Finally Demon, Toa's toughest lieutenant, was seen beginning to nod. Toa was suddenly alone.

'We give up our guns?' he asked.

'Not in haste,' Titoko said.

'The land we have lost?'

'We warm it with no further fires. As it was won, so is it lost. Beyond that, no more.'

'The land we have not?'

'We work.'

'Is that enough to say?'

'By a man of courage. By one who now knows what must be said. By you, cousin.'

Silence grew, and grew longer.

'One year?' Toa asked.

'One,' Titoko said.

'Then perhaps one,' Toa was heard agreeing.

Sounds of relief rose from those seated close to the fire.

'We speak with the one voice?' Titoko asked.

'And drink from the one spring,' Toa said.

'So welcome the year of the lamb,' Titoko said. 'Welcome the year of the daughters.'

'I trust the British are likewise enlightened,' Toa said.

'They will be,' Titoko promised. 'Your grief, cousin, is mine.'

Titoko and Toa embraced.

'We lack the lamb,' Titoko noted.

'True,' Toa said.

'Bring forward your daughter,' Titoko urged. 'Such a year must begin well.'

'How?' Toa asked.

'If we are one, let it be celebrated.'

Toa found cause to smile at last. 'This day, cousin,' he confessed, 'has been much in the making.'

Titoko looked tactfully at the ground.

'Bring my daughter,' Toa ordered.

Rihi presented herself at the campfire. She looked defiantly at her father, with even less delight at Titoko.

'It is agreed', Toa explained, 'that we are again a tribe of one mind. No longer will we point the canoe of our ancestors both upstream and downstream. No longer will we chance wrecking all in the rapids.'

Rihi's face said that her father had best beach his speech.

'There is custom in such matters,' Toa told her. 'Custom says it is good that a man of one party should take a woman of the other as wife. This shall be so here.'

'Here?' she said.

'Now,' he said. 'You are that woman.'

'To be passed on as you wish?'

'As I say.'

Rihi's bitter eyes spoke best for her. 'The man?' she asked.

Titoko thought it time to speak out. 'That question', he said, 'is better answered by me.'

'And unneeded,' Toa protested.

'Who knows?' Titoko said. He told Rihi, 'I am older than I should be. You are younger than is fair. Is that just to say?'

Rihi's face said it an honest statement of matters.

98

'That being so,' Titoko went on, 'might I better share your bed in spirit?'

'Spirit?' she said.

Toa's face was pained. 'What do you say?' he asked Titoko.

'That her life might be more interesting, and mine longer.'

'This is not what I have in mind.'

'It is surely what I have,' Titoko said.

'That you take her in spirit alone?'

'Flesh will not be lacking. The performance of my envoy will not be poor. Your daughter will not weep.'

'I think I am beginning to,' Toa said. 'Envoy? What envoy? Who?'

'Bring out the Yankee,' Titoko said.

There was no delay in the nuptials. In the interests of tribal union Titoko thought rite desirable. Since Toa's priest had perished in the forest flight, he took on himself the task of reciting from a mildewed Hauhau text with Kimball and Rihi before him.

'Should a man wriggle with a woman,' he read, 'do not say it is evil. If they wish each other, it is right that they wriggle. Should a woman wish a husband or a man a wife, they have but to wriggle, once their feelings are firm.' He then asked Kimball, 'Are your feelings firm?'

'About wriggling?'

'As my envoy.'

'Considerable,' Kimball confessed.

'You?' Titoko asked Rihi.

'Yes,' she said, with no show of modesty.

'Then', Titoko urged, 'proceed to the better part of this business.'

'What would that be?' Kimball asked.

'Serving me well,' Titoko said.

Enough was as good as a feast, with sweet courses to follow. Kimball woke to dawn birds, and Rihi's black hair beside him. He slid from their fern couch to relieve himself in neighbouring growth. On his return he met red-eyed Big. After a night on picket, his carbine shouldered, Big was smoking and warming his legs beside a small fire. Kimball sank weary beside him.

'So,' Big said with sleepy smile, 'there is life.'

'Bed beats hell out of a grave,' Kimball admitted.

'Titoko preaches that the food of night sweetens the food of day.'

'If that's his religion, it looks like I caught it.'

'You are now in his debt,' Big said.

'Titoko's?'

'Better to you than Toa. Toa had been long baiting his hook.'

'With Rihi?'

'Titoko fed the bait to you, and left Toa the hook. Thus was Titoko saved from temptation. You, for his purpose, were a gift from God.'

Kimball was silent for some time. 'Whose God?' he asked.

'No Methodist's,' Big said.

Before summer's end Titoko led the tribe back to lowland. They found the British gone and the territory quiet. By the time autumn's snow coloured the mountain, a new village had risen deep in tribal forest. Vegetation was uprooted and ground broken for early spring sowing. Meanwhile there was fern root and fish, berry and bird. It was a winter better suited to Big the hunter than Demon the warrior. A reliable traveller reported that the British army, with its last campaign fought, was leaving New Zealand. Regiment after regiment had been seen breaking camp and marching to ports. Officers and men not discharged to take up land in the colony were boarding ships to England while bands played farewell.

'The 57th too?' Kimball asked.

'The 57th also,' the traveller said.

Kimball's day was considerably brighter.

Titoko shook his head in wonder. 'So the Yankee was right,' he said. 'The surprise is that it is so soon.'

'Listen better,' Toa said. 'They leave guns, they leave scoundrels to settle. The colonist government can rally men by the hundred should it be wished. We may yet curse the day when the regiments departed. Their officers sometimes had conscience.'

'With Kepa to do their killing,' Titoko said.

'We can't have everything,' Toa said.

Another traveller bore Toa out. Colonists were forming their own army. These Sunday soldiers drilled fervently and turned out often for musketry practice. More, riders in a new uniform had been seen abroad. Mostly discharged soldiers, they were constables recruited by the colonial government to caretake the peace and suggest to old rebels that they had best remain beaten.

A third traveller had outlandish intelligence. The last British march on Taranaki had left rumours of a white warrior afoot in the territory, an accomplished killer of colonels, with a name useful to terrify children who thought to wander from home. 'Look out,' they were warned, 'or Kimball Bent will get you.' As it travelled the colony the tale was growing no smaller. Penny-a-line scribes were bettering it daily.

The traveller produced soiled scraps of newspaper. The most excited said that Kimball Bent was the last peril left in the colony. It seemed that this fiend in Maori garb had been responsible for inspiriting old rebels, also for punishing Hauhau firepower; even now he was possibly training Maori rebels in the use of the new breech-loading carbines. So long as Kimball Bent was loose, the writer argued, no corner of the colony could be considered safe for Christian colonists. Another item said that a Sergeant Flukes, now of the Armed Constabulary, formerly of the 57th, described himself as all too familiar with the disgraced deserter and bloodthirsty outlaw Kimball Bent. 'Bent', Sergeant Flukes was reported as saying, 'always was a bad lot. Rest assured that I have a plan to tear him root and branch from the colony.' Asked what that plan might be, Sergeant Flukes declined to explain. 'The fact of the matter', he added, 'is that when I took my discharge in New Zealand I had it in mind to settle an old score or two. Bent left with lashes owing. A noose would now be too kind.'

Winter crept into Kimball's lower bowel.

'Who', asked Titoko, 'is this Sergeant Flukes?'

'A corporal when I knew him.'

'He hopes for further promotion.'

'That is a thought,' Kimball agreed, and tried not to think it.

Toa, on the other hand, was grieved. 'No mention of you,' he said to Titoko. 'Nor any of me.'

'Be grateful,' Titoko argued.

'This is what it has come to,' Toa said. 'This Yankee steals women. Now our good name.'

The colonist constabulary marched to no music. Flute, fife and drum had gone with the regiments. In spring a silent patrol, under the command of a colonist colonel named McDonnell, rode up the coast road from Wanganui looking for work. They found mockery rather than menace. After an ample issue of rum, McDonnell ordered his men to prove their worth. Moving inland under a white flag, they fell on a Maori village whose people had followed Titoko's example and returned to low country. Confused colonist intelligence said that the Hauhau commander called Bent might be brazenly resident there. After the white flag was lowered and volleys split Maori dwellings, the constabulary sank men who showed their faces. Women were taken and used. Still lurching and roaring, the raiders at length shot up one of their own, a looter mistaken by his companions for the white renegade. Otherwise the daring of Colonel McDonnell won praise and promotions. A Private Tonks, formerly a drummer in the 57th, had been given corporal's stripes for vigour beyond the call of duty. The colonial press reported that the natives had been promisingly cowed by the show of firepower. As for its first purpose, Lieutenant Flukes, another promoted survivor of the action, gave it as his opinion that the capture of Bent was only a matter of time. He announced that he was dedicating himself to the hunt for the American double-dealer. 'We'll make it still hotter for him,' the lieutenant pledged. 'Even the surliest Maori will soon find Bent an intolerable presence in their midst, as indeed did we of the Diehards.'

As a prophet, Flukes had promise.

Titoko consulted Toa, and together they conferred with Kimball. 'This', Titoko explained, 'is a matter of sorrow to me.'

'More so to me,' Toa said. 'What of my daughter?'

'A summer's absence should be sufficient,' Titoko told Kimball.

'For once,' Toa said, 'my cousin and I are agreed. We cannot war on behalf of the United States of America. For one thing we lack a navy.'

'You want to be quit of me,' Kimball concluded.

'Until colonists cool,' Titoko explained. 'Especially this man Flukes.'

'One bullet would have done it,' Kimball mourned.

'A second might spark a new fire in our fern,' Titoko explained.

'How will Flukes know I'm gone?'

'I shall enlighten him,' Titoko said. 'I may invite him to this village to show him you are not among us. We will argue that he dreams you.'

'Good luck,' Kimball said bitterly.

Next morning Big was waiting with three horses. Kimball and Rihi mounted two, and Big the third. Hine was in attendance, Toa and Titoko too. Laments were left behind as the journey upland began. They rode the first day in silence, and much of the second. On the third Big led them up a long ridge, and on to a summit. Trees teemed away into the heart of the land. On the horizon were volcanoes, smoky cones draped with snow in a land all but lifeless. They had stopped mercifully short.

'Count off one hundred days,' Big told them. 'On the hundredth my fire will warm this place.'

'One hundred,' Kimball said with no pleasure.

'They will fast pass,' Big promised. 'Colonist passion could pass sooner.'

Kimball shook his head. Big didn't know Flukes.

'There's another way of looking at it,' Big suggested.

'What other way?'

'You are the one rebel left worth the hunt.'

'Thanks,' Kimball said.

'So nothing pleases you.'

'Not much,' Kimball confessed.

Rihi was heard asking faintly, 'Where are we?'

'Safe,' Big said.

'More trees,' she sighed. 'More rocks. More rivers.'

'Another home you can call your own,' Big agreed.

'I could manage with smaller.'

'In good time,' Big said.

'I have heard that before too.'

'Two warnings,' Big told Kimball. 'First, the rats are big here. Build a storehouse on legs to keep your food above ground. Second, never leave Rihi alone long.'

'Because of the rats?'

'Worse. If a voice calls from the forest, forget it.'

'Voice?' Kimball asked.

'One calling you,' Big said. 'Or her. Especially her. Sit and say nothing. Let Tara Pikau call himself hoarse.'

'Tara Pikau?'

'A demon who collects female parts. He wriggles women silly. Those wooed into his territory never return to tell the tale.'

'The men?'

'Sillier. White-haired and babbling fools.'

'He sounds a bigger bugger than Flukes.'

'In his territory,' Big said. 'It begins near here.'

'How do we know which his territory and which not?'

'Easy,' Big said. 'The eels in his rivers are red.'

With advice given, Big rode home. That afternoon Kimball and Rihi raised a shelter just above a ferny river flat on the sunny side of a long valley. Kimball carried his carbine into the woods to drop pigeon while Rihi arranged their dwelling. When he returned, before dark, it was complete with a bush bed. Rihi reposed there already.

'Come,' she said, lifting her arms.

'Now?'

'How better to make the days pass?'

'Well,' he suggested, 'there's keeping ourselves alive. Hunting and fishing, collecting fern root and cooking. Not to speak of warring with rats.'

'You mean there's no more to life than that?'

Sulky Kimball tried to think.

'Remember Tara Pikau,' she said.

'What about him?'

'It is known that he makes off with unhappy women.'

'What are you telling me?'

'Five wriggles a day,' she said.

By morning Kimball judged his marriage safe. Though he dreamed of rivers rising tall with red eels, rats were his first grief. The pigeon he had shot were consumed overnight; likewise dried eel carried from Titoko's camp. It took him all of a day to build a larder on long legs. Next morning he found the legs chewed. Another raiding party might have it down.

'There is an easier way,' Rihi suggested.

'So what would that be?'

'To keep them fed and fat.'

'For what?'

'Eating,' she said.

'Don't say any more,' he warned. 'You could vex me considerable.'

After ten days Kimball had mostly emptied the valley of game; pigeon and pig failing to succumb to his barrage fled to higher ground. By their thirtieth day in the wilderness Kimball, still under siege, found the fashioning of rat snares a less desperate proposition than he earlier supposed. Rihi's dishes of rodent, if a little gamey on first taste, proved the least of local evils. The mosquitoes were murderous and the hill country climate no kinder. Hell-splitting thunder banged overhead, and lightning hissed in on the rain. The river crashed in flood and drove them to higher ground. And there was always the chance that Tara Pikau was trying to tempt Rihi from his bed. That called for craft too.

On their fifty-first day he decided exile might now be all downhill. With a precipice thrown in, that proved the case. On a sunlit morning, after he had wandered downriver to wash, he returned to find Rihi missing. At first he thought bodily function had taken her into the fern. Soon he began calling her name. He had no reply. Matters looked even less favourable. He found his rifle and began stalking trouble. He pushed upriver, still calling, his voice ringing back from the rocks above. Finally a gorge filled with foaming water gave him no footing at all. He clambered into new territory and found it as stony. It also remained empty of Rihi. About to call quits, he crossed a small creek and bent to drink. A creature flashed underwater. It might have been red. It might not. Kimball failed to consider its colour further. He dashed, crashed, and tumbled. Foliage shifted to reveal the river below and nothing resembling terra firma underfoot; he embarked upon space. That was as much as he remembered of his voyage; he disembarked in Eastport, State of Maine. There were square-riggers loaded with lumber. There were pipe-smoking fishermen in seaboots picking their way past baskets of lobster and herring. Regret and relief fought within him as a gang plank creaked underfoot and familiar sounds and smells grew. He shouldered his sea kit and stepped shakily ashore.

'You been a long way, old fellow,' a loitering seaman judged.

Old? Kimball considered his beard. It was long and pure white. He also leaned on a stick. There was no arguing with appearances.

'A wicked long way,' he had to agree.

Two figures in black rose to block his return to known woods and meadows. There was a long-faced and top-hatted undertaker with a coffin made of Maine pine and an underling with a single white lily. Kimball understood the coffin was for him. The lily was to crown his coffin as he was borne to the burying ground. The undertaker, on further consideration, looked gauntly like Flukes, more so when he trained a revolver. The underling, brawnily like Tonks, no longer held a lily. Gripping carbine and bayonet, he had disembowelment in mind.

Kimball's yell must have given heaven a fright. He dived deep into the Atlantic and failed to come up for air.

'Quiet,' Rihi said.

He was floating in sweat. Rihi was pushing him back on to their bed. Her face became less misty, their forest home too. Regret and relief battled again, and this time relief seemed to have the better of it. He began not to struggle and heave.

'Can you hear me?' she asked.

'Maybe,' he said.

'Good. You must be better.'

'Better?' he asked weakly.

'Than you were,' she explained.

'I've been ill?'

She bathed his brow with chill water. 'I wondered if Tara Pikau had taken you.'

'I thought he'd grabbed you.'

'I hid only to tease. I didn't think to find you washed up cold on the riverside, and then in a fever.'

'Long?'

'Long enough to think I was to be a widow.'

'And how long was that?'

'Ten days.'

'Well,' Kimball suggested, 'things could be worse.'

'How?'

'Like ten more without you,' he said.

On the hundredth a fire smoked on the summit Big had chosen.
Kimball and Rihi crawled toward it and found the fire low and
Big snoring loud in the late summer sun. His eyes blinked open
to consider the pair.

'Love won,' he judged.

'Something ample,' Kimball said.

Twelve

Hedged in by high rainforest, hard by a stream, Titoko's new village already looked years settled. Huts of sapling and thatch had hardened into comfortable cabins. The largest was Titoko's. His sleeping quarters had space to spare for companions, and there was an outer room in which he could attend to the less welcome passions of his people. He had named the village The Beak of the Bird. 'A bird has two wings and but one beak,' he explained. 'Also our tribe.' The village was not far from the foot of the mountain, and cooled by its weather. Titoko refused the felling of more trees than needed to let sunlight in. Even dead and half-hollow trees on the outskirts were left upright. He was also firm that tracks to and from the settlement should be tight, permitting just walkers and riders in single file. Neighbouring woodland was opened for cultivation. Pickets were posted only to discourage wild pig from rooting out crops. Packhorse trains, loaded with produce for sale in colonist communities, were sent plodding off in search of pounds and pence. For resurrected Kimball, however, Titoko's Eden had a taint.

'Flukes?' he finally chanced asking.

'He came,' Titoko admitted. 'A most nervous man. When we rode to meet him he saw you beyond every tree. The man has begun to believe his own lies.'

'He needs to be a hero.'

'Do you?' Titoko asked.

'Nothing special,' Kimball said.

'Good,' Titoko said. 'When his terror passed we told him that a lone renegade could not come between us and good relations with colonists.'

108

'Did he want to know where I was now?'

'We informed him. In a forest grave, after slow death.'

'He believed you?'

'Half of him wishes to. The other half still hunts you in dream.'

'I know,' Kimball said.

Titoko's sabbath seemed likely to last. He travelled north and south to persuade fellow warriors that lambs and daughters alike flourished best in the absence of battle; that goodwill toward colonists had more to be said for it than the raising of fortresses and digging of graves. Villages fired by arsonist soldiers were forgotten under young fern. Fraying Hauhau pennants finally floated off in the wind; flagpoles weathered and split. Even Toa, with his beard greying down to his belly, saw truce as having a sunny case to state. Corn fluttered tall in village cultivations, and kumara fattened sweet. Titoko prospered too. On his travels he bewitched more women than pleased his wayside hosts.

Martial feats ebbed. Constabulary redoubts had risen to the south, close to the coast, but those manning them thought to leave well alone. To their rear were colonist dwellings and the beginnings of townships. Not all the new faces were pale. Colouring the new communities were Captain Kepa's men, warriors of Wanganui paid off in rebel acres. Along the coast timber trees were lowered to build more dwellings and barns. Then fire leapt into the forest, with grass seed sown in the cooled ash. When clover and cocksfoot greened the debris sheep and cattle were turned loose to flourish. Elsewhere roses and daffodils bloomed outside farmhouse doors. The realm of colonist and constable began at the river of Waingongoro. The Waingongoro was by far the burliest of the many rivers beating from mountain to sea. Mounted patrols made a point of not fording it. Having seen that the Waingongoro's green waters ran mostly as mapped, the quiet men of these patrols turned their horses home.

'I have a surprise,' Rihi said.

Kimball was just home from village chores; autumn's crops were being gathered before winter frost bit. 'What would that be?' he asked wearily.

'How', she asked, 'do you feel about being a father?'
So much for winter.

On a spring day Titoko arrived at Kimball's door. 'We have travel,' he announced.
'Rihi's near time,' Kimball argued.
'She will be fonder on your return,' Titoko promised.
'Why me?'
'I have thoughts to think. I need a listener when I speak them.'
'Your thoughts. Not mine.'
'That is so,' Titoko agreed. 'Yours are of small interest.'
'Yours?'
'The kind thought without women.'
'And what kind are they?' Kimball asked.
'Those I wish not to think.'

They followed the north bank of the Waingongoro. Titoko's eyes were to the south. Where the land lifted he used a telescope. Otherwise the naked eye was enough. He watched for disturbances in terrain and vegetation, considering trails lately cut through woodland, hoofprints of recent travellers. He gave long attention to places where the river was easiest forded. Finally Kimball risked a question.
'What are we looking for?' he said.
'Signs,' Titoko said.
'Of patrols?'
'Men with guns are no longer my worry.'
They remained Kimball's, with one answering to the name of Flukes. 'What is?' he asked.
'Pegs.'
'Pegs?'
'As surveyors leave. Pegs say roads and bridges, with grass soon behind.'
'What will you do if you see them?'
'Look very hard,' Titoko promised.
Next day they followed the river further to the sea, as far as the coast road between Wanganui and New Plymouth. From forest edge, as if waiting in ambush, they watched a lone and unarmed rider taking a ford, and later a couple of dusty colonists on horse-drawn drays.

110

'They take no care now,' Titoko observed. 'No soldiers, no guards.'

'Is that a good thing or bad?'

'Good,' Titoko said.

'That's your land they are crossing,' Kimball argued.

'Once,' Titoko agreed.

'And your last fire is lit?'

'It is cold,' Titoko said.

Others were beginning. On the long way home they saw smoke lifting a mile to the south of the river. They loitered a day to see if the next night's fire was lit nearer the Waingongoro. It rose from the same site.

'A colonist,' Titoko decided.

'Shouldn't we see?'

'I have seen,' Titoko said.

A week later Kimball was told to guide Big back to the riverside from which the smoke had been noted. They returned to report not one nightly fire but three, all no more than a mile south of the river.

'Three?' Titoko asked.

'Three,' Big said.

A month later Big counted five colonists resident. Then hundreds of forest acres took flame. Smoke rioted across the river. When it paled, a few charred trees were seen standing. There were also colonists scattering grass seed in the soot.

Titoko called on warriors to present weapons for inspection. This puzzled many. Titoko had preached nothing but peace for most of a year. The new order said he might have something of a fickle nature in mind. No man had fewer than two firearms on show, and some several more. Titoko wandered among those paraded, taking a shotgun here, a fowling piece there, an elderly musket elsewhere. Finally two or three score weapons were heaped in the village centre.

'There is a time for weeding,' Titoko told the assembly.

Mutters from the ranks said that some differed. Demon seemed likely to enter louder dispute. Toa was most troubled.

'Why this?' he asked. 'Why now?'

'Those who think to hold all, lose all,' Titoko answered. 'You no longer hold all, but nor have you lost all. As it is with weapons, so with land. We hold what we can, lose what we must.'

He did not need to push his thought further. With the gathering ended, he had Kimball and Big load the weapons on a narrow dray built to negotiate tight forest trails. Demon and Toa lingered to argue.

'Where are you taking them?' Toa asked.

'Where they are useful,' Titoko explained.

'With no men to shoulder them?' Demon protested.

'This is a travelling party of two,' Titoko said.

'Two?'

'Big will be the other.'

'Travelling where?' Toa said.

'To a fight we must win.'

'You make no sense, cousin,' Toa said bitterly.

'You try to,' Titoko said.

As Kimball heard it, the pair bumped seventy miles south on their dray, far into territory held by late enemies. Titoko was again in an English suit, and Big also made it his business to look less unnerving. The harvest aboard was not of a kind seen travelling the Queen's highway before. Colonists and Kepa's Maoris left crops and livestock to watch the two rebels pass. Where enough old enemies stood in awe, Titoko made a speech of calm character, discharged a weapon to prove it deadly, and smashed it against the dray; finally he stamped the pieces underfoot. 'Yet another creature thirsts no more for the blood of men,' he announced. By the time Titoko and Big arrived in the garrison town of Wanganui the coast road was littered with ruptured weaponry. In the town Titoko's passion as a disarmer grew even warmer. As crowds gathered his speeches lengthened. At their climax he fired off and smashed three weapons at a time. When sought by colonial officials he made his meaning plain. 'Without earth we are empty hides,' he said. 'Land is our bones and blood. Let nothing be taken north of the Waingongoro.'

He shattered the last weapon left in his dray. There were smiles, handshakes; even promises. Titoko thought himself understood. One disappointment was that he failed to shake the hand of his most willing foe, the Prussian soldier of fortune called Major Many Birds. Embittered by the persistence of peace, more so by meek colonist commanders, Many Birds had retired to continue fighting the war at his easel. Colonists were pressing money upon him to kill more Maori in paint.

On the social side, however, Titoko was finally seen meeting an even more attentive enemy, the Maori known as Captain Kepa. Maori onlookers sighed as the pair pressed noses, shared breath, and swore friendship. Their past differences, they agreed, had been in error. Whether fighting against Britain or for Britain they were men of the same mind in their love of land; both wished the best for their tribesmen. Though Big felt Titoko's tributes to the Wanganui warrior fell short of flattery, and Kepa himself might have sounded more likely had he returned an acre or two, Titoko himself travelled home with a faint smile.

'So it was a success,' Kimball said.

'As sport,' Big agreed.

'What are you saying?'

'Titoko is not thinking to let fate bed with him twice,' Big said. 'He took the poorest guns from the village.'

South of the Waingongoro more forest burned and more rough farmhouses rose. From the riverside, on a still day, the sound of hammer and saw could often be heard. Grass, on the other hand, grew silently.

Kimball's problem was elsewhere, and of his own making. In the middle of a November night Rihi asked him to run for her mother. Hine came fast, followed by other women of rank. Rihi screamed while forceful women hauled her this way and that, finally into a squatting position. There were chants and prayers aimed at opening the avenue between Rihi's young legs. Hine pushed her knees into Rihi's abdomen to speed events. In the glow of a lamp the wrestling women shone with sweat.

'You'll kill her,' Kimball protested, mostly unheard.

Big, woken by the commotion, removed Kimball from the scene when the women announced him a larger problem than Rihi.

'Your courage is not in question,' Big said. 'Many a warrior flees.'

He dragged Kimball into his own dwelling. Rihi's screams, however, could still be heard.

'As battle is to man,' Big said, 'so birth to women.'

'There must be a difference,' Kimball argued.

'Listen again,' Big said.

Rihi's cries did not diminish.

'Maybe not, then,' Kimball said.

'That is how it is,' Big said. 'While woman's war burns, men fly a truce flag.'

'What does that mean?'

'Rum,' Big explained. 'And a melancholy head in the morning.'

He saw that his companion felt no further pain. Kimball woke next day to a slap on his face and Hine's face looming near. So far as he could determine, she was informing him that he was the father of a fine son.

'Son?' he asked hoarsely.

'The first,' she said. 'The second was a daughter.'

Rihi was bloody, shaken and emptied. A swaddled baby in each arm, a fighter flaunting loot, she rose arrogant from gore and grief. It was shaky Kimball who needed support. 'Your daughter,' she said. 'Your son.'

He found nothing easy to say.

'Look,' she said fiercely. 'And then look longer.'

'I'm looking,' he argued.

'There is work for you,' Hine told him.

It seemed he had business with earth and sky. He took the afterbirth and buried it where none would ever walk on it; the umbilical cords were hung high in a tree, as close to heaven as he could climb.

Grandfather Toa had his grudging say. 'Some looked for an omen,' he explained. 'A boy would say that our tribe was now in need of new warriors. A girl would say that daughters now served best. Instead, matters are mixed.'

Titoko too was early with oratory. 'Let it be said', he told those gathered, 'that the Yankee twig now grips Maori soil with two roots.'

It was one way of looking at it. For the life of him, Kimball failed to find another.

Thirteen

Through the first months of the new year Kimball's offspring were heard nightlong and as much of day as they could damage. Names were decided. The boy would be Wiremu, the girl Meri; or William and Mary. Nature set them apart more than names. Lean Wiremu had nervous eyes and a sad wail. Meri was plump, bold-eyed and shrill, already her mother's daughter. Tribal peers allowed Kimball to be a parent only in passing. A male taking women and children seriously won the contempt of self-respecting warriors. Nor did he fare well with women. Rihi began to find her children more engaging than ever her husband had been and sought the company of like-minded females. Taking their example, she bawled him out shrewishly for sloth. The largest bundle of firewood and fattest basket of food failed to please her. She had become weighty in pregnancy and wasn't looking lighter. Seeing Kimball scorned, Big offered to take him hunting. Hine, if he read her eyes right, promised sport too. Faithful Kimball went hunting.

Summer cooled fast on the March afternoon Big rode into the village to report pegs seen north of the Waingongoro.
'How many?' Titoko asked.
'Enough,' Big said.
'For a bridge?'
'Where a road would travel.'
Titoko sat thoughtful.
'What do you want me to do?' Big asked.
'Dig them out,' Titoko decided.
'Alone?'
'Are the pegs too many for one man?'
'Those who place them may be.'

'Take Toa, perhaps,' Titoko suggested. 'Not Demon. Nor guns.'

'I hear you,' Big said.

Kimball, hovering nearby, made himself seen.

'Not you either,' Titoko said.

Big went out with Toa and rode back to report no difficulties. Neither constable nor colonist had been sighted. The pegs had been dug out and burned. A week later, however, there were new pegs in place. These too were taken.

Toa was roused again. 'Is this peace?' he asked Titoko.

Titoko was quiet.

'There will be more,' Toa promised. 'Each a bayonet in our belly.'

'There will be no dead surveyors,' Titoko said.

'Just one?'

'None,' Titoko said.

'Then a party of my men camped as warning.'

'That is to go to them. Let them come to us.'

'For what?'

'The better to know their thinking.'

'What more need we know? They think grass.'

'Then the better for them to see we do not agree.'

'We have watched forest burn. We have watched grass grow to the river. Why should they care that you fail to agree further?'

'Roads can be ploughed and bridges fired. Such acts may be of the night with no culprit seen. Unless we will it, they win no highway. That is our strength.'

'For what?'

'To hold what we have.'

'And how little is that?'

'For us to learn,' Titoko said.

A melancholy magistrate named Booth rode out of the south. He had white collar and black tie and was flanked by lesser officials and armed constabulary. Sensitive to negotiations with natives, Booth took a modest stance outside the village until he received Titoko's summons. Then he rode into the village alone. Furtive Kimball posted himself to Big's ample rear. Booth had a map drawn by draughtsmen in New Zealand's new capital of Wellington. The map showed land which had been formally confiscated in consequence of the late warring. Land confiscated was shaded. Land left rebel was not. Booth asked Titoko to observe where a splendidly straight line had been drawn. This line, by its nature, failed to notice the curves of the Waingongoro; it leapt through them. Here and there shading reached north of the river.

Titoko tipped the map right and left and shook it a little, as if hoping something might fall out. Then he rolled it up briskly and returned it to Booth. He cleared his throat. 'When I ride beside the Waingongoro I see no line,' he announced. 'I see tree, rock and water.'

'Nonetheless,' Booth said.

'Or should I look heavenward?' Titoko asked. 'Is that where this magical line lives?'

'It has been placed according to the best information available.'

'By men who see nothing of tree, rock and water?'

'It is not incumbent upon those who draw maps to have personal knowledge of the terrain. They are intimate with government requirements in respect of confiscation. They know the cost of war must be met by sale of land. Further, they have surveyors' reports.'

'You tell me this line is the work of blind men?'

'In a sense,' Booth had to agree.

'Send men with sight,' Titoko suggested.

'Maps cannot be redrawn frivolously.'

'They are holy scripture?'

'For present purposes, perhaps,' Booth said.

'Are surveyors as the priests of this religion? Their pegs as the cross of Christ?'

'You overstate the case,' Booth argued. 'The fact is that the health of this colony depends on the drawing of lines.'

'Your colonists, Mr Booth, dwell south of the river.'

'True,' Booth said.

'We dwell this side.'

'What is your point?' Booth asked.

'We all see tree, rock and water.'

'On the part of colonists, in light of the past, there is a human reluctance to cross the river.'

'And we do not cross the river for poor-tempered purpose?'

'For which we remain uncommonly grateful,' Booth said.

117

'So we are agreed,' Titoko argued. 'Our line is made by our mountain's waters.'

'Men who draw lines', Booth explained patiently, 'provide for the requisite acreage, not whims of alpine water.'

'Alas, Mr Booth.'

'Must we feud on that account?'

'Men feud better for a bend of river than for a line none can see.'

'Settlement north of the river can be left for later debate,' Booth said. 'It is to the point that the river must be bridged, and a road provided.'

'For what?'

'Progress,' Booth said. 'Such a road will reduce the distance between New Plymouth and Wanganui. Colonist and Maori alike will travel comfortably this side of the mountain, rather than labour around the coast road.'

'Who will pay for such road, such bridges?'

'Those who use the route. A little more land will be taken and sold.'

'Meaning we must.'

'It is to the advantage of all. With bridges, men travel dry.'

'As will grass seed,' Titoko said.

'Let me make myself clear,' Booth announced. 'The pegs to the north of the river will be replaced, next time under my supervision, with constabulary present.'

'Let me make myself even more clear, Mr Booth. I will give no order to remove pegs. Nor will I give an order not to remove them. With no order given it is therefore not necessary for me to be in attendance.'

'What of your warriors?'

'I say nothing of warriors.'

'It is said elsewhere in this colony, Titoko, that you are no longer your own man.'

'Me?' Titoko said with surprise.

'It is said that a bitter outcast pushes you to conflict with Britain's Queen.'

'Outcast?'

'The American called Bent.'

'The man is no more,' Titoko insisted.

Kimball, for appearances, melted away.

'Reports persist of his presence in your camp,' Booth said.

'Moreover, there are reports from other locations.'

'Other locations?' Titoko mused.

'The length of the island.'

'Wondrous,' Titoko agreed.

'There is no smoke without fire. There is only one construction to be placed on the reports. The man is riding the island to recruit tribes for rebellion. He never fails to make an appearance where there is a squabble between Maori and colonist. The descriptions do not always tally. Some think him tall and dark, others short and fair, but the nationality is the same. Reports also say that his intentions are no longer disguised. He wishes to win New Zealand into the fold of the United States of America.'

'Are dollars offered?' Titoko asked solemnly.

'Sums have not been mentioned.'

'Then he is of no interest to me,' Titoko said.

'Is your word that Bent has not been responsible for the removal of the surveyors' pegs?'

'My word is that you need calmer colonists, Mr Booth.'

'I do not hear you plainly, Titoko. Did Bent have a hand in removing these pegs?'

'Is that what you wish to hear, Mr Booth?'

'It is what many may suspect.'

'Very well. When he rode in with his column of American cavalry, we had not the heart to discourage him.'

Booth failed to smile. 'Alliance with so pestilential a wretch could be judged harshly.'

'How?' Titoko asked.

'As treason. Am I to take it that you acknowledge Bent's existence?'

'It is enough that I acknowledge yours, Mr Booth.'

'For the moment I shall attribute removal of the pegs to petty vandals,' Booth decided with unease. 'Infamy is doubtless what Bent seeks. It is not for me to argue that the British colonist is saintly. But better the devil you know.'

'South of the Waingongoro,' Titoko agreed.

Kimball rose from hiding as Booth cantered away. On the south side of the village he joined with his party. One pushed his horse toward Booth and began talking fiercely. He had small eyes, a thin mouth, and the rank of constabulary lieutenant;

119

there was no mistaking Flukes in a New Zealand mile. Booth was soon shaking his head. When the men of the party pointed their horses south, another constable, bulkier than most, looked back toward the village. It was Tonks.

Kimball put in an appearance in a less exposed part of the village.

Two days later Booth returned, as promised, to the Waingongoro. Also as promised, he came with a party of constables and colonists. Signal poles rose and surveyors' lines were taken from the south side of the river. Pegs were driven in on the north side. The enterprise was observed by Demon and Big, out on patrol. Big reported that the colonists made the affair a picnic. Food was consumed on the riverside, and a good deal of drink. There was cursing and jousting, and firearms were discharged rather freely, though not in the direction of Demon or Big. At day's end constables and colonists rode south. Demon and Big then pushed their horses down to the river and lifted the pegs with no ceremony.

Day followed day, and Booth made no return to preach the commandments of Wellington's map-makers. It was a week before Titoko knew why. There were Irish troubles on the southern goldfields, with riotous Fenians and Orangemen cracking each other's heads. Available constabulary had been ordered south to keep the peace. Booth's constabulary had been considered available. With just half-trained colonist militia to hand, he must have thought better of pegging the north side of the river.

'Give the Irish our guns,' Toa said.

April was mild, with snow faint on the mountain, the sun still warm. In the middle of the month, Big returned from riverside patrol to announce quiet at an end. Impatient colonists, rather than wait on return of the constabulary, had crossed the Waingongoro. They had begun a plank bridge, across which they might soon push horses and drays. Two of the intruders had felled timber on the north bank and raised waterside dwellings of slab and thatch. Meantime they were clearing scrub and heaping it to burn before winter.

'There,' Toa said to Titoko. 'What now?'

Titoko was silent.

'There will be others as bold,' Toa predicted.

Titoko remained silent.

'Next summer their grass will grow where we stand.'

Titoko shook his head wearily, but still failed to speak.

'Do you still think to tell them', Toa mocked, 'that we do not agree?'

'They can be warned.'

'Warned how?' Toa asked. 'Warned when?'

'I am trying to hear what I think,' Titoko said.

'I hear their laughter,' Toa said.

'In that case,' Titoko sighed, 'no guns.'

'No guns,' Toa said.

'And no crossing to the south side.'

'No dead,' Toa agreed.

Kimball woke at dawn next day and heard horses. With a few whoops, Toa's party was gone.

'Is it war?' Rihi asked sleepily.

'Just more trouble,' Kimball explained.

'What is the difference?'

'Considerable,' Kimball argued.

'Like what?'

'Titoko,' he said. 'He's got a new woman.'

Wiremu and Meri, having taken turns to lament the night through, now began a bitter duet.

'There's the war,' Kimball said. 'You didn't wriggle with Tara Pikau when I was in fever?'

'I wonder too,' she said.

In autumn dusk Toa rode back into the village with his party straggling behind. Triumph was plain. Both colonists had been surprised unarmed. They were given time to gather their goods before being escorted vigorously back across the river. Their half-built bridge was demolished, their dwellings fired. Bags of grass seed were tipped into the Waingongoro. The north bank of the river remained rebel with not a shot fired.

'No man crossed to the south side?' Titoko asked.

'Not even Demon,' Toa said.

'Good,' Titoko said with some force.

'Tell me where the good resides, cousin,' Toa said.

'If we say the river makes the line, not maps, then we respect it too.'

'To what end?'

'Ours,' Titoko insisted.

Toa accepted this grudgingly. 'What now?' he asked.

'Nothing,' Titoko said.

'They cannot let this pass.'

'They will not if it suits them best. They will if it suits them better.'

'How will we know?' Toa asked.

'When they next cross the river,' Titoko said.

'With words or bullets?'

'With one or the other,' Titoko said.

'That is putting off the day,' Toa protested.

'I see worse than British north of the river,' Titoko observed.

'I fail to, cousin. Worse?'

'Us to the south,' Titoko said.

Toa was surprised. 'You are thinking that far?'

'Further,' Titoko claimed.

'In what respect, cousin?'

'In respect of what sixty warriors do with the British Empire,' Titoko said.

'Do?'

'When we govern it,' Titoko explained. 'Perhaps we should sell.'

Booth returned with an escort of armed and surly colonists. Again he stood off from the village and waited on Titoko's summons to enter. On receiving it he rode forward alone, leaving colonists behind. This time the magistrate was more tense.

To Titoko he said, 'I bring a cartridge and a white handkerchief. The choice is yours.'

He held both articles up for Titoko's inspection. There was a silence. Titoko lifted the white handkerchief and left Booth the cartridge.

Booth smiled faintly. 'So it is peace,' he said.

'Unless you talk war, Mr Booth.'

'I am not here to pass judgement on what has been done,' Booth said. 'Nor to defend those headstrong people who thought to cross the river before rights and wrongs had been aired.'

'Then they were wrong?' Titoko said.

'In the way of timing,' Booth agreed.

'You mean that it is not good now, but good later, for them to cross the Waingongoro?'

'They took land they understood to be theirs.'

'I know of no such understanding.'

'That is because our discussions are less than complete.'

'You are telling me, Mr Booth, that such discussion means more giving of land?'

'Adjustment,' Booth said. 'Had you considered my map with more care, you would have noted native reserves.'

'I saw it big-hearted with ravine and swamp.'

'Map makers', Booth sighed, 'manage with what God gives them.'

'They do wonders with what no man has.'

'I put it to you that it is in our common interest to make the map work.'

'We have always known our boundaries,' Titoko said. 'A hill here, a rock there.'

'Such boundaries, I beg to remind you, were built on old tribal battle. We are speaking of more charitable arrangements.'

'Blood talks longer than ink,' Titoko said.

'Heaven forbid that it should again be so,' Booth said stiffly. 'Meanwhile I am obliged to point out that you have given offence to private property. I talk of dwellings and fences destroyed.'

'My regrets to Mr Private Property. Inform him that his dwellings and fences were built of our timber.'

'I shall place that argument before the authorities. They may accept it in extenuation this once. Not again.'

'What are you talking, Mr Booth?'

'Civilized procedure,' Booth said.

'Let Mr Civilized Procedure dwell with Mr Private Property south of the Waingongoro,' Titoko said amicably.

'That is your word?'

'My wish. Not yet my word.'

'When would I know it your word?'

'The day we dwell within a fortress. As you see, Mr Booth, that is not yet the case.'

'Matters', Booth said uneasily, 'remain far from clear.'

'I know only that your constabulary is too far to the south to make your maps work. I know also that you know it.'

'Let us see each other as men of good faith,' Booth pleaded. 'I have problems with hell raisers on my side, as you have on yours. Between us we can make good sense prevail.'

'I see appetite prevailing, Mr Booth. A nibble here, a nibble there, before the bite is made.'

'See us as reasonable,' Booth urged.

'With my bad eye,' Titoko promised.

Booth joined muttering colonists and rode back across the Waingongoro. At least Booth did. Some colonists remained on the north bank of the river, loitering with intent. That night four horses grazing near the village were looted. Morning brought uproar. Big tracked hoofprints to the Waingongoro. They disappeared into a ford and rose again on the colonist side of the river. On Titoko's order he followed the prints no further and returned to the village.

'Must we sit here,' Toa asked, 'and await further pain?'

In tribal council Titoko sat embattled. Even men long loyal asked the same question. Most were for chastising pursuit. Heads did not need to be counted; firearms could be.

'There is a quiet view to be taken,' Titoko finally said.

'We have turned the other cheek,' Toa protested. 'Better to bare our bums and have done.'

Titoko looked to Big. 'Was the way the horses went hidden?'

'The path was always plain.'

'To the river?'

'And beyond.'

'They could have swum the horses downriver to conceal their route?'

'They could have,' Big agreed. 'They did not.'

'So', Titoko said, 'it was an invitation made?'

'Invitation?' Big was puzzled.

'To cross to the south side,' Titoko suggested.

'They seemed unworried by pursuit,' Big allowed.

'Or were asking it?' Titoko persisted.

Toa was impatient. 'This is no news, cousin,' he told Titoko. 'The theft was shameless. And why?'

'Why, cousin?' Titoko asked.

'They have no fear left.'

'You wish to refresh it?'

'There is but the one way.'

'Your wish may be theirs.'

'I do not hear you, cousin.'

'I speak', Titoko said, 'of a prod here, a prick there. Of goading.'

Toa considered this, and was quiet. 'And of ambush south of the river?' he asked.

'I think not.'

'Favour us with what you think.'

'They wish sufficient trouble', Titoko explained, 'to speed the return of Booth's constabulary.'

'Who knows?' Toa said with indifference.

'Worse, of Kepa's warriors. Colonists wishing to swallow both banks of the river might bite with Maori teeth.'

'You say theft is to be forgotten?' Toa asked.

'I am saying what I see. Perhaps Many Birds back too.'

'Horses have gone,' Toa said. 'There may be more taken tomorrow.'

'Better horses than bait. Tonight sentries can be placed.'

'And that is all?'

'For now,' Titoko argued.

'No,' Toa said.

'No?' Titoko asked coolly.

'No,' Toa said.

Others were as rebellious. Kimball saw Titoko losing his people. Even Big, gazing at the ground, looked an unreliable lieutenant.

'Then,' Titoko announced wearily, 'perhaps just the horses brought back. No riding warriors. No arms. The horses will be taken by night as they were taken from us. Three men or four will be enough to the task.'

Toa thought on that. 'Perhaps seven or eight,' he said finally.

'No more,' Titoko said in defeat.

Toa rose smiling. 'Good, cousin,' he said. 'For a time you worried me.'

Titoko stood stiffly. 'I worried myself,' he said.

Next morning was bleak. Cloud bulking about the mountain brought chilly drizzle. Toa counted off seven fit men, and placed them in Demon's charge.

'Better a man who cares less for battle,' Titoko said.

'Big?' Toa asked.

'Big,' Titoko agreed.

'Better Demon,' Toa said as further rain fell.

Titoko appeared to see no future in argument with his wild men or, for that matter, the weather. When Demon's party rode south, Titoko retired to his dwelling, and a new female find, and was not seen for some hours.

The day had another difference. Unease made Rihi sociable. At least she leaned on Kimball's shoulder. 'Tell me it's nothing,' she asked.

'It's nothing,' he told her.

'True?' she shivered.

'True,' he lied.

Fourteen

Finishing their chore, Demon and his party rode back to The Beak with all of eight horses. The four stolen beasts had first been observed by daylight, but were later difficult to claim in the dark; the raiders thought it better to be safe than sorry. Horses taken by honest mistake had therefore been brought back rather than left loose in the forest. The descent on farms had been too swift to be challenged. No shots from woken colonists had been heard to their rear.

'What more would you ask?' Toa asked Titoko.

Titoko, who looked smaller daily, was not of a mind to say.

'Well?' Toa persisted.

'Fewer horses,' Titoko said.

Thinking not to make bad worse, he left for manly matters to the rear of his dwelling. Next day a fever took him further from sight.

On a wintry May morning, much as expected, Booth and a reinforced retinue emerged from the forest again. Horsemen wound one by one from the trees with revolvers and carbines ill-concealed. Some hung back warily. The bolder let their anger carry them all the way into the village. Their hoofbeats were sudden and brutal. No disciplined constables were on show.

Nor was Titoko. This time it was Toa who faced Booth.

'Where is he, then?' Booth asked.

'Too ill to talk,' Toa announced.

It might still have been true. Titoko had not been seen outside his dwelling for days. Meanwhile Kimball made himself small.

'You will do the talking?' Booth asked Toa.

'For Titoko,' Toa agreed.

'I am grieved,' Booth said. 'Your men have been as rats raiding the potato pit in the dark.'

'Our horses were taken,' Toa said. 'Our horses are back.'

'Your complaint should have been to me.'

'We no longer have complaint,' Toa said comfortably.

'Vengeance begets vengeance,' Booth protested. 'The rule of law prevails in this colony.'

'What should you have done?' Toa asked.

'Considered your complaint,' Booth said.

'Do you know our horses?'

'No,' Booth conceded.

'Then how consider it?' Toa said.

'I am still prepared to examine witnesses,' Booth said. 'Meanwhile, until the matter is decently adjudicated, I ask the return of the beasts.'

'To where?'

'The farms from which they were taken.'

'You have a sense of humour, sir,' Toa said.

Booth brightened with sweat. 'My information is that eight horses have been taken. How many would you claim stolen, at most?'

'Four,' Toa allowed.

'There you are,' Booth said. 'Two wrongs do not make a right.'

'They make an improvement,' Toa said.

'The law is not in your hands,' Booth announced. 'I deal with felons and administer fines in this region.'

'What are you asking, Mr Booth?'

'That you surrender those tribesmen responsible.'

'I ask that you surrender those colonists responsible.'

'You know that to be impossible, in these fraught circumstances.'

'First our land,' Toa observed. 'Then our horses. Now our men too. Is this what I hear?'

'I should be receptive to a plea of mitigation. With evidence heard, your people would likely be freed with a small reprimand after the court hearing.'

'Likely?'

'Almost certainly.'

'In that case, Mr Booth, why should they be surrendered?'

'Because there are procedures of a correct and proper kind.'

'Demon?' Toa called.

Demon made himself tall among villagers.

'Are you one of Mr Booth's felons?'

'Me?' Demon said with interest.

'Did you steal horses?'

'I rescued horses,' Demon said.

'Now let your people confess,' Toa suggested to Booth.

No colonist offered a sound.

Toa gazed at Booth. 'So arrest Corporal Demon,' he urged quietly.

Booth made no move. There was a longer silence. Colonists who had pushed into the village were uneasy as tribesmen pressed around them; their weapons could be wrestled away. Worse, they could be in the line of fire from overwrought companions to their rear.

'Is Demon not sufficient?' Toa asked. 'Would you arrest more?'

Booth answered in smaller voice. 'I shall personally take charge of the horses,' he offered. 'They will be the subject of lawful inquiry.'

'I think that is not enough, Mr Booth.'

'It is the fairest I can offer,' Booth said.

Booth began to think how to remove himself. Then a voice lifted to Toa's rear. Risen from his bed, Titoko stood at the door of his dwelling. Depleted and shaky on a cane, his hair awry, he had rigged himself out in one of his more respectable suits, without finding time for a tie. The stiff collar of his shirt jerked above the neck of his jacket as he spoke. 'Mr Booth?' he was saying.

'Titoko,' Booth said gratefully.

Titoko pushed forward. The crowd gave him a path to Booth. 'You have a problem,' he said. 'So also do we.'

'That is undeniable,' Booth said.

'It is not about horses,' Titoko suggested.

'Your point is taken, Titoko,' Booth said. 'You talk keeping of peace?'

'I talk of listening, Mr Booth,' Titoko lifted his cane. 'Quiet,' he commanded. Then, 'Listen, Mr Booth. Listen now.'

Booth put on a patient expression. Silence grew around them. Birds fluted and chimed overhead.

'You hear?' Titoko asked. 'You hear the bird in the tree?'

'Just so,' Booth agreed.

'Listen longer,' Titoko asked. 'What do you hear now?'

Booth was briefly silent. 'The same,' he confessed.

'Not the tree in the bird?'

'It fails to make itself apparent,' Booth said, rather baffled.

'That is your problem, Mr Booth. You hear us as but the bird in the tree. You are deaf to the tree in the bird.'

'I will try again, Titoko,' Booth promised testily. 'First we must remove obstacles to goodwill.'

'I see such obstacles to your rear. Speed them home with their weapons.'

'Empty-handed, Titoko? You must see that impossible.'

'Then what is their price to be?' Titoko asked. 'One horse or two, or must it be three?'

Booth worried at a number.

'Then,' Titoko urged powerfully, 'take five.'

Booth was ambushed. 'Five?'

'Five,' Titoko said.

Toa's face was not an uplifting sight, nor Demon's.

'Why the higher number?' Booth asked at last.

'Let it be our song from the tree. We wait on yours, Mr Booth.'

'Very well,' Booth said. 'There will be no arrest made. I shall see this in the nature of a provisional settlement.'

'Good,' Titoko said.

'You offer a generous compromise, Titoko.'

'Fools must,' Titoko said.

Others, Toa loudest among them, found the transaction less pleasing. After the last colonist hoofbeat had gone from the forest, and Booth too had followed, there was a sour tribal council.

'Our face is in the mud,' Toa argued. 'Our mana is gone.'

Titoko remained silent.

'What is such peace worth?' Toa asked.

'What would war today have been worth?' Titoko said.

Toa was at a loss.

'A few horses?' Titoko mocked.

'So what are you thinking?' Toa asked.

'That war is worth more,' Titoko said.

130

'Did I hear war, cousin?'

'You heard thought,' Titoko replied.

For a time men heard themselves breathing, their neighbours too. Titoko had no more to say.

He was on less feeble show the day a traveller arrived with news that the armed constabulary was back from the south. This traveller had just crossed the Waingongoro. He had seen a constabulary patrol interesting itself in the riverside. Several men, and a surveyor, had crossed to the north bank. They thought on the terrain at length and measured elevations on both sides of the river. They seemed to be choosing the site of a fresh redoubt. Such conversation as the eavesdropping traveller heard said that they were waiting on better weather for its building.

'On the north bank?' Toa said.

'Perhaps,' the traveller said.

'They think to fence us in,' Toa told Titoko.

'Or themselves,' Titoko said.

'You think the best,' Toa protested.

'Let worse do the walking,' Titoko argued.

The traveller further disclosed that there were senior officers in the patrol, among them familiar martial faces. Aside from the bulky and bristling colonist colonel named McDonnell, there was another mounted menace in a major's uniform, a man marked off from other men by the haughty set of his jaw, likewise by the bowie knife in his belt and the bright scarf billowing from his neck.

'Many Birds,' Titoko said.

'He is back,' the traveller agreed.

Titoko sighed. 'I heard the man had retired to paint pictures.'

'He must have forgotten the colour of warriors,' Toa suggested.

Titoko shrugged.

Toa recalled, 'You once had the wish to make yourself better known to him.'

Titoko was quiet.

'You called him the one colonist fit to fight,' Toa persisted.

'Perhaps,' Titoko said.

'He may still think you the Maori most worth his bullet.'

'In battle,' Titoko insisted.

'With Many Birds at the river, also McDonnell, what else do we have?'

'That thought is mine to think,' Titoko decided.

'When is it allowed us?' Toa asked.

'When I order it,' Titoko announced. Finally he asked the traveller, 'Were all this party white?'

'No Maori,' the traveller said. He knew Titoko's next question. 'No Captain Kepa.'

'Good,' Titoko said.

'What are you saying?' Toa asked.

'Worse has yet to pull on its boots,' Titoko said.

Kimball managed his own word with the traveller. 'Were there lieutenants with the constabulary party?' he asked.

'Three or four,' the traveller said.

'One lean and mean?'

'All of them,' the traveller said.

'But one sourer than owl's piss?'

The traveller thought for a time. 'There was one such, now I recall him,' he said. 'Not a lieutenant. A captain.'

Flukes must have found a few Irishmen to make miserable.

That afternoon Titoko rose before Kimball. 'Farewell your family,' he ordered.

'Again?'

'Tomorrow,' Titoko said.

Rihi, when Kimball reported to her, was moody. 'Where is he taking you?'

Kimball shrugged. 'Even if he told me, I wouldn't be wiser.'

'He's running away,' Rihi decided.

'Maybe,' Kimball shrugged.

'Titoko fears losing his name as a warrior.'

'Who says?'

'My father.'

'Toa would,' Kimball said. 'What do you say?'

'I am my father's daughter.'

'Who is it wants no war?' he asked.

Rihi was quiet.

'I asked you a question.'

She fidgeted, for some time.

132

'Well?' he asked.

'Me,' she had to agree.

He knew where she was weakest. 'Louder,' he said.

'Me,' she said. 'I want no war.'

'So be your husband's wife,' he ordered.

Titoko set out in rain on a late May morning. Their muddy path was seldom plain more than five paces; trees above were fluttering phantoms. Dirty cloud reared where the mountain should have been on show. Near its foot they slept in a shattered Maori hut with a scrap of roof left for shelter. Kimball wrecked the dwelling further to win wood for a fire. Titoko rested close to flame after they had eaten.

'How long have you been with me?' he asked.

'I haven't been counting,' Kimball claimed.

'Come. One year? Two?'

'Three,' Kimball said.

'You have seen much.'

'One way and another,' Kimball agreed warily.

'And you may see more.'

There was a silence.

'You're telling me something,' Kimball decided.

'That is correct. I ask you to forget nothing.'

'Why me?'

'Your chances are better.'

'Chances?' Kimball asked cautiously.

'Of telling the tale.'

'Why can't you?'

'I am the tale,' Titoko said.

'And I'm the wrong teller,' Kimball argued.

'Why would that be?'

'A son of a bitch called Flukes is the main item in mine.'

'That can be cured.'

'He might be a bugger. He's not worth a war.'

'We are learning what is,' Titoko explained.

'I don't know that I like the sound of that.'

'I don't know that I do,' Titoko said.

There was another silence.

'I have no son,' Titoko explained. 'Thus no grandchildren. It is not an unusual condition.'

'I guess not,' Kimball said.

'It is not always grief. Women wriggle with me as pleasure, not duty. Husbands are safe. Their sons are of their own making, never of mine. On the other hand, what is a man without children?'

'Happy,' Kimball decided with gloom.

'Or grandchildren?'

Kimball shrugged. 'I wouldn't know.'

'We must repair matters,' Titoko announced.

'What is it you want?'

'A grandson,' Titoko said.

'You're looking at me.'

'That is correct.'

'For this tale you want told?'

'You understand.'

'I need to think on it,' Kimball protested.

'I have done the thinking necessary.'

'And I have no say?'

'I need another eye.'

That was old news. Kimball was quiet.

'Therefore I make use of yours,' Titoko went on. 'Not to show me that which I wish to see. That which I do not.'

'That's not easy.'

'I never said it would be. Quick. Where is my fault?'

'I guess you're a little proud,' Kimball said. 'More than that. Proud of being proud.'

'You tell me I am vain?'

'You said it. Not me.'

'Also that I cannot think myself wrong?'

'You said that too.'

'You give me no wisdom at all,' Titoko said with disgust.

'I didn't ask for the job,' Kimball said bitterly.

'There is no more you wish to tell me?'

'As a matter of fact,' Kimball said, 'there is.'

'Such as what?' Titoko asked.

'You piss me off something powerful,' Kimball said. 'And not only me.'

'That is more interesting,' Titoko judged.

'You know your people are leaving you.'

'Because I wish no war?'

'Because no one knows what you want.'

'What, if I listened to whispers, might I hear said?'

'That you are too pleased with yourself.'

Titoko sighed and was silent.

'And too proud of your reputation to risk it again,' Kimball said.

'Not that I fear it?'

'Not as I hear.'

'Fate arranged that I warrior.'

'It's arranging ample again.'

'The once was enough. It is not my need.'

'Then your luck left on the last tide.' Kimball announced, wrapping himself in a blanket.

Titoko asked, 'How soon before Toa takes the tribe?'

'A week maybe. I wouldn't bet.'

'I must,' Titoko said. His snores were slow coming that night.

In the morning cloud was lifting and rain lighter. The temperature was no easier, with breeze frosty in their faces. Much of the mountain had been whitened by overnight blizzard. The land lifted underfoot; forest had begun winning back the old Maori trail, sometimes hiding it altogether. As they hacked their way higher snow tumbled from tree-tops and melted in their hair. They camped the second night in a cave behind a waterfall, beside a smoky fire. Outside their shelter wind grieved among trees. Titoko silently worried at an itch on his leg. 'A week,' he said.

'Or less,' Kimball told him.

'What then?'

'Toa mowing hell's meadow.'

'My thought too,' Titoko said. 'Thank you for thinking it.'

'That's what grandsons are for,' Kimball suggested. 'And, if you don't mind me asking, why are we here again?'

'Go to sleep,' Titoko said.

Morning shed more light on their situation than Titoko wished to. A mild nor'easter was blowing. Sun felt into the forest. The colours of moss, lichen and fern grew among trees shedding fat drops of moisture. Ringing waters also announced thaw. As they climbed again the vegetation began to grab less. Soon it was no more than knee-high, and then shreds of scrub among snowdrifts. The wind rose from a mumble to a grumble. Sooty mist raced toward them, met sun, and backed off. The mountain heaving overhead, such as they could see of it, had lost all style and become ugly ridge and cliff, crevasse and canyon. Sudden avalanche shook the ground. Half the mountain looked to be heading downhill; uncovered crags crawled dark from haze.

'You need go no further,' Titoko said.

'How long do I wait this time?'

'As long as I take.'

'You might be dead.'

'I shall judge that,' Titoko said.

Kimball sank under a blanket and watched Titoko push skyward. This time his wait was shorter; it was no more than an hour before he sighted a faint fleck on the skyline taking Titoko's form. He was stumbling downhill as if in panic, snow whipping away from his feet. As he came nearer, he failed to see Kimball; he now seemed blind in both eyes. When he hurtled past without a word Kimball set out in pursuit. It was some time before Titoko thought to slow his descent; Kimball caught him slumped in snow near the tree line.

'You're a bugger for punishment,' he said.

Titoko breathed heavily.

'So what was it this time?' Kimball asked.

'Nothing,' Titoko said.

'You said that last time.'

'Last time I looked into nothing.'

'This time?'

'Nothing looked into me.'

'You're telling me something,' Kimball concluded.

'Is there choice?'

'So it's war.'

'More or less,' Titoko sighed.

'How much less can it be?'

They sat in silence.

'So,' Kimball asked finally, 'how much more can it be?'

'When peace is no better than war, war must be made worse.'

'What does that mean?'

'War the way it was,' Titoko said.

'With the Hauhau?'

'With tried gods of war. No angels are necessary. No scripture.'

136

'That doesn't sound healthy.'

'The Hauhau were faint-hearted,' Titoko said.

'How do you reckon that?' Kimball marvelled.

'It's not just the killing,' Titoko said. 'It's the eating.'

'The eating?' Kimball asked faintly.

'The eating,' Titoko said.

Kimball felt his genitals shrink.

They travelled down the mountain with mist faint at their feet. A rainbow of bright orange, with a pale edge of blue, lifted from forest and leapt to far plain.

Fifteen

They were much of the way down the mountain before Titoko ended their silence. 'The notion', he judged, 'is not to your taste.'

'Since you're asking,' Kimball said.

'It is far from mine either,' Titoko confessed.

'Then why?'

'We have swallowed shit.'

'You're talking people.'

'That is so,' Titoko acknowledged. 'Shit is less nourishing.'

'All the same,' Kimball said.

'You are thinking your neck.'

'And my family,' Kimball agreed.

'I have far cousins. Safety could be arranged.'

'What would that mean?'

'You with your own tale.'

'What of yours?'

Titoko shrugged.

They travelled for some time in silence.

'Do I hear your reply?' Titoko asked.

'I'm listening too,' Kimball said.

Watchers were sent to note movement along the Waingongoro. Messengers rode out to distant tribesmen with Titoko's word. The scouts returned to report the riverside quiet, but for lone colonists milling timber and fencing the south bank. The messengers arrived back with poor news and few recruits. Other tribesmen, old allies, were cool about walking warrior trails. Titoko's sabbatical speeches had been taken to heart. His second thoughts failed to move them. Anyway, they argued, Titoko had been languid too long; he had best prove his quality as a commander again. They would wait. They would see. Their message was that one war had been enough, two terrible, and thought of a third altogether deranged; Titoko's people were free to fight if the grave was their wish.

'So we have just ourselves,' Toa said sourly.

'How many do you tally?' Titoko asked.

'Less boys?'

'And fighting women.'

'Seventy,' Toa said.

'No more?'

Toa said, 'Constabulary and armed colonists number more than five hundred within two days' ride. Ships could bring hundreds too.'

'You say we need more warriors?'

'Further thought,' Toa said. 'To get more warriors, we must win a triumph. To win a triumph we need more warriors.'

'On one view of the matter,' Titoko said.

'Is there another?' Toa asked.

'Making each warrior worth ten.'

'No warrior has more than one life. We have just seventy to lose.'

Kimball looked at Big's shiny face, then at calm Demon's, finally at Titoko's. First he felt terror. Then he floated free of all that he wasn't.

'Seventy-one,' he said.

There was a thoughtful silence. Titoko told those near him, 'Move to one side. This is my grandson. He now sits with me.'

'Christians came to tame the Maori horse,' Titoko told tribesmen. 'Colonists came to ride it. Now they think to bolt the stable door.'

'What are you telling us?' Toa asked.

'To spit out the bit, shake off the saddle, and run wild again.'

It was most of forty years since his people had warred in traditional style. There were few left familiar with ritual and recipe. An enfeebled old tribesman, long due for death, was borne from his bed, and told to instruct warriors in the pleasing of the war gods as their grandfathers had. Though he wandered far mists, this tribesman at least found the old rites for battle impossible to forget. To prove themselves worthy, warriors

139

had to bite the cross bar which supported their rumps in the village latrine. The latrine was a location too disgusting for malign spirits, and thus suited for first prayers. The reek of fresh dung not only prepared warriors for feats of offensive nature; it also reminded them that all things earthly had a foul end. Further, until combat was past, their flesh was not to be weakened, nor their ties to this world strengthened, by communion with women. Faltering in this respect was fatal to a war party. Warriors enamoured of flesh were famously slow to imperil their lives. Final purification came at the nearest river, which warriors entered naked for baptism and blessing so that they might then set out to slay sound of spirit. When battle began the first foe taken should have his chest split swiftly, his heart removed and pressed to flame. If the north-west wind lifted fumes from the singed organ, the favour of the war gods had been won. If not, rapid retreat was in order. Following triumph, as a final humiliation, the foe must be reduced to food. Preparations were not to be hurried, and prayers recited. There were correct cuts and incorrect cuts; human meat was best left to make its own sauce with a light seasoning of convolvulus.

In the end the old tribesman's lecture left little unsaid. Even Toa shrank. 'This?' he asked Titoko.

'You wished war,' Titoko pointed out.

'Not of the old kind.'

'Tell me better,' Titoko said.

'You think to win us back to war gods between today and tomorrow?'

'I think to win,' Titoko said.

Toa, even more on the wane, went into a long sulk.

Kimball was less worried by war gods than by human spectres. Night after night his sleep turned ugly with Flukes. Flukes never failed to have the dutiful Tonks in tow, often a hundred men more.

'Why are you yelling?' Rihi woke him to ask.

'Dreams,' he confessed.

'Mine too,' she said.

If Titoko had fidgets about fate, they weren't showing the day he picked his first war party. It meant balancing a carved wooden staff on his thumb and forefinger and holding it horizontal in the wind. Its point swayed, perhaps of itself, perhaps guided by gods, until it came to rest on a warrior. The warrior was asked if his heart beat powerfully within him. The wait was such that his answer was sure. Big was chosen, Demon too. Toa was not. Twelve were finally grouped to punish the timbering of the village latrine with their teeth. Toa was a dismal witness, with Kimball even further upwind.

Titoko fired his raiders before they left. 'We allowed colonists to the river,' he said. 'We gave them fresh territory to gaze on. We thought they would respect the river. They do not.'

'Your order?' Demon asked.

'Remove them from the river,' Titoko said. 'There shall be no further building of bridges, fences, or dwellings. Push them all the way back to their redoubts and there let them be.'

'Killing?' Big asked.

'Two,' Titoko ordered.

'No more?' Demon was baffled.

'Just two,' Titoko insisted. 'One body might be seen as a poor-tempered mistake. Two show us earnest.'

'All the same,' Demon argued.

'Two serve as well as twenty,' Titoko said. 'Other colonists will withdraw from the river with no further spurring. The more we kill, the more we chance casualties. I wish twelve to return.'

'With those slain?' Big asked cautiously.

'Not with farmers,' Titoko said.

His face said further questions were unwelcome. That left farewells. Hine led a group of women to the centre of the village. They wore brightly dyed flax kilts, and feathers in their hair; their faces glowed with ochre. Kimball was slow recognizing Rihi among them. Even so it was difficult to see her inflamed face as that of the war-fearing woman who shared his bed nightly. With small balls of flax spinning from their wrists, they swayed, chanted, and sang to ensure the chosen twelve were of one heart. To confirm their potency the men answered with a crashing of feet, a slapping of limbs, and hoarse voices chanting in unison. The chant said the world was the warrior's, all earth, all sky. With weapons high, knees bent back, they leapt from land with tongues protruding. When they came to rest, at last, the forest was quiet; a falling leaf would have been loud.

'Go,' Titoko ordered.

*

141

It was frosty dusk when the raiders returned. As they rode into the village fellow warriors, fretful for news, emerged from their dwellings. Titoko was slower to make an appearance.

'Twelve went out,' Demon reported. 'Twelve return.'

'Dead?' Titoko asked.

'Three,' Demon said.

'The order was two.'

'We came upon three felling trees and sawing timber. One was slain in our volley, the others wounded. They were finished with tomahawks and left where they fell. We burned dwellings and took firearms and horses.'

Titoko could have looked more elated. 'Then it was a good day,' he said.

'It might have been worse,' Demon agreed. 'What now?'

'Worse,' Titoko promised.

As he turned into his dwelling, his eye lit on Kimball. 'Sabbath is ended,' he announced. 'Monday is here.'

'I noticed,' Kimball said.

In two days there were no farmers within five miles of the Waingongoro; some were already further than fifty, and still travelling. Armed constabulary, on the other hand, were less easily moved; they remained walled in their redoubts, with earthworks larger and stockades taller. From their nearest redoubt they ventured out only to build another, one meaner in size, but better placed to overlook Titoko's territory.

'What of us?' Toa asked.

'Us?' Titoko queried.

'It is time to retire inland,' Toa argued. 'To look out a large hill and see to our own defences.'

'You are fighting another war,' Titoko said.

'Another?'

'The last.'

'Which might have been won.'

'And was not,' Titoko said.

'We do not leave?'

'Not our own land. It means we kill only as needed.'

'What is it you wish, cousin?'

'In this world?'

'Have we another?'

'I wish a line all men can see.'

'A line?'

'One no colonist can cross.'

'That would content you?'

'In this world.'

'You hasten us to the next,' Toa grumbled. 'To persist on low ground means grief.'

'Theirs,' Titoko said. 'Ours is to make it.'

Toa was baffled.

In faint morning light Titoko took up his carved wooden staff to determine the wish of the war gods, and certainly his. Again its point came to rest, one by one, on twelve warriors. Once more Toa was not of them. Demon was, and Big.

'This', Titoko told the twelve, 'is a patrol.'

'Of what nature?' Demon asked.

'To determine the health of our territory.'

'No more?'

'Also to persuade the men of the constabulary to give thought to their employment.'

'How is that to be?' Big asked.

'With a killing,' Titoko said.

'One?' Demon asked.

'More means risk.'

'We are not talking', Big said, 'of an attack on their redoubts?'

'We are talking of your twelve alive,' Titoko said.

'You wish a patrol ambushed?'

Titoko shrugged. 'If numbers are comfortable, and one a straggler.'

'Otherwise?'

'You watch. You wait. You return. Not empty-handed.'

'With a head?'

'The rest,' Titoko said.

'War', Demon protested, 'will not be won with one corpse.'

'Nor will it be lost,' Titoko said. To Big he added, 'Where your constable is felled, this message will be left.' He passed Big a folded sheet of paper. Big looked at it with interest.

'Be in no speed to read it,' Titoko advised.

As the patrol rode off Titoko asked Kimball, 'How is that, then?'

'You're vexing them considerable,' Kimball said. 'They never fought a war like it.'

'Who has?' Titoko said.

'You're making it up as you go along?'

'Mostly,' Titoko admitted.

'What is the message?'

'Of kindly nature. It tells the constabulary that they are free to travel roads to the south of their redoubts.'

'To the north?'

'They are informed that the first of them is already food for birds of the air, beasts of the field, and men of my tribe.'

'Sweet Jesus,' Kimball whispered.

'There will be no grace spoken,' Titoko said.

The party commanded by Demon and Big hid in fern and scrub for two days, the large constabulary redoubt always in view. They watched sunrise and sunset; they waited through rain and frost. They saw sentries pacing above the stockades and observed the men in the watch tower yawning; they heard bugle-calls dividing the constabulary day. Their warrior minute came on a sunlit morning with the grazing of horses outside the redoubt. Four men were assigned to this duty, two keeping watch with rifles. One of the horses wandered to graze close to the trees; the rebels in hiding remained quiet. Soon one of the constables set out in search of the missing beast. He took one pace too many toward the forest and made the further mistake of turning his back on the trees while pausing to piss. He was not permitted a cry of panic. His leg was grabbed, then an arm, and in the same second a tomahawk all but took his head from his body. Another blow opened his chest. After clumsy fishing within his interior, his heart was fetched warm into the light of a winter day and singed with matches. The drift of the fumes proved promising. With no further delay the man was quartered and trimmed to convenient form. Titoko's message was placed in the cleft of a stick where the constable's unnecessary parts were scattered.

Triumph was not clear when twelve unscarred warriors arrived back at The Beak that afternoon. They dismounted and unsaddled their horses in silence. Watching villagers were as quiet. When Titoko appeared four parcels were placed near his feet by Demon and Big.

'As you asked,' Demon said, and drew back.

'What is it you bring?' Titoko asked ritually.

'Food for the war gods,' Big answered with no pleasure.

Titoko did not push himself to investigate. Toa, however, thought to make a last plea.

'It is not too late to think again,' he urged Titoko.

'Of what?' Titoko asked.

'Of letting this man be buried with decency. All else may be forgotten and forgiven. Never this. It will be said that you, Titokowaru, led his people back into the dark.'

'You talk Methodist, cousin.'

Toa looked at his feet.

'Are men of the constabulary safe within their redoubts,' Titoko asked, 'or are they not?'

'This far,' Toa said.

'Do we wish to draw them out,' Titoko asked, 'or do we not?'

Toa was silent.

'Prepare the oven,' Titoko said.

The winter day was early waning. In the smoky dusk villagers gathered silent again. They were fewer in number; many warriors found reason to remain in their dwellings, pleading fatigue and forest fever. Kimball was early among those shaky of heart and uneasy of stomach. When curiosity won, he didn't get much past his door. There was no escaping the smell of meat. Titoko took a commanding stance before tribesmen. The oven had been emptied, and its contents, bedded on steaming potato, were set before him in flax containers. Big and Demon were prominent among the warriors parading. Toa stood apart. 'In this war,' Titoko was saying, 'there will be no waste. We not only make one warrior worth many. We likewise make one dead enemy worth ten.'

Toa remained sour. 'How?' he said.

'That will be seen,' Titoko promised.

'Let us observe this miracle,' Toa challenged. 'Let us see you choose your portion.'

Titoko ignored Toa. 'Our old people knew that no enemy is truly beaten until he is killed,' he went on. 'They also knew that no enemy is truly killed until he is eaten. More than his flesh has gone. His mana has flown too.'

'Choose your portion,' Toa persisted.

'Was this man of rank?' Titoko asked Big.

'A constable,' Big said.

'Merely?'

'Only,' Big confirmed.

'Then it is not fitting,' Titoko announced. 'A general perhaps. Even a colonel.'

'You are telling us,' Toa said, 'that it is for others to partake?'

'I know my own mind,' Titoko said.

'It is your appetite that interests us.'

'Men who take orders are necessary. In war, am I seen carrying a weapon?'

'That has not been your choice in the past.'

'It is still not. Yet I order others to slay.'

Toa was silenced.

'A fool of a leader', Titoko said, 'can find men who do as he does. For war I wish men who do as I need.'

'You are talking to me,' Toa judged.

'You, cousin, remain free to mount a horse and ride where light leads you.'

'I am not sure I hear you,' Toa said. 'I am not sure I wish to.'

Lesser warriors were in difficulty too. Most were restless, some easing into shadow.

'It will be enough,' Titoko decided, 'if one man alone ensures that our tribe is as good as its word.'

'That man is not you?'

'I wish to see who would make this war work,' Titoko said.

There was a long quiet. With Titoko's rite near rout, Big stepped forward. His voice said one thing; his eyes something else.

'Give me the meat that is mine,' he asked.

Demon, with less flinching, advanced too. 'And mine,' he said.

Silent Toa, his head low, was the third to take a container.

There was no rush from the ranks. Quiet came early to the village that night. Victuals surplus to need were buried at a distance from the village. For a time, restless in bed beside Rihi, Kimball wished he knew how he felt about Big, Demon and Toa. With daylight again it seemed not to matter. The world was no worse for wear.

146

Sixteen

Pickets about The Beak were doubled. Scouts watched approaches to the forest. Emissaries rode to inform past tribal allies that battle had been joined with colonists and constables. Next morning no warrior was idle, and for that matter only feeble women. Fortification of the village had begun. Titoko had not only forsaken the notion of hilltop strongholds; it seemed he also wished to forgo traditional trenches, moats and parapets. Lines of heaving men lifted logs from the forest and sank them around the village. Logs larger still were split for horizontal reinforcing and lashed into place. Loopholes were formed along the front of the wall at intervals of two paces and hidden by bunches of brush. Toa thought Titoko's defence line indecently shallow, little more than a rough fence, too flimsy by far. An enemy would meet with no barrier until he was upon the village; the palisades had but to be breached once for the village to be naked. Also fields of fire from the loopholes were limited and the palisades could be torched by attackers crouching low. Toa's perplexity was shared; mutters became mutinous. Finally, with displeasure, Titoko took doubters into account. 'What is your grievance?' he asked.

'You tempt disaster,' Toa argued.

'To turn it,' Titoko claimed.

'You ask them to our palisades.'

Titoko did not deny it.

'With the village surrounded,' Toa went on, 'we would never fight our way out.'

'Nor will we,' Titoko promised.

'Nor could we,' Toa insisted, 'with our numbers.'

'What is your count?' Titoko asked.

'The same,' Toa said. 'More than seventy and less than eighty. No desertions, and few newcomers.'

'Your count is faulty,' Titoko said. 'I see a hundred times as many.'

'A hundred?' Toa was baffled.

'Or more. For every man a hundred friends.'

'Where', Toa asked, 'is this magical force?'

'Look about,' Titoko suggested.

Toa considered forest. 'I cannot see these allies,' he confessed.

'Look again,' Titoko said. 'Count again.'

'I see but limb and leaf,' Toa insisted.

'As our guests will.'

Understanding dawned in Toa's face. 'You talk trees?'

'The smaller will do our skirmishing, the larger our killing. Trees give no ground. Nor men in them.'

'And this', Toa marvelled, 'is your defence?'

'Who speaks defence?'

'An ambush?'

'A net.'

Toa shook his head. 'You have talked much of custom.'

'That is so,' Titoko agreed.

'Our grandfathers fought where sky was witness.'

'And died there.'

'Great canoes are not to be hidden.'

'They split faster in sun.'

'Courage was seen.'

'Custom interests me, cousin, as it serves carbines. And better the breech-loading kind.'

Titoko left Toa to think. He failed to confide much in Kimball either. Pious camp gossip said he now communed with the war gods nightly. Since Titoko's dwelling neighboured his, poor-sleeping Kimball knew more reliably that his commander's devotions were shared with soft-footed women short on attention elsewhere. With Titoko himself overdue to swear off wriggling, he might have been making peace worth waving goodbye.

As days passed the palisades were more plainly a target to tempt enemies fast. Most of an acre of fern and scrubby growth was trimmed from the front of the village. Firing platforms, with footing for three or four warriors, were hammered together and lashed high overhead in foliage. Among leaves along the forest edge there were rifle pits large and small joined by tunnels. Dead trees with rotting centre were hollowed until they became tiny redoubts loopholed to serve marksmen squeezed within. Titoko walked the ground again and again, climbing vine ladders to the firing platforms, peering through loopholes, until sure all death's acre could be sown evenly with shot.

Then warriors were herded into the forest to begin slashing fresh trails, most leading nowhere, circling back upon themselves. Soon men were losing themselves in their own maze.

'Now skirmishers,' Titoko said.

Springy saplings alongside trails were stripped of branches and leaves, bent to the horizontal, twisted to one side, and then fastened with flax. Strangers in the forest had only to brush the vegetation once. The flax fastening would be tripped and the intruders felled by the sapling sweeping the trail. An incautious warrior, wanting to test the device, was scythed from his feet, and left mourning loss of vision.

The forest grew even more evil with maze and man-trap. The problem then was that it failed to swarm with bitter and blinded foemen; it remained empty of all but sweet-tempered birds.

To ensure shot of character, Kimball was returned to his old trade of armourer, this time as overseer, with ten warriors toiling to his order. Casting fires burned daylong, into the night, often until dawn. Useful metal came to light in the village, much of it hoarded against a needy day; likewise small kegs of gunpowder. When raw material ran short, he had men scavenge the countryside for buttons and buckles to make lethal, and barter with distant tribesmen for stored powder. Otherwise he couldn't afford to be fancy. Trial proved the bladders of pigs and sheep good cover for carbine cartridges and, when they became scarce, the innards of eels. Titoko turned filled cartridges between his fingers and saw no fault.

'Your tally?' was all he asked.

'Enough,' Kimball promised.

'See weapons are worthy,' Titoko ordered.

Rusty barrels and splitting stocks arrived by the score. Though Big arrived to help, Kimball had few hours to call his own, most of them clouded with Rihi's melancholy.

'What happened', she asked, 'to the war that wasn't to be?'

'I'm just helping out,' he explained with patience.

'Helping Titoko shame my father,' she raged damningly.

'Toa wanted war first,' he pointed out. 'You can't have it both ways.'

There again he was wrong. When Rihi finished flaying him with words, tiny Meri and Wiremu punched him awake before first light. Family life was never short on nightmare. When his eyes did flutter shut, there was Flukes.

Scouts and emissaries rode back to The Beak with a mix of news. The sweet was that land south of the river had never looked emptier. Not only colonist farmers had fled. More than a score of constables had discarded their uniforms in fern and, in long underwear or less, pointed themselves at the healthiest horizon. On the other hand noisy drilling had been noted in the vicinity of the redoubts, also musketry practice heard. The colonist colonel named McDonnell and Major Many Birds were interestingly ill-tempered, seldom speaking to each other, and beatings of faint-hearted men were frequent. Their commanders mounted few patrols, and those they sent out made no attempt to cross the Waingongoro and breach the forest; they seemed to be waiting on reinforcement. Certainly Titoko was, and there the news was sour. Neighbouring tribesmen were not impressed by the ambush of harmless colonists and the slaying of a lone constable. Titoko, they judged, was playing with war. His pagan rites, not least his tribe's recent diet, gave them further excuse to think twice; even unrepentant Hauhau judged man-eating unhelpful, a likely offence to the Holy Ghost, certainly to the colonial government. Their chiefs washed their hands of Titoko in messages to the authorities. 'Let seagulls peck his corpse,' they said. 'We leave him to his fate.' Some even protested a wish to join in Titoko's crushing. Just five unruly and unpromising recruits to Titoko's cause drifted into the forest with ancient firearms shouldered. Less reckless Maori made a point of not taking forest trails which wound near The Beak. Titoko's war looked to be perishing for want of interest. Not only was he finding few friends; he was lacking a foe.

With midwinter past, and further warrior weather wasted, Titoko grew even more peevish. He had Big and Kimball called from their dwellings. To Big he said, 'You have long been considering the British redoubts.'

'The larger and the smaller,' Big agreed.

'You have also kept count of constabulary seen.'

'True,' Big said.

'And there has been little change?'

'But for desertion,' Big said. 'More than a hundred sit in the larger, few more than a score in the smaller. The larger is solid, the smaller still in the making.'

'Their commanders persist in the larger?'

'McDonnell and Many Birds both,' Big said. 'They never show their heads long, even riding the three miles between the redoubts.'

'They think better days?' Titoko asked.

'And more men,' Big suggested.

'Perhaps Kepa's Maori?'

'Who knows? The colonists seem happy to sit.'

'With an enemy ten miles distant?'

'More wondrous still,' Big allowed.

'It might be thought they need awakening?'

'You are thinking it,' Big said.

'That is so,' Titoko said.

'You are also thinking Many Birds,' Big decided.

'Now and then,' Titoko confessed.

'And drawing him out.'

'Perhaps,' Titoko said.

'What of the colonist colonel? McDonnell?'

'With Many Birds gone we can rely on McDonnell to take fright.'

'What do you want of us, then?'

'More knowledge of the smaller redoubt. The weaker.'

'To what end?'

Titoko shrugged. 'McDonnell and Many Birds must be roused to leave the large redoubt. Many Birds is the more promising. The colonel will need shaming.'

'You wish a patrol,' Big concluded.

'Of quiet nature.'

'Why the Yankee?' Big queried.

'He has knowledge of British faces.'

This could not be argued. Kimball shifted from one foot to the other.

'I wish to know where weak is weakest,' Titoko went on. 'You have brushed noses with the British before.'

'Last time', Kimball said, 'things got a little aggravating.'

'This time', Titoko explained, 'crawl close but to listen.'

'What do you want?'

'What they are saying. I wish to know them better, their habits and spirit. Watch when sentries change. It is then that men are less wary. The retiring sentries are sleepy, the new still yawning. Consider how much they show themselves. All knowledge will be welcome.'

'For what?' Big persisted.

'To place marksmen with small loss,' Titoko explained.

'You are talking attack?'

'If man-eating cannot fire them,' Titoko said, 'massacre must.'

In creek-cut country south of the Waingongoro, the small colonist redoubt paid respects to the past by perching on an outer rampart of an abandoned Maori fortress. The place had been deserted since siege and treachery worked its fall; the heads of its last inhabitants shrivelled on stakes until they were skulls. Haunted with dying curses, the site was said to have a poisoned climate of its own. It was a place most Maori circled, making it more helpful for police purpose. It overlooked forsaken colonist farms and half-fired fernland. To the west the Waingongoro washed the edge of Titoko's forest, with the mountain bright beyond. Smoke from The Beak, deep in the forest, must have been plain on a clear day.

All possible approaches to the redoubt were unkind. Big and Kimball closed with it in the feeble light of late afternoon. Tall fern and flax, flourishing in the swampy low ground of old Maori moats, gave skimpy cover. Then they made higher ground. Big wriggled forward a yard or two, then signalled for Kimball to follow. Progress was slow and sodden. At length, pushing apart scrub, the pair peered out on the redoubt. The place was not of powerful size and plainly unfinished. It was hardly more than twenty paces square, with tiny bastions flanking east and west corners. Within rough earthworks were tents and a thatched guardhouse. Men looked to be uncomfortably crowded within. They had been obliged to raise their cookhouse outside the redoubt wall.

Big held up a hand for silence. A detail armed with shovels was labouring in mud to lift the outer ramparts higher. The squelching of their boots could be heard; also their sad obscenities. Half the earth they moved slid back upon them. Some sighed and furtively smoked. Soon a familiar and muscular figure rose on the slippery wall above them. Kimball flinched from old habit. 'If you fuckers don't finish,' Tonks warned the toilers, 'you sleep outside tonight. You hear?'

'We hear, corporal,' a sullen man was heard to agree.

'And you know what that means?' Tonks asked.

'That bugger Bent,' the sullen man suggested.

'Fresh tucker for Titoko's table,' Corporal Tonks promised. 'Me, I think the old bastard's got no taste. There's none of you fit for dog food.'

Light rain began falling. Tonks jumped back into the redoubt. Few of his hounded men found enough energy to spit at his departing posterior.

Kimball had his first useful intelligence. Recent weeks hadn't given his reputation a rest; his chances of old age were still on the lean side. On the other hand martial fires were not burning bright.

There was a third item. Where Tonks was, Flukes should be.

Satisfying himself on commonplace matters, Big gripped Kimball's shoulder as a sign to withdraw before dark. They crouched among trees to the north of the redoubt, smoked, and whispered.

'What did you see?' Big asked.

'Some poor silly sods,' Kimball said.

'Meaning what?'

'Four bob a day for wet feet, a cow of a corporal, and Titoko too.'

'Sympathy does not serve us,' Big suggested.

'What does?'

'Parapets barely five feet tall. They will not raise them much higher.'

'That's all?'

'The outer trench hardly six feet deep.'

'And?'

'Sad workmanship. The parapet is not finished with timber. Not even sandbags. Therefore, no loopholes. Those within cannot shoot without showing themselves above the earthwork; they cannot even enfilade their outer trench in safety. Further, the fools whose work this was have also failed to see that the guardhouse masks the field of fire of men in the east bastion. The gate to the redoubt is left with small protection. As for those defending the west bastion, they will tangle themselves in their tents should they rush to reinforce the east.'

'There must be something you haven't thought of,' Kimball argued.

'Not fucking much,' Big said.

They made their second approach to the redoubt after midnight, crawling close enough to hear the resonant belching of sentries. It seemed the parapet top was too greasy to tread; the two constables on watch, moving in reverse directions, were obliged to pace around the outside of the redoubt. Sometimes, as they passed, they exchanged a bitter word. Sometimes they smoked. Often they told themselves that all was quiet. Once they had something like conversation.

'What do you reckon?' one asked the other.

'I seen better nights,' the second observed.

'Something has to happen.'

'Tell fucking Flukes.'

'He only takes orders.'

'Who bloody doesn't?'

So much for Kimball's largest suspicion. Halfway to dawn it was sure. The sentries woke Corporal Tonks; Tonks roused the garrison. There was pissing, spitting and farting. Muffled sighs, groans and curses finally said all fit men in the redoubt were standing to arms. Then Tonks was heard addressing his commander. 'All present and correct, sir,' he reported.

'And all quiet?' Flukes was heard asking.

'All quiet, sir,' Tonks agreed.

'Good,' Flukes said. 'To your post, corporal.'

An hour or two passed. There were just flutters of movement and stifled coughs until the eastern sky paled. Then a detail of three left the redoubt for the outer cookhouse. By sunrise men were breakfasting on hot tea, damper bread and bacon. There was talk and tobacco smoke.

As day grew Captain Flukes rose on part of the parapet planked as an observation post. He had binoculars in hand. Tonks climbed into place beside him. Their voices as plain as their profiles, they were no more than a dozen yards from where Big and Kimball shivered in deep fern. In keeping with promotion Flukes now sported a clipped martial moustache, a louder voice and larger vocabulary. He strutted a yard left, a yard right, trained his binoculars toward the mountain and lowered them again.

'Look to a further inspection today, corporal,' he told Tonks.

'Major von Tempsky, sir?' Tonks asked.

'The Prussian,' Flukes agreed.

'What's his worry, sir?'

'Us,' Flukes said.

'Not before bloody time,' Tonks argued.

'He tells the colonel that occupation of this redoubt has become reckless. He urges Colonel McDonnell to reinforce it or withdraw.'

'Decent of him, sir.'

'Major von Tempsky, corporal, has no interest in your welfare or mine.'

'What is his interest, sir?'

Flukes lowered his binoculars. 'Titoko,' he said.

Tonks was quiet.

'He argues,' Flukes explained, 'that one strong redoubt, with safety in numbers, is sufficient to turn Titoko. Surplus constables might be used to harass him meantime.'

'Harass?'

'Until Colonel McDonnell has something looking like an army.'

'You don't harass that old nigger a little. You do or you don't.'

'So the colonel seems to think.'

'What does he say?'

'Nothing mortal men can hear. He muses much in his tent.'

'I don't know that I hear right, sir,' Tonks said. 'The boss has got a bad case of the shakes?'

'Or common sense,' Flukes said.

155

He paced the planks again, Tonks to his rear.

'You don't tell me what you're thinking, sir,' Tonks said.

'Of your old comrade Bent, corporal. There are days when I fancy I smell the filthy wretch.'

Kimball's world grew still.

'You can't take him serious, sir,' Tonks protested.

'No?' Flukes said coolly.

'Or the nonsense men talk, sir.'

'Do nothing to discourage it if it keeps men sharp.'

'They don't talk about Titoko's men. They mutter about Bent's bandits, sir. There's a bloody great laugh.'

'He is less to laugh about, corporal,' Captain Flukes said stiffly.

Tonks took the rebuke. 'No, sir.'

'Desertion, disloyalty, treason to one's own. What more can one ask?'

'His skin, sir,' Tonks suggested.

'You shall have it,' Flukes promised. 'Meanwhile look to the major arriving before noon.'

'The devil we know, sir.'

'Perhaps so, Tonks.'

'What do you think Titoko's up to next?'

'He is better not dwelt on, corporal.'

'I can't help thinking, sir.'

'Give yourself more to think about,' Flukes said.

'That an order, sir?'

'What does it sound like?' Flukes asked.

Soon afterwards Tonks resumed booting constabulary arses.

'Do we wait on Many Birds?' Kimball said.

'No,' Big decided with speed.

They scuttled through fern and found trees. By night they were back at The Beak.

'So spirit is weak,' Titoko said.

'And flesh no better,' Kimball explained. 'Many Birds wants to withdraw men from the small redoubt until numbers are happier.'

'McDonnell?'

'The colonel', Big said, 'wishes war to leave him alone.'

'There is no talk of Kepa's tribesmen?'

'None,' Big said. 'Perhaps Kepa asks better money.'

'It can be said that the men of the redoubts are not ready?'

'It can surely be said,' Big agreed.

'Good,' Titoko announced. 'So we force them to attack before they are.'

'Meaning?' Big said.

'We strike the small redoubt to empty the large.'

Toa, standing off, finally made himself part of the conversation. 'For what?' he asked.

'A showing,' Titoko argued. 'Who was it said that to win more warriors we must have triumph?'

'I also said, cousin, that to win triumph we need more warriors.'

'A little fire lit in the British beard might leave a large glow.'

'Perhaps,' Toa said.

'It is also', Titoko said, 'a task for no more than twenty. For one constable, one warrior.'

'An attack on a redoubt needs better numbers,' Toa said.

'Not in the correct circumstance. Not with the correct leader.'

'You?'

'You, cousin,' Titoko said warmly. 'This is your chance.'

Toa was surprised and wary. 'This is sudden,' he said. 'Why this? Why now?'

'It may have been a dream,' Titoko said, 'in which I saw you as victor.'

'May?'

'I dream many dreams.'

Kimball failed to imagine how Titoko found the time with furtive females diving into his bed.

Toa needed convincing too. 'This dream, if you had it, said nothing of my death?'

'Not in my hearing,' Titoko said gravely.

'You would not wish it?'

'Never,' Titoko vowed. 'The least warrior lost on this mission would be grief to me. Grief in your case, cousin, goes without saying.'

'It might hearten me to hear it said.'

'So I say it,' Titoko offered. 'Who would care to console Hine?'

That was an interesting question. It left Toa quiet. Finally he asked, 'Where will you be?'

'Here. The better to make The Beak bite when they follow you back.'

Next day Big mapped the redoubt in the dirt outside Titoko's dwelling. He then lectured Titoko, Toa and others present on the lesser virtues of the outpost. Finally he warned, 'Those in command are not all fools, much as we wish them so. Their discipline is cruel. They turn men out in the middle of the night knowing Maori custom is surprise in the last hours of dark.'

'We attack earlier?' Toa asked.

'Later,' Big said. 'They ease with first light.'

Toa turned to Titoko. 'What of this redoubt when we have it?'

'Have I spoken of taking it?' Titoko asked.

'Perhaps not,' Toa said, puzzled.

'I have not,' Titoko insisted. 'I do not.'

'What is it you ask?'

'Righteous shooting,' Titoko said.

Titoko's plan took Big's judgement into account. As men of the redoubt relaxed with first promise of light, thinking more of breakfast than battle, a small party of warriors would make itself known. Those of this feint would discharge weapons at the emerging cookhouse detail to signal constables within the redoubt that attack had begun. The party would then rush the outer trench of the redoubt to draw constabulary fire. With no more than a small and madcap Maori party on show, the constabulary should be tempted to rise in strength on the shoulders of the parapet. As they directed their weapons down on the warriors in the trench, the redoubt's defenders would be arranged as birds on a branch. At that point a main force of marksmen, sited on high ground Big had noted, would train volleys at the flash of British weapons. Two or more flights of shot might be possible before surprise was lost. All constables showing themselves should by then be silenced. At the least the garrison should be lamenting large casualties.

'What then?' Toa asked. 'We rush their gate?'

'Look into my eye,' Titoko said.

Toa tried.

'The dead one,' Titoko ordered.

Toa reluctantly shifted his gaze.

'What do you see?' Titoko asked.

'A sight that grows no more charming,' Toa said.

'You see a frontal attack,' Titoko said. 'This eye learned the lesson. There will be no argument with the bullets of Britain. You turn. You return.'

'With the task unfinished?'

'The challenge made. No close fighting. No casualties to slow your return. You retire before sunrise. Also before Many Birds rides in from the large redoubt. Your shooting will surely be heard. When he arrives with relief, he will not persist long to number his loss. We must look to his fury carrying him into the forest.'

'You rely on it?'

'I know it,' Titoko said.

Since Many Birds could yet convince McDonnell to recall Flukes and his men, attack was planned for the following morning. Titoko took up his carved staff again and twirled it to choose Toa's twenty. Nineteen were determined. Then came a problem. The staff pointed at Kimball. This, on the face of things, vexed Titoko; he tried again. Once more it failed to pass Kimball.

Titoko shook his head in wonder. 'Something powerful is at work,' he pronounced.

'Something wrong,' Toa argued.

'Wrong, cousin?' Titoko asked.

'I do not wish the responsibility of this man. If he fails to return, my daughter, perhaps also my wife, will see the fault as mine.'

'All to the good,' Titoko said. 'His presence in your party may interest you in caution.'

For a third time the staff chose Kimball.

'Explain this,' Titoko said.

Toa failed to. Likewise Kimball.

'Who', Titoko asked, 'commands the redoubt?'

The question was unnecessary. Titoko knew.

'Captain Flukes of the constabulary,' Kimball answered.

'The man who most wants you dead?'

'The same,' Kimball said.

'Much is explained,' Titoko said.

Toa was silenced.

Titoko lowered his staff. Kimball took up a carbine tested and oiled with considerable dedication; also cartridges as sound as any he had overseen.

'You have but the one chance,' Titoko told him. 'Soon he will be one captain among many.'

'I know,' Kimball said.

'And fetch me Many Birds,' Titoko urged.

'That may not be easy,' Kimball said.

'Better with this,' Titoko argued. He gave Kimball a folded sheet of paper. 'Ensure this is seen.'

'Do I read it too?'

'Should you wish,' Titoko said.

Kimball parted the paper. The communication was short, and in Titoko's firm hand:

> To the coward who calls himself von Tempsky. To the Prussian who poses as warrior. To Many Birds who fails to fly. This is Titokowaru's word. Though a thousand men march against him, Titokowaru shall be found in The Beak of the Bird. Should all the men of these islands march against him, Titokowaru shall be found in The Beak of the Bird. Should even all the British Empire march against him, Titokowaru shall yet be found in The Beak of the Bird. I shall not die, I shall not die. When death itself is dead I shall be alive. Come. I wait. I hunger. This is all. I, Titokowaru.

'Is the meaning plain?' Titoko asked.

'If a thing's not worth saying three times,' Kimball judged, 'I guess it wasn't worth much the once.'

'You don't have to be a hero,' Rihi said.

'Who's trying?' Kimball asked.

'What is it, then?'

'I could use sleep,' he told her.

'You might get it,' she argued. 'A long one.'

'The dreams might be better,' he said.

Rihi wasn't alone with fears. Big also had them. 'I like this less,' he told Kimball. 'If Titoko gives Toa charge there must be a reason.'

'A good one?'

'A bad.'

'He wants Toa to fail?'

'Not to succeed well.'

'Why would that be?'

'To encourage the colonists a little. Too great a triumph might leave them cowardly.'

'Titoko's thinking casualties?'

'He is surely thinking to shut Toa up,' Big said.

Kimball survived the stench of the latrine and the shock of mountain water. Warrior virtue presented no problem; it was weeks since Rihi had permitted a worthwhile impurity. With rites done, Toa's party moved out of the village on a cold July morning. By late afternoon they were labouring out of the forest and crossing the Waingongoro. They were then fewer than three miles from the redoubt. Toa rested his party until dusk. Then they moved forward to determine that the redoubt remained occupied. Finally Toa held up his hand for silence; warrior whispers stopped. Soon British cries drifted downhill. Corporal Tonks, it seemed, had discovered pickets smoking and gambling and was bashing them to rights. It was cover Toa needed. With dark, and few rustles and mutters, he had men divided between the positions Big's inspection suggested and Titoko ordered. Marksmen under Big, Kimball too, took up ground fewer than fifty paces south of the redoubt. Those under Toa, the feint, crawled into place closer to the outer trench.

The moonless night had no surprise and less comfort. An owl or two sounded from the hills. The sentries muddily shuffled; wind conveniently whimpered. Without tobacco, not even a rum issue, cramping and shivering warriors massaged their limbs for warmth. They pissed furtively and their stomachs rumbled loudly. For nourishment they swallowed pork as salt as Lot's wife and washed it down with canteens of icy water. The rest was as Kimball and Big had last seen it. With much of dark gone, men of the garrison were roused. Tonks was heard speaking, Flukes too. Silence grew as men stood to. Perhaps two hours were left to first light.

In the last minutes, Toa crawled up to his marksmen. 'Shoot only with sight of a constable,' he ordered.

'How can that be?' Big asked. 'We shall have but their flashes.'

'You will have light,' Toa promised.

'Only with day,' Big said. 'By day Titoko orders us gone.'

'Day may come sooner,' Toa said mysteriously.

He slipped away to his assault party.

Big muttered obscenely.

'What's wrong?' Kimball asked.

'Toa.' Big was bitter. 'Bad is beginning already.'

'So what now?' Kimball asked.

'The time of lies,' Big said.

'Whose?'

'Yours,' Big shrugged. 'Mine.'

'Toa's?'

'Best of all.'

Big ordered weapons loaded. Many marksmen had two. There was a flexing of limbs, a faint rattle of metal.

Day and death moved nearer. Pearly cloud to the east signalled voices within the redoubt. As the horizon paled Corporal Tonks was heard ordering the cookhouse detail to take up duties. The gate opened and closed behind them. At least their appearance went to plan. Then nothing began to. They were not shot from their feet by Toa's men. Instead, as they left the redoubt, the sky's glimmer had an earthly echo. Flame wisped from the cookhouse, then bright gusts. As fire mounted the three unarmed constables of the cookhouse detail were seen marooned on open ground between the redoubt and the burning outbuilding. They looked left and right, their surprise plain.

Kimball heard Big's groan. 'This', he predicted, 'will surely be seen, and bring Many Birds soon.'

'Perhaps,' Kimball said.

'Games,' Big said.

There was panicky shouting within and without the redoubt, and confusing commands. The three of the cookhouse detail were bawled at by Corporal Tonks to extinguish the fire, then roared at by Captain Flukes to retire with speed. Orders sank under clatter, curses, and the crackle of flame. Rebel shot might have made sense of the uproar, but no shot was heard.

'Where', Big said in despair, 'is Toa's challenge?'

162

When it came, it was not the kind ordered. While the exposed detail dithered, men of Toa's party, armed for close combat, leapt into the light. They circled the Britons briefly, determined first blows, then sank their tomahawks. Shock rang in the redoubt; constables began climbing parapets to get in shots. Corporal Demon, the most conscientious aggressor, continued working with calm. He split the chests of the slain for his companions to tug out their hearts. With British shot still failing to trouble them, Toa's reddened performers fed the hearts to fire. Then only did they move more or less to plan. They grabbed up firearms, discharged them, and danced brazenly, with eyes rolling and tongues showing, toward the outer trench of the redoubt. Finally they bared their arses at the foe, and rushed. The wind whipped a tide of sparks along the ground behind them; hell looked to be emptying of devils. The defenders of the redoubt lifted into view, showing more than head and shoulders, at last making targets.

'Fire,' Big sighed.

The downhill volley swept exposed constables off their feet as they tried to cleanse Toa's trench. One constable crumpled on a parapet edge; the other toppled with a short cry into the redoubt. A third, clutching his head, was tugged to safety. Others seemed to be stung.

Kimball, looking to his next shot, watched for Flukes to rise from a parapet, Tonks too as bonus. Then he had no view at all. Fed by chopped fuel, perhaps by a store of oil, flame shook from the green thatch of the cookhouse roof; dark smoke rolled over the redoubt. One moment Big's marksmen had enough light to level an army; the next there was nothing but murk lit with sparks. Somewhere in the fog Toa's men were befuddling the defenders. Whatever Flukes' men were, they were not targets. Big's marksmen could do no more than round out the confusion with blind volleys.

'We have no task here,' he judged. 'We must rush the redoubt too.'

It was the last thing Titoko wanted.

'To take it?' Kimball asked.

'To make it worth leaving,' Big said.

'And Toa?'

'To save him too,' Big said with regret.

The next minutes were mad. Running, stumbling, Big led

163

his party at the redoubt. The smoke was choking; shouts and shots grew. They found Toa, Demon and two surviving men in the outer trench, chancing shots over the rim of the parapet. Where British heads should be, however, was space. One of Toa's warriors lay dead, and another was expiring. The sky, when seen beyond smoke, was dangerously bright.

'Their dead?' Big asked.

'Perhaps ten,' Toa claimed.

'I think five,' Big spat.

'Better than nothing.'

'Nothing is what we soon will be.'

Enfilade fire ended their feuding. Captain Flukes had gathered his rifles in the redoubt's west bastion. A warrior beside Kimball was taken from his feet; another had his shoulder sliced. The shadowy Britons sank from sight before fire could be returned. Worse, Many Birds might already be saddled and riding fast with a relief column.

'Give them more to remember,' Toa decided. He ordered, 'Rush their gate. Smash it open with tomahawks.'

Big differed. 'This is not as Titoko said.'

'It is what I do,' Toa said.

'If it pleases you to draw fire, we must end it.'

'If that is your wish,' Toa said.

'It is not my wish,' Big said.

There was a pause. 'Thank you,' Toa said.

'Come,' Big told Kimball and other marksmen near. Under smoke they scrambled from the trench to find ground with a larger view of the west bastion. As they readied their rifles Toa's tomahawks could be heard crashing into the gate. Within the redoubt Flukes was crying orders. Five Britons rose from the bastion with barrels depressed on Toa's attackers. Then another surfaced. The sixth was Flukes emptying a revolver. There was flash on flash, and cries as Toa's men were hurt.

'Now,' Big ordered his party.

The sound of the volley lifted across creek and gully and leapt back as long echoes. As fumes lifted four constables were seen lost to their feet. A fifth, Corporal Tonks, crawled slowly from view. The survivor was Flukes, magically intact, and determined to deliver the last bullet in the chamber of his revolver. Then he thought better of defending the bastion.

It was day, minutes short of sunrise.

'Enough,' Big announced.

'Flukes?' Kimball appealed.

'He will keep,' Big promised.

'Nothing surer,' Kimball said bitterly.

With the British gate still solid, Toa too began seeing retirement as worthwhile. Big's rifles drove British heads low while Toa's men retired to safe ground. Big also furnished fire while Kimball ran forward with a knife to pin Titoko's invitation to the redoubt.

Otherwise disappointment did its best to undo him. 'Flukes?' he called.

There was a muffled sound inside the redoubt.

'Flukes?' he called again.

'Bent,' Flukes could be heard telling fellow survivors. Then, louder, 'Bent?'

'Me,' Kimball agreed.

'What is it you want? Surrender?'

'You,' Kimball said.

'Me?'

'Come out and get me.'

Silence said nothing was further from Flukes' mind.

'Life', Kimball pleaded, 'isn't worth it with us both arsing about.'

There were several slow seconds before Flukes was heard again.

'Do your worst,' he shouted. 'We of this redoubt fight to the last man.'

Whoever he was telling, it wasn't Kimball. Flukes had a hero's medal in mind.

Trusting to Big's marksmanship, Kimball sped clear. Nevertheless Flukes risked making his feelings plain; his farewell tickled Kimball's scalp as it passed.

They reached the river, an hour after sunrise, with an eye to Many Birds' relief column riding to cut them off. Warriors staggered from boulder to boulder, waded chilly water, and then dropped with fatigue among the first trees of Titoko's forest. Wounded were borne across the Waingongoro slowly on litters, or leaning on comrades' shoulders; four dead had been left. For a time nothing but gasping and groaning could be heard.

'This', Toa announced, 'is no place to halt.'

Big did not agree. 'I shall wait,' he said.

'We are not challenged. A rearguard is not called for.'

'Watchers are,' Big insisted. 'If Many Birds thinks to follow, better Titoko is informed soon.'

'So you will wait,' Toa said.

'With the Yankee,' Big said.

'Is he necessary?' Toa asked.

'As a runner, his legs are younger than mine.'

'There are other warriors.'

'He angers me less,' Big explained.

'I will require accounting if he fails to return. Titoko too.'

'Titoko already requires much accounting,' Big said hurtfully. 'Four dead. More wounded.'

'What are you telling me?'

'That I wish not to hear the tale now to be told.'

'Tale?' Toa asked with innocence.

'Of a redoubt held by one hundred fierce Britons,' Big said.

Toa thought not to hear. He began herding men along the leafy miles left to The Beak. Big and Kimball settled into a dry site with a large view of riverside.

They sagged and dozed in turn, one always on watch, until noon or near after. Then far, faint sounds had them both sharply awake. Hoofbeats, snapping scrub, the rattle of harness; and not least, British voices.

Major Many Birds' column, arriving from the direction of the punished redoubt, came into view. There were some forty men urging hard-ridden horses down to the river. Many Birds of the curled moustache and curly hair rode stiff at the head of the column, orange scarf fluttering in feeble sunlight. Sooty Captain Flukes, riding beside him, cut a more cautious figure. Pickets were pushed out, to protect the flanks of the column, and the main party made slow approach to the water. There they halted. The ford did not tempt them. Men pointed to a dribble of Maori blood dried on the rocks; earnest interest was taken in a shred of shirt which had served as a rebel bandage. Wooded ground on the far side of the river, where Big and Kimball crouched, was then scanned. Voices rose.

'At the least, sir, it can be said that they passed this way,' a lieutenant reported to Many Birds.

166

'At the most?' Many Birds asked drily.

'They wait on the far side, sir.'

'Just so,' Many Birds said. 'Then covering fire had best be arranged.'

'Sir,' the lieutenant said.

'Twenty rifles should be sufficient,' Many Birds judged. 'The remaining men will make the crossing.'

'Is it your intention to push on to The Beak?' Flukes thought to ask.

'Where else?' Many Birds asked.

'It could be said', Flukes protested, 'that enough is enough.'

'Your meaning is not plain, captain.'

'Catching the brown buggers on the hop is one thing,' Flukes said. 'Following them into their forest is another.'

'Then,' Many Birds said, 'I ask volunteers.' In louder voice he added, 'Those who wish their slain comrades to go unavenged will retire to the rear.'

No man moved.

'You, Captain Flukes?' Many Birds inquired.

Flukes thought not to retire either.

Marksmen were placed; horsemen arranged at intervals along the riverbank.

'Know this before we cross,' Many Birds announced. 'Death on the battlefield is God's gift to the bold.'

The notion failed to rouse a colonial cheer.

'Before we best the powers of darkness,' Many Birds persisted, 'let each of us make a small prayer.'

The silence following should have interested any gift-giver in the sky. It certainly allowed approaching hoofbeats to be heard; a hoarse shouting followed. A second, smaller party of Britons was moving urgently up the south side of the river. At the head rode a half-dressed constabulary commander with a twitching face.

'Colonel McDonnell,' Big whispered to Kimball.

'What now?'

'Woe,' Big promised.

The quivering colonel, when he stayed his horse, had difficulty making himself heard. Finally he asked Many Birds, 'What in damnation do you think you are doing, man?'

'Giving hot pursuit,' Many Birds said.

'The devil you are. Whose notion was this?'

'Mine,' Many Birds said.

'Insubordination has brought you one court martial,' McDonnell observed. 'A second may not go amiss.'

'Sir?' Many Birds asked with indifference.

'My instruction', McDonnell said, 'is that present circumstances do not provide for the river to be crossed. Has that been cancelled?'

'Not in my hearing, sir,' Many Birds allowed.

'Well? What is your plea?'

'Circumstances no longer suit inaction, sir. We are the slave of events, not their master. We cannot be seen cowed by a few threadbare cannibals. I asked for volunteers only. Volunteers only were to make the crossing. Challenge has been made. Challenge must be met.'

'Challenge?' McDonnell bristled.

'Titoko's. The longer he treats us with contempt, the more rebels we may have in contention.'

'Has this challenge', McDonnell asked shrewdly, 'been made specific?'

'Our dead are specific, sir.'

'Are we', McDonnell persisted, 'talking of formal challenge or are we not?'

'I cannot deny the existence of such a challenge, sir.'

'To you personally?'

'To me,' Many Birds said.

'May I take that as a plea of mitigation?' McDonnell asked.

'You may not, I think,' Many Birds decided.

'May not?'

'Unless this is an inquiry or court martial. In such an event I should feel obliged to state that continued occupation of the outlying redoubt was never my wish; that I foresaw casualties of the kind suffered. And was ignored.'

'You would?'

'As duty,' Many Birds confirmed.

'Am I to take it that you wish my command?'

'Take what you must,' Many Birds suggested.

McDonnell took a deep breath. 'What am I to do with you?' he asked.

'Your difficulty, sir.'

'Indeed,' McDonnell observed. His gaze fell on a useful bystander. 'Captain Flukes? What is your view?'

Flukes was uneasy. 'In what respect, sir?' he asked.

'In respect, damn it, of your colleague.'

'It's not for me to pass judgement, sir,' Flukes pleaded. Flukes might have the costume of a captain; he still wore a corporal's heart on his sleeve. Flukes' eyes moved from the colonel to the major, and the better horse to back.

'Then I must help you, captain,' McDonnell said. 'Has Major von Tempsky behaved with credit today?'

'Within my gaze,' Flukes said warily.

'Be precise, man.'

'He brought relief to my garrison, sir. Wounded were treated and carried away. Then the major set out in pursuit of the enemy.'

'So much may be forgiven him to that point?'

'In a manner of speaking, sir,' Flukes said.

'Then?' McDonnell asked.

'We arrived here, sir. On the Waingongoro.'

'Quite. And you were prepared to countenance his folly?'

'I made my feelings plain, sir.'

'And then volunteered?'

'A captain cannot be seen a shirker.'

'You were aware that the act was at odds with my order?'

'Maybe I was carried away myself, sir.'

'What, Captain Flukes, do you think I am? Half your garrison slaughtered. Most of the rest wounded. And yet your defences never breached. Do you think I feel happy?'

Flukes lowered his eyes and looked at a point forward of his saddle.

'It is enough that in place of reliable soldiers I suffer second-rate scum,' McDonnell said. 'It is not my intention to tolerate makeshift officers too.'

'No, sir,' Flukes said, further humiliated.

'Moreover, it may be that someone will soon be called to account for the night's misfortunes. Much as the major may sullenly wish it, I do not mean my head to roll, captain.'

'No, sir.'

'The loss of men could well be attributed to your laxness.'

Flukes had a good eye for doom and demotion. 'Or cunning in the Maori plan, sir,' he protested.

'Cunning, Captain Flukes?'

'Treachery, sir. By someone knowledgeable about British procedure. The culprit showed himself shamelessly.'

'You are talking again, I take it, of your vagabond American?'

'I observed him with my own eyes, sir. And exchanged words.'

'I am more interested in shot which may have been.'

'Rounds placed in his vicinity left something to be desired, sir.'

McDonnell leaned low and weary on his saddle. 'In the past, Captain Flukes, you have confided in me to the effect that the talents of this fellow Bent are less formidable than many in this colony suppose.'

'Based on personal experience, sir. He was an unsatisfactory soldier.'

'And yet a worthwhile warrior?'

'It's true I'm thinking again, sir.'

'Pray do, Captain Flukes. Would you had second thoughts sooner.'

'Perhaps, sir.'

'And made him a more pleasing soldier in the first instance.'

'It was not for want of trying, sir.'

'In future it might be seemly if you bragged less, in the public prints, about bringing Bent to book.'

'Perhaps, sir,' Flukes said with a face growing longer.

'You appear to have made an enterprising enemy.'

'I don't know that I'd go that far, sir.'

'Just how far would you go, Captain Flukes?'

'To even the score, sir, the miles remaining to Titoko's camp.'

'You might do better to talk less of a score and more of a sore. A running sore on the colony's rump. And surgery.'

'Maybe, sir.'

'Which we shall indeed perform in due course.'

'Such is my hope, sir,' Flukes said humbly.

'It would seem', McDonnell observed, 'that I have at least heard your plea of mitigation.'

'Sir?'

'Major von Tempsky seems determined not to plead a hot rush of blood to the head. To frustrate him I will take it as said. Your excuse also appears to be plain. In this morning's near misadventure, and defiance of a standing order, you were as obsessed with slaying Bent as the good major appears to be with finishing Titoko.'

'If that is how you see it, sir.'

'I am obliged to,' McDonnell said. 'Beggars can't be choosers.' He lifted his reins, and wheeled his horse. In a voice loud enough to reach the furthest man, he announced, 'Let retirement proceed in orderly fashion.'

Big and Kimball watched horses turn and British backs group on the far side of the river. Shaping into a column, they began the climb to safe ground.

'Well?' Big asked.

'Well what?'

For some reason, Big wasn't shouldering his carbines.

'Do we', he asked with mischief, 'give a good lie a chance?'

'What lie?'

'By the time we are home we may need one better than Toa to tell.'

'Like what?' Kimball asked.

'Beating off a British horde,' Big suggested.

'Titoko', Kimball pointed out, 'doesn't need them beat off. He wants them this side of the river.'

'A pity,' Big said. 'So the lie will have to be that of the pair who tried to draw them out. Of two against sixty.'

'You think it's worth it?'

'If you want one worth telling.'

Kimball took thought. The British were fewer than a hundred paces distant and departing fast.

'It is over to you,' Big said. 'I have enough to make old age worth living.'

'I can't see the harm,' Kimball decided.

'Nor me,' Big said.

Steadying themselves against trees, they each discharged two cartridges. Big split his between McDonnell and Many Birds, with no reward. With one target and more malice, Kimball had greater chance to excel. His first shot flew over Flukes' capped head. The second, with better elevation, sank Flukes' horse; it collapsed, all kicking legs and agony, beneath the cursing captain. Otherwise the British response was encouragingly calm.

'There,' McDonnell shouted to Many Birds, pointing across the river. 'See what I mean? An ambush was set.'

Many Birds shrugged.

McDonnell unsheathed his sword and held it high. 'Give the bastards a volley,' he commanded.

Men dismounted, ran to clear ground, loaded their weapons, and knelt to discharge them. Shot crashed across the river. Birds flashed and fluttered; twigs, leaves and chips of bark showered around the two in hiding.

'And another,' McDonnell called, flourishing his sword.

The second volley gave up as much din and smoke, and also did no more than let a little light into the forest. It was made different from the first, however, by an unholy howl from Big. With a last, chilling gurgle it was gone. A telling hush followed.

'What', Kimball whispered, 'was that for?'

'A corpse to count,' Big explained. 'They may feel better.'

It seemed to be so.

'Take your horses,' McDonnell was ordering his men. 'Captain Flukes? You may share mine. Let withdrawal proceed.'

As Britons departed, Big found voice. 'In the matter of lies honours may be shared,' he judged.

'How would that be?' Kimball asked.

'McDonnell surely counted five Maori dead from the volleys. Captain Flukes perhaps more.'

'Many Birds?'

'I never saw him looking,' Big said.

It was night when they approached The Beak. The forest was still; they heard only the rustle of their own feet. Where foliage parted they looked for the tree-top glow of cooking fires to guide them on. There was no such glow; there were no such fires. They stood puzzled at the dusky edge of the space cleared before the village. Everything remained cold and quiet. On the far side of the clearing palisades rose dimly. A lone owl made itself heard.

'Titoko fled?' Big said with disbelief.

He took a step clear of vegetation. It looked to be his last. The first firearm, somewhere above, heralded a hellish boom. Shot skipped and clattered. Streaks of light and clouds of sparks lit the clearing. Big fell to earth, Kimball fast behind.

'Stop,' Big pleaded. 'Stop.'

In the din he had to cry mercy for much of a minute.

'Halt,' Titoko finally called from somewhere in gloom.

His message was slow reaching remote marksmen; Kimball and Big covered their heads until the last had been heard. When they looked up it was to see Titoko making a torchlit approach through curling powder smoke.

'What', Big asked, 'was that?'

'Poor shooting,' Titoko said.

Later there was food and warmth. Flames reddened the village palisades. Where there was not mourning there was celebration. Titoko kept aloof. Having suffered a list of Toa's deeds, he was not disposed to be wearied by another. He stopped Big and Kimball short.

'All you tell me', he said, 'is that Many Birds still fails to come.'

'Not for lack of heart,' Big said.

'Do we have war?' Titoko asked.

Big shrugged.

'Not to make a song about,' Kimball said.

For a time Titoko was silent.

'I had a hymn in mind,' he said.

Seventeen

Mystifying days passed, then weeks quieter still. It was a month before Colonel McDonnell mustered enough men and outrage to ford the Waingongoro and argue with Titoko's forest. As Titoko's watchers told it, the colonel pushed four hundred constables and militiamen down to the river on a murky August morning. Officers were mounted, men mostly not. At the riverside McDonnell thought to rouse foot-weary ranks with a last chime of sabre. The more he tried to fire them, the faster August rain fell. Many Birds could be seen aloof and apart, in the shelter of a tree, coolly sketching the scene as his horse shifted under him. 'This force', McDonnell told his lessers, 'is the largest band of armed colonists to take the field in New Zealand. True that we are here to hunt down and destroy no more than a last few mangy Maori outlaws. Nonetheless they are to be treated with respect. No quarter will be asked and none given. Finally, let us give thanks to our politician paymasters who have seen the error of their miserly ways. For once we are not lacking in firepower. Let it never be said we were lacking in spirit. Forward, and Titoko take the hindmost.'

McDonnell launched his men across the river into gloom. Splashing and spray diminished. Trees and thick creepers grew higher around.

At The Beak, Titoko had warriors rehearse their parts; they spent most of the same morning racing to position, climbing trees, ducking into rifle pits and miming shots. Children and most women had been sent further into the forest, nearer the mountain. Rihi, Meri and Wiremu were among those moved to safety. Kimball was thus ensured of night after night devoted without interference to Flukes. For once he wasn't aware of whispers and heavings of women passing the time of night with Titoko. Not that the village had emptied altogether of females. Hine, for one, remained with the warriors, carbine on her shoulder and cartridge belts crossed on her breast. It was her intention, she said, to see that her fool of a spouse survived, or at the least died with no further shame. Most in the tribe were agreed that Toa had made the attack on the British redoubt costly by disrespect for Titoko's orders; Toa's standing had further diminished, and Titoko's suffered not at all. Titoko was the father of triumph, Toa the begetter of grief. Titoko could not have arranged Toa's silencing better, and surely had. Even Corporal Demon seemed to think distance from his old superior healthy. He was more often seen conferring with Titoko in the matter of grieving colonists. Toa, roaming unloved through the camp, looked to Kimball as a companion. There too his luck failed to improve. It was also Kimball's impression that anyone close to Toa risked life and limb.

'Your wife is my daughter,' Toa protested. 'You are next to a son.'

'The way things might look,' Kimball conceded.

Toa leapt on the quibble. 'What do you mean look? Look? Look?'

'Rihi discourages me some.'

'She still shares your bed.'

'Without any hot suppers.'

'Rihi is a girl of moods.'

'And most of them foul,' Kimball pointed out.

'I might have done well to let her run wild,' Toa mused. 'She might have been less taken by a Yankee stranger.'

'You're saying it's my fault?'

'What are you to her now? A warrior among many.'

'What else am I supposed to be?'

'A bolder one,' Toa said. 'Have your will with her. Make yourself master. If needed, throw her over your shoulder.'

'I don't see you up to that with yours.'

'True,' Toa mourned.

Hine was a safe twenty paces off, gazing skyward at rain cloud with Demon and Titoko. Her back, as was now mostly the case, was turned to her husband.

'There is always more than one path through a forest,' Toa argued. 'If you can't win, woo.'

175

'With what?'

'Promise her Maine. Tell her you'll take her there.'

'How? When?'

'When the war is done. Promise her no more forests and forts. No ambushes and escapes. You cannot fail.'

'How am I supposed to get her there?'

'That is your difficulty,' Toa shrugged.

'We're going no place when this is finished. You know it too.'

'Rihi is a trusting girl,' Toa insisted.

'So you want me to lie.'

'Better my daughter smiles.'

A scout arrived running to say that McDonnell's column was more than a mile into the forest. The question was whether they would persist many more miles in mountain rain. Titoko's lips were seen moving. He might have been cursing; he could have been praying. Either way he was urging the rain past.

Soon it was crashing with no consideration for soldier or warrior. As the first black flight of clouds emptied, followed by blacker, forest tracks turned into creeks. High ground produced sputtering waterfalls; low ground grew lively with lakes; rising torrents all but submerged the men of the colonist contingent. They waded, spluttered, and sometimes swam. When watercourses were negotiated, there were Titoko's mazes and mantraps. These did their work too well. Cursing men fell back blindly upon others, and officers failed to rally them with drawn revolvers. Some thought they saw misty Maori spies among streaming trees, and might not have been mistaken. Wild shots set off mad volleys. An aggrieved rout was soon in the making, with moaning wounded on litters. Though McDonnell raged, and Many Birds fumed, their column broke into scattered parties of a score or less. Such parties had one thing in common. Blundering back and forward, enfeebling themselves further, they were pointed everywhere but at The Beak. The most stricken were limping toward the safe bank of the Waingongoro; others were labouring into southern forest without sighting the mangiest rebel.

When the news reached Titoko, he picked out three parties of twelve and ordered them west, east and south.

176

'To what end?' Toa asked.

'Enlightened shooting may still herd them north.'

'To here?'

'As cattle to a yard,' Titoko agreed.

'You don't lack ambition,' Toa observed sourly.

'We have little else,' Titoko said.

The day passed slowly. Titoko made forays south to see to the work of his shooting parties. With other tribesmen Toa and Kimball sat on a firing platform high in the trees. Sometimes the sound of far firearms rose above the clatter of rain. Toa twitched. Kimball smoked. Aside from a trickle of bird turd down his face, nothing troublesome put in an appearance. The din of combat became even more distant. It was dusk when the first warriors ambled home, and dawn before last stragglers were tallied. Britons had not been shamed into making a manly target. Even their commanders took a large interest in life and looked for a fast way out of the forest. Pursuit had finally been pressed. Several constables and colonists had been seen dead, and others had been noted staggering away supported by comrades. Titoko took no satisfaction in damage done to the retiring colonist column. He sorrowed for that which had not been.

'What more must we do?' he said.

'What must McDonnell?' Big asked.

The second question was first answered. The dripping remains of McDonnell's harried column grouped outside the forest. With wounds bandaged, and rum under their belts, they rallied to march on two Maori villages whose occupants had been pleased to keep a distance from Titoko. Children fell underfoot as Britons rushed with bayonets fixed; males who might be tallied rebels were slain; women and untrampled children fled toward the mountain. Their villages were then burned. Surviving menfolk with a grievance arrived at The Beak to volunteer for Titoko's army. One of the more vengeful had already taken a British life; he had ambushed and shot a messenger from the battle front and taken the dispatch the man was carrying from McDonnell to the colonist government. Given to Kimball to decipher, it made lusty reading. McDonnell was pleased to announce that, though much outnumbered, he

177

had left at least fifty Maori dead. Titoko was all but thrashed into submission, and collapse of his rebellion was surely at hand.

When Kimball finished reading the letter, there was a long and reflective silence. Big was first to speak.

'He makes honest men of us,' he said.

With shooting finished, women and children arrived back at The Beak. Kimball's feelings were mixed. The arrival of Meri and Wiremu was one thing; the return of Rihi another. He grabbed the twins up in his arms. He failed to attach himself to his wife. She looked over the camp, and at Kimball, and saw nothing to please her.

'Is there danger?' she asked.

'Not so you'd notice,' he told her.

'Colonists?'

'Gone.'

'Until the next time.'

'It's not my God damn war,' he felt obliged to explain.

She pushed into their dwelling and found more excuse for complaint. In a week the place had become a sad bachelor outpost. So long as peril persisted, and picket duties, he had been sleeping where he fell, eating when he could. There was a flax basket of pork bones. Beds were unmade. There were muddy garments discarded; there were fleas.

'You live like a pig,' she told him.

He shrugged.

'And smell like one,' she sniffed.

He let insult pass. 'Keeping house', he announced, 'is not warrior work.'

'How would you know?' she mocked.

That set him in motion. He gathered up his children and took himself from the dwelling.

'Where are you going?' she demanded.

He stalked off to Hine and invited her to care for her grand-children. With Meri and Wiremu in reliable hands he returned to Rihi. She was outside their dwelling, still shocked.

'What', she asked, 'was that for?'

'This,' he said. With his shoulder he hurtled into her midriff, emptying her of breath; with his arms he snatched up her legs and tipped her over his shoulder. Her hair hung in the mud;

178

her legs protested wildly. Her screams roused the camp. There were sightseers to the right, to the left, soon all around. Men were inclined to mutters of approval; women to expressions of awe. With attention drawn to Rihi's humiliation, he heaved her indoors. He fancied he heard faint applause to his rear. Rihi remained aloft.

'You are a warrior's woman,' he told her, 'or you are not.'

She said nothing, and whimpered.

'Say it,' he suggested.

She failed to. Lamentation mounted.

'Let's get it over with,' he pleaded, his own gloom growing.

Tears persisted, whines and sobs. At this stage, according to Toa, he should make his conjugal point. The notion failed to rouse him. Instead he dropped her into a musty heap of blankets.

'Get yourself another man,' he said. 'I'll live with Big.'

'There is nothing new in the world,' Big told him later that night. They had eaten; they were covering themselves with blankets.

Kimball was quiet.

'Not with women nor war,' Big added.

'Is that all you can tell me?' Kimball finally asked.

Big shrugged.

'So bugger you too,' Kimball said wearily. Sleep was all he had left, and even there he might have to join battle with Flukes. As it happened, he did not. Flukes, or his phantom, was off duty that night. When Kimball closed his eyes the world emptied of women and war. He did not even hear Big depart to oversee the night's pickets.

After midnight, perhaps in the darkest hour before dawn, he was half woken by a whisper of feet. As his blankets lifted there was a rush of cool air over his body. Female flesh began pressing claims. More, this dream was mounting him.

'Rihi?' he asked with awe.

His staff rose and was ridden; Kimball sighed, shook and emptied. He had never known release sweeter. His partner in pleasure surged this way and that, her long hair sweeping his body, in as much disarray.

'Rihi?' he said again, between breaths.

179

'That', Hine informed him intimately, 'is better seen as a trial.'

'You?' he said, altogether woken.

'Me,' Hine said.

'What trial?' he asked.

'To see who is faulty,' she explained. 'I have seen, to my own satisfaction, that you are not lacking.'

'What are you talking about?'

'Your marriage,' she said. 'My daughter.'

'A fine way to start talking about it.'

'I can think of less pleasant.'

It was unseemly to argue.

'Tomorrow,' she said, 'your wife will wish her warrior.'

'She'll have to say it,' Kimball insisted.

'She will,' Hine promised, 'when I warn her of women breaking down your door.'

'Women? What women?'

'It would be immodest to name them,' she said.

Reunion was quiet, Rihi chastened, and also shamefaced. After his return, they nursed their children to sleep.

'I am sorry,' she said finally. 'I have been no wife.'

'I hear you,' he said.

'And you have been patient.'

'Maybe,' he said.

'It's war,' she argued. 'Never knowing what next. Who will live and who not.'

'I reckon.'

'Wiremu? Meri? Will they? Will I? Will you?'

Kimball shrugged.

'Once I was all a chief's daughter should be.'

'Once I was all a soldier shouldn't,' he told her.

Their love-making was on the shy side. Her body had the spirit he remembered, though something was lacking. 'Here,' he said inspirationally, and heaved her above him.

She was perplexed. 'What is this?' she said. 'Where have you been?'

'Don't ask,' he said.

He woke later, and felt for her face. He found open eyes and fresh tears.

'What is it?' he asked.

'Most things,' she said.

He thought on that. Toa couldn't always be wrong.

'It's time', he told her, 'to talk Maine.'

'Maine?'

'Where we're going,' he explained. 'When war is all done.'

'You've never said this before.'

'I'm saying it now.'

'Tell me,' she said.

He did until dawn. By the time he had her walking Maine woods he was hearing her laugh. Near neighbours took her mirth to be the sound of playful love-making. They were not necessarily wrong.

August passed quietly. It was suddenly September, with the air mild, the mountain often cloudless, rivers less muddy, and trees at the forest edge bright with yellow flower. Cooped in their smelly redoubt, Britons won no joy from spring. Colonel McDonnell's employers must have begun questioning his reluctance to push out patrols and establish himself further on the territory he claimed to have conquered. They may even have deduced from his prudence that his triumph over Titoko was made more of fancy than firepower. Overnight there were scores of fresh faces on view in the vicinity of the redoubt. The weak, wounded, and bush-weary had been retired. New tents had risen, and the racket of musketry practice grew.

Titoko was conferring with lieutenants when a scout brought news of fresh colonist clatter. 'Many Birds?' he asked.

'He is still to be seen cursing,' the scout reported.

'Good,' Titoko said. Then he asked, 'Maori?'

'A few come and go.'

'Kepa's?'

'Wanganui tribesmen,' the scout agreed. 'They ride to the redoubt, talk with McDonnell, and ride home again. They never remain long.'

'Negotiations,' Titoko concluded. He looked to Big. 'Kepa must ask more than money.'

Big shrugged.

'If you were Kepa,' Titoko said, 'what more would you be asking McDonnell?'

'More than money?'

'And more than loot or land.'

'Command,' Big suggested.

Titoko was thoughtful. 'Maori leading Briton?'

'Who knows?'

'Britons answering Maori orders?'

'Without McDonnell and Many Birds, it could yet be.'

'It must not be,' Titoko decided.

'Never?'

'The day a Maori steers the British canoe is the day we are dead.'

'Our tribe?'

'All who differ. One Maori pitted against another, using the British to pay off old scores.'

'As Kepa?'

'Our old tribal wars will seem kind.'

'What are you saying?' Big asked. 'That we keep McDonnell and Many Birds alive?'

Titoko was slow to answer. 'Perhaps McDonnell,' he said.

'You cannot mean that.'

'I thought not to see the day when my least problem was Many Birds.'

Demon then had his say. 'Kepa could be asking the right to say no to McDonnell's orders.'

'Perhaps.'

'You would if you were he,' Demon persisted.

'True.'

'Well?'

'I have no time to be he,' Titoko announced. 'I have too little to be me.'

In the second week of September the redoubt emptied and the British marched. The first of Titoko's scouts to reach The Beak reported just a small and sullen-faced force of Kepa's Maoris on show. They rode apart, and were disinclined to converse with colonists, especially not with McDonnell. Altogether a column of five hundred men, with McDonnell and Many Birds at its head, waded into the Waingongoro. This time McDonnell thought better of an inspirational speech; the river was crossed with terse orders and tight teeth.

At The Beak, with women and children again gone, Titoko ordered fires lit in the village, and damp fern heaped on the flames to speed smoke above the trees. 'This time,' he explained, 'they have no excuse for losing their way.' He would retain just ten warriors to man the palisades; the rest would reside high and low among forest leaves.

He retired to his dwelling, and was some time gone. On his return he was squeaky neat in his best English suit; his tie was knotted, his shoes polished, his hair brushed. Finally he planted a top hat between his ears. No one had seen Titoko more elegant. Aside from an ancestral war club of wicked dimension, one better suited to oratory than battle, he was unarmed. 'Why such glory, cousin?' Toa asked with surprise.

'Respect for the dead,' Titoko explained.

It was another two hours before the skirmishers of McDonnell's column moved through trees at the south fringe of the clearing. To the north, across tufts of grass and clumps of scrub, they saw palisades and peaceful smoke. The noon sun was warm; leaves rattled in a light breeze. As more men arrived, officers thought to pause. Peering through greenery, braced against branches, Kimball sighted the ringleted rear of Many Birds' head. The range was fifteen feet; Kimball couldn't gun closer. McDonnell was missing. Many Birds' companion in advance proved to be Captain Flukes. The top of his skull made an even more arresting target.

'I cannot believe our luck, sir,' Flukes whispered.

'Don't,' Many Birds ordered. 'Go back and tell the colonel to push up men.'

'And you, sir?'

'Tell the colonel I shall feel further for the enemy.'

'Thinking to find them?'

'What', Many Birds asked with irritation, 'does that palisading look like to you, captain?'

'Very Maori, sir.'

'And what would you think to find in such palisades?'

'Loopholes, sir.'

'Indeed, captain. And behind each a Maori marksman. That is where we shall find them. The Maori, Captain Flukes, fights only in accord with grand principles. Those principles require them to inflict damage on the enemy from within a fortification.'

'Yes, sir,' Flukes said dutifully.

'Fortunately for us, their tactics never vary; we always know where they are.'

'Yes, sir,' Flukes agreed.

'Such fortifications are also meant to mask escape. If we linger, we lose them.'

'Yes, sir.'

'I mean to begin drawing their fire. The task may slow us for a time.'

'I understand, sir.'

'I shall need reinforcement. Tell the colonel he must make his peace with Kepa and have the wretch move his Maoris forward to cut off Titoko's escape. As for the colonel himself, he must attack in strength.'

'That sounds like an order,' Flukes observed.

'Colonel McDonnell may make what he wishes of my demand,' Many Birds said. 'Ground is not to be abandoned. Nor am I to be.'

'I take your meaning, sir,' Flukes said.

'I trust he does also,' Many Birds said. 'Inform him that the enemy is now available. And that it may be a bitter day for the craven.'

'In so many words, sir?' Flukes asked.

'As profanely as possible,' Many Birds ordered. 'Go, man, go.'

Flukes obediently doubled back into the forest to hurry McDonnell. Many Birds, with curved sword and revolver, ordered advance. Dozens of Britons broke cover and moved into the clearing. They looked little to right or left, and least of all overhead; they had eyes only for the palisades and the first puff of Maori fire. Some way across the clearing Many Birds placed half his attackers in reserve, to provide cover, and pushed toward the palisades with the rest. For a time there was just the sound of boots and breathing. They were within thirty paces of the timber wall when Titoko's call was heard; it was surely meant to shake out the first shot.

'Come, Many Birds,' he challenged.

The small volley from the palisades smoked away two of the major's assault party and left others examining the earth at close quarters. The attack halted, with a crouched and impatient Many Birds looking to his rear for the arrival of McDonnell's main force. Big, in command of rifles in the western vegetation, and Demon in the eastern, had warriors hold their fire. Until colonists grouped in greater number, it was a duel between Titoko's tiny garrison and Many Birds' few skirmishers; the men of the trees were mute.

More Britons gathered at the southern approach to the clearing, among them McDonnell with Flukes at his side. There was a third and taller figure to be taken into account. Tonks had not only returned to the land of the living; he now sported the stripes of a sergeant. Meanwhile McDonnell considered the imperilled ground ahead, and Many Birds' marooned skirmishers.

'The man is a monster,' he announced.

'Titoko, sir?'

'The Prussian. Is no one to relieve me of this affliction?'

'Nevertheless, sir,' Flukes urged, 'he requires reinforcement.'

'Requires?' McDonnell blustered. 'Requires?'

'Requests, sir,' Flukes said.

'Damn the man,' McDonnell said. 'He wishes to commit me to attack.'

'I wouldn't know, sir,' Flukes said feebly.

'Was he, or was he not, ordered to wait on my arrival?'

'If such an order was given, I dare say he was, sir.'

'You dare say?'

'I dare say I was out of earshot, sir.'

'Shall I tell you how that sounds to me, Captain Flukes?'

'By all means, sir.'

'You have decided our soldier of fortune will finish this day a hero. You also see him as your next commander. Kepa surely does too. Where is the confounded fellow? I am not deceived, Flukes. To speed von Tempsky's promotion you are all conspiring to foul my reputation.'

'Not me, sir,' Flukes protested.

'I shall see you a corporal again,' McDonnell vowed. 'Better still, reduced all the way to the ranks.'

'You wouldn't do that, sir,' Flukes said.

'Can I not?' McDonnell mused. 'Give me good reason, captain, why you should not be under arrest.'

Flukes, had he looked up, might have seen a reprieve in the making. Still trying to train his carbine, Kimball had gone a foot too far out on a limb. There was a loud crack; and a long, sad and one-sided sound of branch arguing with bark. Little of Kimball's life fluttered past as his descent gathered speed; everything else did, including his cocked carbine. Vegetation exploded and twigs and leaves scattered as he banged from one branch to the next. One pulled him up short and allowed him a second to grab at sound timber. Careering on its own course, his carbine thudded down on Tonks's neck and, in much the same moment, managed to trigger itself. The sound was mistaken as a signal by Demon, Big and others high in the trees. Most of fifty fresh Maori rifles joined the fight; the forest edge filled with shot from three sides. Winded Kimball, climbing again, was aware of distress mounting below.

'Shit,' Tonks was groaning.

'They are upon us,' McDonnell roared. 'We are outnumbered.'

'Return fire,' Flukes screamed.

'Hold fire,' McDonnell raged.

'Attack,' Many Birds pleaded.

'Where is Kepa?' McDonnell shouted.

'Forward,' Flukes called.

'Take cover,' McDonnell urged.

With several orders too many, pandemonium proceeded apace. Within the woods the attackers were terrified by tree-top snipers and ricochet shot. Beyond leaf and vine, where they might sight the enemy, matters were even more fatal. Metal sped in from both earth and sky. Even dead trees sprouted firearms. Circling men sagged as shot showered on them. Wrapped to a tree-top without a weapon, Kimball was limited to a craftsman's interest in the carnage; he saw next to no rifles jamming and few defective cartridges discharged. On the other hand dismayingly few were directed at Flukes or Tonks when they bobbed into view. A few men had rushed to reinforce Many Birds. Those who failed to reach him were silent on the ground. With a despairing look back, seeing McDonnell and the main force sluggish, the major rose, scarf fluttering, and pointed his sword at the palisades. If doing or dying was his choice, it appeared he preferred both at the double. 'Advance,' he ordered with grievance. A score of survivors stood with him. If nothing else the battle seemed due to end with a bang. Mostly it did, and with many. Many Birds made ten paces toward the palisades while shot split earth at his feet. Then he jerked back and fell. Others tripped and toppled across him. The rest abandoned their weapons and ran. Men who had failed to go forward followed their example. Even Titoko's warriors seemed awed by the mild manner of Many Birds' departure. It deserved a crack of thunder or bolt of lightning or both. All it won was a lull in the shooting. The clearing emptied of all but smoke, corpses and crawling wounded. Finally, through haze, warriors could be seen advancing afoot. Some knelt to place shot among departing Britons; others swung tomahawks to quieten the wounded. The most bitter sight of all, for colonists alive, was that of Titokowaru, warrior chief of Taranaki, a floating nightmare in his best bib and tucker, his terrible face looming under a top hat. Soon there was just the sound of constables and militia cursing and crashing away into forest.

'Retire,' McDonnell could be heard crying, more and more distantly.

'Retire,' Flukes echoed faintly.

The battle for The Beak was finished, though Titoko thought to make more of a good thing. Without a moment for breath, and none for mercy, he called Big and Demon down from the trees, and ordered them to hunt McDonnell's men back to the Waingongoro. To Toa he said, 'One thing remains to trouble me.'

'Kepa?' Toa asked.

'He failed to offer himself. Nor one of his men.'

'He showed wisdom,' Toa suggested.

'Kepa is no coward.'

'No,' Toa agreed.

'So what game does he play?'

'Always his own.'

'Just so,' Titoko observed. 'What does that say to you?'

Toa shrugged.

'That his wish was to watch colonists die,' Titoko said.

'You think it?'

'I know it. His day has gone well.'

'Why would he wish that?' Toa asked.

'Don't ask,' Titoko said.

Finally his eye found Kimball. 'You have little to say, grandson,' he observed. 'Will we hear more of men of Maine?'

'They never took the piss out of Britain better,' Kimball allowed.

187

'So we have something to hymn?'

'To Tuesday's tune,' Kimball suggested.

'Wait on Wednesday,' Titoko said.

Big and Demon struck at departing Britons until there was no light left in the day. During dark they limited themselves to tomahawking stragglers and still later, as dawn grew, to pushing shot at British rumps as they made the river crossing. Ragged Britons began discarding weapons and deserting as soon as their feet found the far bank. Then Kepa's missing men appeared on the skyline. They rode silently into view, sat silently on their horses, and watched the last of McDonnell's men cross the river. They thought not to play even a shy part in proceedings. Finally they rode off without a word said.

At The Beak Titoko had corpses collected and counted. There were just three of his own to be mourned; Queen Victoria could tally ten times as many, not to speak of expiring wounded. Kimball looked from one face to the next. Not even the most disfigured could be mistaken for Flukes. Titoko could have been happier too. His grievance was that there were Britons alive. Fewer would have been if McDonnell had followed Many Birds' example. Titoko's plan had not allowed for colonist collapse.

Carcasses were stripped and heaped. On command order, however, Many Birds was left uniformed and apart. Titoko considered his victim at length, and in silence. Still staring, the Prussian seemed to have shrunk, and still to be shrivelling. There was a drying tomahawk gash in his temple; otherwise his face was undamaged. Breeze blew through his ringlets. Titoko knelt finally to close the man's eyes. Then he tipped his hat in salute, took up Many Birds' sword, and drew back. Only Toa risked a question. 'What ails you, cousin?' he asked. 'Can't you believe him dead?'

'I miss him already,' Titoko said.

The last task was to dispose of the dead to advantage. Titoko had a pyre in mind; one which might smoke black over the forest and glow through the night. The message to Britons left in the territory should be plain.

'A pyre?' Toa puzzled.

'As I say,' Titoko agreed.

'Are we man-eaters one day and the next day not?' Toa challenged.

Titoko was interestingly silent.

'I heard you forceful on the subject, cousin,' Toa observed. 'I also heard you say that you must have a foe worthy of your appetite before you partook.'

'Well?' Titoko asked.

'You have one now,' Toa pointed out.

'It is my feeling', Titoko disclosed, 'that Many Birds needs no further killing.'

'That is not my argument,' Toa said.

'He will burn on the pyre,' Titoko announced.

'Why?'

'One warrior's favour to another.'

'There will be no man-eating this day?'

'Those inclined may partake. But not of Many Birds.'

'What makes him so different?'

'Debt,' Titoko explained. 'I wished a bold foe. The boldest obliged.'

'You forgo spreading of fear?'

'It is spread,' Titoko said.

Finally a random constable, for the few inclined, was reserved for the oven. A second and larger oven was filled with lambs lifted from colonist flocks. Hungry Demon, back from a last scouring of the forest, was indifferent to what form food took. He lifted the first meat to hand. It was a hand. He hesitated hardly a moment.

To Titoko he said, 'Will we hang?'

'If we fail ourselves,' Titoko said.

'Then better for a man than a lamb,' Demon said.

By the month's end it was known that the Governor of New Zealand, in the name of Queen Victoria, had placed a price on the outlaw named Titokowaru dead or alive. The rate for the aforesaid rebel's head, until further notice, was one thousand pounds.

'One thousand?' Titoko said.

'Kepa may see it as fair,' his informant suggested. 'Many think the price set to tempt him.'

'Unless he asked it himself,' Titoko suggested.

'That too is possible,' the informant agreed. 'Also five pounds is offered for each of your warriors, fifty for your lieutenants. A colonist newspaper also offers a sum for the American called Bent, should he be slain.'

'Better than mine?' Titoko asked with interest.

'Better than fifty. One hundred pounds.'

'May his cartridges improve,' Titoko judged. He took thought for a time. Then he said, 'The Governor is free with his money.'

'So some would say,' the informant said warily.

'What would a just price be for his?'

'The Governor's head?'

'You heard.'

The informant shrugged. Titoko ordered his purse brought. It was not fat. He rattled within the purse, and after calculation removed three coins to cast on the ground.

'I make my bid,' Titoko said. 'Let it be known that I offer two shillings and sixpence for the Governor's.'

'This is all?'

'I am not sure of the sixpence,' Titoko said.

Eighteen

The British Empire reeled five miles back from the Waingongoro, took thought, and then retired twenty miles more. Bandaged and bootless men wrecked and fired redoubt after redoubt as they hobbled south. When they could flee no further with decency, they dug themselves into a hill with a disheartening view of the territory they had lost. Death, wounds and desertions meant that Colonel McDonnell had fewer than one in four of his fighting men left; he would be lucky to muster fifty rifles. Kepa's Maoris, still less impressed by the company they kept, marched home to bed with their women, harvest flax, plant kumara, and reconsider their connection with Queen Victoria. It was not even clear that McDonnell could be counted a useful enemy. Spies said physicians arrived regularly from Wanganui to treat his melancholia. Aside from short appearances outside his tent to denounce his men as disloyal swine, he was seldom on show. The sound of breaking bottles was often heard from his quarters. One of his aides, a lieutenant with a sharp sense of shame, bit on the barrel of his revolver and coloured his tent with brain and blood. Others saw mutiny as serving their situation best. Captain Flukes, the only officer left looking likely, arrested malcontents for trial in Wanganui and imprisonment in Wellington, until escort details made too great a drain on constabulary manpower. He then had to survive insubordination with only the fists of Sergeant Tonks to cow the survivors of the colony's first army. Flukes' voice, the spies said, seldom rose above a sad whisper. As spring warmed Kimball had a dream or two he could call his own.

Titoko had problems too. Like McDonnell, his first was with numbers, his second with morale. Unlike McDonnell, his woes

were those of a winner. His sober army of seventy was overnight a high-spirited hundred. In a week he had scores more
rowdily looking for work. After weeding out boobies and
windbags, he could field two hundred men or more if he
wished. More was not his wish. Fewer moved faster and
argued less. When he had enough new faces to embitter with
discipline he began turning volunteers back to their villages.
Meanwhile the unruly arrivals, not to speak of their women
and children, were mouths to be fed. Stray cattle, wild pig,
and lost sheep steamed daily in large ovens. The slaughter
suggested the territory might soon be emptied of meat. Titoko
thought building of eel weirs and planting of crops urgent, and
said so in tribal council.

'Crops?' Toa asked. 'We have colonist gardens to the south.'
Titoko was silent.

'So when', Toa asked, 'do we cross the river?'
Again Titoko seemed determined not to hear.

'Well?' Toa said.

'We have made the line,' Titoko said.

'And you think that enough?'

'I have long thought it,' Titoko said.

'You would trust them to the south bank again? Next time
with gun carriages?'

Titoko, one way and another, seemed in pain.

'Do we wait on them to come?' Toa challenged. 'Or see they
do not?'

Other voices lifted, of the same mood.

'If we cross the river,' Titoko asked, 'where do we stop?'

'Old land is to the south,' Toa observed.

'True,' Titoko had to agree.

'Land no longer held by one British gun.'

'And more yet beyond,' Titoko observed.

'Much,' Toa said cautiously.

'Kepa's?'

'Among others,' Toa conceded.

'Think more on it,' Titoko urged. 'If we march, where do
we stop?'

Toa, who knew a knotty question, was silent.

'Wanganui?' Titoko taunted.

Toa shrugged. 'Perhaps.'

'Wellington?' Titoko persisted.

Toa was thoughtful.

'Or London?' Titoko asked.

'Where Britain's Queen dwells?'

'You heard.'

The assembly was quiet.

'What are you telling us?' Toa asked finally.

'My thought,' Titoko explained.

'And that thought is to cease now?'

'While we are victors.'

'With more to be won?'

'My thought is that if we lose view of our mountain we also are lost.'

'If we fail to move south you leave our old lands an orphan. With free highway, Kepa and the colonists have rope to choke us.'

'You talk fear,' Titoko said.

'I talk from a tribesman's heart,' Toa claimed.

There was wary approval from tribal seniors around.

'Must we be blind boulders rolling?' Titoko asked.

Tribal seniors were silent.

Toa was emboldened. 'One deed asks another,' he went on. 'What warrior deed does not?'

Titoko was quiet.

'I know it,' Toa said with even less mercy. 'You know it.'

Titoko failed to agree. He ended the assembly and tribesmen dispersed. Some were soon saying bitterly that, with the battle of The Beak won, Titoko's heart was no longer in war; that he was afraid of chancing his recovered mana against colonist guns.

'Tell me what I wish not to know, grandson,' Titoko asked.

'War's got you by the balls.'

'The march south must come?'

'The way things are.'

There was a long silence.

'I know,' Titoko said.

Next morning Titoko ordered Big and Kimball to attend him. Candles fluttered low in the interior of Titoko's dwelling. There was pen and paper before him. His fingers were ink-stained and his eyes were red; he had seen out the night with no sleep and surely no woman. 'Cut your hair,' he

193

told Kimball. 'Also your beard. A small English moustache will serve best.'

'What for?' Kimball asked.

'To pass more presentably. As for attire, make free with my wardrobe.'

'What is this, then?' Big asked.

'Travel,' Titoko explained.

'Not again,' Kimball protested.

'I am not asking much,' Titoko said. 'A message delivered, and reading brought back.'

'Reading?'

'Newspapers.'

'The Yankee and I are going behind British lines again,' Big concluded.

'That is correct,' Titoko agreed.

'To Wanganui.'

'We understand each other,' Titoko said.

'The message?' Kimball sighed.

To the colonists of New Zealand, Titoko's communication read.

Salutations to you. This is a question to you. To whom does England belong? To whom does this land upon which you stand belong? The heavens and earth were made by the Creator and men and all things bearing fruit therein were likewise His work. If you know that the Creator made these, it is well. You were made white men, and the land of England was given you for your tribe. I was made Maori and New Zealand was the land given mine. Why have you not taken thought? You forget that there was a great gulf fixed between us – the ocean. You, ignoring that, leaped from your place to mine. I did not leap from my place to yours. I have taken no yard of your land. Let it be that you take no yard of mine.

This is my word to you. Away with you. Away with you all. Leave my land for your own across the ocean. Then arise that you may be baptised, and your sins washed away. Sufficient.

From Titokowaru.

'Do you', Titoko asked Kimball, 'detect error?'

'It's holy enough,' Kimball said.

'Is that a fault?' Titoko asked, rather beady.

'A little goes a long way.'

'What are you telling me?'

'We called ours the Declaration of Independence,' Kimball said.

There were sixty miles to Wanganui, more again on sly forest trails. They bypassed McDonnell's disconsolate colonist outpost with not a shot fired. Six days later, after looting farmhouses left empty, and passing up a chance to scatter a nervous constabulary patrol, Big and Kimball rested their horses in a grove of giant fern and gazed down on Wanganui. It was all of three years since Kimball looked on a town. As civilization went, he had seen worse. Without the Union Jack above the port, the place might have put him in mind of Maine, even of Eastport. At the mouth of a wide river there were jetties, two-storey buildings, warehouses, factories, offices and public houses. One or two hundred dwellings climbed above river level. Drifts of smoke said that the place was still in business. There were a few large houses with bright gardens and brick chimneys. There were many poor hovels with potato plots. Much of the riverside was coloured with the cultivations of Kepa and his tribesmen. Their white, shingle-roofed and prosperous dwellings were scattered around. Away from the river colonists' sheep grazed green fields. They could see citizenry abroad, colonists and Maori on horseback or afoot; and sometimes in banging buggies. Maori canoes, bringing in bundles of flax and bags of wheat for milling, and bearing away trade goods, moved up and down the river. A ferry slung on a long cable was working from the north bank to the south, carrying people, horses and drays heaped with personal property. They had to be colonist families in flight from farms to the north of town. Meanwhile fishermen in whale-boats laid twine on the ebb tide. There were ships in port, trading schooners and a steamer or two. There was also the sound of hammer and saw. Stockades were prominent; so too were barracks, watch-towers, and sentries. Voices reached them faintly as a guard changed. Landward, at least, Wanganui was luxuriantly fortified.

'One of those ships down there', Big said, 'could need a deck-hand. Kimball Bent might be forgotten.'

'There's a hundred pounds saying he won't be.'

'A pity about that,' Big agreed. 'Some would not think the worse of you if you looked for luck elsewhere. Why not?'

'You get interested', Kimball explained, 'in what happens next.'

'You'd better,' Big warned.

With the short approach to the town unpromising, they waited until late afternoon, then worked their way up the north bank of the river. Near cultivations Big found a small river canoe with a pair of paddles. After they tethered their horses, Kimball discarded kilt and cape, and dressed himself in Titoko's hand-me-downs. There was even a bowler hat to lend him spirit. They had a Colt apiece and a handful of rounds to keep bedlam at bay.

In spring dusk they paddled slowly downriver. The town's defenders had thought only for the menacing north; the settlement's waterway left an open back door. The sounds of dogs, horses, chickens and children grew around them. There was also a rich smell of dung and dead fish as they cruised close to waterside dwellings. Kimball peered at a window with curtains undrawn and saw a candlelit family at supper. A bearded father in braces sat at the head of the table while a mother in apron spooned out food; around them were the clean faces of children tiny and tall. Kimball had the melancholy notion he might be missing out on apple pie. As dark grew they drifted quietly among jetties bristling with barnacles and arrived at the port. There was the smell of salt and tar, the sound of river lapping against hulls, and mariners' voices. On the decks there was the flare of matches as pipes were lit. A creaky accordion sounded from a riverside public house. Big shipped his paddle, grabbed at a pile, and swung the canoe under steps washed by water.

'You have Titoko's words?' he whispered.

'And a little spending money,' Kimball said.

'Understand this,' Big went on. 'You are now on your own. I cannot take on a town.'

'How long do I have?'

'An hour,' Big said.

'Then?'

'I recall you with affection,' Big explained.

Beyond the steps were the rough planks of a jetty. Beyond the jetty was sandy roadway strewn with stone. The sound

of the accordion stopped. On both lumber and land his
feet began to ring uncomfortably loud. The bright windows
of the public house lit his way; otherwise Wanganui was
darkening fast. His first problem was to deliver Titoko's
proclamation to a likely door while he still had a little light.
Warehouses loomed around, also a fragrant brewery, a smoke-
house, a timber yard, rope and soap factories and a flour
mill or two. None looked tolerably official. Dodging drains
with a stench, he pushed his feet toward the centre of the
settlement. There were few townsfolk about at that hour. He
found doorways and alleys in which he could loiter until they
passed. Shops grew dimly, just their upper windows lit. He
made out an emporium, an apothecary, then a bootmaker's
and a saddler's. Turning a corner, he came upon the courthouse, no less, and the town lock-up. Rough, wooden,
and reeking, the building failed to say much for Queen
Victoria. There was a moaning and mumbling from those confined to its rear. At its front were two constables with rifles
in hand, and a corporal warming his hands over a brazier.
None of the three faintly lit faces was familiar. Kimball skir-
mished forward, taking shelter in shadow while he looked
out the terrain. The corporal by the brazier removed a flask
from a rear pocket and passed it to his companions to sample. Both drank with relish, then the corporal too. Kimball
thought it time to interfere. 'Best of the evening to you,'
he said.

The corporal, flask to his lips, looked up in fright. 'Do I
know you?' he asked.

'You will when I report to your superior,' Kimball suggested.

'What does that mean?' the constable said uncomfortably.

'Drinking on duty. And worse.'

'Worse?'

'There is', Kimball explained, 'the matter of the fellow I just
saw climbing from the window of his cell.'

'What fellow?'

'The big Maori bugger. Maybe I'm wrong. Maybe he's not
one of Titoko's. Maybe he's not leading Titoko into the town.
Maybe you're not due for a raid. You three seem mighty
quiet.'

'Raid?' said the corporal.

'If Titoko was here, who'd bloody know?'

The trio were in panic. The corporal shakily cocked his carbine.

'If I were you,' Kimball went on, 'I'd do a quick count of heads.'

With no further encouraging the three raced to the rear of the building. There was a crash of bolts. Kimball heard a large timber door grumble open and shut, and shouting begin. Before din became too distinct he took Titoko's document from his jacket and slid it under the courthouse door. Then he whistled off into the night. As a bad bastard he might soon be worth every colonist pound.

Titoko might need newspapers; his courier needed a drink. The night was clear and starlit. Inland sky promised a moon as he hiked back to the port. He heard the public house accordion again, and from that moment his mission was lining up two birds for one stone.

Lettering under a lantern advertised HONEST JOHN'S ALES AND SPIRITS. He moved past hitched horses and stole a wary look in the window. At the bar, yellow with lamplight, were a score of seamen and off-duty constables; there were three or four on-duty whores. Music made the scene even more promising. Kimball tipped back his bowler, adjusted Titoko's watch-chain, and marched into the establishment. Honest John was a fleshy jeezer with a vast ginger beard. He took a sincere interest when Kimball, trying to remember money, let a handful of coins crash on the bar. The sound also impressed nearby drinkers, and won a wistful smile from a whore. 'Whisky,' he said. 'The most truthful malt you got.'

'You're new,' Honest John said.

'Just in,' Kimball agreed.

A fast sample of the pub's best malt proved tolerable; it suggested the need for a second.

'Who'd you be, then?' Honest John asked.

'What do I look like?' Kimball said.

'A speculator,' Honest John said. 'Another sod with more money than sense.'

'You could be right,' Kimball agreed.

'Land, is it?'

'I hear some's going cheap.'

'To the north,' Honest John said. 'Me, I wouldn't pay a penny an acre.'

'You're talking rebels.'

'The wildest,' Honest John said.

'I been bush for weeks,' Kimball explained.

'The politicians are all going crazy.'

'The newspapers?'

'Them too.'

'It looks like I could use some fresh reading,' Kimball concluded. 'You wouldn't have one?'

'Today's from Wanganui, or last week's from Wellington?'

'Both,' Kimball said. 'Before you fetch them, my glass has gone empty.'

The filling of it further reduced Kimball's heap of coins. Emptying it did marvels for morale. The men at the bar didn't know him from Adam, and the whores were playing Eve. The musician, when not looking mournful into middle distance, was mostly interested in sucking up colonial ale. Taking in the lie of the land, Kimball otherwise noted only a lone drinker looking deep into a dry glass at the far end of the bar. Life in the forest considered, he hadn't seen less menace in years. Honest John returned to the bar with a bundle of print.

'Twopence and they're yours,' he said.

'They look used to me,' Kimball objected.

'A penny,' the publican said.

Kimball pushed a shilling across the bar. 'And a malt or two more,' he asked. 'If things are like you say, I could be looking for a fast way out of town.'

'Lucky for some,' Honest John said. 'Tell me, what's that sound in your voice?'

'Sound?'

'Which part of the old country?'

'I'm a wandering fellow,' Kimball explained. 'I was a fair time in San Francisco.'

'If I didn't know better I'd think you was Yankee.'

'I fool myself too,' Kimball confided.

'Watch your words here,' Honest John warned.

'Why would that be, then?'

'Bent. He gives Yankees a bad name.'

'Bent?'

'Don't tell me you never heard of Kimball Bent.'

199

'Who'd he be, then?'

'A cut-throat bastard running wild with the rebels. The next mayor of Wanganui.'

'How was that name again?'

'Bent. Like in crooked.'

If Kimball ever doubted that he was born light on luck, he was sure before his sixth malt. 'Bent?' said the sad solo drinker at the end of the bar. 'Did I hear someone say Bent?'

He lifted his head slowly. He had a boozer's colour and watery eyes. Kimball couldn't place the face, but for a fact it was familiar. Irish, and army.

'That's right,' Honest John sighed. 'We was talking Bent.'

'I seen the bugger nearer than you now,' the face said.

'So you keep telling us,' Honest John said.

'He snuck up on me while I was washing at a river,' the boozer told Kimball. 'Held a gun to my head. Cleaned me right out of clothes and money. Riding a white horse, he was. Leading a hundred warriors. Wanted me to join him.'

'Where', Kimball asked with interest, 'might this have been, then?'

'Up country. Before I took my discharge.'

The man grew memorable. In winning news for Titoko, Kimball had seen the Irishman last as a bitter soldier, bathing in the buff, among hundreds of others as sour. A sad sack from the 14th, if he remembered right. Also, as he remembered, the bugger suffered no more than a bruised bum when Kimball took off from Flukes.

Meanwhile the malt was working. He asked, 'So this Bent put a gun to your head?'

'Like I said.'

'And cleaned you out of clothes and money?'

'That's right,' the boozer swore.

'And wanted you to join him?' Kimball asked carefully.

'I might of done worse,' the boozer confessed.

'What are you now?'

'Nothing to speak of,' the man lamented.

'That's where you're wrong,' Kimball said.

'How would that be?'

'I'm looking at a fucking old fart of a liar.'

'Easy,' Honest John said. 'The story does no one no harm.'

'And no one no good,' Kimball said.

'Why should you care?'

A good question. Kimball's voice was winning stares.

The publican observed, 'You was just saying you never heard of Bent.'

'For a fact,' Kimball agreed, on the late side.

'So how', persisted the publican, 'would you know what's true and what's not?'

Roused, the old sod had the last word. Mustering his legs, he closed shakily with Kimball and considered him at length.

'I never forget a face,' he said with dignity. 'Nor a voice.' To all in earshot, he announced, 'I'm looking at him.'

'Looking at who?' Honest John whispered.

'Bloody Bent,' the old sod said.

By rights there should have been considerable uproar. Instead there was powerful quiet. Honest John set an example by backing off slowly. Then drinker after drinker, constable and seaman, did the same. Even the whores lost their voices. The accordion hiccuped and halted. As space spread around him Kimball calculated that he had half a minute before someone played hero. He took up the newspapers with his left hand. With his right he hauled the Colt from inside his jacket. It was cruelly slow to come free. The occupants of the bar proved marvellously patient. A whore began to whimper. Another finally screamed. She had reason. The Colt, when he chanced training it, had a jumpy life of its own. Without even trying he had everyone covered.

'You want money?' Honest John whispered.

'The door,' Kimball explained.

Honest John was nothing but helpful. 'Behind you,' he said.

Kimball looked over his shoulder. Four paces, maybe five.

'Look at it this way,' he suggested to present company. 'We're all in a fix.'

No one thought to argue.

'I need to walk away through that door,' he explained. 'Does anyone want different?'

No one was saying so.

'One thing more,' he advised. 'I wouldn't talk about this. For one thing no bugger's going to believe you.'

Aside from a sobbing whore, there was silence. He took a pace toward the door. Then a second.

'For another,' he added, 'you're not to know whether I got my white horse hitched outside. Nor a hundred warriors.'

That was worth two more paces. He took a large breath as he levered the door open and backed into the dark.

'I left a little change on the bar,' he pointed out. 'Drinks are on me.'

Tangling in twine, banging into barrels, and tripping on lengths of lumber, he argued with most obstructions on his race to the river. The commotion rising to his rear tended to end when his Colt discharged, though he was the one most at risk; the blast took away the toe of his left boot and the last of his composure. He toppled down damp steps in the dark and crashed into the canoe, with Big a useful cushion. They began paddling fervently upriver. The shouts behind grew faint. Finally the shots too. Ahead was river silvered by moon, their tethered horses, and the long ride home.

'You're drunk,' Big said.

'Mellow,' Kimball claimed.

'And what the fuck was that about?'

'So you buy the newspapers,' Kimball said.

Titoko spent much of a morning enlightening himself with the *Wanganui Chronicle* and the *Wellington Independent*. A former imperial colonel called Whitmore, more recently a breeder of shorthorn cattle, had been recalled to the colours. He was to preside over what survived of the colonial army and undertake the defence of Wanganui's colonists. Colonel McDonnell had been retired. 'Not before time,' a Wanganui scribe said. 'There is no further point in disguising the fact that the recent affray with Titokowaru is the most disastrous martial event in the history of this colony. We wish the distinguished Colonel Whitmore well with his endeavours. May he now serve New Zealand as he has the Empire in the Crimea and in the campaigns against Africa's Kaffirs. The time for excuses is past. The time for a man of action is here. The position is critical. Another triumph for the cannibal captain called Titokowaru might mean the colony aflame with war again.'

As for the editor of the *Independent*, he urged the public to shun cowards lately discharged from the colonial militia, and pleaded with Wellington's publicans to let them go thirsty.

Toward Titokowaru's warriors he was no more considerate. 'Since when', he asked, 'have ignorant and uncivilized savages had the better of the white races in matters military? There is only one conclusion to be drawn. This is not Titokowaru's work alone; he is the willing tool. Let there be no mistake. The hand of an evil genius discloses itself in this unspeakable affair. The name is already familiar to our readers. We talk, of course, of that curse on the lips of the colony, the renegade American called Kimball Bent. It is time for resolute extermination of Bent and his fellow beasts. Let no mercy or scruple be shown. It is not just that people are in peril. The taxation will be ruinous. The colony could soon be bankrupted.'

'That is promising,' Toa said. 'They talk money.'

'And me,' Kimball said, in some pain.

Also, in an urgent black column of print, the colonial government asked the colonists of Wellington not to panic prematurely. There was no cause yet, an official advised, to pack bags and look for a ship.

'Wellington?' Titoko said. 'We have yet to see Wanganui.'

'Speak for yourself,' Kimball said.

Titoko was less taken by another item. The heading read MAORI ACHILLES PROMOTED. The rest said that the celebrated friend of Queen Victoria, Wanganui's Captain Kepa, had been promoted to fill the vacancy left by the decease of Major von Tempsky.

'Achilles?' Titoko asked. 'Who is this Achilles?'

'A Greek jeezer,' Kimball said.

'A warrior?'

'The way I heard.'

'Did he win?'

'Until he was buggered by a bad foot.'

'How could that be?'

'His mother was a god. She dunked him in hell's river to make him a hero. Only she didn't dunk right. She didn't let go his heel. The rest of him was solid. In a fight his heel let in arrow.'

'Have Kepa's feet', Titoko asked, 'been seen poor of character?'

'Not in pursuit,' Demon said.

'What of mine?'

'Sound,' Big judged.

The item further said that Major Kepa would now have sole command of the Maori contingent in the campaign against Taranaki's rebels.

'It is as you thought,' Big observed.

Titoko was quiet.

'Could it have been other?' Big persisted.

Titoko shrugged.

'Your worst fear is not yet,' Big said.

'No?' Titoko inquired.

'There is no talk of Britons taking Kepa's orders. Maori only are named.'

'Perhaps so,' Titoko said.

'Colonel Whitmore is commander of the colonist force. Kepa must still answer to Whitmore.'

'Then we need more knowledge,' Titoko said.

'What more do we need know of Kepa?'

'Of Whitmore.'

'How would you wish such knowledge won?'

'By winning,' Titoko said.

Toa took a large breath. 'We are marching south? Toward Wanganui?'

'Watching our feet,' Titoko said.

Nineteen

It was most of a month before they moved. Pigeon were potted, pork salted and eels dried for nourishment on the journey. Kimball and Big oiled and fired discarded British weapons to establish the worth of the Queen's armourers before passing out cartridges and carbines. Then Titoko pushed scouts ahead under Demon. They were to ensure the territory was safe and otherwise make themselves useful by levelling fences and firing farmhouses and bridges. Finally a baggage train formed and the march south began. After they forded the Waingongoro and found open ground, fires were lit on the reconquered land. With flames climbing high the mood that dusk was festive. Forage parties dug potatoes by the barrel from colonist gardens; fat cattle were slain for the ovens. The spring night was warm and starlit, with no more than slight shelters needed. Even Rihi managed a small smile.

'Is warring done?' she asked Kimball.

'Is that what you want to hear?'

'Please,' she said. 'Is it done?'

'All but, maybe.'

'How much is but?'

'Ample of everything. Especially their arses.'

'Then Maine?'

'Fast,' he promised.

Celebration found its way into their marriage bed.

Next morning, so far as Titoko's tribesmen could see, the coast curving south was theirs. The thorn in its side was the base McDonnell had built, and where Colonel Whitmore was said new in command. Titoko camped inland and had the base watched. There were two hundred men in occupation, few of them Maori; Kepa's tribesmen still made no showing. Those resident seldom showed themselves outside their stockades; there was next to no patrolling. With the Queen's highway hazardous, and bridges burning, supplies and men had to come in by sea. Ships stood off a river mouth, short of noisy surf, and longboats bobbed into shore. Reinforcements were rowed in. Unrepentant cowards were rowed out. The vigorous activity intrigued Titoko. Finally he thought to see for himself. He led a party within earshot of the redoubt to listen to Colonel Whitmore rebuking newly arrived recruits for their drilling and demeanour, promising death, damnation and longer lashings unless they bettered themselves before battle. Titoko thought the jaunty colonel's rage pleasing, especially the ripe quality of his curses.

'A man much in love with himself,' he judged. 'Even more with his orders.'

'Meaning what?' Toa asked.

'Corpses,' Titoko said.

Firelight floated over his face as he sat with Kimball that night. 'Whitmore', he said, 'may give me the win I want.'

'What was The Beak if it wasn't a win?'

'It was good,' Titoko said. 'It could have been better.'

'So the next fight will be?'

'Wednesday's must.'

'Why?' Kimball dared ask.

'We can destroy two armies. Three would ask too much of our warrior week, more so of fate.'

'That is not what you tell Toa,' Kimball observed.

'It is what I don't tell myself,' Titoko said.

'What else don't you?'

'Morning's tide is mine. Evening's must be Kepa's.'

'You could raise a larger army.'

'As could he.'

'So what is this for?'

'The next win. Who needs a tale only of loss?'

Toa began to seem less melancholy company.

Senior tribesmen met. Whitmore's outpost might be isolated; it was also a challenge.

'Push them a little,' Toa argued. 'They have but the sea to their rear.'

'You talk attack on their ground?' Titoko said.
'Of making them swim. The coast would be ours.'
'Then?'
'Wanganui,' Toa shrugged. 'Why not? We have seen colonists flee.'
'We have yet to see Kepa flee,' Titoko said.
'What is your thought, cousin?'
'Of taking no land more than our own.'
'And Whitmore?'
'We pass him by.'
'If Kepa's men rise before us, Whitmore's could trouble our rear.'
'My thought also,' Titoko said.
'So what are you saying?'
'We make Whitmore follow,' Titoko said. 'We keep him in view.'

The march south resumed next day. To leave Whitmore sure of their direction, Titoko pushed a small party of warriors out to his right. Their task was to taunt, to ride just within rifle shot of the constabulary outpost. They floated a few improvised pennants; they fired off a few rounds. Finally, more boisterously, they dismounted and bared their arses at the cooped colonists. Sharp cracks heralded asthmatic shot dropping to ground. Colonel Whitmore was seen on a parapet bellowing at his frustrated marksmen, and beside him, even more bitter, the captain called Flukes.

Two days and twenty miles later, half the distance to Wanganui, Titoko called halt and began looking inland. Another day passed before he followed up an old bullock track and found a site to interest him. It was a place where two great gorges all but met. Between was a belt of burned-off land, a hundred paces wide, with bush-darkened gullies hiding gorge walls. The character of the place could not be seen from coastal approach; it all looked level. Lifting beyond was a lately fortified hill. Tribesmen camped on its summit had been a target for imperial gunners two years before. There were ruins; there were graves.
'You think to rebuild?' Toa asked.
'I think to think,' Titoko said.
There was no further conversation. It was an afternoon warm

with early summer. Titoko found shade and slept, while others of his party grazed their horses and grumbled.

'He tells us nothing,' Toa protested.

Titoko woke refreshed, with decision.

'Bring our people up from the coast,' he told Toa.

'They will ask questions,' Toa said dourly.

'And they will have answers,' Titoko promised.

It was some time before the column arrived. Toward dusk Titoko walked downhill with Kimball. He appeared to be pacing out ground.

'Tell me what you hear said,' he finally asked.

'Toa thinks you could do better.'

'When does Toa not?'

'He thinks the hill.'

'And I think the flat.'

'I can see.'

'I have slept on this land. Also dreamed.'

'I should have known.'

'I looked over my shoulder. I saw a battle behind.'

'The last one?'

'The next.'

'Over your shoulder?'

'Already fought.'

'In the Maine woods,' Kimball said, 'we got a bird called the fillieloo. Maybe it exists. Maybe it don't. Hundreds of hunters reckon they seen it.'

'What is this creature to me?'

'It flies backward to see where it's going.'

'It is no Maine bird,' Titoko said. 'It is Maori.'

Titoko continued looking out ground. That between the gorges took his fancy more and more. Later, with his people about him, he had his tribe's fires lit north, south, and west. Where a fourth might have flamed, to the east, was where he stood lone long after dark.

Next morning was noisy. Women prepared food for hungry workers. Juveniles gathered palm fronds and saplings for shelters. Patrols were sent riding north and south. Other warriors were abroad from first light, attacking the forest; there were explosions of leaf and branch as trees toppled and rolled. These

208

were split, trimmed to pointed posts, and dragged to Titoko. With his back firmly turned to the hill he was using short sticks to mark out a palisade line between one gorge and the next, crossing ground levelled by the old bullock track. Beyond the track, to the west, the line took off at a sharp angle, ending where ground fell to forested gully and bare gorge; to the east it also felt toward broken ground. The line was irregular in one other respect. It enclosed nothing; the rear was naked. Toa was not the only one unsettled; Big and Demon hid their surprise better.

'A single line?' Toa finally asked.

'Sufficient,' Titoko said.

'Again I see nothing strong.'

'Good,' Titoko said. 'May they see weakness too.'

Fires burned by night to throw light on warrior labour. Post after post was lifted and heaved into holes; digging of trenches began.

It was midnight before Big told Kimball to quit. 'Look to your woman,' he urged. 'It may be your last chance.'

Kimball climbed up to the hillside camp. Family fires were guttering low, with a few women still waiting on their men. Rihi was one, sitting outside their family shelter. Wiremu was fretful and feverish in her arms; healthier Meri was asleep inside the shelter. He sat with them in silence. Warrior voices, and the sound of chopping and hammering, rose uphill. In the flash of the fires Titoko's toiling warriors were small shiny shapes.

'It begins again,' she said.

'Who knows?' he said.

'I know,' she said.

Wiremu grew quiet. She put him to bed.

'Come,' Kimball said. 'You too.'

'Take me to Maine,' she asked.

'So listen a little,' he said, holding her hand and beginning to talk.

Her head soon rested comfortably on his shoulder. Unless he was much mistaken, he had won back his wife.

Late next morning patrols made their return. The first, from the north, said Colonel Whitmore and Captain Flukes had left their outpost and were marching in force; their contingent had been strengthened by another steamer call. Most of three hundred men had been tallied on the move. The patrol from the south reported a second band approaching. They included Kepa's people, Major Kepa himself, some untidy Wanganui militia, and scores of blue-uniformed constables freed from garrison duty. Perhaps three hundred men, perhaps four. A day's march separated the columns. When they met there would be six to seven hundred rifles.

To slow them, Titoko dispatched Demon and other devout marksmen to snipe at the columns from high ground, and then to retire with speed. By the time their pursuers climbed inland and thrashed back and forward through fern, looking to silence them, marksmen would be well on their way home. Meanwhile the columns would be moving warily, with more time won for Titoko's wall.

In two days the palisades were pushed seventy paces to the east; then, at an angle, fifty to the west. Where the wings met a command bastion rose on stilts; smaller bastions were built east and west. Some of the lumber looked a little shaky, as Toa didn't tire of pointing out. Titoko's interest was more in the nature of the ground than the character of the timbering. At The Beak he had offered an open front to win the enemy near; here he was tempting them with open flanks. Those thinking to encircle his position would be confused by growth and gully and thwarted by gorge. Meanwhile Titoko worked to make his line more discouraging. Rifle pits were dug along the front of the palisades and concealed with sod and brush. Banked parapets, behind loopholes, made a second firing line for kneeling warriors. Finally, large and small bastions allowed for a third layer of fire to take attackers from their feet.

After inspection, Titoko saw nothing worth improvement. 'Sleep,' he told weary men. The palisades were lightly manned. Sentries were placed to separate women on the hillside from warriors on the flat. Silence and abstinence was the order of the night. Fires were cooled too.

'Morning?' Kimball asked.

'Morning,' Titoko said.

Demon was given charge of the night's last watch.

It was a damp night, unseasonally cold and misty. Under the command bastion, wound in a blanket, Kimball woke to faint light. Big, earlier tumbled beside him, had gone. Quiet feet were on the move. Warriors were nudging others awake. Kimball climbed into the bastion and found Big beside Demon. Both men signalled silence as they peered into the mist. It thickened here, thinned there, as breeze played through it. At first, as mist moved, Kimball picked out no more than patches of fern and scrub and shadowy stumps along the line of the old bullock track. Then one of the stumps shook itself apart from others; another followed suit. Both sank suddenly. Other shadows floated into view and vanished as fast.

'Tell Titoko their scouts are here,' Big whispered to Kimball.

Titoko had set himself apart from his men, in a commandeered constabulary tent to the rear of the palisades, close to where the women camped, without so much as a sentry in attendance. He claimed to think battle better in solitude. Kimball approached with caution. 'Titoko?' he called. 'They are here.'

'Many?'

'Enough.'

Titoko appeared from his tent, dressed fit to kill. 'Fast or slow?'

'Slow.'

'Good,' Titoko said. 'Help knot my tie.'

Titoko took his place in the central bastion. With whispers and signals he sent skirmishers east and west. They were to place themselves on gully lips, at the edge of the bush, to tease outflankers toward the gorges. The rest of his men, weapons in hand, ran silent to pits and parapets along the palisade line. Big was given the long eastern wing to command, Demon the short western. Since no one said otherwise, Kimball stood watch beside Titoko and Toa in the central bastion. Demon raised his arm from the west bastion to show himself placed; and soon Big from the east. The shadows in the mist had ceased movement; the mist itself was slow lightening. There was the far whinny of a horse and a faint rattle of harness. Otherwise even light rain was loud.

'Cousin?' Toa asked nervously. 'How do you see this?'

'Two volleys,' Titoko said.

'Then?'

'The terrain does the talking.'

'And we?'

'We take an interest,' Titoko said.

There were more minutes to wait before colonist boots became audible and mounted in number. The mist filled with movement. Shadows were no longer single; they rose and fell dense up the old bullock track. One wave of constabulary sank to train carbines; another raced forward. Kimball had never seen colonists moving so efficiently before. A passionate young captain appeared to be hurrying a hundred men forward to test the centre of Titoko's line. Behind was surely a second hundred and likely a third. Flukes and Whitmore, and for that matter Kepa, were not yet on show. Forty paces out from the palisades the storming party paused to fix bayonets. Then they rushed. As they closed with the palisades their sound was all hard breathing and boots. Twenty paces out they were still moving with spirit. Titoko lifted an arm to the west. Demon, from his own bastion, acknowledged the message. In the same moment fifty rifles flashed along the west front, their roar billowing behind. The first layer of fire, at ground level, took legs from attackers. The second struck among them at chest height. Others in the first line, not least the panicked young captain, were pushed further east when Demon mounted his second volley. As they fled shot they placed themselves in the sights of Big's marksmen at a range of ten paces. Titoko lifted his arm again, this time toward Big, and let it fall. The east palisades flamed too; streams of sparks became a leaping cataract. The storming party, taking shot from two sides, bunched and bobbed, shedding men as lightly as leaves; the young captain floated free to join those prone. Survivors spun back upon others unscathed. Some tried to bash their way back to safety with butt and boot. A tardily heroic lieutenant, risen from the rear, counselled against cowardice with a revolver in hand. The few he inspired pushed along the palisade line, looking for entry, and found no way forward at all. Smoke began giving them cover; Big's second volley failed to bite as cruelly as his first. Soon enough men were on the move to the open east of the palisade line to interest Titoko, more so when a hundred dangerous newcomers struck off from the bullock track in the same direction, looking to outflank the line. To a man they were Kepa's tribesmen; and at their head, by far the burliest, was Kepa himself. Bouncing across the ground, swinging his major's sabre, full-throated Kepa had never looked livelier.

Titoko ordered Big, Demon and half their warriors from pits and parapets to skirmish east and west. 'Stand off', he advised, 'until you see faces.'

Shooting rose left and right, out of view of those in the command bastion. Titoko failed to stir himself, or give further orders.

'Should we not see?' Toa asked.

'I can hear,' Titoko said, lighting his pipe.

Most lifting voices were colonist. Blundering from gullies to be baffled by gorges, Whitmore's men were making easy targets. Single shots, rather than volleys, seemed to be sufficient. Short cries, soon silenced, said carnage was mounting. Meanwhile, to the front, perhaps a hundred paces out from the palisades, Whitmore and Flukes, and constabulary held in reserve, were making an appearance through haze. Looking far less jaunty, Whitmore viewed dead and dying, and cursed. He had cause to curse louder when Kepa was heard commanding his tribesmen to leave the field to foolhardy colonists. As retiring Maori flew past his position Whitmore called on Kepa to persist in forcing the issue. Kepa's reply, so far as could be determined from a distance, was a long and dry laugh. The issue was forced. Failing to encircle his enemy, Whitmore now found his own flanks turned. Survivors of the first assault were flailing right and left, and mostly to the rear. Captain Flukes, revolver in hand, was failing to persuade those in flight to take a calmer view of Titoko's firepower. Even the ranks of men in reserve looked shaky.

Kimball, meanwhile, lifted his carbine and took sight on Flukes. The range was eighty paces. Then he felt his firearm pressed downward.

'No,' Titoko was saying. 'I need him.'

'Flukes?'

'And Whitmore.'

'Why?'

'To hold others,' Titoko explained. Above the sound of battle, he cried, 'Attack.'

Groups of skirmishers under Big and Demon grew at each end of the palisade line and moved forward, pushing volleys. Men of Whitmore's reserve force began to fall. The colonel had the choice of returning fire or retiring. While he came to decision he ordered a platoon forward, under Captain Flukes, to slow rebel advance. This met with Titoko's approval.

'The man has promise,' he judged.

'Flukes?' Kimball said.

'Whitmore. Flukes is now yours.' He gave a louder order. 'Of others kill many, but Whitmore is not to be slain.'

'Not?' Toa queried.

'Not,' Titoko said.

'You fear Kepa in command?'

'I fear not fighting fools.'

Others in the bastion thought to test their marksmanship. Kimball took sight again as Flukes came on. At fifty paces he was improving as a target. Kimball steadied himself, felt for the trigger, and heard roar. The problem was that it was not his weapon at work. Flukes spun, dropped his revolver, and clutched his shoulder. Kimball's shot, a whisker too late, split air and not Flukes. Sergeant Tonks rushed his damaged officer to the rear. Others, without good excuse, joined in the flight.

Hine lowered her smoky carbine. It seemed she had limbed Flukes. Kimball swallowed his obscenity.

'I wished you to see my shooting,' she whispered with menace. 'Also your fate should you again deceive my daughter.'

'Me?' Kimball said with surprise.

'You,' she said. Her eyes had no humour. 'No one knows better than I that you have been unfaithful.'

'It takes two to go behind the woodpile,' he argued.

'Your story,' she said.

She moved to Titoko's side to place her next shot. Kimball thought to stand clear.

Meanwhile Colonel Whitmore was ordering men to hold their ground. When he found himself lonely he ordered them to retire. The second order was heard.

The rest of the morning was given to letting even more light into colonist ranks. In sixes and sevens, then in twos and threes, they were not allowed a headlong rout; they were forced to return fight all the way back to the coast. Finally Titoko called his killing parties home so that casualties might be numbered. One warrior was dead, his neck broken when overbalancing from a bastion, and another had shot himself in the foot. Sixty colonists had been left slain or dragged from the field. Survivors of the assault would make much of never seeing a rebel face that morning. Colonel Whitmore, with keener vision, would count Titoko's two hundred as a thousand insane savages. Fewer would leave his report too painful to read. Even Titoko found totals puzzling. A second tally of his force turned up only grazes, sprains and one broken toe.

'We saw little of Kepa,' Big noted.
Titoko was quiet.
'He gave no orders,' Big observed.
'Nor did he take them,' Titoko said.
'True.'
'Or leave dead behind.'
'You are saying something,' Big concluded.
'A little of Kepa is enough,' Titoko said.
A little of other things were too. When a fleshy constable was prepared for the oven by fervent newcomers, Titoko took himself elsewhere. Those who partook were told to keep their distance from those who did not. That especially meant Titoko. Warriors could make what they wanted of this. Mostly they did. Man-eating was out of style. A field of stiffened colonist dead, soon with a reek, gave meat a bad name.

Twenty

'Where,' Rihi asked, 'is Maine now?'
'Still in the United States,' Kimball told her.
'Why aren't we?'
'That's a shorter story,' he said.
Kimball now had a cross to carry. Rihi had the hammer and nails.
'You promised,' she pointed out.
'I've been getting this side of another fight,' he said.
'More than that.'
'Trying to righten a piss-cutter of a captain,' he admitted.
'Maine was to shut me up?'
'I'm not saying it didn't,' he allowed.
There was a long and sombre silence.
'How far to Maine?' she asked.
'It depends on the winds.'
'So how far from Wanganui?'
'A small way,' he said carefully.
'How small?'
'Jeezly small.'
'What do you mean, jeezly?'
'Bloody. Bloody small.'
'And is Wanganui a jeezly small way?'
'It's looking a bloody small way,' he said.

That was Toa's thought too, with battle a day or two gone.
'Are we to sit here?' he asked Titoko.
'With a peak climbed, a warrior rests.'
'You are talking fame?'
'I am thinking peaks.'
'There are others taller.'

'The one on my mind is our own.'

'Taranaki?'

'A few miles more and it will no longer be seen.'

'Whitmore will return. The colonists must.'

'Not soon,' Titoko said.

'Give them ground, and their return will be sooner.'

'Ground before us begins to be Kepa's.'

'Much of it sold to colonists,' Toa said.

'They gave Kepa's people their price.'

'Kepa has never been fussy about fighting for our acres. Why faint of heart about his?'

'Because then there is no end,' Titoko said.

'You are saying Kepa matters?'

'And we.'

'You are not talking Wanganui?' Toa said.

'That is correct, cousin. I am not.'

'What is it you want?' Toa asked.

'War my lieutenant. Never my leader.'

Toa took another tack. 'We have come this far with two hundred warriors,' he said. 'What might we do with two hundred more?'

'Think lazy,' Titoko said. 'Not lean.'

Titoko's army fattened all the same. Soon there were four hundred armed men on show. Neutral villages to the rear of their march began glowing with belligerence. With news of a war in which only colonists were killed, scores of fair-weather warriors mounted their horses or shouldered weapons and fearlessly marched. Daily new volunteers appeared on the skyline, or rustled from scrub, hungry for a helping of Titoko's mana. They tended to sulk or discharge weapons, by way of protesting their spirit, if Titoko suggested their arrival late in the day. Even some of Kepa's tribesmen, thinking to their future and recalling kinsmen among Titoko's people, stole out of Wanganui to offer their services. To prove their quality as turncoats they brought rumour and colonist newspapers, Titoko's need for print now being famed. Rumour and reading informed him that the British Empire was singing small and falling back further. Seventy miles of coast, from the Waingongoro to Wanganui, was his if he pleased. Newspapers told of Wanganui townsfolk taking ship south, of food shortages, even of Kepa's people packing. Panic had also bitten the capital. Wellington's louder politicians were asking for a genuine British general, rather than counterfeit commanders, and the return from Britain of ten thousand Queen's infantry. Colonel Whitmore, after offering his resignation, had been persuaded to raise a fresh force to subdue Titoko.

'What is your thought, grandson?' Titoko asked.

'You're in trouble,' Kimball said.

'Think further.'

'You have won all you needed to. And more than you're going to.'

'Say what I wish not to hear said.'

'You don't want to go forward.'

'That is not new.'

'And you cannot go back.'

'That is so,' Titoko acknowledged.

There was a silence.

'You have seen Wanganui,' Titoko said.

'Enough of it,' Kimball agreed.

'What is our chance?'

'A snowball's in hell.'

'With Kepa ahead.'

'Even without.'

'Without?'

'If it isn't a warrior called Kepa, then another Maori with a mind to colonist cash.'

Titoko sighed. 'My thought too.'

'So why are you asking?'

'Because it has to be said.'

'And not by you.'

'Not loudly,' Titoko agreed. 'I wish not to know my own mind.'

'So you use mine?'

'Correct,' Titoko said.

'Arseholes to you, then,' Kimball said. 'There's one other thing.'

'What would that be?'

'You can't sit here. No one wins the same battle twice.'

'I know,' Titoko said.

The Battle of Strewn Whites, as Titoko thought to call it, was in the first week of November. Before the second was gone,

with colonist silence queer, he decided the time had arrived
to pay the devil a day's march. The move muffled those who
most despaired of his sloth. It satisfied firebrands looking for
work. One by one colonist farmhouses began blazing; smoke
hung dark on the land behind. Travelling the dusty colonist
highway without challenge, and behind a few yawning scouts,
Titoko's column came to rest an easy ride from Wanganui.
Calling a halt at a ford, Titoko crossed the small creek in their
path, urged his horse up a rise, and reined the beast in. He
looked north and south and was silent. When he signalled,
Kimball and Toa rode up to join him, and Demon and Big
returned with the scouts. Sunset was colouring cloud and
horizon. There was nothing in the place promising death of
any but a commonplace kind. It was easy coastal plateau,
grassland patched with ploughed acres and crops, backed
by low hills patchy with fern. Hills dark with old growth
reared inland. Otherwise the land fell away slowly to lakes,
dunes, and surf. The sound of the sea was distant; a little
breeze fluttered through long grass on the road edge. Horses
began grazing.
   'I think here,' Titoko announced.
   'For tonight?' Toa queried.
   'And as many nights as needed.'
   'This country is too open,' Toa protested.
   'Who knows?' Titoko said.
   'Where is our advantage?'
   'It may be seen,' Titoko said.
   'You would camp on their highway?'
   'And wait for them to travel it again.'
   'Whitmore?'
   'Or worse,' Titoko agreed.
   'What is your thought, cousin?'
   'That our presence here will soon be known. We may make
it felt sooner.'
   'To what end?'
   'Wanganui could yet empty of people. Constabulary will also
be obliged to venture out from their stockades. To camp here is
to call them cowards.'
   'And they may yet call us mad.'
   'The worse for them,' Titoko argued.
   'Are you thinking to draw the line again?'

'I am thinking that we have taken the land for which we battled.' To Big he said, 'Can our mountain be viewed?'

'From inland a little,' Big said.

'There,' Titoko said. 'I am thinking no further.'

'There is much you are not saying,' Toa observed presently.

Titoko pretended surprise. 'What would that be, cousin?'

'You have stopped short of Kepa's tribal lands.'

'That is true,' Titoko allowed.

'There is but another river to cross. You cannot face it, even now.'

'I can face a Maori who fights for British shillings, even for bounties. I cannot face one who fights for his own acres. Then there are two of us.'

'You and he?'

'That is not my war.'

'What is, cousin?'

'A last worth fighting.'

'For that you choose this place?'

Titoko was thoughtful.

'Right on their road?' Toa persisted. 'You choose this?'

Dusk was coming in fast. There were already stars in the sky. Downhill the halted column was turning restless. Horses whinnied; women gossiped and children whimpered; warriors lit their pipes, looked impatiently to Titoko, and waited on orders.

'The place chooses me,' Titoko said.

Kimball felt a faint shiver or shudder; it didn't much matter which. Either someone had just shat on his grave, or someone had not.

Later, Titoko confided, 'I am losing the time. Is it Thursday or Friday?'

'Thursday, I guess,' Kimball said, 'with the feel of Friday.'

'Then better Thursday,' Titoko decided.

'Better?'

'Who needs a new sabbath soon?'

Mornings still had the sweet chill of spring. Afternoons were heavy with summer's first heat. Evenings did not cool uncomfortably. For most of a week there were few complaints heard.

220

Tents rose, and shelters were built, before Titoko asked much of menfolk. Living off the land had never been easier. The unfenced countryside had homeless livestock to be herded for slaughter. Colonist potatoes were there to be dug. Fish and clams could be won from the shore. Within vengeful rides there were further dwellings to be plundered and fast-riding colonists to be sniped; there were soon none left farming north of Wanganui. Constabulary patrols were seen riding up the coast. They were not attacked. Titoko wished them to observe what they might, and then ride home to report.

Finally he had a muster of warriors. 'We have come this far,' he told them, and was quiet.

As silence grew longer, his mystified men finally agreed they had.

'There are those who think further,' he informed them.

That was no news either. Toa had been urging a livelier insult to Wanganui. He looked for support among newcomers, those who had not lived the Battle of The Beak, nor even the Battle of Strewn Whites. Those who had fought both were deaf to Toa and took Titoko's orders. Among such was Demon, and especially Hine.

'If there are those who would march on a colonist town, let them be heard,' Titoko suggested.

There was a silence. 'What is your thought, cousin?' Toa asked.

'To let such men move,' Titoko explained. 'To let them form up with their firearms and march south as one.'

'While you remain with the rest?'

'Here,' Titoko said.

There was a longer silence. Kimball saw the challenge meant. Titoko, still trying to think lean, was as vexed by his numbers as by colonist quiet. A war party might rid him of the reckless and leave remaining warriors easier to manage. Colonist calm could also be ended. Whitmore's constabulary and Kepa's tribesmen might be tempted up the coast before they were ready. A foiled raid could serve Titoko well.

Toa seemed to see it too. There was no one quieter.

'Good,' Titoko said, though his face said otherwise. 'Do I hear silence?'

There wasn't a whisper. Titoko's live eye was busy. Even his dead one looked in business.

'Let me continue to hear it,' he said.

With his force gone to domestic duties, Titoko began looking over landscape to see what it told him. Big and Demon stood attentively near; Toa was a little further removed. After walking this way and that, looking seaward and landward, Titoko called his senior men on to a horseshoe-shaped clearing of colonist land abutting the road. To the rear the ground fell to a slow creek and lifted ferny and forested beyond. The ground they walked was sheep-grazed grass; a few black stumps rose here and there.

'What', he asked Big, 'is a fortress for?'

'For defence,' Big said.

Titoko's eye travelled to Demon. 'Your thought?' he asked.

'To impede,' Demon said.

'Toa?' Titoko said.

'To deter,' Toa said.

'You all three say the same,' Titoko observed.

'As does custom,' Toa said.

'Custom', Titoko went on, 'also says there is no defeat in fleeing a fortress. Is that not correct?'

'When the enemy has been hurt,' Toa agreed.

'When further fight is not wise,' Demon offered.

'When the work of the fortress is done,' Big said.

'And that is custom?' Titoko asked.

'Allowing for firearms,' Toa said.

'Thus you all talk of fortresses which fail to defend, impede, or deter?'

Big and Demon were thoughtful, and Toa was cautious.

'I ask where you have been,' Titoko continued. 'I ask what you have seen.'

'Small battles made large,' Toa said.

'Such as The Beak, and the Battle of Strewn Whites,' Demon said.

'They have much in common,' Titoko said.

Big took the point. 'Our fortification was not surrendered,' he said.

'No?' Titoko said.

'The enemy thought it wisdom to flee.'

'What does that say?' Titoko demanded.

'That the fortifications were not on hilltops,' Big said helpfully, 'and thus not surrounded.'

'It says more,' Titoko urged.

'That there was guile in their nature,' Toa said reluctantly.

It was Demon who had the answer wished. 'The fortresses were false,' he said. 'They were not for defence.'

'So what are you telling us?' Titoko asked.

'There was only attack. There could be but attack.'

'I am beginning to hear you,' Titoko said. 'And you, perhaps, me.'

'What do you ask of us, then?' Toa finally said.

'More than a fortress,' Titoko said. 'A machine.'

'Machine, cousin?'

'One to eat an army and spit out the pieces.'

'Here?' Toa marvelled.

'The best there has been,' Titoko promised.

Battle with Titoko's site was joined the next day. With the sun just above the horizon and dew bright underfoot, Titoko and Big worked over the ground. Titoko had a plan, with which he paced this way and that, and Big had hammer and pegs. Where Titoko called an order, Big hammered in a peg. The distances between the pegs left onlookers silent. With no sod turned it was plain that the fortress would be the largest seen since Methodists talked Titoko's people into the building of churches. Finally parties of warriors swarmed across the terrain with axes and saws, picks and spades. Parties moved out to fetch forest timber and retrieve galvanized iron from collapsed colonist barns and dwellings. Firearms were reserved to the few left to idle on picket or patrol. Summer grew warmer daily. November was almost gone; December was due, and perhaps a third colonist army. Kimball was seldom permitted a patrol. Work went on rain or shine, and there was an abundance of both. Trenches grew deeper and ramparts higher. At day's end Kimball crawled from the fortress caked with clay, sawdust in his hair and wood chips in his whiskers.

'Is this getting us to Maine?' Rihi asked.

'When we've dug past hell,' he told her.

The fortress rose in the form of four merged crescent moons. Titoko's plan provided few straight lines and next to no angles. The four curving walls were bound by round bastions. Each was eighty paces in length before it curled into the next. Each was double palisaded with fifteen-foot logs, and then curtained with light growth, allowing a gap at the base through which fire might be placed. Each wall served as a mouth. Attackers closing with the walls would find themselves bitten right and left by enfilade fire before they could begin to show fight. Meanwhile the deep trenches within the fort were covered with timber, iron, and a considerable thickness of soil. While rifle shot fell feebly away from the outer walls of the fortress, shells lofted within would sink and splutter. Robust underground rooms were also meant to survive artillery. Tunnels between would allow parties of warriors to move fast from one crescent of the fortress to another without danger. To warn of peril a watch-tower stood a strong thirty feet tall at the centre. Provision was made for events thereafter. Storage pits were packed with potatoes, barrels of salt beef, potted pigeon, wild honey, and gourds of drinking water. Access to creek and forest would be gained by covered walkways. Warriors should be able to win refreshment even under colonist noses. Rifle pits were placed at the edge of the forest to establish this advantage. Warrior by warrior, family by family, the fortress was occupied.

Work didn't stop. Titoko took satisfaction in pointing out hasty workmanship, and especially in ordering sweaty warriors to pick apart portions of the fortress and put it together; again and again he walked around it, halting to view it this way and that, to ensure there was no fault in the arrangement of firepower. He climbed to the watch-tower often, to consider its parts better, and seldom descended without ordering warriors to begin toil again.

The first colonist approach came at the end of November. Colonel Whitmore rode the highway up from Wanganui and made himself seen at six hundred paces with a new and bright troop of cavalry. For a time he inspected the fortress through binoculars. If his first thought was to test the spirit of his recruits, his second thought was not. He flaunted them forward, he wheeled them back. Then he did the same again. After a few shots had been fired Titoko saw no point in his entrenched warriors interfering with martial affairs. After an hour of colonist cantering he observed, 'I cannot see Kepa. What does that mean to you?'

'No grave-digging detail,' Kimball said.

'Officers?'

'Just a lieutenant or two.'

'Then he has other men hidden,' Titoko decided. 'He wants us on open ground.'

'I guess,' Kimball said.

'It also means that he has a fear of this place. The longer he looks, the worse it will seem.'

After another hour, Whitmore himself failed to see the point in his performance; he ordered his men to retire. Titoko's newcomers jubilantly discharged weapons; his veterans merely expelled breath.

That night the sentinels in the fortress watch-tower gave a cry. 'Horses,' they warned. Warriors woke to weapons, and raced to ramparts. The night could not have been darker; there was no moon and few stars. Titoko climbed the watch-tower, Kimball close behind. 'What horses?' Titoko shouted at the sentinels.

'On the road,' they reported.

'Where?'

'Here,' said a brisk British voice outside the fortress. 'Titoko?'

Titoko peered into the night, and saw nothing.

'Titoko?' the voice asked again. It seemed thirty paces off, perhaps less.

'Who is that?' Titoko asked.

'Your foe,' the voice said. 'My white flag cannot be seen. I think dark a wiser protection.'

'Colonel Whitmore?' Titoko asked.

'The same,' the voice said.

The night grew quieter.

'What do you want, Whitmore?'

'You most of all,' Whitmore said.

'My head?' Titoko asked.

Whitmore sighed. 'I too find bounties distasteful.'

'Where is Kepa?'

'Not many miles from here.'

'Would he say the same?'

'I know him eager to march. My word is his.'

'The worse for him, then,' Titoko said.

'It need not be,' Whitmore argued. 'We could all yet see sense.'

'Your sense?'

225

'Common sense, Titoko. Your fortress promises to make many widows.'

'It is not meant to make friends,' Titoko said.

'This campaign is a graveyard of good men in more ways than one,' Whitmore went on. 'Major von Tempsky, alas, is no more. Colonel McDonnell, though alive, appears to wish he were not. I am talking of reputations left ruin.'

'Yours?'

'Even yours,' Whitmore predicted. 'It may finally be said that success swelled your head. That this was blind folly, and reaching too far.'

'I hear you, Whitmore.'

'And I you, Titoko. We are neither of us fools.'

'Have you spoken, Whitmore?'

'As one wearied man of war to another. I came to find the warrior who not long since talked peace. He who smashed weapons and preached kindness to orphans.'

'The warrior you wish?'

'Just so,' Whitmore said.

'The fool is dead,' Titoko claimed.

'I sorrow, Titoko, not just for brave men fallen, but for brave men who must.'

'Begin praying for them, Colonel Whitmore,' Titoko said.

'Let me be blunt, Titoko. Do you wish Wanganui?'

'I am not saying I do,' Titoko said. 'I am not saying I do not.'

'But you wish us in suspense?'

'I wish you no comfort,' Titoko agreed.

'Peace is not an impossibility. Were you to end menace, and surrender some ground, even vengeful colonists might see talking of terms as no mortal sin.'

'Surrender ground, Colonel Whitmore?'

'This highway. Your stronghold.'

'Ah,' Titoko said.

'I need hardly tell you that your presence makes life difficult for Wanganui. The town is losing its hinterland, and too many people. Moreover, this coast of the colony has become impractical to administer. The road cannot be travelled, nor rivers safely crossed.'

'Is there more good news?' Titoko asked. 'You are not speaking of the travelling of the road, Colonel Whitmore, or the crossing of rivers.'

226

Whitmore was silent.

'I hear colonist grass,' Titoko persisted. 'I hear you no more.'

'Then hear another voice, Titoko. I have with me a man of goodwill, well known to you. Magistrate Booth.'

'Booth?' Titoko said. 'Here?'

'No soldier, Titoko. A man convinced of the virtue of a mission such as this. More, a man who was willing to ride here alone. I could not, of course, countenance so dangerous an initiative. Ignore me if you must, but Mr Booth deserves your respect.'

'When I have heard him,' Titoko said. 'Booth?'

'Titoko,' a new and shaky voice said.

'You have something to say?' Titoko asked.

Booth cleared his throat. 'Things have reached a lamentable pass since last we talked, Titoko.'

'The laments are yours,' Titoko said.

'There are graves the length of this coast. Not to speak of dismembered young fellows mouldering in fern. None deserved so frightful a death.'

'It is not for me to say alas, Mr Booth. What do you ask?'

'Do be a good fellow, Titoko, and stop all this fuss.'

'That is all?'

'No rebel has made his point more. News of your feats has spread far and wide. In London it has begun to be said that colonist avarice has made desperate bandits of the Maori. Such sentiments cannot but be heard more often. Even among fair-minded colonists you have won, if not sympathy, then a lively respect.'

'Are you such a colonist, Mr Booth?'

'I see anger where there was injustice. It is my regret that I fanned the flame. Confiscation of rebel lands was never a policy of my making. Reasonable voices are urging its end.'

'Reasonable voices, Mr Booth?'

'Shamed voices, Titoko. Christian voices.'

'It is queer, Mr Booth, that such voices are not to be heard until the sound of the gun.'

'With this visit I am trying to make amends, Titoko.'

'I try to hear you,' Titoko said.

'I see, if you do not, that this must end badly. No fortress lasts forever. No fortress can.'

'Go on, Mr Booth.'

'We have curbed wild men before, Titoko. It is still in our power to call them back from the pit.'

'You are making an offer?'

'Not at this juncture,' Booth confessed. 'It is not in my province.'

'Then why are you here?'

'I am thinking toward a gesture on your part, Titoko. An offer could well follow soon.'

'What gesture?'

'Give your word you will not breach Wanganui. That you will march no further. That is all.'

'You ask that?'

'Much could be forgotten. The climate would be auspicious for a fresh beginning. New outrages must foul the air more.'

Titoko was quiet.

'I can no longer plead with you as one churchman to another,' Booth persisted.

'That is true,' Titoko said.

'On the other hand, I recall your sermons. They thrilled even those to whom the Maori tongue was a mystery. Most to the point, they shone with compassion.'

'What is this to me now?' Titoko asked.

'I cannot believe you now devoid of charity. The town of Wanganui is in a pitiful state. Numbers destitute grow daily. There are even beggars to be seen. Is this what you wish?'

'It is not my wish, Mr Booth. It is war's.'

'Think again on that score too,' Booth urged. 'I have seen Colonel Whitmore training new and more reliable recruits. I have seen Kepa gathering fresh men. Not just his own tribesmen now, but others more distant, Maoris who see more mana in humbling the great and terrible Titokowaru than in racing to his side.'

'I hear threat, Mr Booth.'

'You hear grief, Titoko. Think. You may see a hill of colonist dead. There may be a Maori mound as large.'

Titoko was silent. Looking for weakness, Booth thought he had found it.

'In pity's name call a halt here,' he pleaded.

'You ask much again, and offer little, Mr Booth. As it was with your maps, now it is with war.'

228

'What is it you are saying?'

'I am saying no,' Titoko explained. His voice could have been louder.

'No?' Booth queried. His voice was small too.

'It is not my wish to tell you twice,' Titoko said.

'So I must return empty-handed?'

'As you came, Mr Booth.'

There was a pause. Horses shuffled distantly in the dark.

'May I risk a further question?' Booth called.

'If it is your pleasure, Mr Booth.'

'Does the American rogue persist at your side?'

'What is it to you, Mr Booth?'

'Bent could yet be helpful,' Booth suggested. 'It is thought more and more, in your favour, that you may not be held responsible for your more scandalous deeds.'

'Why not?' Titoko bristled.

'The fact of the matter, Titoko, is that in their despair colonists still cannot bring themselves to believe that simple tribesmen alone have administered their whipping. They look for larger cause. They see such in Bent. It might help matters, now or later, if you confessed yourself foully misled.'

'And gave him up?'

'As token of your sincerity. Bent might be of much use in arriving at an accommodation with the colonial authorities. There is still time, I should like to think I have not heard your last word.'

'I should like to think I have,' Titoko told him.

'No doubt. But there is no shame in second thoughts.'

'Ride home, Mr Booth, and take Colonel Whitmore. I promise a safe hour before I order men in pursuit.'

'Thank you,' Booth ventured. 'That is a beginning.'

'That is the end,' Titoko said.

Horses were then heard moving south on the Queen's road. The men of the garrison remained at their posts until the last colonist sound faded. It seemed Titoko was never going to speak; Kimball, on the other hand, felt need of neighbourly conversation.

'You don't want the town anyway,' he said.

'No?' Titoko said.

'Where's the skin off your arse? You could give them Wanganui.'

229

'Better you,' Titoko said in poor temper.

Kimball thought not to crowd his luck; he tacked home to Rihi by way of waves of warriors rising stiffly from battle positions.

'What does tonight mean?' she asked.

'Nothing fancy,' he said.

If Titoko had second thoughts, he was near with them next day. Kimball was returned to armoury duty, and the making of shot to see out a summer siege. The problem was that siege failed to begin. December came. Whitmore went. Fresh Maori hue and cry on the far coast of the island required subduing. With Whitmore went most of his constabulary, and much of his militia.

Titoko again failed to share his thoughts, unless with Big.

For Big vanished between one day and the next. No explanation was made by Titoko. Some said they had heard Big's horse galloping in a northern direction before daybreak; others said west. None said south. Either way, he was gone.

Wanganui's defenders were thinned. Whitmore had left the town largely in the care of Major Kepa, his tribesmen and allies. Also, said spies, the captain called Flukes, his wound healed, was again to be seen strutting above the town's stockades and hounding men within. He appeared to have charge of the whites who remained resident. Patrols were never pushed more than a mile or two toward peril and showed pace only when pointed home to Wanganui. Nervous sentries were shooting each other at night. Others were drunkenly feuding with knives, doing Titoko's work for him.

Tales of the town's weakness warmed Toa. 'Wanganui waits for us,' he confided to Kimball.

'Tell Titoko,' Kimball said.

'You might tell him better. Let it be your thought.'

'To fight Kepa?'

'Kepa might again see wisdom in withdrawing to let colonists fight their own battle.'

'And might not.'

'Kepa has his own need.'

'So have I,' Kimball said.

'His is still to command colonists.'

'Mine's getting your daughter to Maine.'

'Talk of Maine was to win peace,' Toa said with disgust.

'I've lied myself out. Now I reckon I mean it.'

'Then you would do well to think Flukes,' Toa urged slyly.

Kimball was quiet.

'There is no Whitmore to push men between Flukes and your bullet.'

'There's bounty-hunting bastards as bad,' Kimball argued, though other faces were faint.

'That is fair-minded of you,' Toa said. 'Yet with Flukes gone to your gun the interest of others may wane.'

Kimball slept little beside Rihi that night; his heaving and sighing owed nothing to lust. Rihi's complaints grew louder as the night lengthened. Sometime after midnight he dressed, gathered his carbine and cartridges and began to depart before the twins made a chorus.

'Where are you going now?' she yawned.

'Just looking out the way to Eastport,' he said.

It could even be true. He certainly meant to be first to catch Titoko's ear when he woke. Titoko's tent sat solitary to the rear of the fortress. Kimball dozed out the rest of the night beside a smouldering fire nearby. Sometime toward dawn he woke to stealthy movement, a shadow. Thinking an intruder afoot in the fortress, perhaps an assassin, he lifted and trained his carbine. Seconds later he lowered it. The shadow was womanly; it disappeared under the flap of Titoko's tent with no sound. A footloose female leaving her snoring husband's bed for Titoko's wasn't one of life's larger surprises. What then happened, however, was. Hardly a minute had gone before the flap of the tent lifted again; the shadow was speeding back the way she had come. Either Titoko was a faster shot than anyone knew, or he was ailing something wicked.

Dark lightened; dawn came. Titoko rose into the morning.

'What do you want?' he asked.

'A hearing,' Kimball said.

'Begin,' Titoko said irritably.

'The way I see it,' Kimball said, 'this war's going no place.'

'And you wish to?'

'One way or the other.'

'Toward Wanganui?' Titoko asked.

'I guess,' Kimball admitted.

231

'You have been talking to Toa.'

'If you don't want Wanganui, why are we here?'

'Did I say I didn't want it?'

'I haven't heard you say you did.'

'If I need it I wish it as fruit starved on the tree,' Titoko said. 'If we dig at roots here, dig at roots there, it will soon have no nourishment.'

'Maybe. But we're eating ourselves out of victuals too.'

'What I don't wish is Kepa.'

'I notice,' Kimball said.

'Tell Toa that I have heard his complaint.'

'There's more than Toa grumbling.'

'Many?'

'Too many.'

Titoko was thoughtful. 'What would satisfy them?'

'A job of work.'

'Is manning this fortress not such?'

'Not when there's only flies to fight off,' Kimball said.

There was a call from the watch-tower. 'A rider,' the sentinel reported.

'North or south?' Titoko asked.

'North,' the sentinel said. With wonder he added, 'Big is back.'

Big was gaunt and his horse lean. Titoko took him to his tent. Eavesdroppers were warned away. Warriors were silent, hoping for a whisper from the tent to reach them. It was hours before Big was free to leave the tent to look out food, and nightfall before he confided in those fit to hear.

As Big told it, Whitmore's departure had left Titoko puzzling. It might mean that other once powerful tribes were also thinking to rally against the colonists. Titoko had heard rumour of sympathy from tried and unbeaten rebels camping armed in the heart of the island; Big had been sent to divine whether such rumour was correct. He pushed his horse across mountain range and river, and a hundred miles of forest. Mount Taranaki was soon long behind. Steaming volcanoes grew to the east, and bitter desert patched with thorn and spiny grass. At the end of the journey, before he had breath, he faced a large assembly of old rebels. Some were welcoming, many not. They were men who had lost land, but not a good opinion of themselves, in battling Britain's best regiments. After six sluggish years that good opinion was shaken. While they dwelled in retirement, trading with colonists outside their forest sanctuaries, a warrior of lowly tribe had begun to make them look small.

'Who is this Titokowaru?' they asked Big.

'A Maori who says no to colonists,' he told them.

'What is his authority?'

'Scores of colonist dead, and many more fled.'

'But who?' they persisted. 'Who was his father, his grandfather? What is his warrior line?'

'Are these things of importance?' Big asked.

'The man is an upstart,' he was told.

'Who of you', Big asked, 'has won back one colonist acre?'

The challenge made him no friends, but left a long quiet. The assembly grew angrier as the days passed, and other retired warriors rode in to hear out Titoko's emissary and have their considerable say.

'Titoko has shown what can be,' Big told them.

'What, friend, is that?'

'Colonists crouched in their ports. Perhaps soon leaving this land to live in their own.'

A shaky, white-haired chief stood with Bible in hand. 'I wish to speak', this Christian said, 'of custom long thought forsaken. Is that which we hear true?'

Big was in difficulty. 'Titoko', he said, 'thinks beliefs best which sorrow colonists.'

'You talk eating of men.'

'I talk eating the enemy.'

'Brothers in Christ,' the old man objected.

'And soldiers of Satan,' Big said.

'I thought never again to hear it,' the Christian said.

'You hear it now,' Big said, 'as you did from your fathers.'

The old man sighed. 'My ears say that you have no shame.'

'Your ears hear a warrior,' Big insisted.

'What of Titokowaru?'

'The order was his.'

'When punishment falls, those serving him must answer to the greatest chief of all, our saviour Jesus Christ, and trust to His mercy.'

'What war did he win?' Big asked.

The Christian, deciding not to hear, sat with injury done.

Big appealed to those about, 'There is more to this war than meat.'

One famed chief, a man of comfortable girth, now in receipt of colonist favours, thought to argue. 'You have borne here the tale of a man who takes no risks.'

'And therefore wins battles.'

'Of small character,' the new chief said.

'Of good character,' Big said.

'I see smoke faint in fern.'

'Flame is your wish?'

'It would be of interest,' the man said.

'How much flame?'

'Wanganui.'

'That is another thing,' Big said.

'That is correct. It is a town.'

'It is also a Maori the colonists call Major Kepa.'

'And Titokowaru fears Kepa?'

'He fears himself more.'

'Kepa? What does he fear?'

'Not Maori bleeding Maori.'

'Your answer is interesting.'

'Also true. Kepa risks losing profit from colonists and land taken behind British guns. Most of all losing the smile of the Queen.'

'He is better Titokowaru's problem.'

'Is that an honourable answer?' Big asked.

'A wise one. Is Titokowaru's wish that we war with Kepa too?'

'Titoko's wish is that you listen.'

'Tell Titokowaru to show us Wanganui. Then we could well.'

'To learn?'

'To see the way the tree falls.'

At the end of the assembly, there was no rush to arms or faint promise of an uprising to draw off constabulary and militia from Titokowaru's lone war with the colony. It was merely agreed that Big had shown himself honest in debate, and deserved better than a return to Titokowaru with nothing in hand. Emissaries were therefore sent riding south to Kepa, asking him in the name of all Maori to stand aside and let Titokowaru fell colonists without further hindrance.

'That is all?' Demon asked.

'All,' Big said. 'The emissaries should have reached Kepa. Their horses were faster than mine, their trails better known.'

'What', Kimball asked, 'does Titoko think?'

Big shrugged.

Titoko was not seen that evening, nor most of the next day. In late afternoon he called others to him.

'There are those not happy to wait for Wanganui,' he announced.

'That might be said,' Toa answered cautiously.

'Do I hear others?' Titoko asked.

Big was quiet. Demon at last said, 'I am this way and that. I see this fortress ready. I also see their garrison small.'

'I see another of no faith,' Titoko said.

'Faith is not lacking,' Demon protested. 'Days may be. Whitmore could be back soon with numbers, and our chance gone.'

'You too would think to test Wanganui?'

'It could leave me more peaceful,' Demon allowed.

'In respect of my judgement?'

'That too,' Demon agreed.

'Then a raiding party is necessary,' Titoko decided.

'To Wanganui?' Demon asked.

'Surely within sight of its walls.'

'A challenge?'

'Made by you.'

'Me?' Demon asked with surprise.

'That is correct.'

'Why not Toa? It is his notion first.'

'You promise warriors less troublesome. Toa promises nothing.'

Toa, though his lips moved, failed to speak. Big, on the other hand, did. 'That is half the reason,' he judged. 'You wish to know Kepa's will.'

'That is correct,' Titoko said with calm.

The raiding party, with Demon at its head, rode out on a late December morning. The sea was bright, the land never greener. There were eighty riders, new men mixed with old campaigners. Big was left behind for his health and Toa for his humiliation. Kimball, on the other hand, was judged fit to pursue his difference with Flukes. A mile or two south, he pushed his horse alongside Demon's.

'Understand this,' Demon said. 'Our mission is to prove Titoko wise.'

'You're saying we're not serious?'

'I am saying we are,' Demon explained. He did not enlighten Kimball further.

'What if we're a success?'

'It will be Titoko's triumph.'

'And if we're not?'

'We, not he, will be seen makers of folly.'

'So Titoko wins either way?'

'As Toa surely cannot. Should Kepa stand aside, and let colonists alone war for Wanganui, who will hear his name shouted through the land?'

'It might make him happier.'

'Not Titoko,' Demon said.

They crossed gully, dark river and gorge; loud parrots lifted from overhead trees. Now and then Demon detailed men to remain in place as guards on the trail.

'Don't we need them?' Kimball asked.

'They may be useful survivors,' Demon explained.

'And not the rest of us?'

Demon shrugged. 'Who knows?'

'You're not hopeful,' Kimball said with foreboding.

'Whatever happens, and whatever not, Titoko must have warriors to man his fortress. Also, if needed, to build it bolder.'

'Meaning he's in love with it,' Kimball said.

Demon shrugged. 'As a woman.'

'There's none had him tighter.'

'That is your thought?'

'Lately,' Kimball confessed.

Demon kept his to himself.

The miles left to Wanganui were journeyed slowly. At dusk they saw the river with a last gleam of light, and lamplit dwellings above the port. They also saw walls, and heard bugles. As night became blacker, the lights of the town thinned. Finally there was just the twinkle of a steamer standing off in the river, a lantern swinging on a moored schooner, and a glow from militia redoubts.

'With light,' Demon promised, 'we learn more.'

Kimball didn't doubt it. 'Whether Whitmore's still gone?'

'Whether Kepa is not,' Demon said.

There were two empty farmhouses outside Wanganui's northern defences, both in distant view of sentries on dawn watch. Demon sent men with matches to move on these dwellings before dark was gone. The rest were ranged nearby, with cover and height.

Fire took the farmhouses at first light. Martial noises were soon heard. One blazing farmhouse might be the work of God; two had to be Titoko's. Uncertainty followed on the uproar within the stockades. It was all of ten minutes before a gate opened and the first horseman appeared. Kimball borrowed Demon's binoculars. The horseman was Flukes. He was in argument with others to his rear. Then others began braving the gate. More minutes passed before a muster was plain.

'No Kepa,' Kimball said with interest.

'Not yet,' Demon said.

Made bolder by the absence of Maori musketry, Flukes' troop pushed their horses into a canter. They had a thousand yards of pasture and cropland to cross. The distance was enough to string Flukes' men out considerably. First came Flukes, Sergeant Tonks, a couple of corporals, and a clutch of constables. Then for fifty yards there were strays in single file. Finally, beginning to bunch, there were men with misgivings about the enterprise, or with notional horses, or with both. By the time Flukes was in range of Demon's marksmen, the troop was strung out for two hundred yards between the fast-riding men and those to the rear. A minute later Flukes and his advance group were under Demon's guns. Frustrated Kimball sighted and resighted his carbine as Flukes began moving past. Demon refused the order to fire.

'Why not?' Kimball whispered.

'Because the last shall be first,' Demon insisted, 'and the first last.'

'You're talking Flukes,' Kimball protested.

'Ambush wisdom,' Demon said.

'Flukes is their captain.'

'Your way we lower only men to the fore, while the fearful flee home. My way, we lower many more. Flukes must turn back to help.'

Flukes passed without misfortune, and then strays. When the rearmost riders jogged into range Demon lifted his arm. He was a long time letting it fall.

The first volley did considerable damage, mostly to horses. They tumbled and screamed, men spilling too. Less maimed horses, losing their riders, began sprinting free. A second volley aggravated the confusion. There were more horses expiring, and stunned and bloody militia standing to shoot. Further shot struck among them as warriors began firing at will. Constables not staggering away made themselves small, shooting blind from behind their perishing beasts.

Meanwhile Flukes wheeled his advance guard, ordering horsemen back toward their embattled fellows. Horses had no mind in the matter; men, for a time, did. Flukes swung a sabre, urging them on. It was a minute or more before he had men in presentable formation. He fanned them out in two wings, and rode hard at the centre, pushing uphill toward the smoke and flash of the ambushers. Demon's marksmen would soon be shooting point-blank. With that thought, Demon gave the order to reserve shot until ordered. Kimball watched Flukes close with his carbine. A hundred paces, eighty; Flukes kept coming on.

Then a warrior let his gaze wander back toward Wanganui, and gave out a cry. Surging through the garrison gate were mounted men by the score, mostly Maori, and behind one of their own. Without tunic and insignia, a white shirt billowing behind him, Major Kepa still looked a leader. His horse was making short work of the ground, and his beefy lieutenants were riding hard too. Behind them more and more tribesmen, mounted and afoot, thronged from the garrison. The Wanganui plan was now clear. Flukes' mission had been to draw fire; Kepa's was to kill it.

With Flukes rearing to the right, Kepa looming to the left, Demon found only one order useful. 'Retire on the volley,' he said.

A warrior in early flight crashed into Kimball as he fired; his shot travelled well to Flukes' west.

The rest of the volley did no more than slow Flukes as

Demon's men made for their horses. One thing was proved. Wanganui's defences were on the mean side of middling.

By noon they had made most of the distance home. Wary of ambush, Kepa and Flukes failed to press their rear. Demon's men rested their rumps and watered their horses when he judged it safe. Metal was cut from legs, arms and a thigh, and wounds bandaged. Two warriors whose horses had been shot away were counted lost to bounty-hunters. With regrets uttered, Demon propped himself against the same tree as Kimball. 'We know all we need about Kepa,' he judged.

'I had him all but salted down,' Kimball grieved.

Demon's gaze was distant. 'Not Kepa,' he said. 'Never Kepa.'

'Flukes,' Kimball explained.

'You're telling me something,' Demon decided.

'Piss on ambush wisdom,' Kimball said.

There was a long pause. Demon took note of his companion's face.

'Shit on it,' he said.

Twenty-one

The new year dawned foul; storm after storm struck from the west. Trees lost leaves and limbs and finally fell; creeks became gusting rivers. Afoot in the uproar, Titoko found drainage of the fortress site considerably less to his liking. He ordered out men. Waist-deep in water, warriors struggled along trenches to find tunnels sloppy with silt and ramparts eroded. A bucket brigade was busy, and soon toilers with shovels. Discontent made no showing as repair went on. Weather-lashed warriors understood that they were labouring for their lives, and by nightfall most found bed a black grave. Then storm subsided to a daylong dry gale; finally Titoko's people woke to bright, still and humid morning. If some thought the return of summer licence for an easy life, they were wrong. Titoko saw even less excuse for slacking. Ramparts were reshaped and reinforced with brush bound into clay. Palisades were curtained afresh and spoiled foodstuff replenished. The crescent moons of the fortress frontage again hid nothing feeble.

Titoko made daily inspections. It seemed he might have another month to fault his mistress. Meanwhile he was seen with no other.

Having found a fight he could win, Whitmore left enough graves on the far coast to impress his superiors and returned to Wanganui. Men placed to observe the port reported ships unloading men and munitions, and a new town of tents rising behind Wanganui's bastions. Then matters became mysterious. Whitmore took ship up the coast, bypassing Titoko's fortress, and set foot on land lost to the colony. He lit no fires in the manner of Maori rebels. With a few dozen armed constabulary at heel he seldom halted long enough to hoist the Union Jack.

Titoko's scouts shadowed him as he moved. First he pushed north to Taranaki and struck through forest to the site of The Beak. There he spent a long day thinking on Titoko's palisades, and burying charred bones. He ordered palisades axed and the fortress razed, down to the last splinter, before he departed. Then he rallied his men and marched south to the site of the Battle of Strewn Whites and spent a long day there too. Decomposing colonists were dragged from scrub and interred under cairns and white crosses. Otherwise he walked the ground without pleasure, shaking his head and shouting at subordinates. Again he looked thoughtfully at the ramparts and palisades which had impoverished his manpower. He clambered into trenches and climbed wearily out. Finally, as at The Beak, he ordered the place destroyed. The remains of the fortress burned nightlong, the glow seen across miles of countryside and coast, as far south as Titoko's new quarters. With no casualty to count, Whitmore and his men sailed home to Wanganui to report triumph.

'Taking empty fortresses?' Demon said. 'What game is this?'

'Fighting lost battles,' Big said, 'and looking for lies.'

'There is more,' Demon decided.

'They wish nothing left,' Titoko said. 'No trace, no memory. Also of us.'

'You think that?' Toa asked.

'I know it,' Titoko said.

There was silence for a time.

'We are thinking to hear you,' Big said, 'and are not sure we do.'

'We must make this week of the warrior harder to forget.'

'With who to hear us?'

Titoko shrugged. 'I think of the far side of Saturday, of those Maori who make no move to help and will live to lament it. They will have sons.'

'What would you wish said?'

'That we did not fail brother Maori. That brother Maori failed us.'

'What of those serving Kepa and the Queen?'

'We make it more bitter for them to answer their sons.'

'Your meaning is not plain,' Demon objected.

'Let their orders be Whitmore's. Let them see themselves small.'

'I still look into muddy water,' Demon protested.
'The war I wish', Titoko explained, 'is no war of warriors.'
'You must see that wish vain.'
'Kepa has twice left the field to colonist commanders.'
'Because he saw folly.'
'Because he was not his own man,' Titoko said.
'And you are?'
'When not with a woman,' Titoko said with conviction.
'Amen,' Big whispered to Kimball.

By the end of January Colonel Whitmore's sorties into abandoned fortresses had surely begun to unsettle his paymasters. They must have asked for something more stirring. For Whitmore put out stronger patrols, and then deployed road-builders to ensure a more tolerable route to Titoko's fortress. Titoko thought not to delay the work, or Whitmore, and discouraged sniping. Now and then Whitmore rode out to inspect their labour, also to view Titoko's fortress from far. Titoko viewed Whitmore. No greetings were exchanged. Whitmore was busy with his hands as he lectured his retinue on the mysterious character of the fortress. After pointing west and east, he clapped his hands together, as if trying to crush the place into friendlier shape.

'What do you think he looks for?' Titoko asked Kimball.

'Trouble,' Kimball suggested.

'Trick,' Titoko said.

'What trick would that be?' Kimball asked.

'He has been to The Beak and seen the ruse there. He has been to the place of the Battle of Strewn Whites and seen the ruse there. He now looks to the next.'

'Is there?'

'Surely,' Titoko said.

'I must have missed it,' Kimball decided.

'The trick this time is that there is none,' Titoko explained. 'This fortress is what it says. A fortress.'

'You think he won't figure that?'

'Not on the first day. Perhaps on the third.'

'What happens meantime?'

'Melancholy,' Titoko said.

On the last day of January Whitmore marched in earnest. Titoko's impressed scouts tallied two thousand men moving, a force three times greater than any colonist army seen. Squadrons of cavalry protected their flanks. Ten much-drilled divisions of armed constabulary, each of seventy men, were on show, and then company after company of colonist militia, followed by Kepa's brown hundreds. Finally there were teams of oxen dragging drays piled with provisions and horses hauling gun-carriages. After long weeks of waiting, it seemed Whitmore was biting the bait. Titoko's four hundred were drilled for the last time and refreshed in their duties. All but a few pickets were called back to the fortress. Those left outside were told to bury themselves in growth, let Whitmore's skirmishers pass without challenge, and use their eyes and ears before returning to report.

On the first day of February Whitmore's force camped within two miles of the fortress. At daybreak next morning the advance guard of the colonist column came into view. Cavalry began to parade at five hundred paces. Shot warned the horsemen to keep their distance. As their mounts reared they were even more of a mind to. Whitmore and his aides took up position in a shady grove of trees. There they were joined by a dour and resplendent Major Kepa. His womenfolk must have been busy; his uniform glowed with more braid than a British general, and his hands were white-gloved. Soon gunners and guns arrived. Much discussion followed, with use of telescopes and field glasses. At length something was decided. There was shouting and movement. Officers cantered this way and that.

Titoko, in the watch-tower, took Demon's telescope.

Kepa had ridden out of the confusion to take up a position to Whitmore's right. An assortment of Wanganui warriors were moving with him; but not warriors alone. The men falling in behind him were of mixed colour, as many with white faces as brown. Captains, one of them Flukes, arrived to flank Kepa. To show whose word prevailed on Whitmore's right they saluted their commander. Even the colonist army seemed awed.

Titoko saw what he had to, until he believed it, and returned the telescope to Demon.

'Tomorrow he could sit in Whitmore's saddle,' Titoko said.

Demon shrugged. 'Colonists need him more than he needs them.'

'So who needs us?' Titoko asked.

No one in the watch-tower chanced an answer.

'It had to happen,' Demon said presently.

'Not today,' Titoko said.

He lowered himself from the watch-tower and left observation to Demon. His order for the morning was for a score of marksmen to maintain a weak fire. Whitmore's skirmishers were just to be teased. 'We need them nearer,' he said.

With more shouting, echoing down the ranks through sergeants and corporals, the army shook itself out. Lines of skirmishers formed, and behind them men with picks and shovels. By noon Whitmore's saps were within two hundred paces. Parties of colonists and tribesmen leapt from trench to trench to take over the digging. By late afternoon the saps were an easy pistol shot from the south face of the fortress. Behind them, guns and mortars were heaved into place. Titoko's interest was still on the wane; he climbed to the watch-tower only when called.

'They make no move to encircle,' Demon reported.

'No,' Titoko said.

'There must be a reason,' Demon persisted.

'This time they trust nothing,' Titoko said.

'Then it is working,' Demon said.

'Well,' Titoko agreed.

He ordered marksmen reduced to a dozen.

Finally a man left behind colonist lines scrambled back to the fortress to report. He had eavesdropped on talk between Colonel Whitmore and his senior officers. Some had pleaded for investment of the fortress before nightfall. Whitmore's angry answer was no. He thought he had observed rifle-pits to the rear of the fortress. They might be significant of desperate proceedings in store. 'It is all too probable, gentlemen,' he told them, 'that this fortress is yet another fake. Look how little fire is pushed from it. Where are Titoko's massed rifles?'

'There is only one way to learn,' Major Kepa said. 'Attack.'

'On my order, at my pace,' Whitmore said.

'The worm's?' Kepa inquired.

'That which sanity asks,' Whitmore said.

'That which the enemy,' Kepa said.

Whitmore ignored all of such mood. It remained his view that battle had best begin the next morning. Positions taken up through the day would be held through the night. Soon after daybreak bombardment of the fortress would begin. Field guns and mortars would shell it for a full hour. The moment bombardment finished, the fortress would be rushed. Warriors left living would be slow manning their parapets and soon overpowered. Whitmore's centre would close with the fortress, keeping pace with Major Kepa and his right wing. This could be taken as meaning that the right wing would clash first with the fortress, that Kepa had the work. The left would be held in reserve, ready to fill gaps should such appear in the course of assault.

The news was not cowing.

'Gaps?' Demon said. 'There will be but one, where an army has gone.'

Titoko turned to Big. 'Are we to kill them all?' he asked wearily.

'Even Kepa,' Big promised. 'Their battle plan could have been made by you.'

'It was,' Titoko said.

Most things considered, he might have raised a smile.

An hour before sunset impatient gunnery officers thought to rehearse their weapons before battle began. Titoko's fortress was given its first test. Observing the preparations, he ordered all but a few warriors into bunkers. First mortars thumped out ranging shots. Their shells played with terrain outside the palisades while gunners struggled to right their elevation. Then six-pounder Armstrong guns began banging. One overhead shell chipped a palisade before whining away; a second sank into soft earth at the centre of the fortress and, after a hiccup of protest, was not heard from again. Those following also failed to make an alarming impression. A wealth of dirt rose, but no warrior cry. Finally a rider from Whitmore began shouting at gunners to stop heartening the enemy. Warriors climbed from the bunkers, carbines in hand, to report little damage and no death. Underground they had suffered no more than cramp, and seen only wisps of earth falling. The superstitious were saying that Titoko had but to turn his blind eye on Whitmore to silence colonist gunners. Finally Titoko ordered those with no duties from the fortress. For warrior constancy, he wished women, children and the old safe in nearby forest before dusk. This meant Rihi, Wiremu and Meri. Carrying his daughter and son, with Rihi bent under their goods to the rear, Kimball hurried down a covered walkway to the creek; he forded it and set his family on high ground among trees. Other women and children, along with elderly warriors, were fighting for the best locations from which to view affairs of the morning.

'I'll be back to fetch you tomorrow,' he told his wife.

'When?' she asked.

'Soon as things go quiet.'

'When will that be?'

'Maybe an hour after the first shot,' he said.

'Then what?'

'We pick and choose our ship,' he promised.

When he returned to the fortress the sky was red with sunset. Toa was at Titoko's side in the watch-tower. Colonist fires burned by the score in the distance. Breeze carried the smell of bacon, coffee and beans. There was a cease-fire of sorts as food was consumed. Now and then one of Whitmore's men shouted an obscene challenge at those in the fortress. They were answered with silence. In frustration their language grew fouler.

'We have had our feuds,' Toa was saying to Titoko.

'We have,' Titoko said.

'All between us is now forgotten,' Toa promised.

'To the good, cousin,' Titoko said.

'I see fate in this.'

'Fate, cousin?'

'What else is at work here?'

'Me,' Titoko suggested.

'Then let it be said that I see the greatest of warrior generals. I see his greatest triumph growing. The gentlest of my grandchildren will boast I was with you this eve.'

'And tomorrow? Or is this your speech of farewell?'

'Never,' Toa vowed. 'I say only that I mean not to close my eyes. I wish this night to last.'

'See those on watch remain as wakeful.'

'They will hear my tongue,' Toa promised, and left.

Titoko looked at the fires burning outside the fortress and listened to the loud curses of men doomed. 'Answer me, grandson,' he said. 'Is this what I wished?'

His voice was cold.

'Mostly,' Kimball said.

'Why, then, is it now not?'

'Now you've got it?'

'Just so. What does this tell you?'

'That there's no pleasing some.'

'It tells me that the next world might make more sense.'

'The next?' Kimball asked with unease.

'I see none in this.'

'Tonight,' Kimball protested, 'is no time for talk like that.'

'When better?' Titoko said. 'Tomorrow the tale is yours to be told.'

'Already?'

'The better for saying I did what I must.'

'If that's the way you want it,' Kimball promised.

'The rest is best left,' Titoko explained.

'The rest?'

'Britain's regiments back. And more Kepas, and more.'

'And only one Titokowaru?'

'My eye sees no other.'

'You have never spoken defeat before.'

'Because it was not to be spoken,' Titoko said.

'You always knew?'

'From Monday.'

Kimball was a long time thinking, longer speaking. 'Holy shit,' he said.

Stars grew brighter as cooking fires cooled. Titoko ended his silence.

'Tell me,' he asked. 'Must tomorrow come?'

'Unless you settle with the sun. You arranged the rest.'

'So it must be Friday already.'

'How do you see Saturday?'

'I don't,' Titoko said.

'Maybe you've been too long on the labouring oar,' Kimball argued. 'I never seen a man who needed bed more.'

'Strange you mention it,' Titoko said.

They clambered down the watch-tower to solid ground. Titoko walked toward his tent. Warriors not manning ramparts and bastions were asleep in battle bunkers. Titoko's tent was the only habitation left above ground.

'Whisper in my ear after the middle of the night,' Titoko

ordered. 'If Kepa has a warrior surprise, it must be before dawn. Thereafter Whitmore's orders will prevail. Bombardment, then blind attack.'

'It doesn't bear thinking about,' Kimball said.

'It must,' Titoko argued.

'You're telling me something,' Kimball decided.

'That I am not to be troubled. Tell Toa I need no sentry.'

'None?'

'None. You alone disturb me. On no account Toa.'

'What if there's alarm?'

'If others cannot war without me, they must learn.'

'That sounds like you're quitting.'

'No more than needed,' Titoko said.

Most of the fortress was dark; oil lamps and candles burned below ground. Kimball found his way to Toa slowly, tripping on earth upturned by colonist shelling, and passed on Titoko's wish.

'No sentry?' Toa said.

'And quiet.'

'This is not Titoko of old.'

'He's the best judge of what he needs,' Kimball said.

Titoko surely was.

For the first of the night there was no serious shooting and little of it lucky. Toward midnight rifles began to discharge with more sting, backed by excitable cries. The most troubling flashes were to the fore of Kepa's position. They said Kepa was pushing men from their saps to draw fire and test their spirit. One guess was that he was hoping to tire and unnerve the garrison with gunshot and abuse. Another was that he hoped to steal a march on Whitmore and wrestle a rampart from Titoko before the morning's bombardment. A third guess was a feint, with Kepa about to test the fortress elsewhere. The problem was how much firepower was needed to halt him. If rifles were called up along the south face of the fortress Whitmore would have warning of his difficulties with daylight. On the other hand a weak reply might give ground to Kepa. Demon and Big weighed one guess against another; Toa backed and filled.

Meanwhile a rifleman arrived from the palisade line to report. 'There is a colonist voice calling,' he said. 'It asks for Bent to be heard.'

Kimball crawled up to the palisade line. Shot cracked into timber overhead. Finally he chanced a word. 'Hello?' he shouted.

There was an order given on the far side of the palisades. Bang and flash thinned.

'Bent?' a familiar voice asked.

'Me,' Kimball agreed.

'This is the last we're likely to talk,' Flukes said.

'I reckon too,' Kimball said.

'I wanted you to know', Flukes bragged, 'that I've as good as got a hundred pounds in my hip pocket.'

'I'd keep your cash in a bucket,' Kimball advised.

'A bucket?'

'The one you're due to kick,' Kimball explained.

'Still the comical bugger, aren't you, Bent?'

'Still the horse's arse, aren't you, Corporal?'

'Captain,' Flukes said.

'Corporal,' Kimball said.

Flukes tried a shot in the direction of Kimball's voice. He missed by a Maine mile. A dozen other shots hit in hard behind. Kimball thought to suspend hostilities.

A more vexing problem was that Kepa was still owling around outside the palisades. 'The fortress must be alerted,' Toa said. 'Titoko must be woken and told.'

'He says not until after the middle of the night,' Kimball announced.

'Which is near.'

'Not yet. And I alone disturb him.'

'You alone?'

'He said on no account you.'

'Why not?'

Kimball shrugged. 'Orders are orders.'

'Of a queer kind.' Toa was all suspicion. 'Did he say Demon was not to disturb him, or Big?'

'Not in those words,' Kimball had to admit.

'Why do you think that might have been?'

'Because he knew they would not,' Kimball suggested.

'Holding this fortress comes first,' Toa said. 'You have a duty.'

'To see Titoko is peaceful,' Kimball argued.

'Let it be on my head,' Toa said with grievance. 'Why is it always for me to anger Titoko?'

Big, nearby, thought to suggest, 'Because you have the gift.'

Toa ignored him. 'Come,' he said to Kimball. 'You alone shall wake him and I alone shall address him.'

To see their way to the rear of the fortress, Toa carried a sputtering lantern. They walked in its shy glow; shouts continued to mount outside the fortress, and palisades were tipped with light as firearms flared. Finally they arrived at Titoko's tent. Kimball stopped.

'Go on,' Toa urged.

Kimball lifted the flap of the tent. Toa raised his lantern. For a moment nothing made sense. Then too much did. Aside from his lean old legs, little of Titoko was on show. This was because there was a shiny brown back rising and falling above him. Titoko, beneath, was a long way from war. The curving back belonged a woman. The owner of the back turned her face into the lantern's light. It had to be Hine, and was.

Toa's howl, long to be recalled, largely by those who never heard it, lifted high into the night. Other things moved slowly. Hine uncoupled and covered her lower parts with a blanket. Titoko calmly raised himself on an elbow. Toa's reason for sorrow remained of uncommon size.

'This,' Toa stuttered.

'This,' Titoko sighed.

'And tonight,' Toa said.

'You are soon to the point,' Titoko said.

Though he wavered, it seemed Toa was not to strangle Hine or strike Titoko. To Kimball he said, 'Fetch Demon. Fetch Big. Fetch all with the stomach.'

The message Kimball took away made him a messenger worth shooting. There was only one language useful. 'The war's fucked,' he told those entitled to know.

There was a quick council, the most warlike Kimball had ever watched. Lesser warriors were warned away while battle line was drawn between their commanders. On one side was Titoko; on the other almost everyone. Two weak lanterns lit stricken faces. Demon could not have been more downcast;

Big could not bring himself to speak. No one was heard more often than Toa. Hine sat defiantly apart while her husband raged.

'You asked custom of us,' Toa said.

'True,' Titoko said.

'You asked tribute to the war gods again.'

'That also is true,' Titoko agreed.

'You even asked man-eating.'

'As all here know.'

'Yet you yourself did not partake.'

'For reason made known.

'Or because you did not believe in it?'

'I still carry no weapon in war. I hear no complaint that I order killing.'

'I ask what you believe, and what you do not.'

'I am not sure I hear you, cousin. I surely partook of your wife because I believed in her.'

'The eve of fight?'

'As it would seem.'

'Not only custom, but sense, says men must be fresh for a fight. Not just humble warriors. War-leaders too.'

Titoko shrugged.

'So there is one warrior code for others, another for you. How else explain this?'

'Fate,' Titoko said.

'Come, cousin,' Toa said. 'Fate?'

'I thought to feud with it a little,' Titoko claimed.

'To tempt it?'

'To argue.'

To others assembled, Toa said, 'I trust all hear him plain.'

Reluctant nods here and there said that most did.

'I understand your grief, cousin,' Titoko said presently.

'It is more than a husband's grief,' Toa argued. 'It is more than adultery.'

Titoko did not disagree.

'It is tonight of our nights,' Toa said. 'A great army ranged against us, and victory in hand.'

'I hear you,' Titoko said.

'And this. How can it be?'

Titoko was in difficulty with an answer.

'You must have known that a fortress holds few secrets. You

251

must have known the chance of discovery great. Was it your wish?'

Titoko was mute.

'Was it?' Toa persisted.

Titoko shook his head.

'What does that mean?'

'It means', Titoko confessed, 'that you ask a fair question.'

'Who would risk all for a rogue's wriggle?' Toa taunted.

'The rogue who is wriggling,' Titoko said.

'Your answer is shameless.'

'My answer is mine,' Titoko said.

'More regret would be fitting,' Toa argued.

'I admit an unwise wriggle. What man cannot say the same?'

'But on the eve of battle?'

'Alas,' Titoko agreed.

Demon broke in. 'You could have waited.'

'I have,' Titoko said. 'And for what?'

Gunfire rose outside the fortress. Among other things it said morning was arriving sooner than helpful.

'You forgo trust,' Toa said finally. He turned to others. To Demon he said, 'Has Titokowaru's warrior word gone?'

Demon was some time answering. 'Gone,' he judged.

'Big?' Toa asked.

Big was even slower. 'Gone,' he said.

'Need we hear others?' Toa asked.

Others appeared to think not, though sighs were heard.

'There,' Toa said. 'To Kepa you may be worth one thousand pounds. To us, not a penny.'

Hine's voice rose. 'Wait,' she said.

'It is not for a disgraced woman to speak,' Toa told his wife.

'You wish to take Titoko's triumph,' she went on. 'You now have the chance.'

Toa was silent.

'Perhaps it was meant,' she persisted.

'Meant?'

'By those who work through Titoko. His gods.'

'In whom few believe. Perhaps not even he.'

'They have not failed us this far.'

'What are you telling us?' Toa mocked. 'That his gods were working through you?'

252

'It is not for me to say,' she answered modestly.

'There may be prettier reasons for faithless wriggling,' Toa said. 'I have not heard them.'

Demon weighed in. 'It is almost tomorrow,' he announced coolly.

'That is so,' Big said.

'Outside our palisades are two thousand men,' Demon said.

'What are you saying?' Toa asked.

'It is time for one voice. Perhaps for one word.'

'What word is that?'

'Fight,' Demon said.

'Or not?'

'Whose word must it be?' Demon asked.

With Titoko present, reply was difficult.

'It seems to be mine,' Toa said.

'And the word?'

Toa was slow to speak.

'Tonight cannot be secret,' Big said. 'Even poor-witted warriors will see much wrong. All will be troubled with thought of fatal omens. All will be fearful when Whitmore orders advance and Kepa attacks.'

'This', Toa told Titoko, 'is what you have brought us to.'

'The word?' Demon said with impatience. 'We have few hours of dark.'

'There is just one word possible,' Toa decided. 'That which is not victory, and that which is not defeat.'

'Withdrawal,' Big concluded.

'Before dawn,' Toa said.

'Outside this fortress,' Demon protested, 'we are fish in Kepa's net.'

'Within too,' Big said, 'with no Titoko to make it work.'

'And that is now impossible,' Toa said firmly. 'Who among you can trust the order of a man who fails to respect his own?'

'So it is over,' Big mourned. 'This fortress. All.'

Titoko sat alone. No one met his eye. No one tried.

'Let it empty within the hour,' Toa announced. 'Let departure begin.'

'Am I allowed voice?' Titoko asked.

'If it must be,' Toa sighed.

'Let most begin moving. Let women, children and the weak

253

be well served with rifles. But let there also be a firm rearguard to turn those who pursue.'

'What are you asking, cousin?'

'Carbine and cartridges,' Titoko said.

'At this late hour? You?'

'Also volunteers for such a rearguard.'

'Which you think to command?'

'I think to serve,' Titoko said.

'Remorse does not become you, cousin.'

'It may better my aim.'

'Has Titoko been heard?' Toa asked the assembly.

Voices agreed that Titoko had.

'Also his wish for volunteers to fight rearguard beside him?'

That wish, it was clear, had been heard too.

'Volunteers', Toa said, 'may now make themselves known.'

There was a silence. At length, in difficulty, Big stirred. 'I am such a volunteer,' he announced.

Demon was next to speak. 'And I,' he said.

'I wish those who have been through the fire,' Titoko said. 'Others can flee to their villages and deny knowing me. I wish only Monday's warriors, those of the seventy with me from the beginning, those who now know death nothing to lament.'

'Men of despair?' Toa asked.

'Those who know their best fate is to be hunted as pig.'

'Their worst?'

'Not to be thought.'

There was a second silence.

'That must mean me,' Kimball said.

Titoko thought for some seconds before his reply.

'It must,' he agreed.

Titoko finished with forty, all of them familiar, none of them feeble. Two hours before dawn Toa left the fortress with three hundred or more warriors; they were to gather up women and children as they pitched into the dark and picked their way to high forest. For those of the rearguard there was no chance for farewells. Titoko ordered them into ramparts and rifle-pits to keep up fire from the fortress so long as wisdom allowed. An hour before dawn he let it fall away. Fight from the fortress was ended.

'Move,' he whispered.

At the rear walkway of his fortress he stood to one side and allowed men to pass out. It was plain he would be last to leave. It was also plain he was making a farewell. Fires and lamps had been left burning to persuade besiegers that the place was still occupied; the ramparts and palisades rose in a ghostly glow. After letting his eye wander Titoko turned to his companion.

'Well?' he asked.

'Maybe', Kimball said, 'it was too good to be true.'

Titoko thought on that.

'When was true good?' he asked.

Whitmore was left to level his third empty fortress.

Twenty-two

It was Titoko's thought that his rearguard would have three hours' advantage on pursuers. One hour to dawn; one for Whitmore's bombardment; one for Kepa to find the fort lifeless. Disbelief, celebration and the breaking out of rum might kill an hour or two more. Thereafter the speed of pursuit would depend much on Whitmore's lungs and Kepa's legs. The rearguard would move closer to the coast than the main party, leaving a trail meant to draw the colony's army. The point of their existence, Titoko told his forty, was to make a target; they were to let Toa and those with him win safety by chancing the interior.

'Meaning what for us?' a veteran asked.

'Meaning sons and daughters live,' Titoko said. 'Meaning the tribe.'

'As it must be,' said the warrior.

'I asked volunteers. Need I ask again?'

He did not. Their warrior chore was to lead death a dance. To beckon it they left fires smouldering behind them to suggest ten times their number. On the other hand it was not Titoko's thought that his rearguard succumb. Firearms were cleaned, cartridges counted, and watch kept for their hunters. As day followed day, and Titoko's men wearied, the fires behind them grew brighter; on the sprightliest tally there were a thousand men gaining on them. No count said fewer than five hundred.

Summer did not diminish. Clay crackled underfoot, and dry scrub rattled in breeze. Skies remained cloudless, even the tip of Taranaki with no wisp; their days were never sweetened with rain. On the tenth day of flight, through country too open, Titoko ordered a move inland, and broke his rearguard in two.

Each party, from reverse directions, and leaving two trails, sweated up a long, creek-eroded plateau and met on its summit. An old conflagration, smoking upland, had left rock outcrops as islands in a head-high sea of new fern. A cooling wind roved through it. It was as good a place as any to rest and refresh men; its other possibilities were plain only to Titoko. 'Here,' he said.

'For tonight?' Big asked.

'And morning,' Titoko said.

That evening, out towards the coast, army fires began burning. Kimball looked inland, toward sunset, forests, and the centre of the island. It was easy to fancy Toa's refugees trickling through that sour territory, scrambling across creeks and fording rivers, gathering wild honey and berries, daily more lean. Light left the land; mountain merged with mountain and mountain with sky. A lone tear dried on his cheek. Demon rose before him, and eased his buttocks to earth.

'Whatever you are thinking, it is better not thought,' he advised.

'The children are small,' Kimball said.

'They have their mother.'

'She could be stronger too.'

'You may see them again,' Demon said.

'This rearguard isn't going to make heaven fast.'

'Your fear', Demon decided, 'is still Flukes.'

'He gets no easier to kill,' Kimball admitted.

'I shall make it my business,' Demon promised. 'You have a warrior's word.'

'I'm obligated,' Kimball said.

'And I to you,' Demon said. 'I need a last interest.'

Kimball thought to ask, 'Why me?'

'You fought my war,' Demon said.

Soon after sunrise, with all signs promising, Whitmore pushed his column toward the plateau. As the land lifted, the trail divided. Whitmore was obliged to split his force as Titoko had. Major Kepa took two hundred men uphill to the left; Captain Flukes took two hundred to the right. With the rest in reserve, Whitmore awaited happenings on low ground. These were not long coming. Titoko placed most of his rifles in fern to the rear of the plateau, where the land fell away to river. There was to be no early discharge of weapons, and then of but a round apiece.

Fire was to be held until Flukes' party and Kepa's were about to meet on the summit of the plateau. The signal would be a shot from Titoko's carbine, his first of the war, perhaps also his last. This scheme baffled many in the rearguard. For one thing, thick fern gave them no field of fire. All would have to fire blind. 'So sight on birds,' Titoko told them with indifference. He scuttled away to observe the approach of Kepa and Flukes. The sound of stumbling, cursing men rose nearer; Kepa could be heard gruff and, at a greater distance, Flukes blaspheming. The two parties grew quiet as ground levelled off. The foremost of each, fearful of ambush, began pushing more slowly, trying and failing to keep the fern at arm's length. What could not be seen, not by them, was that they were closing with each other.

Soon there were several hundred careful men afoot on the plateau. Titoko's round was not heard until the last moment. A second later forty loud firearms whipped fern. Then two or three hundred weapons joined the din. Titoko arrived back on the lip of the plateau. 'Depart,' he ordered, and his men began to plunge off its rear.

The shooting behind did not thin. Flukes' men, and Kepa's, were briskly engaged. Between shots there were shouts as the colony's riflemen successfully stalked each other, or fell upon their fellows with weapons of close combat.

Panic persisted for minutes. Embarrassment finally got the better of battle, with Kepa raging halt and Flukes screaming cease-fire. As they brought men to heel, and counted casualties, Titoko had more chance to argue his party away. His men eased down the rear of the plateau, rock by rock, and crossed shallow river. On the far side were trees.

Titoko waded to dry ground, climbed into shade, and dropped beside Demon. Demon was training field glasses on the plateau. No pursuers made a showing.

'I may have heard a more worthwhile shot,' Demon said. 'I cannot recall it.'

'Thank you,' Titoko said.

'On the other hand their casualties could have been greater.'

'Who knows?' Titoko shrugged.

'Perhaps an ambush as they cross the river,' Demon suggested.

'That is not my thought,' Titoko said.

'What is it, then?'

'Disappearance.'

258

'Again?'

'We began with three hours to live. We might make it three days.'

'And that is to be called triumph?'

'It is not to be called death,' Titoko said.

Near noon on the fifteenth day, travelling closer to the coast, they passed the remains of a riverside settlement. There were beached canoes on the near bank. Across the river a large grove of peach trees climbed a slope. All glowed with ripe fruit. Dropping weapons and swags, Titoko's parched warriors swam or paddled to the far side, and swarmed into the shade, grabbing at fruit and stuffing their mouths until juice dribbled down their chins. When they were sated, some began gathering more for the journey; others heaved rotten fruit playfully at each other, scoring succulent hits. There was even the sound of men laughing. Meantime Titoko interested himself in the countryside. He absently sampled one peach, no more, and spat out the stone.

'Sufficient,' he decided, to considerable dismay.

'You are thinking sore bellies?' Big asked.

'As I recall it,' Titoko said, 'the Bible instructs us to give the enemy food if he hungers, drink if he thirsts.'

'And you think to leave them good fruit?'

'To guard this crop until they come.'

Life with Titoko was never short on surprise. 'Are we', Big asked, 'Methodist again?'

But Titoko was serious. 'Begin placing men,' he told Demon.

'To what end?' Demon asked.

'Sore bellies,' Titoko said.

Demon was slow understanding. Then he smiled for the first time in a fortnight. 'I hear you,' he said.

Weapons and swags were gathered and brought across the river. Marksmen were placed close to the peach grove. Others were arranged on high ground to the rear. The sun could not have been hotter. Men sought shade where they could, and lazily waited on events.

It was close to day's end before these took a sober turn. First dusty colonist scouts rode up to the river. Before long Whitmore's full column began to arrive. Land about the orchard swallowed down forty warriors in seconds. Whitmore, Kepa and Flukes appeared on the riverside. They appeared to be deciding their campsite for the night. Whitmore and Kepa turned their horses back; Flukes remained at the river. He was not lonely for long. Sergeant Tonks rode up and pointed across the river at the peach grove. Flukes finally nodded his head. Tonks soon had canoes retrieved and a forage detail formed. Men launched themselves across the river with much the same passion as Titoko's warriors had shown. There was splashing and high-spirited shouting as they grounded their canoes, staggered uphill and fell on the fruit. No more than two or three of the party were armed; the rest had bags to be filled and lumped back to the river. Meantime, they gorged. Meantime too, warriors cocked carbines.

The forage party ventured further into the grove, and finally several men put in an appearance on the far side. Titoko was first to his feet. 'Now,' he was calling. Warriors likewise leapt from the ground and levelled their weapons. At close range their volley sank two constables, and left a third foundering. Survivors turned in panic to face blast from behind, warriors afoot in the grove, twigs smashing, and fruit exploding like sticky grenades. Two more of Tonks' men tumbled mortally. Others, skidding on trampled peaches, collided with each other, and with trees. Titoko called up his party and pushed pursuit to the south edge of the grove. As the foragers fought to gain the river, and their canoes, they came under even more powerful fire. Men trying to hold a canoe steady, for Tonks to clamber aboard, made easy targets; the canoe overturned, taking Tonks too. It drifted downriver with just his bobbing boots to be seen. Those who found the south side of the river were those who swam. Even so, some were shot as they rose from the water.

Flukes was busy keeping his head down and calling up rifles to return fire. He failed to order another river crossing. Nor, when he rode up, did Whitmore. Volley after volley struck across the river, riddling nothing but fruit. By dusk it must have become plain to Whitmore and Flukes that they were warring with a quiet peach grove. They were left with a crop of corpses.

'That', Titoko judged, 'was better than nothing.'
'You are too modest,' Demon argued.
'I have to be,' Titoko said.

That night storm thundered inland; by morning the uncrossed river had risen four feet and was promising to roar higher. No army could have mastered it, no horses, no men. The peach grove gave Titoko better than three days. He pushed his rearguard faster through sea mist and rain.

'Now three weeks,' he said.

They crossed more colonist countryside and left it behind. As they closed with Mount Taranaki, and limped into the territory of cousins, they looked for hospitality and found little. Villagers who might have welcomed Titoko weeks before, and asked him to test their sons, now had bitter faces and failed to meet his eye. Titoko's disgrace might soon be their grief; Whitmore's marauders, not to speak of Kepa's, were unlikely to differ between Titoko's loyal warriors and those lately misled. Demon and Big had to plead for shelter. Titoko sat humble and apart while charity was asked. When comfort was offered, it was never for more than a night, and seldom other than cold meat, a hut filled with fleas, and a thin blanket. The meaning was plain. More than one man who had volunteered for Titoko's rearguard sound of heart now found that muscle missing a beat. In the morning a blanket would be empty and another warrior gone. Where Whitmore's rifles failed to trim Titoko's forty, Maori dread did. In days his rearguard was a tiring score.

On the thirtieth they approached the place where meeting was planned with Toa's column. It was an old upland refuge, hidden in a region of precipice and ravine, to be found only by paddling and carrying canoes upriver and then by blind smashing through growth. They arrived on a storm-bitten acre sheer on three sides. As a last resort the height had promise; it held little else. There were dank, half-rotted cabins coloured with rain, crawling with rats, and reeking of old grief. Those who had used the place had left no defence works; its steep situation had been its security. Graves said death had been a patient besieger. Meanwhile the place was deserted, with nothing to suggest recent visitors, nothing of Toa and his party. Titoko ordered his men to scavenge what they could, and make cabins tolerable. Soon shooting was heard; their first pig had fallen.

'Toa?' Kimball asked.

'We wait,' Titoko said.

His answer was the same two weeks later. 'They were sure to be slow,' he explained.

'This slow?'

'Or slower,' Titoko said.

Their days held no alarms. Pickets were placed, mostly to doze.

In the third week, with summer cooling, and mornings moist with fog, Big raised an objection. 'You have placed faith in Toa before,' he said.

'That is so,' Titoko agreed.

'It is not for me to say that Toa's misfortunes are many. And more so of late.'

'That is correct,' Titoko said. 'It is not.'

'He may have further thoughts about seeing your face again.'

'He may. He may not.'

'He could disown you, and lead our people over to the colonists. He could ask mercy in return for favours. Many might see Maori wisdom.'

'You are telling me of treachery before it is seen.'

'Before it arrives behind guns.'

'It is not to be thought,' Titoko decided.

'Anything can be thought in this quiet,' Big argued.

Titoko did not disagree. They looked across valley after valley. There was no wisp of smoke, no glimmer of man.

'The husband of Toa's daughter is with us,' Titoko pointed out finally. 'If colonists attacked, he would be early shot down. Toa knows this.'

'Is that why the Yankee is here?'

'When he volunteered for our party, it was not in my heart to refuse him.'

'For your safety?'

'And yours.'

Big took this in. 'I have seen you sly before. You better yourself.'

'I tell you Toa will arrive.'

'And I tell you that it might be well to be sure. Also to hasten his people here.'

'What miracle do you have in mind?' Titoko asked.

'Finding them before Whitmore finds us,' Big said.

'Whitmore or Kepa?'

'Kepa,' Big said reluctantly. 'This is no country for Whitmore.'

Titoko looked out on forest for the last time that day. Finally he turned his back. 'Leave in the morning,' he said. 'Light fires on high points. Discharge shots. You have five days. Hurry them here.'

Big left the camp soon after sunrise, with two young warriors to speed word back to Titoko. Soon after Big had gone Titoko announced another mission. This was Demon's. He was to canoe downriver, toward the coast, and use his eyes and Maori rumour to determine whether danger was near; whether the colonist hunt was continuing, or if the trail of the rebel rearguard was cool. Demon was likewise given five days for his task. The difference was that Demon would journey alone. He needed no messengers; no young warrior could cover the interior faster. One way and another, Titoko had much on his mind. He was short tempered with the band remaining to him; even Kimball kept his distance through the first day and the second. On the third, however, Titoko called him close. The day was chilly and clear. Mount Taranaki, patchy with early snow, lifted beyond forty miles of forest. Some days the mountain looked taller. Most it seemed smaller. Today it was slow making up its mind.

No one was looking at it longer than Titoko. 'It has come to this,' he said.

'This?' Kimball asked.

'He too was hunted.'

'He?'

'Our mountain.'

'I remember you telling me.'

'I likewise told you why.'

'A wriggle too many,' Kimball marvelled.

'Just so,' Titoko said with no smile.

'Hell's bells,' Kimball said, and heard them ring.

Soon there was no more to think.

'You feared this from the beginning?' Kimball asked.

Titoko shrugged. 'Men are not mountains, nor mountains men.'

'Even so,' Kimball said.

'You told me of a warrior whose heel was his weakness, and led him to doom.'

'The Greek jeezer,' Kimball agreed.

'He says no man is born without fault.'

'Maybe,' Kimball shrugged.

'Mine was elsewhere. Must it be recalled that my cock cost a war?'

'Is that what's worrying you?'

'On bad days. I know more bad days than good.'

'You probably reckon right,' Kimball said with regret.

'Right?'

'The tale's buggered. There's no putting it together now.'

There was a silence.

'Try,' Titoko said suddenly.

Kimball thought.

'Go on,' Titoko pushed.

'I guess it can be said you were the one warrior the British couldn't bring down.'

'Couldn't?'

'Not the way a woman could.'

'That has promise,' Titoko said grudgingly.

'That's the best I can make it.'

'You miss one thing.'

'Like what?'

'It was a wriggle worth a war.'

Kimball sighed. 'I've got to tell that too?'

'To be fair,' Titoko said.

There was an even more sizeable silence.

'When were tales ever fair?' Kimball asked.

On the other hand the mountain seemed a sight taller.

A morose wind was blowing the day Big and Demon were due for return. Titoko paced for most of the morning. 'Have our weeks gone?' he asked Kimball.

'Almost,' Kimball said.

'Kepa must know his last chance to strike near, even if Whitmore does not.'

'How do you reckon that?'

'With a week or two more, winter could war for us. Cold, rain, and snow.'

'If we have the weeks,' Kimball said.

'True,' Titoko said.

Demon was sighted climbing uphill toward noon. He was

bruised and famished; and brought news Titoko would have been better without. Whitmore's army now commanded the coast, even if Whitmore did not. The colonel had shipped off to Wellington to be celebrated by his superiors for the toppling of Titokowaru's last stronghold, and for reducing his foe to a contemptible fugitive. In his absence Kepa had command of the army. Hundreds of white colonists, not to speak of his tribesmen, now took his orders without quibble. His column had been feeling through rough country for routes Titoko might have taken. Demon had witnessed the column at work. It closed with a Maori village thought sympathetic to Titoko, left two old men shot, a woman sabred, and survivors interested in talking. Kepa, with Captain Flukes at his side, was on hand to see that information won was of helpful character. It was further ensured by long beatings and torching of dwellings, and promise of more. Queen's Maori and colonists alike competed for duties. Among their chores was one which promised to be profitable. They were smoking the heads of suspect rebels.

'And?' Titoko asked.

'I watched Kepa begin moving again,' Demon said.

'Behind you?'

'Three days behind,' Demon said. 'No more than four.'

Major Kepa was in no mind to let Whitmore again slow him with orders, or to let winter win.

A messenger from Big tumbled into the camp with an untidy story told between gulps of breath. Breaking through bush country, lighting fires on heights, Big had won a signal from Toa's column. It had taken two days to find it, another to get it moving again. This was due to the condition of the party. Hardships had been many. Food was short, footwear rotted, clothing ragged. Women and children were suffering, the elderly too. There had been drownings; there had been burials. Though most warriors were surviving, some of the thoughtful had begun to see more risk in the forest than in the arms of Kepa, and fled downriver toward the coast. The large casualty, however, was Toa. Tribulation had undone him. He was skinny, hobbling and beginning to babble. With his warrior will gone, he was an unfit leader. His wife Hine now led the column more fiercely than any man. Big was pushing from behind, also trying to keep the column alive and moving.

'How far away?' Titoko asked.

'Unless there is more grief to slow them,' the earnest messenger reported, 'two days' walking.'

Titoko found need to think. He moved away, with Demon close behind. Kimball was left with the messenger.

'You saw my wife and children?' Kimball asked.

'All women and children now look the same,' the messenger said.

'The same?'

'Weeping or beginning to weep.'

'My wife might be different,' Kimball said. 'Think.'

'I am thinking,' the messenger protested feebly. 'Do you wish truth, or a tale?'

'Truth.'

'I have told it. Toa's wife leads. Toa follows. And many crawl behind.'

Kimball told himself the tale. If her parents persisted, so might Rihi. So might Wiremu and Meri. So, for that matter, might he.

Demon and Titoko stood on a craggy outcrop above the camp. No outlook was promising. The sky was damp. The land fell leafy from their feet into murk.

'Kepa could arrive first,' Demon said.

'If Big and Hine fail to speed our slowest,' Titoko agreed.

'Think what that may mean,' Demon suggested.

'I do,' Titoko said.

'All could fall to Kepa. Their party. Yours too.'

'What are you thinking?'

'That better some live.'

'To fight again?'

'To tickle colonists a little. To keep them in terror.'

Titoko shook his head. 'There will be no warriors needed.'

'In the new world?'

'In Sunday's dawn, should we see it.'

'I would sooner not,' Demon said.

'Then look to your last fight,' Titoko suggested.

'Your word is no?'

'Death needs you most here.'

'I wished only to know', Demon explained, 'if you had also been thinking my thought.'

'To leave?'

'To save such as might be.'

'What man could not,' Titoko confessed.

'But you wish our forgiveness,' Demon said.

'I led you into war,' Titoko admitted.

'And could yet lead us out?'

'My gun might unsay much,' Titoko said.

'I still hear a man more in need of forgiveness than triumph.'

'In need of sweeter companions,' Titoko said. 'Warriors day after day, with no talk but battle, are a sour diet.'

'Forgive us our manhood,' Demon said.

'Forgive mine.'

'Some days that is more difficult than others,' Demon said.

'My word is still no.'

Demon was quiet. 'When Kepa comes?' he asked.

'Deeds to be sung,' Titoko argued, though his face said different.

That afternoon the camp was a place of whispers. Those who had not overheard Titoko and Demon were soon as knowledgeable as those who had. They were left with only the weather to consider. Kimball listened to faint birds and far water.

Most of the next day passed without news. Toward its end Big's second messenger emerged from the trees. 'Our others remain slow,' he reported. 'They have more rivers to cross.'

Silent Titoko seemed to be crossing them too. Kepa's army was a day nearer.

'We could tell Hine and Big to turn their people back,' Demon argued.

'To what?' Titoko asked.

A little later an outlying picket scrambled panicky into camp. He had seen the smoke of evening fires lifting downriver; he had also heard male voices on the far side of a valley. Neither fires nor voices could be friendly.

'Tomorrow?' Demon asked Titoko.

Cartridges were counted, and carbines oiled again. Fires were dampened at dusk.

Daylight began with a distant shot. It might have been Big or Toa signalling. It might have been one of Kepa's scouts mistaking a pig for a rebel. Titoko was not to be speeded. After thought, he ordered half his men to cover the approach to the camp; the rest, under Demon, were to feel into the forest for the missing column and lead it to the camp without further loss.

'Go,' Titoko told Kimball. 'Fetch your family.'

'Thank you,' Kimball said.

'If we meet Kepa first?' Demon asked.

'Serve yourself well,' Titoko said.

They waded fast river and rose shivering on rocks. Trees edging the river were shiny with dew and menacingly still. Demon, pushing hard, was the first to breach the foliage. Clouds of leaf soon closed out the light. They travelled for an hour before Demon signalled stop. He touched his lips for continued quiet. Then they all heard. At first the noise seemed no more than the rustle of another river. It became a soft gasping, sighing, and moaning; the sound of weary humans, not water, moving in mass. A few yards of growth further and they came upon people toiling haggardly up a gully, arguing with the crumbled edge of a creek, and mostly failing and falling. Demon's party had happened upon the middle of the column. There were muddy women; there were near naked children; there were sunken-eyed warriors. Demon's men began helping people to reliable ground. Kimball bent to a creature who seemed a woman. For one thing she had a child bundled on her hip. She staggered against him, and whimpered. Then her eyes said the woman was his wife.

'No,' he said.

Rihi had no voice to argue. He grabbed up her bundle and looked into the wrinkled face of his daughter. Meri was alive too, though he might not have noticed. She looked at him through watery eyes, opened her mouth and gave out a sound more a croak than a cry.

'I have no love left,' Rihi whispered. 'Give her yours.'

'Wiremu?' he asked.

'Big carries your son behind.'

Kimball sighed.

'Are we to live?' she asked.

'Ask Titoko,' he said.

They waited on the rear of the column. Skin hung slack from

268

Big's face; his eyes were bloodshot. There was no smile as he surrendered his wriggling package to fresh arms. Wiremu, skin and bone too, saw his father and wailed.

With his children clutching his neck, his wife holding him behind, Kimball helped Hine and Big hike the lost party out of the forest and up to Titoko's camp. Hine was always ahead. Toa had to be aided by men still with strength. Most yards were murder. The rest were just killing.

In the camp nothing was changed for the better. Senior men gathered in the afternoon light to hear Demon argue a move. Big was all but beyond understanding, and Toa sat shamed with his head between his knees. Around them were two or three hundred of the tribe in like disrepair. Warriors of the rearguard were working their way through the new arrivals, trying to fit their families together again. Where they failed, there were sounds of grief. Other warriors were passing out scraps of food and doctoring those in most need. Meanwhile Demon was loud.

'We have waited too long,' he announced. 'More delay cannot be chanced.'

'Nor can a move,' Titoko said.

'We still have a little light,' Demon protested. 'A mile won today is another for Kepa to march.'

'Perhaps.'

'And another to set a good ambush.'

'Who among them would live that mile?' Titoko asked.

'More than likely to live here,' Demon suggested.

'You move them,' Titoko mocked. 'You march them.'

'Kepa', Demon whispered, 'has been waiting on weakness. He could not ask more.'

'And it is weakness not to risk the young, ill and old?'

'It is not strength.'

'I cannot ask more of them,' Titoko said.

'I hear no warrior,' Demon said.

'That is correct,' Titoko said. 'Today you do not.'

There was a silence in which far birds sang.

'And that is your word?'

'If I have command,' Titoko said.

'It is yet to be settled,' Demon insisted.

Whatever appearances said, Toa was now the tribe's leader.

'Let Toa be heard,' Titoko suggested.

Toa heaved unsteadily up from the warrior throng. His eyes had no light.

'What', Titoko asked, 'is your thought?'

It did not seem Toa had one of interest. He looked from left to right, right to left, and shook his head. 'An end,' he said.

'Of character, cousin?' Titoko asked.

'Of character,' Toa repeated.

'And you would trust that to me?'

'You have taken everything else,' Toa said.

Then Hine stood to the rear of the gathering. Cartridge belts again crossed her breasts.

'I shall speak for him,' she said.

'By all means,' Titoko nodded.

'There is but one leader among us. All else is lie.'

'What if I have less will for it?' Titoko asked.

'The more reason,' Hine said.

Titoko took thought. Then he said, 'Let those with empty hands begin weaving ropes, and plaiting strong ladders.'

'What is this?' Demon asked.

'An order,' Titoko said. 'We chance another night, until the weak are rested and ready to move.'

'The ropes, the ladders?'

'To give chance something to grip.'

Demon backed off. Titoko was tolerably in command again.

Kimball placed Rihi and the children in a dry cabin. As for food, he found some half-cooked potato flavoured with pigeon fat. The children collapsed and slept with no urging. Rihi did not. She shivered while he held her.

'Don't go,' she pleaded.

'Where would I go?' he asked.

'Somewhere without me.'

'I'm not', he argued, 'going nowhere.'

Nor was anyone fast. Outside the hut four fit warriors were being ordered down valley to determine whether Kepa's men were near. Those less fit were placed on picket. Men with little worth left were assigned to cut vines or strip and weave flax with women.

'And you', he added, 'won't be going nowhere I'm not.'

'That is a promise?'

'The best there is,' he said.

By the end of the day reliable ladders had been fastened to trees and slung down the ravine to the rear of the camp; they dangled toward a racing river. Thereafter there were footholds cut in steep rock. On the slippery riverside there were a couple of old and unpromising canoes. As a line of escape, it left much to faith.

The patrol sent down valley returned to report nothing but quiet, no fires, no sign of Kepa's force. This troubled Titoko more than a sighting.

'If Kepa has gone to ground,' he said, 'it must be for reason.'

'Reason?' tired Big asked.

'Because he is near,' Titoko said.

He ordered quiet, and had it, but for whimpering infants. Fires were doused too. Titoko pushed rifles forward, to cover the climb to the camp, and placed others to the rear; those to the rear manned the natural trench at the ravine edge. If an advance were made upon the camp, the forward rifles would retire on volleys, carrying women, children and the weak back to the ravine edge and giving them time to depart.

Dusk came, then dark. A faint moon rose beyond busy cloud. Some slept. Most drifted in a dream between sleep and waking. Owls sounded far and near. A shower of rain whispered on leaves. After it passed rocks and trees seemed to be breathing.

Kimball found Rihi asleep in his arms. He pillowed her head with his knapsack and then, thinking to warrior chore, collected and loaded his carbine. Demon had charge of the forward rifles; Big of those to the rear. Titoko padded between the two parties urging both to remain alert. Looking him out, Kimball groped across the camp site, past looming cabin and crag, moving towards Big's position on the ravine edge. Moonlight came and went. Then he lost all sense of direction. For one thing, there were rocks to his right he could not recall on the route before.

'Titoko?' he whispered.

He got no answer. He gave out a low whistle.

'Titoko?' he whispered again.

This time he had a result. The landscape was in sudden

commotion. The rocks to the right were growing in number; there were fresh shapes rising up, seemingly from the pit, certainly from precipice.

'Silence that bastard,' Flukes was ordering.

Kimball discharged the night's first shot too far to the right of Flukes' face. The flash showed Flukes, Major Kepa and marauder after marauder heaving into view. Flukes was training a revolver, Kepa a carbine. Kimball skipped to the right, leapt to the left, and hit ground as the attack burst over him with shot upon shot.

'On,' Kepa called. 'On.'

They were trampling past. Colonist boots collided with his head right and left.

He rose to uproar. Kepa's men, mastering cliffs, sheltering under ledges till dark, had struck the campsite where it was weak. Plunging between Demon's forward line and Big's rear rifles, they had the place to themselves. There were woken women moaning with fright, addled children fleeing, and old men tumbling unclad from cabins to meet tomahawk and bayonet. Neither Demon's men nor Big's could risk fire without felling their own. Titoko could suddenly be heard, in the dark, from Big's position. He was ordering Big's men to hold fire. Demon's, meanwhile, sprinted back uphill to close with Kepa's force. Kimball, thinking smaller, ran toward the cabin where he had left Rihi and the children. The flare of firearms lit less of his way as fighting began hand to hand. Demon's grunting men heaved themselves again and again at Kepa's, looking for a way back through the camp to the ravine escape route. Kepa's men were not easily parted. Demon's challenge also failed to slow the killing within the camp. The first cabin was torched, giving Kimball more light to pick a path among dead and dying. Flukes and Kepa were at work only a few feet away, driving back Demon while men elsewhere split skulls and abdomens. One form reeled toward him and fell. A gust of flame showed him Hine sprawled and bleeding from breast to belly. He cradled her head.

'Rihi?' he asked.

'Look to her,' she said.

He hesitated.

'Go,' she ordered, and fought not to let her eyes close. They closed.

There were new cries in the night. Their meaning became clear. Demon's men had been struck by yet another band of attackers from the rear. They were now trapped between two killing lines. Meanwhile Titoko and Big remained helpless uphill. From their roost on the ravine edge they could make no path for Demon short of levelling tribal innocents together with Kepa's troops. The longer matters were left, the fewer of Demon's party would live. That much was clear. Little else could be. The cabin where he had left Rihi was empty, of the children too. On the other hand his knapsack had also gone, which was hopeful. Moving away, he collided with a couple of constables on arson duty. Behind them, with lit brands, were a pair of Maori as ugly. Thought was called for; and army English.

'What the fuck are you doing?' he asked. 'Captain Flukes is calling everyone into the line.'

'Flukes?'

'Bet your arse. Major Kepa too.'

That checked them. He sped several paces clear before shot danced around his feet.

'That', one constable swore, 'was bloody Bent.'

'Is,' said his companion. 'Do we get him?'

'Fifty-fifty,' the first said.

As they overhauled him Kimball ducked clear of dwellings, crashed into scrub, and lay still. Boots banged about him; bayonets were thrust into foliage. Meantime firing grew downhill. Captain Flukes was certainly and desperately calling men forward. Other cries also said Demon wasn't dying easy. With the best will in the world no pursuer could give more than half a mind to a renegade head in the din of battle; the other half said a bounty-hunter had his own to consider.

'Fuck,' the first constable despaired.

'Shit,' the second agreed.

They hurried away, with parting jabs into bushes. Kimball breathed again.

'Rihi?' he called into the dark. 'Rihi?'

Flames were taking the thatch of more cabins. There were screams from those half-alive within.

'Rihi?' he pleaded.

'Here,' she said marvellously.

Moving toward the voice, he found live flesh underfoot.

273

Passing patches of light showed him two or three dozen survivors hiding behind rocks. Among them was Rihi. Bundled
beside her were Wiremu and Meri.

'I have to get you uphill,' he told the group with authority.
No one differed. He grabbed up his children.

'Come,' he ordered those around. 'Lift yourselves. Run.'

Several began to put gunfire to their rear.

'Please,' he said. 'Now.'

Several more moved.

'Trust me,' he pleaded.

One by one more stood, thinking to live. Others were too
tired to care. There was no time to interest them.

'Don't leave my side,' he ordered Rihi. 'Don't fall behind.'

They ran. There were fewer than forty paces to Titoko and
Big, up ground sloping rockily to the ravine edge. There would
be safety behind their guns, and ladders. Meanwhile Kimball's
people argued with boulder and branch. They spread as they
climbed; Kimball heard hard breathing right and left, Rihi's
loudest as she stumbled at his side.

Then he heard Titoko's voice lift above battle. 'Ready?' Titoko
was calling. Warrior choice had been made. He was mounting
a volley in support of Demon, to the grief of all in its path.

'Drop,' Kimball shouted to his party. Then, to Titoko, 'Stop.'

His first shout might have been heard; the second was
late.

The issue of fifty firearms burned bright through Kimball's
party. There were grunts, cries, and Rihi was no longer at
his side. The children had spilled from his arms as he went
to earth. He groped back toward her. Warriors above, understanding disaster, were dropping their weapons and scrambling
downhill to help. Finally, in the dark, on loose stones, Kimball
found Rihi's head and felt her breath warm on his hand. Near
her neck blood rose even more warmly from a wound. She
sighed. 'My leg too,' she said calmly.

She began sliding away into a gully. Their children were
loud with fright.

'Quick,' he called to helpers.

'Yankee?' Big called back.

'Here,' Kimball sighed.

Then there were stronger arms. Not just for Rihi and the
children; for him too. He had failed to notice the groove made

274

the length of his scalp by a friendly carbine; or, for that matter, his blood mixed with his wife's.

When Kimball put the night together, it was with what must have happened, to make sense of living.

Titoko must have mounted more heartening volleys, reducing and confusing Kepa's men, allowing Demon to battle uphill between them.

Kepa and Flukes must have decided that morning would be less murderous, and done no more than hold ground.

Big's warriors must have held the ravine edge until all who could walk, or were worth carrying, had escaped into forest further upriver.

Hine, like many, must have been left to die.

Toa must have been somewhere. Titoko must have been everywhere. He still had a tribe.

Twenty-three

For days there was the hiss of overhead shot, then the smack of metal on timber, as Kepa's force pushed after them. Parrots screaming from foliage could announce hunters just a hilltop or two behind. There were no large fires lit, no long camps made. Food was fern root and fungus, moss and mushroom; it was a restful season for pigeon and pig as man stalked man. To spare ammunition for desperate encounters, Kimball whittled small pieces of hard wood to size as bullets and pressed match-heads into service to refresh used percussion caps. As a means of stinging pursuers such measures were useful; for the purpose of felling them they were foul. Hourly Titoko's remainder grew feebler, fewer, and indifferent. Drowsy laggards for whom Kepa's tomahawks no longer held terror were left behind with no blessing. Old people pleaded need to rest, took one breath, pitched face forward into mud and failed to rise. Even strong-bodied men sickened, sank, crawled a few yards and moved no more. Others drifted ghostly into mist, and were suddenly gone. Despairing cries could be heard when Kepa overtook them. Scouts under Demon sometimes circled back to track Kepa's progress. They returned to report headless torsos, and once to witnessing encamped colonists and Maori making male heads more fearsome by gouging out their right eyes before curing. The hunters weren't happy to wait on the real Titoko. With the head of a humble warrior worth only five pounds, they were gambling on a fake to win a thousand.

Other things weren't any fancier. Meri weakened in Kimball's arms and failed to take food. Wiremu, only a little less sickly, was passed from woman to woman as they limped higher inland. Rihi's wounds festered as one day after another dawned and darkened; no Maori herb healed her. Her eyes were shiny and her voice a whisper. On better days she knew where she was; better days were few. Four men were needed to carry her litter through swamp and over slimy boulders. Men strong enough to bear the lame and the ailing were soon hard to find. Most were like Toa, just able to place one foot before another and, after a time, do the same again. Even Big seemed half his old size. Demon, with little spare flesh to lose, had legs like sticks. Titoko grew hoarser as he argued people out of loitering in Kepa's path.

'Have you thought', Demon asked, 'of where we are going?'

'I have,' Titoko said.

'Then where are you taking us?'

'Home,' Titoko claimed.

'To our mountain?'

'Where we belong.'

'You are talking open land.'

'I am talking our land.'

Demon grew mocking. 'You think mercy might be found there?'

'A meal may be,' Titoko said.

The day Meri died was one of wind and rain. As it happened, Kimball had his daughter in arms. Rihi was asleep in her litter nearby. Other survivors were resting along riverbank while men foraged in the forest. A few were on watch downriver. For once Kepa was failing to press hard and a daylight halt appeared safe. It seemed to Kimball that he had heard no mutter from Meri for some time. When he parted her blanket, she was already cool, her small face without colour; it looked to be all of an hour since her last breath.

His first difficulty was in making no sound. His second was in easing away from Rihi's litter before she woke.

Big, however, saw Kimball beginning to back off.

Their eyes met. Kimball nodded. Nothing was said. Big took up a large knife and led Kimball into growth.

'Here?' he asked, a few paces on.

There were large trees and small; and fern was thick.

'Why not?' Kimball said.

Parting rock and root, Big carved out a grave. It did not need to be large, nor very deep.

'A stone?' he asked. 'A cross?'
'God should know where to find her,' Kimball decided.
'Then maybe you wish to say something?' Big said.
Kimball tried to think.
'A prayer?' Big suggested.
Again Kimball had a problem.
'I'm prayed out,' he said.

Toward evening Rihi woke long enough to notice him now nursing Wiremu. 'Where', she asked, 'is Meri?'
'With Hine,' he reported.
'Where?'
'Just a little ahead of us.'
'Just a jeezly way?' she said, trying to smile.
'Jeezly little,' he said.
It looked very likely.

There was one prize. Kepa's force was sickening and slowing too. Demon, the only man left to take risks, crept back to army campfires and returned to tell of mounting grief. Colonist was feuding with Maori, and both with their own. Kepa had lost men to torrent and abyss; there were accidental shootings; men were wretched with hunger and moaning with dysentery. Major Kepa's white gloves were long gone and his gold braid was a few threads. The Queen's favourite Maori, for what it was now worth, was a red-eyed and ranting drunk.

They stopped travelling up rivers; they began travelling down. Gorges grew wider, rivers slower and the country kinder. Days passed without a shot heard. On a cold morning, long after they had finished believing in it, they saw their mountain ahead, summit and shoulders shiny with new snow. Under the mountain was level land, familiar forest. Sighs rose from men with the breath, and sobs from women. In Kimball's arms, Wiremu was not to be roused by sounds of rejoicing. Big had another small grave to dig.
    After the burial Titoko thought to call the living to order.
    'I promise you nothing,' he warned.

They moved not toward The Beak, but north. By dark, when they rested, their destination was clear.

'The mire,' Demon said.
'It has eaten invaders before,' Titoko observed.
'So old tales tell,' Demon said.
'Good tales.'
Demon shrugged. 'For those who need them.'
'We do,' Titoko said.

Next morning, the mountain bolder above, they crossed open country without meeting peril. Beyond trees swamp began to glimmer. They were soon wading through mud and dark water from islet to islet. Big knew the way into the centre best, where one old trail led to another, where mud was less likely to drag travellers down. By afternoon they were scrambling aboard the island at the heart of the swamp. Herons hovered on long wings and ducks scattered in small storms of spray. For a time breathless men and women could do no more than marvel at the peace of the place. Before dark hunters were out and bearing back eel and bird; women had old shelters cleaned and cooking fires lit. Demon alone was left with a far gaze.

Big helped Kimball carry Rihi from her litter into a solid shelter. Though her eyes fluttered open, she seemed not to know what they were about. When she was comfortable, they left her to the care of women.

Outside the shelter Kimball felt a rough hand on his shoulder.

'She will not be with us much longer,' Big said.

'She lived through the rest,' Kimball argued.

'Bravely,' Big agreed.

'Why can't she now?'

'What would you wish me to say?'

Kimball was quiet.

'Death is an honest warrior,' Big said. 'He has never lost a war yet.'

The women were calling Kimball back to his wife. Rihi was asking for him. She began asking often.

Solid food in their bellies, after weeks without, sank some warriors faster than shot. Their innards rebelled and they rolled away from the fires groaning and vomiting. Titoko, on the other hand, held down his meal. With no song and dance, he even managed a widow.

Morning came cool and fine. Demon mustered men and put

out a patrol to look for danger. They returned to declare the swamp deserted north and south.

'What now?' Demon asked.

'Patience,' Titoko argued. 'We finish our Saturday safe.'

'Then?'

Titoko shrugged. 'Sunday,' he said.

'In the long view we cannot remain here.'

'We have no long view,' Titoko said.

'Then I speak of the short,' Demon said. 'Soon they must think to surround us.'

'Their net will be fouled.'

'Kepa will drink the mire dry to get here.'

'That', Titoko said, 'is my hope.'

'So this is a holiday?'

'Enjoy it,' Titoko said.

Toa made a poor showing. Since Hine's loss his voice had hardly been heard. Even the death of his grandchildren had passed him by. Now there was his lingering daughter. He dogged Kimball, pleading that he make it his business not to let Rihi die.

'How?' Kimball asked, helpless.

'As I do,' Toa said.

He fell to his knees, and tugged Kimball down beside him. Toa was on talking terms with Jesus again.

In a week Titoko had fifty warriors worth the name. Some kept watch to the south, lest Kepa or Whitmore rear out of the land. Some hunted. Some scouted for ammunition. Two travelled north as messengers to relatives of Titoko's, old rebels who might give refuge. Meanwhile, on the island, survivors of fight and forest made each new day a feast. Boys began to look sturdy again, and girls pretty. The old laughed with less pain.

Even Rihi still lived. Three times a day Kimball sat by her bedside and spooned a warm broth into her mouth. Three times a day, after that chore, he sat silent with Big. Several times more he knelt with Toa.

Early one morning a warrior posted to the southern edge of the swamp arrived back on the island. He had seen distant fires burning nightlong.

'Many?' Titoko asked.

The warrior shrugged.

'Go back and count,' Titoko told him.

'The fires?'

'The men,' Titoko said.

The same day, at noon, messengers returned from the north. Titoko's relatives were offering a wooded fastness for settlement. It sat in territory neither colonists nor Kepa could reach without risking a larger war. There was a condition on the gift. Titoko's relatives wanted no distress. If Titoko was to take refuge in their territory he was not to challenge colonists again; he was not to bring death on more Maori heads.

'You would say yes?' Demon asked Titoko.

'Where is choice?' Titoko said.

'And where pride?'

Titoko was silent.

'Where?' Demon persisted.

'Pride is no ally,' Titoko said.

News from the south said so too. There was a multitude marching or riding in two columns, each numbering more than five hundred. Weary Kepa commanded one, and refreshed Whitmore the other. There were veterans of the hunt in fading rags; there were new men already limping. In late afternoon the columns rested a mile from the edge of the swamp and grew loud with rum. Morning and mire might sober them, if not on the side of mercy.

The picnic on the island was close to an end. Rihi for that matter too. That night she took only one sip of broth.

Next day Titoko sent men to keep watch on the army and report its progress. A party under Captain Flukes was first to test the way. They cursed thirty yards into bog, finally up to their chests, before Flukes feebly called his men to retire. Kepa was next. He ordered his men forward at a bold run. They fared even worse, losing their weapons and almost their lives. He failed to favour them with an order to retire. Fifty yards out, the bobbing heads of his best men could barely be seen. Howling abuse to their rear, Kepa proved no better than colonists at finding a way through.

Rescues took most of a morning. Shouted conferences between Kepa and Whitmore used the rest. It was Whitmore's belief that Titoko should never have been allowed to gain the swamp. It was Kepa's that Whitmore had a whore for a mother. When they had sworn each other out, they sent parties to feel around the fringe of the mire for a happier approach to Titoko. After much talk of tricks learned in taming Africa's Kaffirs, Whitmore had men begin labouring. They chopped and trimmed saplings and collected bundles of brush, rush and long creeper. By nightfall the point of the enterprise was plain. They had fashioned two long, ladder-like carpets of vegetation to lay across shallower bog, and spread the weight of men wider. These proved reliable under the heaviest constables. When one carpet was crossed, another could be spread. Five men with two carpets might travel fifty yards in an hour. Two hundred carpets could carry the army through.

'They could be here in two days,' Demon told Titoko. 'Their scouts sooner.'

That evening it seemed they had arrived. There were shouts from sentries, shots, and more shouts. Then three intruders were manhandled on to the island and brought bound to Titoko. Two were shaky Maori guides. The third was a muddy Magistrate Booth. Titoko ordered bonds cut away.

'What', Titoko asked, 'have I done to deserve you, Mr Booth?'

'My purpose is charity,' Booth claimed.

'Colonel Whitmore knows you are here?'

'Colonel Whitmore does not.'

'Do you wish him to know?'

'In due course.'

'Due course could be a grave,' Titoko said. 'What do you want?'

'To interpose my person between his army and your people.'

'You are trying to be honourable, sir.'

Booth gazed at his feet.

'No hero is needed now,' Titoko argued. 'Not you, not even me.'

'I owe you more than one favour, Titoko. I also know something your enemy does not. I know your heart was never in this. Your head perhaps, but never your heart. God help us if it had been.'

'Thank you, Mr Booth, if I hear right.'

'No native general has panicked the colony more,' Booth said. 'Pray God none will again.'

'Have you something new to tell me?' Titoko asked.

'It may be timely to consider your future.'

'Mine?' Titoko mused.

'I am not here to save innocents alone. It is important you live, even if Major Kepa may need some convincing. Better a settled tribe with a reasonable leader than dangerous and undisciplined bandits wandering the hinterland.'

'Making your task harder, Mr Booth.'

'Just so, Titoko.'

'And life difficult for colonists.'

'That goes without saying.'

'It is better said.'

'Then I say it, sir. Madness must end.'

'You would have me preaching again, Mr Booth?'

'A little Christian fervour might not go amiss. There could well be a Queen's pardon. Even, for that matter, compensation.'

'Compensation?' Titoko asked.

'Of a personal nature,' Booth said.

'I think there is an English word for such money.'

'Honorarium?' Booth suggested. 'Gift?'

'Bribe,' Titoko said.

'This far no rebel chief has found cause to quarrel with sums offered for his use.'

'If I understand right, Mr Booth, you are telling me the thousand pounds bid for my head might better be spent keeping it on my shoulders.'

'If that is the way you choose to see it, Titoko.'

Titoko was quiet. Finally he said to Big, 'Find Mr Booth food and a bed.'

Booth was removed.

'If you are to leave, it must be now,' Demon told Titoko.

'Tonight?'

'Surely tomorrow. Kepa will not give up the hunt on Booth's plea. Nor can Whitmore be seen weak. You will have a day on them. I cannot promise more.'

'You?'

'In slowing them,' Demon said.

'With who?' Titoko asked. 'I have given no order.'

'Alone,' Demon said. 'I will not be travelling.'

'What is this, then?'

'The end,' Demon said. 'You know it also.'

'I thought never to hear desertion from you.'

'In the north you will give your word not to do further ill to colonists? Or to speak ill, even of Kepa?'

'If such is the price.'

'Such is,' Demon pointed out.

'You are telling me that it is not one you can pay?'

'You have your difficulty. I have another.'

'Yours?'

'I still have a fight in me.'

'One?'

'One better fought. It could fester.'

'What is in your mind?'

'Testing the old tales.'

'Of the swamp?'

'Or leaving a true one. This island is to the west of them, and you will be moving north. I shall haunt them from the east and the south.'

'One man to argue with an army?'

'With their rear and far flank. A man who knows where he is can make himself worth fifty. One shot here, one shot there. They will not be quick to discover this island, and your path north.'

'There is risk in this,' Titoko said soberly.

'They could become reckless,' Demon agreed.

Their conversation was outside Rihi's shelter. Inside were Toa and Kimball. They were waiting on Rihi to die. Everything said she must. Her fever was high and her mind far. But she still failed to finish the journey. Toa sat still, his lips silently moving. Kimball, when not cooling his wife's face with moist towel, held her hand. Things were that way until morning.

Outside, in cold light, Titoko began mustering his people.

'The last march,' he promised. 'Our Saturday is finishing. Sunday begins.'

There was human heaving; there were grunts and laments.

Then Titoko looked in the door, Big too.

'All must leave,' Titoko said.

'Rihi isn't done with dying,' Kimball said.

Titoko said, 'We have three days to safety, with the army one behind. We have no morning to waste.'

'You're telling me to leave her?'

'In Mr Booth's Christian care.'

Booth moved into the doorway. 'I mean to remain on the island with the weak and defenceless. It will speed the others. The least I can do is make myself useful.'

'Not with my wife you won't,' Kimball said.

'Your wife?' Booth said, puzzled.

'Kimball Bent's,' he said.

'Dear God,' Booth said. 'You are he?'

'And then some,' Kimball said.

There was a silence. Booth's eyes were busy.

'I expected a monster of more substance,' he confessed.

'I'm still hairing myself up to it,' Kimball explained.

'We live and learn.'

'Or we die and don't,' Kimball said. 'This is my chore.'

'Come,' Titoko urged.

'No,' Kimball said. 'Take Toa with you. I'll chance along later.'

'I am leaving Demon to the swamp,' Titoko said. 'I cannot think you too.'

'In that case look out the wild horses,' Kimball said.

'What horses?'

'To drag me,' Kimball said.

Big said to Titoko, 'You have the warriors to escape the swamp. And the guides.'

'The path north is plain from here,' Titoko agreed.

'And your need for lieutenants less.'

'What are you telling me?' Titoko said.

'I will throw your grandson over my shoulder,' Big announced.

'Now?'

'When his woman is dead,' Big explained. 'Or should Kepa appear.'

Titoko was quiet. Then he promised, 'I will have your head if he loses his.'

'Offer better than Kepa,' Big said, 'and it's yours.'

Toa prayed for the last time beside his daughter. Titoko's people had their swags gathered, their weapons, and soon

285

even the slowest were moving tidily off the island. Toa was finally persuaded to join them.

Titoko lingered with last farewells.

'Remember my message,' Booth told him.

'I cannot forget it, Mr Booth.'

'If it helps, Titoko, I shall inform Colonel Whitmore that you moved out in a westerly direction. That may win you more time on the way north.'

'Thank you, sir. Why?'

'The tree in the bird,' Booth explained. 'Would I heard its song sooner.'

Then Titoko shared breath with Big and Demon.

'If asked to choose between you,' he said, 'I could not.'

Big and Demon were quiet.

'You might have warred better,' Titoko went on. 'You might have warred worse. There is no shame. The war was not yours to win.'

'No?' Demon challenged.

'Not in a hundred Mondays,' Titoko said. 'It was mine to lose.'

Demon seemed about to say something, but thought better. Big looked at the ground.

Titoko nosed in on Kimball. His breath was warm and not especially sweet.

'Grandson?' he asked. 'How is the tale?'

'Improving ample,' Kimball said.

As he left dry ground Titoko looked back the once; he waved the once too. He sank from sight of those left on the island. Soon there was no doubt; he was gone.

Booth withdrew first. 'I must look to my charges,' he said.

Demon had a pair of carbines shouldered; he was already pointed south. 'This way and that,' he said, 'we will be rid of war when today's sun sets.'

'Well rid,' Big said.

They were not inclined to look each other in the eye.

'You have quit Titoko too,' Demon said.

'In my way,' Big confessed.

'With the Yankee your excuse?'

'I would have found another.'

'And you have no plan to join Titoko?'

286

'Unless in the next life. Not in this.'

They breathed quietly, as one.

'There was good in this time, and there was evil,' Demon said. 'War makes the warrior.'

'As I have seen also,' Big said.

'In this case war bettered itself,' Demon suggested.

'You are telling us something,' Big noted.

'That I am not sorry to have known you,' Demon agreed.

'Or I you,' Big said.

Demon turned to Kimball. 'I gave you a promise,' he said. 'Today I may make my word good.'

'Flukes?'

'Should I sight him.'

'No fuss,' Kimball asked.

'No fuss,' Demon promised.

He waded into the swamp, not looking back, and was gone between one clump of flax and the next.

Kimball resumed vigil beside Rihi while Big checked weapons and kept watch. They had carbines, Colts, and a couple of tomahawks. If caught in the mire, they might make their last minutes lively.

An hour passed, with Rihi unmoving in the gloom. Then she sighed. Her eyes opened on Kimball.

'Where are we?' she asked.

'In that cabin I fixed us alongside the woods,' he said. 'The one with the view of Cobscook Bay.'

'I can smell the sea,' she said. 'The pines too.'

'And the blueberries in the fields,' he suggested. 'And cattle turd, and lumber and salt fish. Not to speak of them roses you planted outside our door.'

'What am I doing?'

'Now?'

'Today.'

He took a biggish breath. 'Working over the fire inside, I reckon. Warming the children their supper.'

'You?'

'I've had a cold day hunting, and putting out traps. There's frost on my whiskers and snow on my boots.'

'Then you'd better put your feet up.'

'Not without you've spooned out some chowder,' he said.

'Chowder?'

'Maine lobster. Wicked good. The best.'

'It's ready,' she said.

He fell quiet.

'What is it?' she whispered.

'Things have moved on some,' he explained. 'It seems how we're older.'

'Already?'

'The children have grown and gone. We're looking a little grey.'

'What are we doing?'

'It could be we're tapping maples for syrup.'

'Could be?'

'Or down on the shore collecting clams.'

'Clams?'

'The sweetest,' he said. 'But I tell you for a fact what we're doing.'

'Tell me,' she urged.

'We're filling ourselves with a mess of turkey and cranberry,' he said. 'It must be Christmas, or maybe Thanksgiving.'

'I can't spend all my days cooking,' she said.

'You're right,' he said. 'I reckon to get you to bed when we're done with the dandelion wine. No children around. Why not?'

'You,' she mocked.

'Us,' he said.

Rihi left a sigh unfinished. If she wasn't harboured in Maine it wasn't the fault of the hand on the helm.

Big and Booth had the grave dug. Aside from the silence when it was filled, there were no minutes for ceremony.

'I will say prayers to speed her soul,' Booth promised as they parted.

'She doesn't need heaven,' Kimball argued. 'She's safe where she is.'

The mountain stood bright in the sky. There was the sound of swamp water lapping against land. Birds could be heard overhead and then, at a distance, a lone shot. It had to be Demon's.

'Come,' Big said.

Across the swamp another shot said Demon had the army

in range. This shot called up a chorus of rifles. Birds soared thick to the south.

'Move,' Big said, and bumped Kimball brutally from the rear. Kimball staggered and fell, and was slow to rise.

'What was that for?' he asked.

'Slow arse,' Big said.

They began putting the swamp behind them. For an hour, as they followed Titoko's path north, single shots behind gave them thought. It seemed Demon was still stalking and sniping. Rifles in reply grew angrier. Toward noon there was an awesomely echoing volley. It was followed by bafflingly faint human sound. Thereafter they heard no single shots.

Demon might just have come to the end of his ammunition.

'Faster,' Big said.

At noon, as they breasted the last band of swamp, there was new firing. The problem was that it came not from the south, nor from the east. It was from the north, and near.

'No,' Kimball said.

Just one thought was possible, though neither spoke it.

The firing grew again. Now there were cries. Big's face twitched.

'Hurry,' he said.

They clawed up a bulky log abandoned by flood and looked across reeds, flax, oily water and ooze. Beyond were sandspits, islets and low lumps of land heralding an end to the mire. Birds were climbing high and smoke was clouding territory to their left. As it lifted they saw a cluster of horses tethered by a patch of cabbage palms. Fifty paces beyond were men afoot in blue uniforms, shooting wildly and at will. A constabulary patrol had worked its way around the swamp and chanced on Titoko's stragglers. They made easy marks. Some were shot down as they rose greasy from swamp. Others were driven back into bog, to become circling heads. A few were already drifting face down. It was impossible to see how many were in peril and how many clear. But the rear of Titoko's column was now being whittled. A half dozen warriors appeared on a low hillock, likely sent back by Titoko to push fire at the constables; they were far from enough. One fell before he could place his first shot.

'We have work,' Big said.

Kimball began climbing over the log. Big hauled him back.

'First,' he suggested, 'we live to do it.'

Kimball had never seen Big cooler. There was no fleck of sweat on his face, no shake in his voice. All warrior trails had been walked. All ended this side of Sunday.

'How many do you count?' he asked.

'Thirteen,' Kimball said.

'And how is our ammunition?'

'Five rounds apiece.'

'What does that say?'

'Fancy shooting.'

'You have half the idea,' Big said.

'The other half?'

'We close with them while they are in fever,' Big said. 'Then our task is two. We both pick them off and draw them away from our people. If possible, we tease them down into the swamp to our advantage. Should we fail to fell thirteen men with ten shots, we still have Colts. When those empty also, we have tomahawks and knives. If not tomahawks and knives, hands.'

'It looks like a long day,' Kimball said.

'Bet your bounty,' Big said.

Ducking around reeds and easing through flax they waded to the rear of the killing party; Maori groans and screams said constables were still placing shots with success. Four of the warriors on the hillock were now prone; the others had fled. Big found another log useful for shelter. They peered over it warily. The constables were now fewer than forty paces off, and had faces. The worst and best of it was that one was a captain by name of Flukes. Sergeant Tonks, living his ninth life, loomed at Flukes' side. Of the eleven lesser targets, some were brown and most white. As if on a duck shoot, they scorned cover and bunched badly, shoulder to shoulder, barrel to barrel, on a lip of dry land. They seldom lifted their gaze from the slaughter, giving no thought to flanks or rear. They fired and reloaded without panic, and found time to be ribald between rounds. The poorest marksman would have to work hard to miss them.

Beyond the log hiding Big and Kimball, a shallow channel

of green mountain water wandered into the swamp. Dead slowly nudged down it into their view. First came a fat grandmother. Then children mixed in sex and size. After them drifted an elderly and long-bearded male with his chest opened by bullets.

There was no mistaking Toa. Kimball sniffed.

'Do you wish to grieve,' Big asked, 'or to live?'

'What's that supposed to mean?'

'Taking new breath.'

Kimball's first was difficult.

'Deeper,' Big urged.

Kimball breathed.

'Your first shot will be the finest of your life,' Big promised. 'It will be bettered only by your second.'

'The first?'

'To their centre.'

'Flukes?' Kimball asked.

'Too far to their safe side.'

Kimball had to allow it true. Leaping this way and that, loudly encouraging his men, Flukes was not in clear view.

'No sad shots,' Big warned.

They steadied their carbines across the log, and looked along barrels. They cocked their weapons as one, with no word said. Kimball tasted bile from his belly and salt from his tears. Shifting his carbine a shade, he had one blue uniform after another in view. He breathed, spat, and found a sweet calm.

'Now,' Big whispered.

They fired. One constable crashed apart from his fellows. A second jerked, dropped his weapon, and knelt clutching his gut. Cries grew as Big and Kimball hid to reload.

'Helpful,' Big judged.

This time they cocked their carbines before exposing themselves above the log. The less they showed themselves, the longer their day. Snap shooting, however, also produced result. A third constable was nipped; a fourth, with a sigh of disbelief, sagged to ground. That left nine on their feet, or diving for cover. Flukes had yet to see from which quarter the shots were arriving.

'Where are the buggers?' he shouted. 'Where?'

Kimball loaded fast and looked to place his third shot in Flukes.

'Wait,' Big said.

'Why?'

'Because they are stopped,' Big explained.

'Stopped shit,' Kimball protested.

'Listen,' Big pleaded.

Constabulary rifles were quiet. One wounded constable was coughing wetly, another mortally groaning. Further off there was the sound of running feet, cracking vegetation and fervent Maori voices. Survivors of Flukes' slaughter were breaking out of the swamp, pushing through scrub and flax to take Titoko's trail north.

'You see,' Big said.

'I see,' Kimball had to admit.

'As we live they are safe,' Big argued.

Sergeant Tonks' voice lifted. 'Are we just letting the sods go, sir?' he was asking Flukes.

'We are, sergeant,' Flukes agreed.

'What now, then, sir?'

'We determine the number deployed against us.'

'Out there in the swamp?'

'They have us in range.'

'So no run for the horses?'

'Not yet,' Flukes said.

Quiet spread. Birds settled. The groaning constable left off groaning for life; the coughing constable quietened some too.

'There might be a hundred out there, sir,' Tonks said with unease.

'I would wager on fewer than ten, sergeant. Perhaps five or six.'

'A good five or six,' Tonks argued.

'An excellent five or six,' Flukes said.

'It's your arithmetic, sir.'

'It is,' Flukes agreed.

Minutes went. Big pressed Kimball's weapon down when it looked to be lifting.

'No more shots, sir,' Tonks observed.

'I am not deaf, sergeant.'

'I was thinking the horses might now be worth the risk, sir.'

'I daresay you were, sergeant.'

'There has to be a limit to this, sir.'

'I shall determine that limit, Tonks.'

More minutes. Kimball felt the chill of the swamp icing his balls and creeping to his trigger finger. Then Flukes spoke.

'Perhaps now or never, sergeant,' he said.

'Yes, sir,' Tonks was unusually crisp.

'Dead will be left. Four men will move to the horses with the wounded.'

'Right, sir.'

'The remainder will answer unfriendly fire should it be drawn.'

'That's including you and me, sir.'

'You and I, Tonks.'

'Then, sir?'

'We see, sergeant, don't we?'

'A bugger if we don't,' Tonks said. To constables nearby he added, 'Ready up, you scabby mongrels. You heard the captain.'

Kimball looked at Big, Big at Kimball. They cocked their weapons.

'Those headed for the horses,' Big whispered.

'Not Flukes?'

'Not yet.'

'Not ever,' Kimball said bitterly.

'We have use for horses,' Big explained.

'I got more than a little for Flukes.'

'Strike at their near side,' Big said. 'I shall strike at their far.'

They heard Tonks yell at picked men to run.

Big and Kimball swung their carbines over the rim of the log. They had time to see two wounded men being borne toward the horses on the backs of their fellows. The range was thirty paces. Kimball lucked on the near pair with a shot through a rump; Big spliced the further pair too. Screams mounted.

Big and Kimball were down behind their log again and breathing.

Flukes was shouting, Tonks cursing. 'Retire,' they roared.

Two surviving constables were fleeing back to Flukes.

'Seven on their feet,' Big said.

'And four rounds.'

'We need them nearer,' Big decided.

'Flukes still didn't spy us.'

293

That was plain from obscenities. Big peered over the log toward Flukes' position. 'They have gone to earth,' he reported. 'This could be difficult.'

'Not if we lay Flukes away.'

'How to draw them?' Big pondered.

'Let them see us for a second,' Kimball suggested.

'Or let them see you,' Big said.

'Me?'

'You make a smaller target.'

Big had a case.

'You declare yourself,' Big went on. 'I shoot as they are tempted from cover. To speed matters I need your good wishes, your carbine and last rounds.'

'What do I have?'

'Your Colt. Flourish it in desperate fashion.'

'And not shoot?'

'A full Colt will be needed.'

'When?'

'At ten paces. Better yet, five.'

'You reckon on them that near?'

'When they see you a carcass. Fall with your best cry. Then gurgle a little. After that, quiet.'

'I mightn't be faking.'

'Then the better your scream,' Big said warmly. 'It might help matters to think of our rear.'

'Kepa?'

'He could be led by this shooting.'

'Give me more good news.'

'Time is with Flukes. Kepa could soon have five hundred hunting us down.'

'Nothing's simple,' Kimball sighed.

'So shit first,' Big suggested.

Kimball broke cover in a crouch, frogged through mud, and fell flat on a handy islet. Behind him Big loaded and cocked carbines. Then he signalled.

'Flukes?' Kimball called, rising to his feet with revolver gripped. 'Flukes?'

There was a shaky silence. Flukes stared.

'By Jesus,' he said.

He also found his feet.

'Bent?' Tonks asked, likewise heaving into view.

More men with rifles rose. Two made the mistake of rearing in front of their captain and sergeant. Big's first shot, bound for Flukes, struck one of the two to the rear of his ear. With Kimball commanding their gaze, Flukes' men failed to note Big's location. They also failed to return fire. Big sent away a second bullet to chip a constabulary skull. Kimball, fast on his belly, had to think on dying a second death.

Big loaded the last rounds, cocked, and signalled again. Kimball stood. His performance was no better for rehearsal. 'What's the problem, Flukes? Where are you, Flukes?'

This time Flukes rose shooting. So also did Tonks, and four or five others. Mud swallowed Kimball's face as overhead bullets passed noxiously near. His mortal cry had to compete with the noise of Big's shots, also with the curses of another constable in grief.

'Goodbye Bent,' Tonks was saying. 'That's him, sir. Down.'

'Not before time,' Flukes sighed.

'No, sir. At least we was in at the kill.'

'Indeed, sergeant. An excellent kill.'

'If you don't mind me saying, sir, there should be a medal in this.'

'Not to speak of the bounty, sergeant.'

'Now you mention it, sir.'

'I can assure you, sergeant, that your devotion will not be forgotten. It will be fairly divided.'

'Much appreciated, sir. When do we fetch him out?'

'When we finish with his friend. Until then celebration is premature. Did others also sight that sniper?'

'A fat Maori bugger,' Tonks said, 'behind that rotten log.'

'At the least it now seems that Bent had but the one companion.'

'Yes, sir.'

'So keep up fire on that log. Wear it and tear it. Give him no peace. The wretch may be persuaded to take to his heels. His back will become a better target.'

Face down, frugal with breath, Kimball heard Flukes' rifles begin filling Big's log with lead. More and more bullets churned up the swamp, chowdering flax and timber too. As smelly water rained down, Kimball held tight to his Colt.

'Confound the bugger,' Flukes said, after yet another flight of shot failed to shift Big. 'What are you thinking, Tonks?'

Silence said Sergeant Tonks had quit.

'At the worst,' Flukes went on, 'we may yet have to enter the swamp to silence the fellow.'

'What's the best, sir?'

'There you have me, sergeant,' Flukes confessed.

'We can't piss off without Bent, sir,' Tonks said. 'No bugger would believe us.'

'Did I speak of departing the field, sergeant?'

'Not in so many words, sir.'

'So we are understood,' Flukes argued.

'Sir?' Tonks sounded baffled.

'Men will continue keeping the Maori quiet. Under their covering fire you and I, Tonks, will bring such as we need of Bent to dry ground. Does that sound a fair compromise?'

'It could be worse, sir.'

'Just so, Sergeant Tonks. Bent is the issue here. For our purposes the Maori can go to the devil. And will if he falls in with Kepa.'

'Yes, sir.' Tonks sounded relieved.

'You have your hatchet, sergeant?'

'Ready, sir.'

'You have work for it,' Flukes promised.

Kimball heard boots crash into the swamp. At most Flukes and Tonks were a minute away. Big, to his right, was still strangely quiet. Kimball didn't dare lift his head to see. He didn't risk thinking until Tonks and Flukes were all but upon him. Then he rose yelling and training his Colt. Off to his right, so the side of his eye told him, Big had risen too. Tonks and Flukes were abreast of each other, ten paces off, both firmly possessed of firepower. They ducked as Kimball's first shot travelled between them. Then their discharged revolvers left his ears ringing. As he danced off the islet, backing toward Big, he realized there had been no shot from Big's quarter. Maori oaths to his rear began telling him there would be none; Big's Colt had jammed. Flukes and Tonks were looking even uglier as they advanced, beginning to place shots within a hair of his hide; the men left on the edge of the swamp were keeping up fire too. The rising haze was made half of smoke, half of muddy moisture. A hand fell on his shoulder and Big cruelly whipped his Colt away. 'Down,' Big said, and began emptying the weapon at Flukes and Tonks as they closed. Tonks flinched for a moment as a bullet carved his shoulder; blood trickled from under Flukes' constabulary cap as he came on. Big's next bullets didn't slow them either. Kimball took breath and reached for a knife. So did Big when his Colt sounded for the last time. Behind them carbines were cracking; before them Flukes and Tonks were gunning in for the kill.

Then nightmare swam out of nowhere. First it was nothing human, a beast dripping blood and slime as it burst from the mire. When it heaved above Flukes and Tonks with a howl it shook into the shape of a man. The terrible eyes were Demon's. Some of his face had been shot away, and much of his chest. He had only arms whole to lift a tomahawk.

First it emptied Tonks' skull. With a flick quite as fast it shaved through Flukes' neck, and left his head hanging by sinew and skin. There was a short gush of gore as his heart continued pumping to no point. Then two torsos rolled in red water.

Demon was sinking when Big and Kimball reached his side. Big held Demon's head clear of the ooze.

'That was a good fight,' he said.

'The best,' Demon sighed.

He had taken new shot. There was bright froth from his mouth.

'Dying is selfish,' Big argued. 'Think of us.'

'Think of me,' Demon argued.

The silence was queer. The survivors of Flukes' patrol had taken note of Flukes' failure and fled, leaving dead and dying and most of their horses.

'Now?' Big asked.

'Before Kepa,' Demon whispered.

There was no dry round to discharge, nor Colt to discharge it. Big cut Demon's throat in less time than it took Kimball to look away.

Twenty-four

They buried Demon as deep as they could dig. They had time left to loot constabulary corpses, pick fresh weapons and two likely horses.

They rode the first mile in silence. Trampled fern showed the way Titoko's people had flown.

Then Big pulled up his horse. 'Hold out your hand,' he said.

Kimball was puzzled, but did. One of Big's hands closed over his. Kimball found a lone silver cuff-link in his palm.

'As promised,' Big said. 'You again have the pair.'

'What's that supposed to mean?'

'My life is mine,' Big said. 'Yours is your own.'

'You're telling me something.'

'Trails part,' Big agreed.

'Whose trails?'

'Mine and Titoko's.'

'Ours too?'

Big shrugged. 'If life doesn't bugger you now, it buggers you later.'

'Your way?'

'Buggered later,' Big said.

'Titoko's?'

'You heard Booth talk cash.'

'Titoko didn't listen.'

'The first time. Perhaps the second time too. I think of the third and the fourth.'

'Then?'

Big shrugged. 'Wouldn't you?'

Kimball was quiet.

'I hear him toasting the Queen's health,' Big said. 'Even calling for three loyal cheers.'

'But not yours.'

'Champagne fouls my belly. Three farts would be my need.'

'You're saying more,' Kimball suggested.

'Colonists will never think me amusing.'

'Maybe not me either,' Kimball decided.

'True,' Big agreed. 'Bounty hunters might ride a year or two yet.'

'What are you thinking, then?'

'Wilderness of character. Travelling upriver until the eels turn red. Tara Pikau could be a friend.'

'What then?'

'It is for me to pardon the Queen and her colonists.'

'Meaning you won't.'

'Just a little robbing and raiding. Potatoes here, sheep there. Enough to be free.'

'How free?'

'No orders, no killing. No shouts. A roof, a fire, and a bed. Maybe not even a woman. Not a life to every man's liking.'

'No,' Kimball said.

'Something pains you,' Big said.

'Titoko,' Kimball admitted.

'Join him,' Big urged. 'There may be more safety. Perhaps a faster pardon. And Maine.'

Kimball was quiet. Then he lifted his reins.

'So where are you going?' Big asked.

'Where you are,' Kimball said.

'Think twice,' Big suggested.

'I have.'

'And what does your second thought say?'

'The same.'

'You sure it's what you want?'

'It's sure what I know.'

'Once a rebel?'

'I'll outlaw along a little,' Kimball said.

The mire fell further behind. They journeyed through scrub, with hills heaving dark ahead.

'Who needs lies now?' Kimball asked.

Big didn't think on his answer.

'True,' he said.

They pointed their horses higher.

Near sunset, from some tall point in that territory, an observer might have seen a pair of riders passing, one small and middling pale, the other large and muddy brown. Such an onlooker could have watched them follow up a stony river bed and ford channels with care. Their hoofbeats would not long have been heard. Later a far campfire might have gleamed. When dark passed, and hills coloured with morning, there would be no shadow of warrior, no whisper of men merely mortal.

In Fact

Titoko, or **Titokowaru**, was born close to the slopes of Mount Taranaki, probably about 1823. His father, Hori Kingi Titokowaru, was an esteemed warrior chief. In 1845, five years after New Zealand came under the British crown, the elder Titokowaru embraced both the Anglican and Methodist faiths. His son, however, had committed himself austerely to Methodism years earlier. For him the Anglican faith was 'the church of outward shows'. We know him to have been literate. He was also as knowledgeable about Maori tradition as about the Bible. Neither Christianity nor British rule, however, meant an end to long-standing tribal feuds. Titokowaru's people, the Ngaruahine sub-tribe of the Ngati Ruanui tribe, fought neighbours north, south and west in the 1840s and 1850s and it seems sure that Titokowaru won his first knowledge of war in these decades. It was said of him that, in addition to being a sober and intelligent scholar, 'he was an unusually plucky, dare-devil kind of young man, ready for any mischief'. That corresponds with his later record. He has been identified as saying to his fellow Maori, in 1850: 'Give over war. Do not say I am laying down the law. It is Christ who is saying so.' In 1854 he had begun expressing himself more traditionally. At a large assembly of Taranaki tribes setting themselves against sale of land to European colonists, he is reported to have said: 'My mother is dead and I was nourished by her milk and thus let our land be kept by us as milk for our children.'

That stance, one way and another, was to tempt war. It came in 1860, over disputed sale of land, to the north of the Taranaki region. Though their own territory was in no peril, Titokowaru's people were prominent from the outset, and in the engagements between Britain's regiments and Taranaki's tribesmen it is likely that Titokowaru began winning respect as a tactician and a military engineer. With no decisive result won, Britons warred elsewhere for the next two or three years. (There were up to 18,000 British troops involved at the height of the New Zealand Wars, whereas rebel Maori at most fielded 1,200 fighters, never at any one time: warriors also had crops to harvest and families to feed.)

War eddied about Mount Taranaki again in 1864, with the birth of the Hauhau (or Pai Marire) faith; Titokowaru appears for a time to have been an adherent of this ostensibly peaceful but in fact militant creed. Certainly we know that he lost his right eye in a frontal assault on a British redoubt at Sentry Hill, just outside modern New Plymouth, on 30 April 1864. His was not the only loss. Throughout Taranaki Maori tribesmen saw thousands of fertile acres disappear in the colonial confiscations that followed hard on the fighting. When Titokowaru bursts into the record again, however, it is as a man persuading his people to give over war in favour of reconciliation with colonists. That is where this story starts. It is also where it ends. In between there was a war in which, according to one contemporary chronicler, colonists were 'surprised and out-generalled in every way . . . defeated, massacred, driven back, almost cowed, by the successes of a handful of savages'. It was the most extraordinary of the many wars fought by the Maori in the nineteenth century; it was also to be the first forgotten. The silences of oral history suggest that Maori tribesmen were no more anxious to recall it than humiliated colonists. One may ask why. Facts and fragments of fact are under no obligation to make sense; fiction must.

After the self-inflicted failure of his challenge to the British Empire in early 1869, Titokowaru and his people succeeded in living beyond the colonist pale for two or three years. They then returned in a trickle to their old lands. The Waingongoro River again effectively became the line between colonist and Maori. This roused the ire of, among others, Wanganui's much-honoured Major Kepa. The unforgiving Kepa, now having his own difficulties with colonists, told the New Zealand government: 'If you do not punish the man that has done evil, then most certainly do not chastise me.'

Nervous administrators were not anxious to mix with

Titokowaru again, though he had by then, in the mid-1870s, once more renounced war in favour of pacifism. The notion, as expressed by Te Whiti, a prophet of peace with whom Titokowaru allied himself, was that the lion would be persuaded to lie down with the lamb. For a time it seemed the British lion might. Titokowaru and Te Whiti, for some years, presided over a virtually independent and prospering Maori state under Mount Taranaki. In 1879, however, colonists began fresh sorties across the Waingongoro, again with surveyors as advance guard. This time they came with gifts rather than guns. Chiefs were feasted; their womenfolk were presented with finery. And large sums of money changed hands to persuade powerful chiefs to look more kindly on government acquisition of land. Official instructions were that Titokowaru was 'to be treated with extra courtesy'. At first he was, certainly in monetary terms; his palm was crossed with close to a thousand pounds, the price once placed on his head as a rebel. He was rebuked by his ally Te Whiti for having taken the bribe.

When roads arrived in the region, however, Titokowaru proved not to have been bought. Riding about in a buggy, he helped direct passive resistance against surveyors, road builders and white farmers. The weapon this time was not the carbine, but the plough. Tribesmen ploughed up survey lines, roads, and colonist crops. Hundreds were arrested and imprisoned; hundreds more arrived to take on the work until arrested too. There were protests in Britain and New Zealand at so primitive a land grab. It was called off, but not for long. Among other things white farmers close to Mount Taranaki, angry at government lethargy, and feeling threatened again, briefly declared themselves citizens of a republic. Rancour was as strong elsewhere. In the year 1881 a colonial army of 2,000 marched upon the headquarters of passive resistance, the Maori village called Parihaka where Titokowaru was in residence with Te Whiti. Field guns were set up. The troops marched in. They were met by lines of singing, dancing children. Juveniles and women were soon cleared, and ringleaders of the ploughing protest were arrested, Titokowaru among them. One newspaperman saw him 'crouching handcuffed like a large dog'. In prison he went on hunger strike for a time.

'This is your day,' he told his captors, 'but mine is hereafter.'

303

Though charges against him were dismissed – causing the government to pass legislation to ensure they could not be in future – he was held in a cell for eight months, and finally released on sureties totalling five hundred pounds. By then passive rebellion had been broken. It had proved no better than armed in stemming the British Empire's tidal march. The last duty left to the old and ailing warrior was that of promoting goodwill so that his people might survive. He festively marched his followers around colonist communities to show no harm meant. He also wooed colonists – as they had tried to woo him – with feasts to which hundreds were invited. If the occasion suited, he toasted Queen Victoria. 'I will shower peace upon the people until the end of time,' he promised. Though at first uneasy, colonists finally crowded to shake his hand. They found no giant, but instead an emaciated, one-eyed and altogether harmless old Maori. Was this the Titokowaru who once had the colony feeble with fright?

Yet a last spurt of fighting spirit was left. In July 1886 a small group of Maori non-violently occupied disputed land now farmed by a colonist. Constables arrived on the scene, and angry colonists, and so soon did two or three hundred more Maori. Conspicuous among them was Titokowaru. At first it seemed the affair might end quietly. A Maori meal was cooked, and colonists and constables invited to partake. Instead they began striking vigorously at Maori heads with batons and whips. As tempers mounted, Maori began hitting back. The riot ended with no shot fired and only spots of blood shed. Nine Maori were arrested, including Titokowaru. Now too weak to walk, he was bundled off to captivity in a buggy. He was shipped to Wellington, formally found guilty of 'malicious trespass', and given another month in a colonial prison.

A little more than two years after his last fight, on 18 August 1888, he was dead. Tradition says that his last large gesture was to call for Major Many Birds' sword to be brought from hiding. He broke his old enemy's weapon – how or with what tradition does not say – and ordered it buried. 'Let war be returned to the great nations of the earth,' he urged. It was. The trenches of World War I were just a heartbeat of history ahead.

Titokowaru was interred in a site secret to this day. Two thousand tribesmen farewelled his body before the coffin was closed. Many of those weeping had battled alongside him;

some had fought against him. It no longer mattered which. His war with this world was done. His hereafter had come.

Kimball Bent lived to tell the tale, but never made it home to Maine. After the end of Titokowaru's armed rebellion in 1869 he dwelled as a fugitive in dense forest east of Mount Taranaki for most of a decade. The first fellow white to chance on him there, in 1873, was a colonist surveyor named Skinner. Looking out land for sheep, Skinner came upon an enigmatic American, a man whom most in the colony believed dead and already judged so by military chroniclers. Bent failed to own up to his identity, though no one was fooled; he claimed to be a Samuel Smith, a New Englander who found himself on the Maori side in the course of the New Zealand Wars. Kimball Bent, he claimed, was somewhere else and someone else. (Possibly as many as ten British regular soldiers, mostly Irish, deserted their regiments and offered their services to Maori rebels in the 1860s. Some had short lives. Bent's proved long.) The intrigued Skinner reported that the lines on the outcast's face 'shew he has gone through many hardships'. On the other hand, Skinner 'could not detect any expressions to lead me to believe that he had perpetrated any of the atrocities laid to the door of K. Bent'.

In 1878, five years after his encounter with the surveyor, Bent warily left the forest, canoeing downriver in the company of Maori friends, and at the first colonist town asked after his chances of a Queen's pardon. Either people didn't know what he was talking about or feigned not to. Still in fear of retribution, he retreated to the forest. A journalist hastily on the spot to interview him described him thus: 'Fairly intelligent looking, quiet in demeanour, tidy in appearance, a man who in a good suit of clothes would be presentable anywhere . . . a man of easy and retiring disposition, rather sensitive, without any indication of viciousness, strong passion or boldness.'

Other colonists were less compassionate; it was to be some time before Bent had a suit of clothes, and he was never to be especially presentable in colonial society. 'The intensity of feeling against this man is hard to understand,' one later observer noted. It was still fierce decades later. Titokowaru had been forgiven, his war forgotten, but Kimball Bent was neither. While upriver among Maori tribesmen he tried to announce his continued existence by way of correspondence. The letters were dispatched downriver in Maori hands. They may or may not have been mailed. Those meant for Maine certainly produced no replies from relatives. If Bent's plea crossed his desk, the American consul in New Zealand was not persuaded to take an interest in repatriating his marooned fellow countryman to his birthplace. One version of his life says that he interested himself in native herbs and traditional Maori medicines and became a travelling healer. Apprenticed to a confectioner before he left Maine, he kept his hand in by catering to tribesmen with a sweet tooth; for one Maori function he is known to have cooked sixty-six iced cakes. He took a third Maori wife, after Rihi's death, but seems to have left no issue. He never stopped pleading for a pardon and never got one. With colonists no longer interested in winkling him out, he began visiting European communities but remained a figure of awe and loathing. One writer remembers him paddling into town in a canoe of his own making: 'At the Patea wharf he seemed to be engaged a good deal with his own thoughts, and sat in his boat for a long period, as was the custom of the old-time Maori. He looked a wild man and there was a wild look in his eyes. He was not happy when he came back to civilization.' Maybe not; but he was grateful for a respectable suit of clothes thrown his way by a crewman of a steamer moored nearby.

Formal history fails to tell us much about relations between Bent and Titokowaru when the New Zealand Wars ended. It can be inferred that they remained warm. Informal history says that when the old warrior leader lay dying he summoned his adopted grandson to his side. Bent rode in from a distant village and arrived minutes before death did. 'I am going away,' Titokowaru told him. 'Do not desert the tribe. Remain with our people.'

He would. One may surmise, though, that as his old warrior comrades aged, weakened and died he felt less and less comfortable with the new generation of Maori; that his persisting presence was a puzzle to them. The last of his life was happier. A sympathetic family of South Island Maori, kin to Titokowaru's people, finally gave him a home far from the farms of embittered northern colonists. He must then have been somewhere between fifty and sixty years old. In a sunny community near the sea he became best known for his skills as a carpenter; he built houses and halls to shelter those who now sheltered him. He was also free to exercise a larger talent, that of storyteller. He had, after all, Titokowaru's tale to tell. And at last some seemed anxious to hear. In his old age he was, reported one journalist, 'always willing to talk over the thrilling adventures of his earlier years' and always spoke 'in kindly terms . . . of the great rebel chief Titokowaru'.

Early in the twentieth century a journalist and apprentice historian named James Cowan, looking for frontier tales, knocked on Bent's door and asked for some of his time. The old man did better than grant an interview. He allowed Cowan to make free with diary notes on his early life. The result was a series of highly coloured articles and in 1911 a book called *The Adventures of Kimble* (sic) *Bent*. Failing even to check the spelling of his subject's name, Cowan was bound to get much else wrong. He duly did. Much might be credited to Bent's leg-pulling. Much was surely due to Cowan's failure to audit Bent's story. Anyway he credited Bent with a youthful existence in the US Navy and even half-membership of a mysterious Indian tribe called the Musqua in northern Maine: there is no such tribe. Still anxious for a clean slate, and a formal pardon, Bent denied firing at fellow whites in the New Zealand Wars, and particularly not at his regimental commander (Colonel Hazzard). He admitted only to manufacturing shot fired. The story would not have survived long under cross-examination in a witness box. Cowan, however, was no lawyer and Bent no sworn witness. Otherwise much of Cowan's book is rather overwrought fancy in *Boy's Own* prose. Cowan, who would later write better, could not have been especially proud of the book, and was perhaps even ashamed; he omitted to send Bent a copy. (Bent's friendly local bank manager finally gave it to him, a year or two after publication, as a birthday present. Bent's thoughts on the book are not on record.) But the remarkable tale of Titokowaru's rebellion – and its collapse – was at least in print. Nearly eighty years later a young historian named James Belich, hunting through the records, would set about confirming it in his book *I Shall Not Die* (1989). Without Kimball Bent's testimony, however, there would have been little left for a historian to interpret.

At a time when Bent at last had some comfort, even some

respectability of a colourful kind, distant relatives in Maine apparently began writing to the old man and urging a return home. Perhaps it was too late. He thought, after all, not.

He died on 22 May 1916. He was 79 years old. In Europe, on the Western Front, great armies were massing for an offensive on the Somme, due to take lives by scores of thousand. New Zealand casualty lists, after the Gallipoli disaster of 1915, were already long. The death of a survivor of Titokowaru's tiny war passed almost without notice. One New Zealand journal to record his passing was his neighbourhood newspaper, the *Marlborough Express*. In its obituary it recalled that Bent had been 'regarded as a dangerous rebel with many crimes laid at his door and an outlaw with a heavy penalty on his head. To shoot him and win the award was the eager determination of many.' Finally, however, the *Express* felt a charitable stance overdue. '[Kimball Bent was] more sinned against than sinning,' it judged. 'Whatever his mistakes or wrong-doings he has paid dearly.'

His unmarked grave has long been lost under weeds and wildflowers in a small South Island cemetery. In the North Island there is little left of the forests he knew, the battlefields he survived. The site of the Battle of Strewn Whites is now a few crumbled trench-lines in upland cattle country. The setting of Titokowaru's most dramatic triumph, the Battle of The Beak, has become an always eerily quiet picnic reserve. There is a monument there to the memory of Major Gustavus Ferdinand von Tempsky (Many Birds) and those who died with him. There is nothing of marble or metal in the region to recall Titokowaru and his warriors. The great mire, through which he led his people to safety, has long been drained. Oil-wells pump, natural gas bores flame, petro-chemical industry steams, and dairy herds graze tidy grassland. But the companionless cone of Mount Taranaki, a volcano two centuries silent, still rises coolly from a green wreath of rain forest. On near approach it fills half the sky.

A Note on the Author

Born in New Zealand of English, Irish, Welsh, and Australian convict ancestry, Maurice Shadbolt has published four collections of short stories, several works of nonfiction, and eight novels, including *Season of the Jew* (a Godine Nonpareil, 1990), which was selected by the *New York Times Book Review* as one of the best books of 1987.